Maria Adolfsson (b. 1958) lives in Stockholm where she, until recently, worked as a communications director and now writes full-time. The Doggerland series has been sold into 18 languages to date, and has sold over 160 000 copies in Sweden alone.

FATAL ISLES

Maria Adolfsson

ZAFFRE

First published in Sweden by Wahlström & Widstrand in 2018
First published in the UK in 2021 by
ZAFFRE
An imprint of Bonnier Books UK
80–81 Wimpole St, London W1G 9RE
Owned by Bonnier Books
Sveavägen 56, Stockholm, Sweden

A CIP catalogue record for this book is
available from the British Library.

ISBN: 978-1-78576-837-8

Also available as an ebook

1 3 5 7 9 10 8 6 4 2

Typeset by IDSUK (Data Connection) Ltd
Printed and bound in Great Britain by Clays Ltd, Elcograf S.p.A.

Zaffre is an imprint of Bonnier Books UK
www.bonnierbooks.co.uk

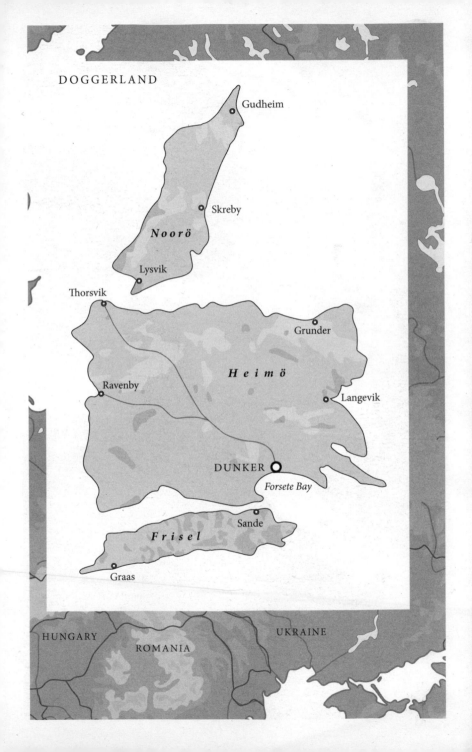

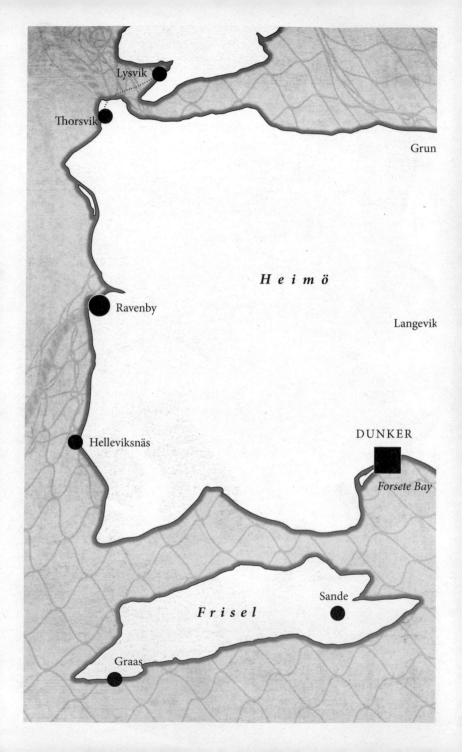

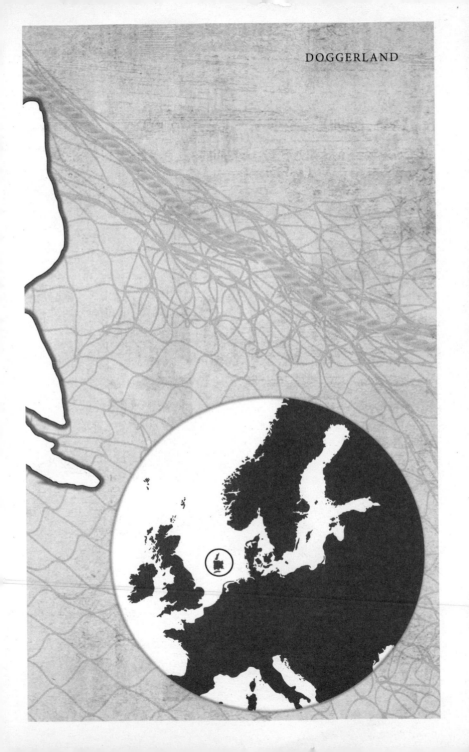

DOGGERLAND

It is not down in any map; true places never are.

Herman Melville, *Moby Dick*

1

She knows before she even opens her eyes. This is wrong. All of this is terribly wrong.

She should be in a different bed, any bed, just not this one. The light snoring from the other side should be someone else's, anyone's, just not his. And with an absolute certainty that slices through all other thoughts, she knows she has to get out. Immediately, this second, before he wakes up.

Slowly, and as silently as she can, Karen Eiken Hornby folds back the duvet and sits up without glancing towards the other side of the wide bed. She scans the hotel room, registering her knickers and bra on the floor next to her bare feet, her dress next to her green suede jacket in a pile on the coffee table, her handbag discarded on an armchair. Beyond them, she can just make out her trainers, peeking out behind the half-open bathroom door.

She plans every movement in order to get out of the door as quickly as possible, listening to the deep breathing behind her back, her own silent and shallow. She does a quick run-through of the necessary steps in an attempt to quell a wave of anxiety churning in her stomach. Then she takes a deep breath before reaching for her knickers and pulling them on in one motion. Carefully, to avoid jostling the mattress, she gets to her feet and feels the room spin. She waits, breathes. Then a series of hunched-over steps to snatch up her bra and tights with one hand and pick up her dress and jacket with the other. Nausea mounting, she continues into the bathroom and quietly pulls the door shut behind her. Hesitates for a split second, then turns the lock. She instantly regrets it when she hears the tiny click from the bolt, quickly pressing her ear against the door. But any sound on the other side is drowned out by her thumping heart and the blood rushing to her head.

Then she turns around.

The eyes that meet hers in the mirror above the sink are blank and strangely unfamiliar. Heavy with self-loathing, she studies her flushed cheeks and the mascara that's flaked and settled in dark circles under her eyes. Her brown hair is hanging limply on one side, while the rest is still tied back. Her long fringe is sticking to her clammy forehead. Resignedly, she studies the devastation and whispers with a gluey, dry mouth:

'You fucking idiot.'

Something turns in her stomach; she only just has time to bend down over the toilet before the vomit starts coming. This'll wake him for sure. She listens helplessly to her own retching, panting as she waits for the next cascade, closing her eyes so as not to have to look at yesterday's leftovers in the toilet bowl. Gives it a while longer, but her insides seem to have calmed down. Temporarily relieved, she straightens up, turns on the tap and fills her cupped hands. Rinses out her mouth and lets the water cool her face, realising it will probably make the black circles under her eyes worse and deciding it doesn't matter. There are no limits to this particular hell.

At almost fifty, she's really reached new lows this time. She feels like seventy.

A quick escape is all she has left to hope for now. To get home so she can lie down and die. In her own bed. But first, she has to get out of here, get in her car and go straight home without talking to anyone, without being seen by anyone. Then a faint glimmer of hope when she realises that on this particular day of the year, she might have a chance of slinking out of town unseen. At quarter past seven in the morning, the day after the oyster festival, all of Dunker is out cold.

She fills one of the toothbrush glasses with cold water and downs it quickly while she disentangles her hair tie with the other hand, noting that it pulls a few long hairs out with it. She refills the glass, pulls on her dress, shoves her bra and tights into her handbag and is just about to put her hand on the door handle when she stops. She has to flush. Even though the sound is bound to wake him, she has to; she can leave no trace of herself behind. With eyes screwed up tightly and a grimace of dread, she listens to the sound of water rushing down into the bowl, followed by the sound of the cistern refilling. She hangs back for a few more seconds, until the sound has subsided to a soft tinkling, then pulls the strap of her handbag over her shoulder.

Then she takes a deep breath and opens the bathroom door.

He's on his back with his face turned to her and for a second, she freezes. Backlit, he looks like he's watching her. But then another thunderous snore fills the room; she jumps as the spell is broken.

Six seconds later, she's gathered up her shoes and opened the door to the hallway. And there, on the cusp of freedom, something makes her turn around. Driven by the same kind of compulsive urge that people have when they pass an accident on the motorway and don't really want to look but have to anyway, she lets her eyes take in the man in the bed. Studies the slackly open mouth, listens to the faint gurgling that accompanies each exhalation.

With a feeling of unreality, Karen studies her boss for three seconds before closing the door behind her.

2

The door to room 507 closes with the sound of rushing air and a faint click. The maroon carpet is soft under Karen's bare feet when she hurries over to the lift and pushes the button. Her pulse throbs at her temples while she uses her index finger to wrench her trainers on. The moment she straightens up, there is a ding and the lift door slides open with a soft hiss.

She's lucky. The reception desk appears to be unmanned when she dashes through the lobby toward the exit with just one quick glance to the side. Then a sudden shudder of anxiety when she realises she has no memory of how she got here. Did they really walk here together? Whose idea had it been? Jumbled memories flash before her like high-speed film sequences: the harbour with her friends Eirik, Kore and Marike, the pub crawl that followed with more oysters and glass after glass of wine. And then a hazy image of Jounas Smeed who had appeared in one of the bars in the wee hours. A few more sequences surface while she moves toward the exit: laughter, bickering, abruptly flaring arguments, drunken embraces to make up and Jounas's face close to hers. Much too close.

Halfway out, delayed by the exasperatingly slow revolving door, she's struck by another horrifying thought: did anyone see them check in?

*

Outside the hotel, the September air is clear and free; she has time for one deep breath before her stomach lurches again. She quickly glances up and down the deserted street and jogs across it with one hand clapped over her mouth. Moments later, she's on the other side of the promenade, leaning over the railing while the wave of nausea slowly subsides. Then a second of relief before the realisation she's been fending off since she woke up ten minutes earlier hits her full on. The worst is yet to come. She has to see him again on Monday morning.

Karen gazes eastward across the bay, toward the harbour. She can make out the forest of bobbing masts in the marina, but the ferry terminal beyond it is as deserted as always on Sundays. The ferry from Esbjerg won't arrive until eight in the evening and since a few years back, there are no boats to Denmark or England on the weekends. Anyone who wants to leave Dogger-land on a Sunday these days has to fly from Ravenby. Through the morning mist lingering above the sea, she can make out the white radar tower of a cruise ship anchored at the farthest end of the deep-water port.

She squints toward the horizon while fumbling around her inside pocket for her sunglasses and cursing softly when they're not in their usual place. Pats down her jacket and concludes that she must have either dropped them at some point last night or left them in the hotel room. Now she's going to have to drive at least halfway back to Langevik with the low sun in her eyes, thirsty and nauseous and with a throbbing headache. A double espresso and two paracetamols are what she needs to not be an immediate danger on the road, but she knows that none of the shops and cafés on the other side of Strandgate are open. At this hour, the day after Oistra, she's likely the only person awake in the whole hungover town, with the possible exception of a rat or two, digging through brimming bins and oyster shells. That thought makes her stomach turn again.

Karen takes a few deep breaths with her eyes closed and her palms against the rough, cool stones of the wall. The fresh air feels good, and the breeze pushes her damp hair away from her face. She turns the back of her neck toward the sun and gazes down at the beach. A colony of black-headed gulls screech around a few poorly tied binbags. Further off, she makes out the contours of another binbag. Next, she realises it's actually a man, sleeping. He's lying on the sand with his coat pulled up over him. Next to him is a shopping trolley, most likely stolen from Qvick or Tema, and now filled with empty bottles and cans. He looks like one of the junkies who hang about by the mall behind Salutorget Square. He's probably going to feel much the same as she is when he wakes up: thirsty, sweaty and with a hangover like a heavy backpack of anxiety. On the other hand, unlike her, he seems to have spent the night in innocent solitude.

From far away, a moped engine makes a half-hearted attempt at cutting through the monotonous sound of the breaking surf. Foamy waves crash against the pier that juts fearlessly out into the sea; a dilapidated sailboat is moored to one of the six dolphins in the bay. She absentmindedly ponders how long it will be before the harbour police head out to shoo it away. More likely than not, they'll let it slide until after lunch at least; zealous as those boys usually are, not even they will have the energy to whip up their hunting instinct before noon this morning.

The end of the pier is still shrouded in morning haze and the outline of the lighthouse at the tip of the thousand-yard breakwater is still blurred. There must have been thick fog last night; she recalls that the bellowing of the foghorn had been unusually persistent. And then another memory: an annoyed Jounas getting out of bed to close the window before climbing back in. She quickly pushes the image down, tears herself away from the railing and starts walking briskly toward the car park over on Redehusgate.

Her car is neatly parked three blocks away, exactly where she left it twelve hours before. The sight of her dark green Ford Ranger in the deserted car park outside city hall immediately relaxes her. In less than an hour, she will be in her own bed, in her own house, behind closed blinds, with sleep giving her a few hours' respite from the relentless self-reproach.

The next moment, she realises she doesn't have her car keys.

3

'How are we doing here?'

The voice behind her is authoritative and a touch condescending. Karen freezes mid-movement, with one hand in her handbag and the other braced against the bonnet.

Squatting next to her car, she has unsuccessfully spent a few panicky minutes rummaging around for her keys. Checked every pocket, felt along the bottom of her bag and then proceeded to methodically pick one item out after the other with mounting anxiety.

Now she curses inaudibly through gritted teeth; what on earth are the police doing out at this hour? Why the fuck are they wasting man-hours and taxpayer money on patrolling streets and city squares when the whole town is asleep? She pushes herself up on stiff legs. Then she reluctantly turns around and tries to squeeze out a relaxed smile.

She only manages a stiff grimace.

A look of horror followed by disbelief flutters across both officers' faces when they behold the devastation.

'Oh, excuse me . . .' says the older of the two and takes a step back, looking embarrassed.

His eyes bounce helplessly between the sooty make-up remnants on the ashen face before him and the items on the ground. His slightly younger female colleague gives Karen one quick glance and then stares, openly curious, at the bits and bobs strewn across the asphalt: a copy of yesterday's paper, a mobile, a half-pack of cigarettes, something that looks like a pair of black tights, a phone charger, a half-eaten apple with bitemarks in its darkened flesh, a bra and a box of condoms.

Karen forces out another stiff smile, her face tense. Then she gestures vaguely at the mess on the ground.

'I can't find my car keys.' She inhales, in an attempt to prevent her breath from reaching the two officers. 'New handbag,' she adds.

'Spent the night in town, ma'am?'

The female officer has squatted down and now looks up with a small smile, as if to signal sympathy and understanding. Karen feels her annoyance growing; what the fuck does this unbearably fit slip of a thing with her bobbing ponytail know about 'spending the night in town'?

'Why?' she asks frostily.

Her penetratingly blue eyes with the golden rings around the pupils – which she knows can cow people into silence – fix on the younger woman, forcing her to look away, and she regrets it the moment she wins the power struggle. What is she playing at?

'It tends to get late after Oistra, so I spent the night at a friend's,' she adds in an attempt to smooth things over. 'But I think I'd better keep looking . . .'

Karen gestures significantly toward her handbag and the jumble of things that still seem to fascinate the female police officer. Just then, she sees a gloved hand reach out, pick up her wadded-up tights and shake them gently. The flat key hits the pavement with a jangle. Two seconds later she hears the familiar beep of a car door unlocking.

'Here you go, boss,' says Police Constable Sara Inguldsen, who has straightened back up and is holding the key out to her with a wry smile.

Unable to speak, Karen accepts the key and watches as the two officers back up a few steps and salute her in unison. Apparently, Police Constable Björn Lange has regained his ability to speak again, too.

'Drive carefully, Inspector Eiken!'

4

The motorway from Dunker to Langevik runs along the south-east coast of Heimö for four miles before cutting across the narrow Skagersnäs Peninsula and continuing in a north-westerly direction for another mile. Karen feels sweat trickle down her back as the artificial chill of the air conditioner simultaneously makes her shiver. Her hands clutch the wheel and she keeps a close eye on the speedometer. Granted, she doubts the traffic division has people out doing speed checks on a morning like this, but the thought of being pulled over by colleagues and having to blow into the breathalyser is about as appealing as another night with Jounas Smeed. And probably as devastating to my career, she reflects. Despite overly generous laws – the result of pragmatic politicians having more to lose than gain from proposing reform – her blood alcohol level is likely above the legal limit. That insight makes her stomach turn to ice and she slows down further. Not that. Never that.

The road is virtually deserted; minutes go by without her seeing another car. Karen relaxes her grip on the wheel and shakes her shoulders a little. Later, after a few hours' sleep, she's going to go over every detail of the night before, obsess about what happened, turn every last moment over and over, scold herself and mete out a sentence of penance and clean-living. Not another drop of alcohol for weeks, no cigarettes ever again, daily runs, weight training and healthy food. It's not her first time; the mindset inherited from her Noorö relatives is deeply ingrained. Not deeply enough for her to avoid sin, but enough to make the worst transgressions fill her with anxiety. Not for fear of God's wrath and exclusion from Heaven; more for the price she will be paying in this life.

This time, her boss at the Doggerland Police Authority is going to put her through the wringer. But as impossible as staying in her job is going to be, she can't see any alternative. A few weeks' leave is hardly going to make the problem disappear, and then what? Roll the dice and quit? Change careers, at her age? She banishes any further mulling about the future, but can't ward off the mounting flood of memories from the night before.

The last Saturday of September. She'd met up with Marike, Kore and Eirik at The Rover for a pint before commencing the traditional oyster eating. Marike had been in a foul mood after a failed firing that had destroyed two weeks of work; something had gone wrong with the new glaze she'd had such high hopes for. To make matters worse, Marike Estrup hated oysters, a fact she'd announced in an unusually thick Danish accent. Over time, they'd all grown used to her quirky mix of Doggerese and Danish, and they had discovered that Marike's accent served as a kind of Geiger counter, gauging her mood; last night, the readings had been off the charts; it had been almost impossible to understand her northern Jutland hissing.

Kore and Eirik, on the other hand, had been in a terrific party mood. Two days earlier, their bid on a house in Thingwalla had been accepted and the two men had spent Friday night worrying about mortgages, arguing about décor and engaging in make-up sex. They'd spent all day Saturday in bed, planning the move, the subsequent housewarming party and growing old together, nestled in a cocoon of bright expectations.

Karen had had a productive Saturday, which had begun with her driving to the DIY store in Rakne. Pleased with herself after sealing seven windows, changing the hinges on her tool-shed door and spending almost half an hour on the phone with her mother without raising her voice once, she'd studied her still-tanned friends in the gentle twilight of the pub. Her own pale skin had made her look tired, almost sickly, which Kore had heartlessly pointed out.

'Sure, but it's my turn next,' she'd countered. 'I should be heading off on Monday or Tuesday at the latest.'

She'd had just a few days off at the start of June, and worked the rest of the summer. While her colleagues were on holiday, she had wrapped up an investigation on her own, written the final reports, tidied up and held down the fort with the aid of temporary staff from the outer precincts. When coyly asked if she wouldn't mind waiting to take her annual leave in the autumn, Karen had been careful not to let on that it, in fact, suited her perfectly. She has accumulated well-needed martyr points, which she can trade during the dogfight over Christmas and New Year's leave.

Contentedly slouched in one of the armchairs at The Rover, she'd announced to her friends that three weeks of holiday lay before her and that she was going to spend the greater part of that time in north-east France while darkness and cold slowly engulfed Doggerland. There, on the farm in Alsace, where she owned a measly portion of the land and vines, she was going to sit around with the others, Phillippe and Agnés, discussing the harvest and comparing it to other vintages.

But first, she was going to celebrate Oistra.

As always, the annual oyster festival began in the harbour, where locals and tourists crowded in between the stands. The oysters hadn't had time to fatten up properly yet, but the first Saturday after the autumnal equinox was the start of a long season and a big celebration was in order. Piles of edulis and gigas shrank and were restocked at a feverish pace while money changed hands and fresh barrels of porter and sweetgale-seasoned Heimö liquor were rolled out by brewery workers, grunting loudly. Sweet black bread with butter was the only traditional accompaniment, crucially important as it kept people from passing out from hunger and intoxication, which is why it was provided for free on the night of the festival, while ads for the festival's sponsors covered every spare surface.

In other words, it was the same as every other year.

Merry and jovial as the mood may be, however, Oistra would usually claim its fair share of victims through drunkenness, fights and the occasional food poisoning. What was not part of the tradition was the recent addition of street food and cheap wine served in paper cups, as was regularly pointed out in outraged letters to the editor from signatories such as 'Preserve our Doggerian heritage' and 'Disappointed Seventy-Two-Year-Old'. The entertainment side of the festival had also improved according to some people – and gone to the dogs according to others. In the past twenty years the folk musicians had had spirited competition from local and international rock bands, excruciating talent competitions, the racket from temporary carnival rides and the shrill shrieking of children.

Last night, Kore and Eirik had scarfed down at least a dozen oysters each and Karen half that before they even left the harbour. Marike had watched their tilted-back heads and greedily open mouths with revulsion.

'Molluscs are not fit for human consumption. They can make you terribly ill,' she said with a mouth full of pulled pork, which made her even harder to understand.

'It's this shit that'll make you sick, not the oysters,' Kore had countered, completely unperturbed, before downing his last bit of Heimö liquor and chucking the plastic cup in a bin while making an inadequate attempt to suppress a burp.

'Bloody hell,' he said, pulling a face. 'It's time for something decent to drink.'

They had continued the evening with a customary pub crawl, during which glass after glass of wine had been accompanied by even more oysters. For the sake of comparison, some of the bars along the promenade served French belons in addition to the local variety; Doggerian custom prescribed patriotic but good-natured booing every time someone ordered the foreign rivals. And it was at the third pub, Café Nova, just as Karen had ordered a glass of Chablis and two belons, that she felt hot breath against her ear and heard a deep voice.

'Detective Inspector Eiken, looks like you're willing to put just about anything in your mouth.'

She'd slowly turned to the Head of the Criminal Investigation Department and smiled.

'Oh no, Smeed, you're not that lucky.'

But an hour and a half later, they'd been in a double at Hotel Strand. What had happened there was something she was now approaching in the same way a person lifts up a rock and looks in horror at what's wriggling underneath. She squints at the sun and the shiny asphalt. Alcohol had played a part, naturally. The generally festive mood, too; after all, it wasn't the first time Oistra had led to sexual mistakes followed by deep regret, or, in the worst cases, divorce. Yet even so, she can't remember a faux pas ever making her feel as remorseful as she is now.

Karen glances out at the sea while the road turns gently to the north. The mist has cleared; the sun is already halfway up the sky; the choppy sea is sparkling. A few great black-backed gulls are cruising on the updraughts, looking like they're contentedly digesting their food and chatting idly, rather than scanning the waves for more fish. She rolls down her window and breathes in the salty air. I'm simply going to have to call the head of HR and ask for a transfer, she decides. Maybe there's a vacancy in Ravenby, or even Grunder, tedious though that would be.

Work had hardly been frictionless, she reminds herself. One by one, her female co-workers had left the department under their previous boss. Eva Halvarsson had given up hope of ever advancing from constable to inspector and had requested to be transferred to the uniform division, while both Anniken Gerber and Inga van Breukelen had relocated to the Frisel district. Karen had clung on, less out of doggedness and tenacity and more because she couldn't face starting over. Not again. But mostly because working as a detective inspector was an effective way of keeping her mind off things she was desperate to forget. Together with about a dozen male and nowadays two female colleagues working at the Doggerland CID, she is responsible for investigating all violent crimes on the Dogger islands: Heimö, Noorö and Frisel. The decision to centralise was made eleven years ago and met with strong criticism from the local police districts, but the protests had subsided as the crime resolution rate went up. Unfortunately, the number of violent crimes had gone up, too, which meant the number of unpunished offenders had stayed constant. And that Karen was able to keep her mind from straying into unwanted territory.

Even so, her qualifications had been questioned when she was first hired – that her degree in criminology from the London Met would offset her lack of 'dog years' as a patrolling officer had not convinced her old-fashioned colleagues. But Karen's work performance had, in time, silenced that criticism. Even so, Jounas Smeed's respect for her as a criminal investigator had, from the moment he became head of the CID, felt grudging, as though he found any recognition of her competence difficult. Instead, he'd immediately established something he himself defined as 'a relaxed jargon between us coppers' as the prevailing tone in the division. The rewards had been instantaneous. Relieved to have a boss who didn't care about discipline and deference, Karen's male colleagues had embraced Jounas Smeed and gleefully taken his policy of 'banter' to intolerable lengths. Karen had grown used to the constant jokes, delivered in the form of little barbs and digs. Or rather, out of self-preservation, she'd learnt to ignore Johannisen's inexhaustible rebuking of feminists and women drivers and Jounas's recurring laments on how impossible it was to understand how women think. She doesn't dignify any of it with so much as a comment. She knows silence speaks louder than protests. Knows that bored yawning is more provocative than loud objections. She's learnt to tune it out, refuses to show her exasperation, well aware that taking the bait will only make it worse. But mostly, she does it because she's noticed that it gives her more power. Jounas Smeed needles her by constantly, trying to get a rise out of her; she needles him even more by not obliging him.

And now I've gone and shagged the bastard, she thinks. Goddamn it!

And, she realises, as she spots the signs announcing the Langevik exit, she knows exactly why they ended up in bed together. It was their power struggle, the ongoing battle between them, that had made them both throw out the rulebook last night. Fuelled by the alcohol, their mutual urge to get the upper hand, had morphed into a pathetic seduction game where both of them had viewed themselves as the clear victor. Intoxication had undone all the rational counter-arguments, had dismissed all the warning bells and instead created a sudden physical desire. A spark that had died as quickly as it had flared up.

The sex wasn't even good, she thinks, not without a level of schadenfreude. Mostly an endless and tedious series of positions, each more uncomfortable than the last, probably aimed to impress. At least the prick was agile for his age. More agile than me, she admits.

She glances in the rear-view mirror, turns on her indicator light and exits. The ramp toward Langevik is paved, true, but the speed limit is forty here and she law-abidingly slows down to just below that. For a moment, she looks away from the road, up toward the steep ridge where wind turbines loom. The rotors spin at an even pace; she can hear the swishing through her rolled-down window. The windmill park runs all along the Langevik Ridge and was, when it was built six years ago, the subject of vigorous protest. The residents of the village down by the seashore had organised meetings; there had been petitions

19

on every shop counter in town as well as between the taps at the local pub. Today, the protests have long since died out and it's been many years since the windmills were a topic of conversation among the villagers.

Karen studies the tall, white towers. There's something soothing, almost beautiful about the revolutions of their slender white arms. Personally, she never had anything against them, not even when the protests were at their most strident. But since a pint of good beer has always been high on Karen Eiken Hornby's list of things that make life bearable, she had dutifully signed her name on every petition; refusing would have made the village's only pub fall silent, would have made every face turn away. But, of course, every attempt to stop the park had been futile; one after the other, the tall white towers had been erected along the Langevik coast and Karen hadn't minded; the sound of the turbines only carries to her house when the wind is straight out of the south-west. But here, just below the turbines, on the gentle slope where the houses are few and far between, seemingly randomly scattered across the slope where the Langevik River meanders down toward the sea, there is a constant whine.

A hundred and fifty yards further on, in a garden sloping steeply down toward the river, there is a movement; a middle-aged woman is trudging up the path from the old washing jetty towards her house. She's dressed in a drab bathrobe and has wrapped a towel around her hair like a turban. Karen feels a shudder of unease before she can push down the instinctive feeling of guilt. Granted, there are a thousand reasons she shouldn't have slept with Jounas Smeed, but Susanne really isn't one of them. They must've been divorced for ten years by now. For a moment, she contemplates honking in greeting, in accordance with town etiquette, but she decides not to. In the current circumstances, she has absolutely no desire to make herself known. Besides, Susanne Smeed doesn't seem to notice her; her eyes are firmly on the ground and she looks like she's in a hurry. She's holding her robe firmly closed and is walking briskly, determinedly. She's probably cold after her morning soak; the water can't be very warm this time of year.

The knowledge that she's almost home makes her relax; she feels exhaustion take an increasingly firm hold of her. She stifles yet another yawn and blinks hard a few times. Just then, a cat crosses the road, head down, every inch a predator, alert and prepared to defend its prey, which is dangling helplessly in its mouth. Karen feels adrenaline rush through her when the seatbelt tightens as she brakes hard.

'Not the time to relax,' she whispers. 'You know what can happen. If anyone knows, you do.'

She continues down the gently sloping road toward the town centre. Here, houses line both sides of the road, but there's still not a soul to be seen. She slows down even more and turns onto the long high street. The outside serving area of Langevik's only pub, The Hare and Crow, is a jumble of furniture. There are still glasses on the tables and a handful of gulls are flapping about among discarded oyster shells. True, there's no need to stack and chain chairs and tables overnight here, like the bars have to do in Dunker, but the pub's owner, Arild Rasmussen, usually tidies up before closing. It would seem Goodman Arild snuck too many unfinished drinks in the kitchen last night, celebrating Oistra just like everyone else.

She slowly drives past the health clinic, passes the corner shop, the closed-down post office, the shuttered hardware shop and the barely surviving supermarket. The old fishing village on the east coast of Heimö is on life support, surviving mostly on the remnants of a historical willingness to go out and protest. But the public demonstrations are growing increasingly tame, choice and price are enough to make most people forget their principles and set their course for superstores and DIY stores. Only Arild Rasmussen's business seems to thrive; The Hare and Crow is still busy most days of the week.

At the end of the high street, the road rounds the old fish market and runs along the harbour. Karen follows the sharp bend and slowly continues down the narrow gravel path between the sea and Langevik Ridge. White and grey stone houses climb the slopes; along the shoreline on the other side of the road, jetties and boathouses jut out into the water. Everything testifies that Langevik, just like all the other coastal villages in Doggerland, had been once populated mainly by fishermen, sailors and the occasional pilot. These days, most of the waterfront properties are owned by IT technicians, oil rig engineers and the occasional arts worker. Behind the simple, grey stone exteriors, wood-burning stoves and tea kettles have been replaced by induction hobs and espresso machines. Karen knows more and more of the boathouses are being turned into extra living space; instead of large rowboats with room for four or six rowers, their weather-beaten façades now hide comfortable sofas in all-weather artificial cane. Their owners spend mild summer nights there, sipping wine, enjoying their magnificent ocean views, without having to worry about broken nets or whether the damn seals have stolen half the catch this time, too.

And maybe she would have done the same, if she could afford it. Karen Eiken Hornby isn't nostalgic by nature. On the surface, most things still look like when she was growing up, and yet nothing is the same. And that suits her just fine.

She turns into the steep driveway of one of the last houses and notes that she's going to have to fill in the trench by the gate if she wants to avoid bumping her head on the roof of the car the next time she bounces into her garden. With a sigh of relief, she kills the engine and sits motionless for a few seconds before opening the door. Exhaustion washes over her again and her legs feel like lead as she walks up the slope to the house. She breathes in deeply, filling her lungs with the smells of approaching autumn. The air is usually a few degrees colder here than in Dunker, and there's no doubt the summer's quickly coming to an end. The birch trees are already turning yellow and the rowan by the tool shed is red with berries.

An enormous, fluffy grey cat is lounging the stone steps by the kitchen door. When Karen comes closer, it rolls over onto its back, stretches out to its full length and yawns, showing its pointy fangs.

'Good morning, Rufus, no mice today *again*? What use are you?'

Next, the cat is up, rubbing against her legs, and before Karen has pulled the key out of the lock, he has slunk inside.

She throws her handbag on the kitchen table, pulls her jacket off and steps out of her shoes in one motion. Then she opens the cupboard above the sink, takes out two painkillers and washes them down with a glass of water while absentmindedly stroking the cat, which has jumped up on the kitchen counter. The sound of increasingly imploring meowing cuts through her headache while she looks for a tin of cat food. The second she puts the

23

bowl down the caterwauling dies down instantly; she feels her shoulders drop. She should install the cat flap she bought, tonight. Even though there are plenty of mice and at least two outbuildings for Rufus to patrol, he apparently prefers to eat in a more dignified manner in the kitchen and spend his days on the living-room sofa. Where he lived before he came limping up her driveway last spring, she has no idea. The notices she'd put up on telephone poles and slipped into people's mailboxes yielded nothing. The vet had reattached his ear, neutered him, splinted one of his legs and put a cone on his head so he wouldn't lick the ringworm medication. Apparently, the ragged cat had come to stay and she was now forced to admit their war of attrition was over: Rufus had triumphed.

To the sound of the cat's chewing, Karen turns on the coffee maker and cuts a couple of slices of bread. Fifteen minutes later, she's gobbled two cheese sandwiches and washed them down with a pint of strong coffee. Her searing headache has mellowed into a dull ache and, suddenly, exhaustion overwhelms her. Without cleaning up after her meal, she drags herself up the stairs to her bedroom, pulls off her dress and lies down on the bed. I should at least brush my teeth, she thinks to herself. Moments later, she's out like a light.

5

The sound is coming from far away, seeping into her consciousness through layers of sleep. When it finally gets through, she figures it's the clock radio, but slamming the button to turn it off has no effect. The digital digits tell her its 1.22 p.m.; it takes her another few seconds to realise two things: she has slept through half of Sunday and the sound is coming from her phone, which she left in the kitchen.

Annoyed, she throws her duvet aside, pulls on her robe, which was draped across the armchair in the corner, and staggers downstairs. The ringing is relentless; she digs through her bag as her stress level rises and fishes her phone out the same moment it falls silent. A quick look at the screen and she's suddenly wide awake. Three missed calls, all from Chief of Police Viggo Haugen.

Karen sits down on a kitchen chair and calls back while her thoughts race. What could the chief of police want? They hardly have a close working relationship. And on a Sunday, too. can't be good news. On the third ring, an authoritative voice answers.

'Haugen.'

'Hi, this is Karen Eiken Hornby. You've been trying to reach me?'

She makes an effort not to sound like she'd just woken up, goes a bit too far; her voice coming out squeaky and shrill.

'I certainly have. Why aren't you answering your phone?'

Viggo Haugen sounds annoyed; she casts about for a white lie. She's not about to admit she has spent half the day sleeping off a hangover.

'I've been gardening and left my phone in the kitchen,' she says. 'It *is* Sunday,' she adds, regretting it the moment she hears how it's received.

'As a detective inspector, you are supposed to be available twenty-four-seven. Is that somehow news to you?'

'No, of course I'm aware that . . .'

The chief of police interrupts her by clearing his throat loudly.

'Well, anyway, something has come up that means you're on duty immediately. A woman has been found beaten to death in her home. Everything points to it being straightforward murder. I want you to lead the investigation.'

Karen feels herself sitting up straighter in her chair.

'Of course. Can I ask . . .'

'I want you to put together the team you need immediately,' Viggo Haugen continues. 'The chief inspector will give you the details.'

'Of course. Just one question . . .'

'Why am I calling you and not Jounas?' the chief of police cuts her off again. 'Yes, I can see why you would ask that.'

The sharp edge in his voice has softened a little; Karen hears him take a deep breath before pressing on.

'The thing is,' Viggo Haugen says slowly, 'the victim is Susanne Smeed – Jounas's ex-wife.'

6

Karen says nothing for several seconds while the information sinks in. The image of a shivering woman in a drab brown robe flickers past.

'Susanne Smeed,' she says dully. 'Are we sure it's murder?'

'Yes, or manslaughter, obviously we can't say at this stage. But according to the chief inspector, she has definitely been beaten to death. There are two constables at the scene and they're adamant on that point.'

Viggo Haugen's voice has become agitated again; now, she can clearly discern the apprehension in it.

'As I'm sure you understand, Jounas can't lead the investigation nor serve as the head of the division while the case is ongoing. I've already spoken to him about it and he agrees, of course. You're going to have to take over until it's cleared up.'

Two seconds of silence.

'Or until we can work out a different solution,' he adds and clears his throat again.

While listening, she's been thinking ahead. Of course Jounas Smeed has to be put on leave. Until they know more, he's on the shortlist of people they need to interview. Slowly but surely, the consequences dawn on Karen. With a mounting sense of unease, she realises she's going to have to interview her own boss. The same boss she left in a hotel room in Dunker less than eight hours ago.

As though her thoughts might give her away, she feels an instinctive need to end the call with Viggo Haugen as soon as possible.

'I understand,' she says curtly. 'I live near Susanne Smeed; I can be there in thirty minutes. Do you know if the scene of crime team has arrived yet?'

'Yes, or they're on their way, the coroner, too, but it obviously takes a while to get out there. It's only been about an hour since it was reported.'

It must have happened sometime after eight, when she saw her alive, and before twelve when it was called in. A window of less than four hours during which someone beat Susanne Smeed to death.

While I was sleeping my hangover off just over a mile away. Bloody hell!

'OK, I'll start calling people,' she says.

'Great, and one more thing . . .'

The chief of police hesitates for a moment, as though looking for the right words.

'As you will appreciate, this is a very sensitive situation. I can't stress enough how important it is that you handle this as discreetly as possible. Leave the media to me, no spontaneous comments and no other . . . Well, discretion above all, suffice it to say. Have I made myself clear, Eiken?'

Go fuck yourself, you pompous arse, she thinks to herself.

'Perfectly clear,' she replies.

With that, the call is ended; Karen runs upstairs, her thoughts racing. Three minutes later, she steps out of the shower and brushes her teeth while she dries her hair with a towel. She can still feel the lingering hangover in every part of her body.

28

I have to eat something before I go, she thinks. I won't make it if I don't. She pulls on a pair of jeans and a dark blue T-shirt and hurries back down to the kitchen. Yesterday's lunch leftovers are in the fridge: a kind of chicken casserole thrown together using whatever she could find in the freezer. She turns the Tupperware container upside down on a plate, shoves the cold lump in the microwave and fetches her black boots from the hallway. A quick glance at the time: twenty to two. Just a moment ago, I thought my biggest problem was that I slept with my boss, she muses grimly as the microwave dings. Only now does it occur to her that she's going to have to postpone her vacation again. She can probably forget about this year's wine harvest in France.

Fourteen minutes later, Karen Eiken Hornby, Interim Head of the Criminal Investigation Department, buckles her seatbelt. She has placed a banana and a can of Coca-Cola she found in the fridge behind the chicken casserole, on the passenger seat. Before she starts the car, she pops two pieces of gum in her mouth to suppress the urge to smoke.

Karen reverses down the driveway, turns out and hears the gravel spray behind her as she tears out of there. While wolfing down the casserole, she'd talked to the chief inspector at the Dunker Police headquarters, who painted a fairly clear picture. The call had come in at 11.49 a.m. A neighbour had for some, as yet unknown reason, peeked in through Susanne Smeed's kitchen window and spotted a pair of feet and legs and a knocked-over kitchen chair. The rest of the body had been hidden from view behind a large fridge. The neighbour, a man by the name of Harald Steen, had at first thought Susanne must have passed out or slipped and hurt herself, and had called an

29

ambulance. The operator who took the call, however, had been switched-on enough to inform the police as well, who had dispatched two constables, Björn Lange and Sara Inguldsen.

Karen had momentarily stopped chewing her chicken when the chief inspector mentioned those names. Apparently, both constables had been on their way back from checking on a burglar alarm that was going off at a house just six miles south of Langevik and had consequently been the nearest unit to Susanne Smeed's house. Within half an hour of being called, they had been at the scene, broken down the front door and immediately concluded that this was neither a case of low blood sugar nor an accidental fall.

Björn Lange had been sitting on the front steps with his head between his knees when the EMTs arrived; Sara Inguldsen had told them they'd come out for nothing.

'Apparently, it's a mess,' the chief inspector told Karen.

7

Karen parks at the end of a long row of cars on the muddy verge outside Susanne's house. The first is the coroner's black BMW, behind that is the scene of crime team's white van. She climbs out and stands motionless in the light rain for a moment. Scans the road in both directions. Down by the house next door, she glimpses a patrol car. Any tyre tracks will be impossible to secure, she realises. By now, most of the villagers will have roused themselves and at least twenty vehicles are bound to have driven by the house.

She looks up and gazes out across the landscape. This part of Heimö – the tall ridge in the north, the rushing river meandering toward the sea, the stone bridges arching across its bends, the heather-covered hills – has been etched into her since childhood. Now, she studies the surroundings with fresh eyes. Without seeing their beauty or noting their still-ness, she matter-of-factly makes note of all possible routes by which a stranger could get here and back without being seen. Ordinarily, it would have been impossible without some of the neighbours noticing. But on this particular day, the most hungover day of the year, the otherwise oh-so-curious villa-gers likely had other things to worry about than which cars passed by on the road.

'Good afternoon, boss.'

Björn Lange gets up from the front steps when Karen approaches the house. She notices that the constable is looking several shades paler than when they had met that morning and that his hand seems to tremble when he salutes her.

'Good afternoon,' she replies and smiles. 'Is this your handiwork?'

She nods to the door at the top of the steps. One of the panes in the leaded glass window has been shattered and two of the edges have been cleared of sharp pieces of glass. Björn Lange nods and quickly starts explaining, as though he's unsure whether she's going to be critical of his decision.

'Yes, it was locked and we didn't know if time was a factor. All we knew was that someone was in there, because the radio was on. I hope we didn't compromise any evidence, but we thought she might need help. We obviously didn't know it was too late . . .'

He breaks off and Karen nods with a reassuring smile while pondering what made the sensitive Lange become a police officer.

'You did the right thing,' she says. 'I've been told it's ugly in there. I'm going to have to talk to both Inguldsen and you later on down at the station, but I suggest you take a couple of hours off now and go eat something. Where is she, by the way?'

'She's over at the neighbour's house, the one who called it in. The old man was still here when we arrived and wasn't feeling well, so she drove him home. Apparently, he's got problems with his ticker.' Lange makes an awkward gesture toward his heart.

Karen curses inwardly. A lone female constable accompanying a witness who can't be written off as a suspect. What the fuck were they thinking? She happens to know that old man Steen does in fact have a heart condition and wouldn't be capable of killing so much as a kitten, but that's not something Sara Inguldsen and Björn Lange know anything about.

'All right, then head down and keep her company,' she says tersely, refraining from scolding him. After her embarrassing early morning run-in with Lange and Inguldsen, she's on the backfoot; this will have to be what makes them even.

A conspicuous warmth and a faint smell of smoke greets Karen when she opens the front door. Something burning, or traces of it. She's looking into a square hallway with a flight of stairs leading up to the first floor. To the left of the stairs is a mahogany-coloured dresser with open drawers, and on the floor in front of it are scarves, gloves, a clothes brush and other things she can't identify. Through the door further in on the right, she glimpses a beige sofa and the edge of a plush blue living-room carpet. There are faint noises and mumbling voices coming from the door on the left. Bent over a big black bag in the middle of the hallway is crime scene technician Sören Larsen. When he spots Karen, he raises his chin in greeting and hands her a pair of blue plastic shoe covers and a plastic cap.

'Thanks, Sören, is Brodal inside?' She nods toward the kitchen door while twisting her hair into a bun and pulling on the see-through cap. Sören Larsen meets her eyes, his eyebrows raised above his face mask and nods silently.

She knows what that look means. Kneought Brodal is in a mood today. As usual.

Karen takes a deep breath and walks over to the door. At first sight, disregarding the stepping pads, everything looks normal.

Straight ahead is a hob, a workbench, a sink and a dishwasher and above that a row of grey-stained cupboard doors. On the right, on a long granite counter, sits a polished, over-sized machine Karen assumes to be some kind of coffee maker; the shelves above it are lined with various kitchen gadgets, bowls and copper pots. Immediately to the left of the door looms a tall blue cabinet with the stylised biblical motifs that characterise Doggerian folk art. Jonah and the whale is a common theme; whoever painted Susanne Smeed's cabinet a couple of hundred years ago had been inspired by that particular story. An ordinary, fairly pleasant kitchen.

But that impression changes as she continues to take in the scene. Further in is a heavy oak kitchen table, surrounded by three chairs. The fourth is lying on its side. She registers the stepping pads and the numbered yellow plastic triangles, and then her eyes are drawn to the blood, red spatter in an arc just a few feet from her.

'Be really fucking careful, Eiken,' a sharp voice says. 'Pay attention to where you put your goddamn feet.'

Karen takes a few cautious steps along the pads, cranes her neck to see past the big cabinet and gasps involuntarily. It takes her only a fraction of a second to successfully suppress the urge to look away. Expressionless, she studies the woman on the floor.

Susanne Smeed is on her back, her head and neck at an unnatural angle between the floor and the edge of a black wood-burning stove. Her thick robe has fallen open, revealing a cream-coloured nightgown with lace embroidery along the deep neck line. One breast is exposed; Karen notes that it's unexpectedly plump for such a slender body. Susanne Smeed's left hand is

34

hidden, but Karen notes that the other one lacks jewellery but has well-manicured nails painted a subtle shade of pale pink. Her head and upper body are resting in a pool of blood, which has soaked the thick terrycloth of her robe, dyeing the fabric a darker shade of drab. The hair that's not blood-soaked looks well-cared for with blonder highlights on a somewhat mousy base. The legs are stretched out straight; a dark blue velvet slipper still dangles from the toes of the right foot; the other slipper is upside down under the kitchen table.

Neat. The thought comes to her unbidden. Neat chaos.

A technician in white coveralls moves in slow motion around the dead woman, taking pictures from every conceivable angle. There's the soft rustling of protective clothing from two other technicians, who are slowly and deliberately circling the room. Karen knows their silent, measured movements – which to the uninitiated might look like a sign of respect in the face of death – are in fact the product of deep concentration while taping and brushing to collect every last shred of evidence. When one of the technicians moves to the side, it becomes clear what caused the smell of burning: a pile of what looks like the charred remains of a basket of firewood is sitting between the stove and the kitchen table. The flames have licked the wall, leaving a wide swath of soot, dangerously close to the chequered kitchen curtain. She spots her own reflection in the glass and tells herself the dark circles under her eyes must be caused by the portable spotlights.

Karen turns her attention back to Susanne Smeed's head; this time, she forces herself to inspect it thoroughly. Strands of her blonde hair have got stuck in the blood, hiding parts of her battered face. With a growing sense of unease, she registers the crushed ocular bone and the nose that seems to have moved sideways. Her exposed teeth are white behind the split maxilla, giving the impression of a rictus smile. Her eyes are wide open and as empty and blank as on any other corpse Karen's seen: no surprise, no fear, just an endless, grey nothingness.

In the middle of the bloody wreckage, she can still make out Susanne Smeed's familiar facial features. Her unease morphs into a sharp swirling in her stomach; to stifle the nausea, Karen turns to the kitchen table. A bowl containing the remnants of what looks like yoghurt with soggy muesli in it, a basket of sliced rye bread, a tub of butter that has liquefied in the heat, an empty coffee cup sitting neatly on its saucer.

At least you had a cup of coffee after your morning swim, she thinks and lets her eyes linger on the cup's blue floral pattern. But what happened after that?

'All right, Kneought?' she says softly, only now turning to the large man who is clearly having a hard time squatting next to the corpse. She studies the coroner's broad back and is surprised Brodal can actually wriggle into standard coveralls without bursting the seams. 'What have you got for me?'

He replies curtly, without looking up.

'Well, she's dead. How about that?'

Karen ignores his harsh tone and silently waits for the coroner to continue. Brodal's jargon often gets on her nerves, but in this particular case she sympathises to some extent; she knows Kneought Brodal and his wife saw Jounas and Susanne Smeed socially for years, before they were divorced. Brodal must have been more than superficially acquainted with the woman whose dead body he's now examining.

'I got here just after half past one and at that point she'd been dead for at least three, but I'd say no more than six hours,' he says, the frustration in his voice palpable. 'I can't be more exact than that in this blasted heat. For some reason, someone decided to light a fire in that damn thing and then tried to set the house alight.'

Kneought Brodal gestures toward the wood-burning stove in the corner, where one of the crime scene technicians is currently hunched down, peering into the open door. Then Brodal looks up and meets Karen's eyes; she notices that his forehead is shiny with perspiration.

She glances over at the modern, brushed steel induction hob at the other end of the kitchen and then back to the stove. Apparently, Susanne, like so many others, had wanted to preserve certain aspects of the old kitchen when she modernised. She wanted to retain the feeling of an old rustic kitchen while also investing in every conceivable modern convenience. That's how most people go about it. But actually using the old stoves for heat, that was unusual, when the temperature was still well above freezing. Had her morning swim made Susanne so cold she turned to the wood-burning stove? Or was it the work of the killer?

'When I got here, it was a bloody sauna,' Brodal continues gruffly. 'The technicians had finally put the stove out, thank Christ, but it's going to be well-nigh impossible to pin down a more exact time of death. It's pure luck the whole thing didn't burn to the ground,' he adds, nodding to the charred wood basket.

'Lucky for us, perhaps,' Karen replies drily. 'But hardly for whichever stupid bastard's planned to pass murder off as a regular house fire.'

Brodal closes his bag and struggles to his feet. His coveralls strain across his ample gut; Karen worries the flimsy plastic zipper might give at any second.

'Could be, it's up to you to find out. Either way, I'm done here, I'll have more for you after the autopsy,' he says and wipes his brow with his wrist.

'At least it looks like we've found the murder weapon. Have a look at this, Eiken!'

Sören Larsen's voice is coming from the doorway. He's holding up a long iron poker, wrapped in a plastic bag with rust-coloured streaks on it.

'Probably consistent with the injuries on the body, if you ask me,' Larsen says, turning the bloody plastic bag this way and that, looking pleased. 'We found it neatly hung up next to the cast-iron stove.'

'Perhaps,' Brodal says. 'Which is to say, he may have used it to smash in her face, but the cause of death is likely something else.'

Both Karen and Sören Larsen look inquiringly at the coroner. For a second, he looks like he's enjoying the attention.

'My guess is she was sitting on the chair when the first blow landed, but I'm fairly certain that's not what killed her. The second blow didn't do the trick either, but it sent her flying backwards so hard her skull was crushed against the wood-burning stove. Whoever did this is an ice-cold son of a bitch, who was dead set on killing Susanne.'

8

Detective Inspector Karl Björken is at the supermarket, wavering between frozen pizza and fish fingers, when his phone vibrates in his pocket. His eighteen-month-old son Frode is sitting in the shopping trolley's child seat, crying heartbreakingly. His chubby hands strain toward the end of the aisle, where his mum disappeared in the direction of the nappy section. Karl glances quickly at the screen; his dark eyebrows shoot up when he realises who's calling. Karen Eiken Hornby may be his immediate superior, and over the years they have become friends, but she would hardly call just to chat. Especially today.

'Please, sweetheart, Mummy will be right back,' he says as he presses the phone to one ear and covers the other with his hand to block out the noise.

'Hiya, Karen,' he says. 'To what do I owe the pleasure? Have you sobered up after Oistra?'

'Shut up. Are you sitting down?'

'Hardly. I'm at Tema. What do you think I should go for, frozen pizza with ham . . .'

'Listen,' Karen breaks in quickly. 'I need you to come in, there's been a murder.'

While Karen explains what's happened, Karl watches his wife return with dread. She's pushing a trolley filled with three large packs of nappies; it looks like she really has to put her weight into it to get the heavy shopping cart rolling. In the child seat is Frode's twin brother Arne, who's chewing on something. Ingrid Björken's neck is blotchy; she looks utterly exhausted when she gently pries something out of Arne's sticky hands. His infuriated howls echo between the shelves of tinned vegetables and pasta sauces.

When she spots Karl her face lights up and his heart sinks like a stone. He knows that smile – the one he fell in love with almost three years ago and which still sends jolts of electricity through him – will be erased two minutes from now.

Forty-five minutes later, Karl Björken steps aside to let the gurney carrying Susanne Smeed's body out through the front door. Inside, he can see Karen in the hallway, talking to Sören Larsen, whose kinky blond hair looks like a tousled halo around his head. Karl notes that Larsen is standing unusually straight in an attempt to make the height difference between him and Karen less noticeable. Sören Larsen is five feet four inches in his stocking feet – the extra thick soles of his boots add another two inches, but he's still more than an inch shorter than Karen.

She looks focused; Karl has seen that mix of tension and restrained anticipation before. Now she turns her wrist to check her watch.

'Björken should be here any minute,' she says. 'We're going to have a poke around the house and talk to the nearest neighbours; I'm assuming you've got more to do here. I figured we could do an initial run-through at the station at seven tonight. Does that work for you?'

'Seven's fine,' Larsen replies. 'But don't touch anything, you hear me? Even if you're wearing gloves, I don't want you adding fingerprints.'

Karl steps over the threshold with a sigh; the moment his tall and wide silhouette darkens the hallway, Sören Larsen and Karen turn to the front door.

'Oh, there you are,' she says. 'Welcome; looks like we have a big mess on our hands.'

'Definitely murder?' Karl asks.

'Without a doubt. Well, or possibly manslaughter, I suppose, if the lawyer's really bloody good, but certainly not an accident. You can help me have a quick look around the house before we head down to see the neighbour who found her. Brodal just left and the body is being taken away right now, but you can have a look at the kitchen first and I'll brief you on what we know after.'

Karl pulls a pair of shoe covers from Sören Larsen's bag and takes a deep breath before entering the kitchen. Ingrid won't be happy when he gets home. Whenever that may be.

Karen stops in the doorway and scans the room. There's an oat-coloured sofa in front of a low table straight ahead. A pile of women's magazines on the smoked glass coffee table, next to three remote controls that look like they've been placed side by side with meticulous precision. Two black leather armchairs flank the sofa on either side; all three are turned toward a giant TV that covers most of the opposite wall.

Further down the same wall is a fireplace and two more arm-chairs, while the opposite wall is dominated by a large white bookshelf. Everything looks neat, clean and slightly clinical.

Where the kitchen, with its old cabinets and floral china, revealed a desire to hold onto the rustic, the living room looks like it was decorated by someone who simply opened a furniture catalogue to a random page and bought everything in the picture. Karen studies the impersonal interior; there's probably not one piece of furniture older than ten years in here. And yet, the impression is far from modern, if anything it's conventional, bordering on excruciatingly boring.

Then she notices the mantel, where a handful of photographs in gold frames are lined up. She thoughtfully walks over to the fireplace to have a look at the pictures, but is soon interrupted by Karl, who has entered the room.

'So that's what a kitchen looks like after someone gets their head smashed in with a poker. I don't think I'm ever going to get used to it'

'And that's after quite a lot of blood was soaked up by the bathrobe,' she replies without turning around. 'But according to Brodal the poker didn't kill her; the back of her head hit the edge of the wood-burning stove. You can have a look at the pictures tonight, at the briefing.'

Karl does a quick scan of the room and then walks over to stand next to Karen. They study the photographs in silence.

'Her daughter?' he asks after a while, nodding toward the pictures.

They look like they're all of the same person. A girl of about three on a beach. She's smiling toward the photographer, brandishing a red plastic shovel. Then a whiteish-blonde six-year-old with a missing front tooth, wearing a pink ballet leotard and a tutu. An almost-as-blonde girl of about ten, eleven, proudly doing the splits on a gymnastics beam with her arms above her head. Another picture, probably from the same time, shows the same girl, smiling triumphantly from the top of a podium.

'I guess so. Would you mind checking the bookshelf?'

Karl walks over to the white laminate unit.

'I don't know if I'd call it a bookshelf.'

With a weary look, he studies the ornaments scattered between rows of CDs and DVDs. A tiny basket full of porcelain flowers, a coloured glass paperweight, a collection of porcelain horses of various sizes and colours, a Spanish doll in a flamenco dress, a Japanese doll dressed as a geisha. The handful of books fit on two shelves: a smattering of bestselling romances and crime novels, a twelve-volume dictionary, a few thick books that look like some kind of self-help literature. Karl reads the titles out loud:

'*Dare to Be Happy*, *The Path to Your True Self*, *Stop Being a Victim – Seize Life*, *People Who Take*, *How to Cleanse Your Life of Negative Energy*. Oh my God, do you read this crap, too?'

'Every day, can't you tell?'

Karen is now studying the pile of women's magazines on the coffee table. At the top of the pile is the latest issue of *Vogue*. She fishes a pen out of her breast pocket, carefully pushes the glossy magazine aside and finds herself looking into the bored eyes of a model on the cover of *Harper's Bazaar*. Further down the pile are several issues of various magazines full of fashion, beauty and celebrity gossip, alongside a couple of publications about antiques. Karen straightens up and scans the tidy, impersonal room, avoiding the empty windows, looking for anything that can tell her who Susanne Smeed was. Or maybe this is exactly who she was. A woman with no ideas of her own, anxious to have everything looking neat. Anxious to look good *herself*,

43

Karen thinks, remembering the dead woman's manicured nails and the exposed breast. Silicone, no question about it.

She looks at the white walls, which are hung with a few oil landscape paintings, a framed reproduction of a Monet, another by Sisley and two gilded wall sconces with milky glass shades. This could be anyone's house. Any neat, tidy, middle-aged woman's.

'I don't think we're going to find anything else in here,' she says. 'Shall we move on to the upstairs?'

A thick beige carpet effectively muffles the sound of their footsteps. Up on the landing, two doors stand ajar while a third is closed. Karen notes that a golden heart – identical to the one on the downstairs bathroom door – adorns the closed door and decides to hold off on searching the bathroom. Instead, she pushes one of the other doors open and finds Susanne Smeed's bedroom. The large double bed isn't made but looks surprisingly untouched. A fluffy duvet is carefully folded back toward the side of the bed that has apparently not been used. The thick pillow has a pillowcase with the same floral pattern; a faint dent suggests that someone had at some point rested their head there. A pink blanket is folded over the armrest of a small armchair in floral chintz by the window. Across from it there's a home gym with various devices and a display that looks to Karen like the cockpit of a small plane.

'How much do you reckon that costs?' she says, eyeing the monstrosity.

'Well, I certainly couldn't afford it,' Karl says drily. 'And why have such a big bed if she only uses half? Barely half, actually. She must lie still all night long. Does your bed look that neat when you wake up?'

She makes no reply. Her bed is just as big, even though she usually sleeps alone, too. On the other hand, he's right, it really does look like Susanne Smeed didn't move a muscle all night.

'I bet there's a lover in the picture,' says Karl, who apparently doesn't want to drop the subject. 'Home gyms and a king-size bed, she certainly seems prepared, is all I'm saying . . .'

'If that's the case, he didn't sleep here last night, that much is clear. But we'll have to look into it,' Karen says, thinking she's not at all sure she agrees with him. Going through Susanne's house has given her virtually the opposite feeling; to her mind, the whole house exudes loneliness. The hope of a change, but nevertheless an almost unbearable loneliness.

She bends down, gingerly grabs the underside of the left wardrobe door and pushes it aside. Neat rows of hangers with blouses, skirts and dresses meet her eyes. On the shelf above them are stacks of neatly folded tops in every imaginable colour and fabric. At the bottom are pairs of shoes, lined up three deep: a half-dozen pairs of pumps of various colours and heel height, strappy gold sandals, sandals with pearls, other kinds of strappy sandals, two pairs of loafers and, at the far back, at least five pairs of boots. Karen slides the next door open and stares at even more neatly hung-up clothes: dresses, skirts and jackets of various cuts and a couple of thin summer coats. The rest of the space is taken up by tall stacks of shoe boxes, several of them with red sale tags. A rough estimate tells Karen there must be at least twenty, maybe thirty shoe boxes in this wardrobe alone.

'Well, well, well,' she says. 'Seems Susanne had at least one little weakness after all. Look!' Karen steps aside to let Karl see.

'Wow! But then, what woman isn't crazy about shoes?'

He's right, she thinks. Susanne could barely have picked a more vanilla hobby than being a shopaholic. Everything's in excess, yet nothing stands out; everything's tidy, yet completely impersonal. And nothing here explains why someone smashed Susanne's face in with what looks to have been unrestrained fury.

Karl has opened the top dresser drawer and is carefully pushing aside knickers, bras and socks to see if there is anything interesting underneath. He closes it again with a sigh and pulls out the next one. Karen watches him gingerly dig around underwear and tights with gloved hands. Sören Larsen would not be happy if he came in right now.

'Not exactly racy stuff. Not so much as a dildo,' Karl says disappointedly.

'I assume she would keep that in her nightstand if there is one,' Karen replies. 'No, don't get excited; I already checked. Just a few packets of tissues, a bottle of hand lotion and a jar of sleeping pills.'

Karl lights up momentarily but slumps back into dejection when Karen continues.

'No prescription label. They were over the counter until a few years ago; she must have bought them before then. Or abroad.'

Karl pulls out the bottom drawer and feels around under piles of neatly folded slips and nightgowns. Then he stiffens, frowns and draws out something that looks like a big book with a worn blue cover.

'Bingo,' he says. 'A photo album.'

'Better than nothing. We'll have to let the technicians take a look at it first. Let's do a quick sweep of the rest of the upstairs. Then we have to talk to Harald Steen as soon as possible.'

'The neighbour who found her?'

Karen nods.

On the door to the smaller bedroom are traces of screw holes, as though there was once a sign on it. Inside, on a narrow bed with a striped pink bed throw, sits a teddy bear, staring at them from under a poster of four smiling young men.

'One Direction,' Karl says. 'My sister's kids were nuts about them.'

I know someone else who was, too. Karen feels her chest contract. But she says nothing.

Sitting on a white dresser is a small stylised brass tree, with glass-bead necklaces and a small charm bracelet dangling from its thin branches. Above the dresser is a mirror and next to that a gilded hook from which hangs a pair of pink ballet shoes with long satin ribbons. Karen opens the top drawer and notes that it's neatly lined with pink shelf paper, but otherwise empty. When she pulls out the bottom drawer, there's a rattling sound and she discovers two little silver-coloured plastic trophies, rolling about desolately at the bottom of the drawer.

A sense of sorrow pervades the abandoned girl's room. A mausoleum for a lost child, a child who hasn't lived here in many years. Karl looks like he can read her mind.

'Maybe she uses it as a guest room,' he says; Karen wonders whether he's trying to comfort himself or her.

'Yeah, maybe,' she says, unconvinced.

Something tells her Susanne Smeed rarely had company. Each new room they've entered has made the feeling of loneliness grow more pronounced.

A quick look in the bathroom is just as unproductive. The room is dominated by a corner tub with gold taps; the giant

bath is ridiculously oversized. A pink, fluffy rug covers what little floor remains. The bathroom cabinet contains nothing out of
the ordinary: an electric toothbrush, painkillers, vitamins, dental floss, another jar of sleeping pills and a long row of skincare
products and perfumes. Possibly another sign of Susanne's urge
to consume. Karen looks with a degree of fascination at the jars
and bottles with Clinique, Dr Brandt and Exuviance logos, as
well as others she doesn't recognise.

'I doubt we'll find anything else here before the technicians
have done their bit,' Karen says. 'Let's head down to see old man
Steen.'

9

Harald Steen's house is just over two hundred yards down-stream from Susanne's, on the other side of the Langevik River. Karen and Karl follow the muddy path along the water while she recounts to him what Kneought Brodal has concluded.

'Burglary?' Karl asks without conviction and pulls his hood up against the fine rain.

'Maybe. Susanne's handbag was found discarded in the grass by the front steps and there was no wallet in it. Also, some of the hallway dresser drawers were pulled out and the contents looked like they'd been rifled through.'

'OK, so then . . .'

'On the other hand, there was a tea caddy in one of the cabinets with quite a bit of cash in it, which wasn't taken. Seven hundred and fifty marks and twenty shillings to be precise, according to Larsen, so if someone was after money, they over-looked it. Well, the rest you saw for yourself; neither the living room nor the bedroom seem to have been disturbed, only the hallway dresser.'

'Phone? Laptop?'

'So far we haven't found either, which may indicate someone took them. But nothing in the house seems to be missing, at least not the kinds of things your run-of-the-mill junkie nor-mally steals. She had seventy-two pieces of silver cutlery neatly packed in a case in one of the kitchen drawers, according to Larsen, which even the most inept thief should have found. But her car does seem to be missing. I know she drives a white Toyota, which isn't by the house or on the road.'

'Have you put out an alert?'

'What do you think? Johannisen is working on it. And I've called in constables Cornelis Loots and Astrid Nielsen to check with the neighbours if anyone's seen or heard anything.'

'The strangest part is that the front door was locked,' Karl says. 'Since when do burglars lock the door behind them?'

'It's one of those locks that triggers automatically when you close the door. I had one myself; changed it after the second time I locked myself out.'

'And you said no signs of sexual violence?'

'No, not according to Brodal's preliminary examination anyway. Moreover, she was wearing a robe and slippers and was sitting in the kitchen when it happened.'

'Maybe he'd been in the house for a long time. Holding her against her will, letting her get dressed before he beat her to death.'

Karen gives Karl a look, her eyebrows sceptically raised.

'But not until after he served her breakfast? Come on, Karl. How likely does that sound?'

'Well, it might have been someone she knew? I'd still wager she had a lover who snapped.'

'If that's the case, it won't take long to find out. There are no secrets in this village. But you saw the bed; if she had a lover, they certainly didn't spend last night together.'

They cross the plank bridge to the other side of the river and are now on Harald Steen's property. Karen hesitates a moment and then says:

'And there's another thing. I spent the night in Dunker and early this morning, driving home, I actually saw Susanne.'

She tosses her head in the direction of Susanne's house.

'She was on her on her way back up to the house from the jetty, probably after a morning swim. I've seen her do it before and never checked the time, but it must have been about quarter past eight.'

Karl stops and turns around, as though he might be able to see Susanne hurrying up the path. Karen knows what he's thinking.

'Exactly,' she says. 'If Brodal's estimate regarding the time of death is correct, she was probably murdered shortly after I saw her. And no, I didn't meet anyone on the road. But I've asked the technicians to take a look at the area around the jetty, though I doubt it will lead to anything.'

Sara Inguldsen meets them on the front steps of Harald Steen's house. Björn Lange is standing further down the garden; he hastily tries to stub out a cigarette when he spots them.

'Afternoon, boss,' Inguldsen says, raising her hand to her cap.

Karen nods curtly and starts scraping her boots against the edge of the steps to get the mud off.

'Good afternoon,' she says with a quick smile. 'Learn anything useful?'

'Not a lot; Harald Steen has barely put two words together. He didn't see anything inside, but he saw Lange's face when he came back out. And he heard me send the ambulance away, so he pieced it together. His face went completely grey, so I drove him home and left Lange to guard the house on his own.'

51

'Why didn't Steen try to get in to help her? According to the report he thought she'd fainted or fallen down,' Karl Björken asks.

'He tried, he says, but the door was locked. And that much is true; Lange had to break a window to get in. The old man had to go back home first to call the ambulance, then he dragged himself back up the hill to the house again to wait for the ambulance. No wonder he had chest pains.'

'Is he OK now?' Karen asks, putting her hand on the door handle.

'Yes, but exhausted. He's on the sofa in the living room; he may have dozed off.'

'All right, take Lange with you and go get something to eat. You've been at it for a long time now.' It's been a full work-day since she ran into Inguldsen and Lange in Dunker, and at that point they had probably already been on the job for a few hours. She instantly regrets it. There's no need to allude to the morning's mortification.

'Yes, it's been a long day for all of us,' Sara Inguldsen agrees with a grin.

The door to the living room is open. Harald Steen is lying on the sofa, but he's not asleep, or maybe Karen's discreet knock wakes him.

'Oh, it's Eiken's girl, is it? Come on in,' he says and makes as if to get up.

'Don't trouble yourself, Harald,' Karen says and enters, closely followed by Karl. 'Yes, you already know me, of course; this is my colleague Karl Björken. Do you mind if we sit down?'

Harald Steen gestures towards two armchairs upholstered in pilling brown-and-yellow striped fabric. There's a half-empty glass of water next to a small bottle of heart pills on the coffee table.

'Are you feeling better?' Karen asks as she sits down on the edge of one of the armchairs and leans toward the old man. 'It must have been a big shock.'

'Yes, it's worn off a little now. I figured she'd just slipped or fainted. I could never have imagined it would turn out like this. And such a young person, too . . .'

Karen is suddenly unsure how much Harald Steen has grasped of what's happened. Does he still think it was some kind of accident? She leans forward and fixes him firmly.

'Susanne's death wasn't natural, Harald,' she says. 'That's why we need to talk to you.'

For a few seconds, Harald's eyes flit confusedly between Karen and Karl; a moment later, he's struggling to sit up.

'Not natural? But that lady said . . .' He gestures toward the door, where Karen only now realises Sara Inguldsen is still standing guard in her dark blue uniform. Curious girl, that, she thinks. Or ambitious.

'I didn't know how much to tell him,' Sara says quietly. 'I just explained that Susanne Smeed was dead, and that we always call a doctor out when someone passes away in their own homes.'

'That's fine, but you get going now. We'll contact you and Lange if we need anything else.'

Karen turns back to Harald Steen and locks eyes with him.

'Yes, what Sara told you is true, Harald, we always do that. But in this case, we unfortunately have good reason to believe that . . . Susanne's life was taken.'

'Her life was taken.' As though that sounds better than murdered somehow, she thinks to herself, glancing furtively at the small white bottle of tablet. A heart attack now wouldn't just be disastrous for Harald Steen, it would likely obliterate any hope of securing an important witness statement.

'That's why we need your help, you see,' she continues. 'Maybe you saw or heard something that might help us find out who . . .'

'How?' Harald Steen interjects with surprising force. 'How did Susanne die?'

He has now, after an arduous struggle, managed to push himself up into sitting position, his back straight but his eyes still confused and worried. He reaches for the glass of water and Karen notes that although his hand does shake a little, he doesn't look pale.

'Are you all right, Harald?' she asks in an effort to refocus him. 'Is there someone you'd like us to call? You have a son down on Frisel, don't you? Maybe it would be good if he came over and spent the night?'

She glances at her watch: quarter past four. The ferry from Sande runs every thirty minutes on Sundays. Harald's son could be here in a matter of hours.

'No, by all things holy, don't bring him here,' the old man snaps. 'I'll be just fine, don't you fret.'

'Someone else then?' Karl suggests mildly. 'Maybe you shouldn't be alone, at least tonight.' He's leaning back in the worn old armchair and has crossed one long leg over the other to try to find a way to support his notepad.

'The carer is coming at six tonight,' Harald Steen mutters. 'Unless they forget about me, that is . . .'

'Oh, you have home care, do you? How often do they come?'

Harald Steen chuckles and is now looking noticeably pleased, as though he's already forgotten why the police are in his living room.

'Well, since I've had my heart troubles a lady comes twice a day and feeds me, so there's no need to worry about me. She cleans, too, really well. But she's Polish, of course,' he adds, as though that cancels out part of his satisfaction about the services provided.

Karen hears Karl's pen rasp as he makes a note.

'And when does she normally come by?'

'The Polish lady? Well, you see, it varies. Sometimes around eight in the morning and then again for supper. But she uses very strange spices. I've tried to speak to her about it, but—'

'Do you remember when she was here this morning?' Karl cuts him off with a quick sideways glance at Karen.

'Yes, it was unusually late, maybe nine. No, on second thought, it was actually closer to half nine. I know I'd been awake for a long time before she deigned to show up. Had been out celebrating Oistra, I imagine. They are heavy into the drink, the Polish ladies are, or that's what they say.'

Karen and Karl exchanged another look.

'Did you notice anything while you were waiting for your carer to arrive?' Karl asks. 'I mean, did you see anyone or maybe a car near Susanne's house?'

Harald Steen looks surprised.

'No . . .' he says slowly, shaking his head, as though the question is incomprehensible to him. 'How could I see anything? I was still in bed. I usually stay in bed until I after I've had my morning coffee. She does make strong coffee, at least.'

He lights up and Karen sighs inwardly. This isn't going anywhere. They'd probably do better to pin their hopes on the carer having seen someone. She notices Karl closing his notepad, and they make to get up from the armchairs in unison.

'But I did hear the car, of course.'

Karen freezes mid-movement and notices out of the corner of her eye that Karl does, too. They both look expectantly at Harald Steen as they sink back down into their armchairs.

'You say you heard a car?'

Karl speaks with forced calm, as though he's afraid the least hint of excitement could make Steen lose focus again.

'Yes, Susanne's car, that clapped-out Japanese banger. That's why I thought it was strange her kitchen light was on. And the smoke from the chimney, too. I mean, why would she leave things like that? But I could never have imagined . . .'

'Are you sure it was Susanne's car?' Karen breaks in as gently as she is able.

Harald Steen emits an offended snort.

'The noise it makes! Screeching and creaking like an old lady before it gets going. There's no mistaking it. It's the starter, of course; I've told Susanne to get it looked at, but I guess she never gets around to it.'

'And this was before your carer came this morning?' Karl prods him. 'Are you absolutely sure?'

'No, you're right, the Polish lady was here already. It was just after she called out that the coffee was ready. We thought it was a bit peculiar for Susanne to be heading out so early on a Sunday. And the day after Oistra, too. I suppose that's why she was so late,' he adds.

'So late? I thought you said it was early?'

'The Polish lady, of course. She didn't deign to show up until almost ten. Apparently saw her chance to have a lie-in. But it's like they say, even the wool is a heavy burden for a lazy ewe.'

'Around ten? Are you sure?'

'Yes, I remember now, because I listen to the news and weather forecast every half hour. And I had to listen to the same old news several times. But I suppose she'd been out for Oistra like everyone else and had too much Heimö liquor. They drink like sponges, I've been told. The Polish ladies, I mean.'

Karen takes a deep breath and makes one last attempt.

'So you're saying you heard Susanne's car drive off after your carer arrived? Did she hear the car, too, do you think?'

'I should bloody well think so! She said something about how it sounded like the cars back in Poland. Good lass that, at the end of the day.'

They take their leave after asking one last time if Harald Steen wouldn't like his son to come. Karen decides not to wait for the carer. Instead, Karl has written down the number of an Angela Novak from a company by the name of Homecare, whose business card they found on the fridge door.

'So, what do you take from that?' Karl asks while they climb back up the hill.

'He was more doddery than I'd expected. Not too many years ago, Steen was one of Langevik's most prominent residents. He hosted auctions and was considered stingy but very funny, if I remember correctly. But that's a long time ago now. In recent years, I've mostly seen him from afar, out and about in the village.'

'Well, I don't think we can draw any conclusions from the times he gave us; it's hard to tell which if any of them, were accurate,' Karl says glumly. 'Even if one of his many guesses is bound to be close.'

'True, but he might be right about hearing Susanne's car. You'll have to check with Angela Novak. She might have noticed more than he did, as well.'

'If the old man's right, it would mean the killer left in the victim's car sometime just before ten.'

'Well, the car is missing, so there's a chance he's correct. Let's see if Brodal can narrow down the time of death a bit more. I'm going to put the screws on him.'

'When did you put out the alert for the car?'

'As soon as I got here and noticed it missing. But that wasn't until around two thirty.'

'So the killer had hours to get off the island.'

'Only to go to Noorö or Frisel, if that's the case. There's no ferry to Esbjerg or Harwich on Sundays.'

'No, but there are flights from both Lenker and Ravenby. I'll bet you anything that car is going to turn up at one of the airports.'

'So your new theory is that someone planned the whole thing – killed Susanne Smeed and then fled the country? Just now, you thought it was a burglary. Either way, if you're right, they should already have found the car, since the car parks by the ferry terminals and airports are the first places we check.'

Karl Björken shrugs; Karen presses on.

'I spoke to Cornelis Loots, who checked with the port authorities. The only large vessel to leave the island today was a cruise ship that's currently on its way to Norway. It left Stockholm on the twenty-fifth and travelled to Dunker via Copenhagen. Its next destination is Edinburgh and it will be stopping by the

Shetlands and the Norwegian coast before returning to Sweden, I believe. One of those cruises for American pensioners with Scandinavian roots. But I have a hard time seeing why a rich American would spontaneously leave his luxury suite to cycle to Langevik and kill Susanne Smeed.'

'Cycle?'

'Fine, or hitchhike. How else would he have got here? The killer stole Susanne's car to get away, but he didn't leave any other vehicle behind. Either way, I've asked Loots to contact the cruise company to request the passenger list, just to be on the safe side. But if your theory about fleeing the country is correct, we don't stand a chance. The ports leak like sieves.'

Karl walks with his hands shoved deep into his pockets and his shoulders pulled up against the wind. Karen looks at him and knows that she needs to slow down, not inundate him with arguments, like some bloody terrier.

'And then there's all the small boats from Denmark, the Netherlands and God knows where,' she continues. 'We're talking thousands of people who arrived yesterday, most of whom left this morning. Why does every idiot and his cousin have to come here for Oistra?'

Karl chuckles.

'Don't let Kaldevik or Haugen hear you say that.'

Karen knows exactly what he's alluding to. With a shudder, she remembers the Minister of Home Affairs' visit to the police station a few years previously. In the lead up to the summer season, Gudrun Kaldevik had spoken to the gathered employees of the Dogger Police Authority, underlining how important it was for the police to contribute to the enjoyment and security of the tourists through helpfulness and service mindedness. For once,

Karen had agreed with Johannisen when he'd muttered: 'We're not a bunch of fucking tour guides.'

The context of the event had been a notorious case the summer before, when two young, overzealous uniformed officers had taken an intoxicated man into custody. Unfortunately, it turned out the reason the man in question was slumped on a park bench in Stadshuset Park was that he had been assaulted and robbed of his phone and wallet, and the reason he was slurring his words wasn't drunkenness, but rather that he had suffered a stroke the month before. As part of his recovery, the German captain of industry and his wife had decided to travel to Doggerland, a long-standing dream of theirs. The mistake was only cleared up when the wife, having spent three anxious hours waiting for her husband to return to their hotel after going for a short walk, contacted the police. No amount of apology had been able to persuade the couple to stay on the islands. Or, as they had made very clear, to ever return.

The story regrettably received a lot of attention in both local and German media. Minister for Home Affairs Gudrun Kaldevik had been forced, as the political head of the Police Authority, to give about a dozen interviews in German media in her rusty school German, which had led to a number of awkward mistakes and 1 337 063 views on YouTube. As if that hadn't been bad enough, the whole thing had also taken place just six weeks before Dunker was inaugurated as Europe's next Capital of Culture.

There had been dead silence after the minister finished her speech to the gathered police corps; Viggo Haugen had rushed to assure her he would personally oversee an overhaul of local police culture. Holding himself 'personally responsible for a positive culture shift within the Authority', would, however, prove about as futile and idiotic as it sounded.

Karen and Karl continue up the path in silence, listening to the rushing of the river, winding its way down toward the sea. Karen thinks about the inevitable task that awaits her.

'You'll have to try to reach Angela Novak today. And I wanted to ask if you could attend the autopsy instead of me? I'll go have a first talk with Jounas alone. I think it might be best if we don't all both barge in at once.'

'I'd certainly be happy to forego that particular pleasure,' Karl replies with a sigh. 'This must be fucking awful for him.'

Karen is grateful Karl has no idea her first concern isn't Jounas Smeed and his potential feelings about his murdered ex-wife. Further interviews down the line, with more people present, are bound to be unavoidable, but she has to speak to him in private first. For the first time since she left him snoring in room 507 at the Hotel Strand.

10

Karen drives toward Dunker with a knot of unease in her stomach. She drives on autopilot, letting her thoughts wander freely; she knows the road so well she can feel every curve in her body before it emerges, see every new vista the second before it appears.

The coastal road approaching Heimö's capital from the east slopes gently uphill; rolling hills sprinkled with stony pastures and copses of deciduous trees stretch out to the north. White and grey sheep move slowly across the hillsides, grazing methodically, their heads down. The lambs still have a few more weeks to fatten up before the autumn slaughter, and the wool sheep's summer coats still have some time left to grow before the shearers invade the island in a couple of weeks.

On the other side of the road, steep cliffs lead down to the sea, whose presence can always be sensed, as a hushed mumbling or a threatening roar. Today, the fresh breeze is coaxing white breakers from the waves and the sun glints between swaths of cloud scudding swiftly toward the mainland.

Coming in from the plateau in the east, the city of Dunker opens up panoramically. Easing up on the accelerator at just the right moment affords a brief glimpse of the entire bay, the long promenade that runs from the harbour in the west, past the rocky beach and all the way to the yellow cliffs in the south-east. Turning inland instead, there is just enough time to make out the half-moon shape of the town spreading out from the bay, before the road's tight bends start winding down toward the central parts of the city.

Dunker's town planning follows the same tried and tested recipe for segregation of different social groups as so many other European cities. And, as in other places where fishing was traditionally the main means of survival, the sea is at the heart of the town centre. The buildings expand in concentric half circles from the shoreline, and with each circle, the character of the city changes. Along the promenade and the quay holding the sea back, sandstone houses jostle with whitewashed stone houses and low brick buildings. Rising up behind them are much more opulent brick houses, where a succession of factory owners, shipping magnates and the growing middle class took up residence as they climbed the rungs of the Doggerian hierarchy. In Thingwalla, which flanks Dunker Bay in the north-west, large stone houses preside over generous plots of land between sea and forest. Few can aspire to live there, even today; Thingwalla is Dunker's Millionaire's Row.

The next circle consists of Sande and Lemdal, rows of terraced houses built in the twenties and thirties on what was then the north-east and north-west outskirts of town. Neat residential streets that radiate out from the old town, lined by grey stone houses, built during a period characterised by profit maximisation through social development. Back then, concerted efforts were being made in Dunker to build homes that could keep tuberculosis and rheumatism rates low among the workers at the textile mill, the harbour and the soap factory.

By now, almost every house in Sande and Lemdal has been expanded to the max. Every last inch of planning permission has been squeezed out of the long, narrow plots, originally meant to accommodate potato and vegetable patches for each household.

The circle beyond that, counted from the town centre, is made up of blocks of flats divided into East and West Odinswalla; street after street of three-storey houses from the fifties and sixties. The endless sprawl seems unjustified, but the explanation is simple: up until 1972, Doggerian law prohibited building higher than three storeys.

In the last half circle, in the neighbourhoods of Gaarda and Moerbeck, the reformed planning laws have been exploited in full. Here, furthest away from the sea winds, the buildings are all grey, box-like eight-storey tower blocks, erected during the latter half of the seventies. Here, architects and contractors have, in the name of rationalisation, ignored any need for liveable streets, greenery or nooks and crannies in people's everyday environment. There are no cafés here, no restaurants and no street vendors, unless you count the heroin and amphetamine peddling that takes place relatively openly in car parks or on one of the street corners near the two schools. The nightlife consists of rival drug dealers growlingly marking their territories and petty thieves scurrying through the pools of light spread by the few remaining functional streetlamps. Honest folk, who for some reason couldn't make it home before eight in the evening, walk quickly and pull their doors shut behind them with a sigh a relief. In Gaarda and Moerbeck, safety exists only behind locked doors, and for some, not even there. But residents who open their narrow airing windows when the wind is blowing in

64

from the north-west can smell the sweetgale from the wetlands further inland.

Karen drives through Sande and turns west toward Thingwalla. Jounas Smeed likes to stress to his colleagues at the station that his house is located on the exclusive neighbourhood's very furthest outskirts. Even those among them who appreciate their boss's attempts to downplay his background, however, are perfectly aware the Smeed family never has been – and never will be – on the outskirts of anything. Smeed lives in Thingwalla, period.

She studies the majestic, whitewashed stone villas as she slowly follows Fågelsångsvägen down toward number 24. She's only been here once before. During a heatwave a couple of years previously, Jounas had invited everyone in the Criminal Investigation Department to a barbecue together with their colleagues from the Technical Services Unit and the Prosecution Service. It had been relaxed and pleasant in the sweltering August heat.

The meteorologists seem to have got it right. The clouds are stacking up over the island; when Karen opens the car door and reaches for her jacket on the passenger seat, she feels a first gust of cold air, which according to the forecast has blown in from the north-west. She shivers and glances up at the house; blank windows stare back at her. Not a light on, not a movement glimpsed behind the black glass or in the part of the garden that's visible from the road.

Maybe he's not in, she thinks in a moment of irrational optimism. After a moment, she hears the sound of a car approaching at high speed. Karen spins around as a shiny black Lexus comes to an abrupt stop behind her own dirty Ford Ranger. Jounas Smeed stays motionless behind the wheel for a few seconds; their eyes meet. Then he shifts into first and slowly continues past her towards the garage, without so much as a nod.

Karen watches the car go by with a growing sense of unease; this is going to be just as unpleasant as she has feared. She walks up the driveway with heavy steps, catching up with her boss as he closes the garage door. They round the corner in silence and walk side by side towards the kitchen door.

11

'Want some?' Jounas asks, nodding to the bottle of whiskey he's picked up from the marble kitchen counter. Karen recognises her favourite kind from the Groth distillery up on Noorö.

She shakes her head. Jounas takes a glass out of a cabinet and leaves the kitchen. He says nothing, but indicates with a barely perceptible rise of the chin that he wants her to follow.

Karen's initial nervousness is replaced by exasperation as she is forced to traipse after her boss like a well-trained dog. She follows him without a word across shiny parquet floors and plush rugs through the dark house. They pass a spacious hallway from which a wide staircase sweeps majestically up to the first floor. A giant chandelier hangs above a round table with a vase filled with wilted tulips. To the right of the staircase, she glimpses something that might be a study and further on, as they pass the library, she notes green chesterfield armchairs in front of a richly ornamented mantelpiece and dark bookshelves covering the walls from floor to ceiling.

Karen remembers the anxious neatness of Susanne Smeed's impersonal living room. Despite having shared ten years of marriage, the contrast between hers and Jounas's home is almost embarrassingly stark. Clearly, Susanne got no part of the Smeed fortune in the divorce.

Jounas continues into a large rectangular living room and turns the overhead lights on. The sharp light makes Karen blink and the room is suddenly reflected in the windows that cover one of the walls. She walks over to the sliding doors and gazes out at the garden for a minute. An L-shaped wooden deck runs along the side of the house, with a well-equipped outdoor kitchen with an enormous grill and shiny utensils jostling for space under a domed brick roof at one end. Diagonally to her right is a long table with seating for twelve and over by the pool she spots big, comfortable garden chairs under a vast parasol.

He should close that, she thinks. There's a storm coming.

Soft lawns roll gently down toward the sea, still vividly green. Karen can't see it from here, but she knows there's a private sandy beach down there; she eyed it jealously from the water just last summer, sputtering past in her motorboat. Most of the houses around here have their own jetties; exclusive boats are moored to them at this time of year, waiting to be driven the few hundred yards west to the marina at the close of the season.

She raises her eyes to the horizon where the sea has now turned a greyish blue under a rapidly darkening sky. As she does, a gust of wind shakes the parasol and the first few raindrops land on the soft silvery surface of the cumaru wood. I should really tell him to close his parasol, she thinks to herself. Instead, she turns around and notes that Jounas Smeed has lowered his long body into one of four light-grey armchairs, slumping limply with his legs sticking straight out in front of him. One arm hangs down the side of the chair, his fingertips almost touching the floor, while the other balances his glass of whiskey on his chest.

'So, Eiken,' he drawls. 'What's your game here?'

'Well, as I'm sure you understand, I have to talk to you . . .'

'Interim Head of the Criminal investigation Department. I suppose congratulations are in order. Good day at work for you, eh?'

'Come off it. I didn't choose for this to happen.'

'But you're enjoying it. At least admit that.'

'Absolutely. Relishing every second.'

She regrets her choice of words immediately, knowing Jounas is going to seize every opportunity to strike.

'Like last night, then. Why did you leave without saying bye, anyway?'

'Well, why do you think? The whole thing was a mistake. A huge fucking mistake, which I hope we can put behind us as soon as possible. OK?'

Jounas Smeed straightens up a little and takes a deep swig from his glass. Then he fixes her firmly and smiles mirthlessly out of the corner of his mouth.

'OK,' he says. 'What do you want to know?'

Karen clears her throat and slips her hand into her pocket to get out her notepad, then hesitates for a moment and decides not to. The situation is tense enough as it is; drawing attention to the shift in their power dynamic more than is strictly necessary constitutes an unnecessary risk. She hardly thinks memorising the answers to the questions she's about to ask will be much of a challenge. In an attempt to retain at least a portion of the authority he's seeking to rob her of, she remains standing.

'Well, you can start by telling me where you were between seven and ten this morning, please.'

The sound he emits is somewhere between a snort and a dry laugh.

'Come on, is that the best Brodal can do? My God, getting off to a great start, aren't you . . .'

Apparently revived, Jounas Smeed empties his glass and gets to his feet.

For a moment, she thinks he's about to leave the room, but instead, he walks over to a low table. His back blocks her view, but she can hear the sound of metal on glass when the cap of a bottle is unscrewed, and the faint tinkling of more whiskey being poured into his glass. He sways a little when he turns around; it occurs to her that this is unlikely to be her boss's first drink today. He must have had a few strong shots in him when he drove up in his Lexus. Then she recalls her own drive home from Dunker that morning. If the media were to catch wind of the Doggerian police's blood alcohol levels on this day, it would be enough to make them jump for joy. On the other hand, it's only a matter of time before they have something else to rub their hands with glee about. Granted, most of the town's journalists are likely at home at the moment, nursing hangovers, but that respite is about to come to an end any minute. The news of the murder of Susanne Smeed is going to spread like wildfire across the islands.

'Would you mind answering the question?' she says calmly when Jounas Smeed has returned to his armchair. 'What were you doing this morning?'

'Well, I reckon you know that as well as I do.'

He watches her, eyebrows raised.

'I left the hotel at about twenty past seven,' she informs him. 'After that, I can't give you an alibi. What did you do after I left?'

'Twenty past seven, eh? And then you drove home,' Jounas says thoughtfully, ignoring her question. 'Past Susanne's house? You didn't stop by any chance?'

'What the fuck is that supposed to mean?'

'There now. Calm down, love.'

'And what possible reason could I have for killing your ex-wife? You, on the other hand, probably . . .'

She cuts herself short, realising she has walked right into his trap; once again, he has made her lose her control. With just a few words, he's managed to erase years of carefully assembled indifference to his moronic prattling. She takes a few deep breaths and sits down on the edge of the long white sofa. Tenses her back and braces her legs not to sink into the soft cushions.

'Please, Jounas,' she says, forcing herself to sound calm. 'If you could just tell me what you were doing between, all right, twenty past seven and ten this morning. You know I have to ask.'

'I came home around ten, with the hangover from hell,' he replies, unexpectedly compliant. 'Before that, I did what you did, I woke up, threw up and left the hotel with my tail between my legs.'

She ignores the jibe.

'What time did you leave the hotel?'

'At around half past nine.'

'Did anyone see you? In the lobby, I mean.'

'How the fuck should I know? No, I don't think there as anyone at reception, but I didn't give it a lot of thought; I paid when I checked in. When *we* checked in, I mean.'

For a second, she toys with the idea of offering to pay for her half of the room, but she decides against it. The less they talk about it, the better.

'Did you drive home or walk?' she says instead.

71

'I walked. It's only twenty minutes and I needed some fresh air. I left my car parked by city hall. Next to yours as a matter of fact, maybe you didn't notice?'

Had Jounas's car been there? Maybe, but her encounter with Inguldsen and Lange had given her other things to think about.

'Don't you usually use the station garage?'

'I did, earlier in the day. I left work late; I was in a bad mood and was planning to drive straight home. But after getting the car from the garage and driving out on Redehusgate, I changed my mind. Figured it was Oistra, after all, and I should at least have a half dozen oysters and couple of pints before heading home. So I parked in the car park, figuring I'd be back in less than an hour. But that's not how it worked out, as you know.'

I certainly do, she reflects. The Jounas she met later that night must have had a lot more than a couple of pints in him, more like a couple of bottles of wine.

'Did you meet anyone? The next morning, I mean, walking home.'

Jounas looks like he's pondering that; she gets the distinct impression he's play-acting. Given the circumstances, he must have asked himself that already. The moment he found out his ex-wife had been murdered, he must have realised he would be asked to account for his whereabouts at the time of the murder. That, and many other things besides.

'I did, actually,' he says after a while. 'A drunk down on the promenade, looking to bum a cigarette. I gave him one, but I doubt he's in much of a state to give an exact account of what time it was, if you even manage to get hold of him. I wouldn't think he has a fixed address, judging by the stuff he was dragging around.'

'What did he look like?'

'Well, he looked like they normally do, dirty, bearded. He was pulling an old shopping trolley full of glass bottles and junk.'

'And you didn't see anyone else? Didn't talk to anyone?'

'What do you think? How many people did you run into this morning?'

Karen is once again reminded of Björn Lange and Sara Inguldsen and decides to abandon that line of inquiry.

'And then what?'

'I went home and fell asleep on the sofa and woke up when Viggo Haugen called just before one to tell me what had happened. I tried to phone Sigrid after that, but she didn't pick up.'

'Your daughter,' Karen says, recalling the photograph of the gap-toothed six-year-old on Susanne Smeed's mantel.

'Yes, but when I couldn't reach her, I decided to go over. She's prone to not picking up when I call. But I didn't want her to hear about her mum being dead from someone else.'

Karen nods briefly. That sounds reasonable, almost human.

'So, I went back to the station, got in my car and drove up to Gaarda. *Yes*, that's where she lives,' he adds in an annoyed tone, as though this information has provoked raised eyebrows too many times. Apparently, Karen failed to hide her surprise that a future heiress of the Smeed fortune has chosen to live in one of the grey high-rises north of town.

'And did you reach her?'

'Yes, she actually let me in, after ten minutes.'

His tone isn't bitter; if anything, he sounds surprised he managed to get hold of his daughter. One of these days, I'm going to have to find out what that's all about, Karen thinks, but not now.

'How is she?' she asks instead and sees a shadow of annoyance pass across Jounas's face.

'You'd have to ask her. I'm sure you're not planning on holding off interviewing the daughter of a murder victim, regardless of how she's doing.'

His voice has hardened again and he stands up abruptly. Staggers slightly but manages to regain his balance.

'I've nothing more to add,' he says without looking Karen in the eye.

She stands up slowly and says calmly:

'OK, that's enough for now. But I will need to speak to you again, probably tomorrow. Just one more question before I go.'

Jounas has walked over to the window and is standing with his back to her, gazing out at the garden. Outside, the rain has picked up and Karen can see the parasol struggling in the wind.

'When did you last see Susanne?'

'Go fuck yourself, Eiken,' Jounas Smeed replies and slides one of the glass doors open. 'It's time for you to leave.'

The wind and rain hit her face like a slap. The temperature must have dropped several degrees during her short visit to her boss's house. The wooden deck feels treacherously slick under her boots; she gingerly walks down the three steps to the gravel path. Just before she rounds the corner, she turns around and looks into the brightly lit living room. Jounas Smeed is back at the sideboard, unscrewing the cap of a half-empty bottle of Groth single malt. Then she hears the crash of the parasol toppling over.

12

Per Lindgren shuts his eyes and leans back. It almost feels like he's taking off, ever so gently, hovering above the ground, carried forward by the sounds around him. The faint soughing of the still bare trees, the gulls angling in from the sea, peering down at the table, screeching excitedly. You might as well give up, he thinks, nothing here but disappointment for you, and for me. Neither he nor the gulls will be served fish. Not here. Meat is out of the question, of course, it always has been, but fish had at least potentially been on the table. Some had been for it, others stridently against. The majority verdict had been that neither fish nor shellfish would be allowed in the commune, but that eggs were OK, so long as they came from their own hens or ducks.

Per Lindgren smiles when he thinks back to the discussions they had in the run-up to the move. Ingela had threatened to pull her and Tomas out of the project entirely if they started chipping away at their vegetarian ideals. Brandon, who would probably have preferred both eggs and bacon for breakfast, had, after several warning looks from Janet, wisely settled for one out of two. They won't find out what Theo thinks until tomorrow; the Dutchman is arriving a day later than everyone else.

Theo Rep is Janet and Brandon's friend from Amsterdam, and though the others haven't met him, both Janet and Brandon have vouched for him being a good fit. Besides, he actually owns a Bukhanka; Lord knows how he got his hands on a Soviet mini-van, Per thinks. A terrain vehicle with space for a lot of people is exactly what they'll need on the island.

They have six months. That's how long their pooled funds will be able to keep them afloat while they build a shared future on the farm. They're going to have to pinch the pennies, live simply, until they can reap what they sow. Everyone has put in everything they have, contributing according to ability. Tomas and Ingela chipped in a few thousand, Disa is contributing knowledge, Brandon contacts – exactly who they are and what they will be good for is unclear to Per – Janet a couple of hundred pounds she inherited from her grandmother and Theo his Bukhanka and some saplings.

And then there's his beloved Anne-Marie, without whom, none of it would have been possible. When news reached them that her grandfather had died, all it meant was that some old man she'd never met, the father of a father she could barely remember, had apparently popped his clogs. Anne-Marie had never visited Doggerland, was barely aware she had roots there. And now, like a bolt out of the blue, she was suddenly the owner of Lothorp Farm, north of Langevik on Heimö. The names had sounded strange, almost exotic. But then the lawyers had put it to her plainly: if Anne-Marie wanted, they were more than happy to oversee the sale of Lothorp Farm and the extensive parcels of pastureland and forest that went with it. If, on the other hand, they wanted to keep it all, they would have to find someone to look after it. Or do it themselves.

They'd only thought about it for a week before making their decision.

Per starts when he hears the familiar sound of running, laughing children break off suddenly with a thud in the gravel yard. He counts inwardly: one, two, three, and then it comes, the howl. And moments later, Disa's mild Danish voice soothing:

'There, there, you're all right.'

He keeps his eyes closed and hears the crying subside as a second child begins to scream inside the house and then a third one.

'I'm on it,' Tomas announces; Per pictures his friend picking up Love, expertly sniffing to check if the cloth nappy needs changing before taking Orian into his arms, comforting him. Bathing, changing and soothing is Tomas' job, breastfeeding is Ingela's. And Tomas dutifully completes his tasks, even though the children aren't his. So in love is he with Ingela that he'd probably agree to anything to keep her this time. Now that they've finally found their way back to each other after several years apart.

And then Per muses that Tomas completes his tasks with the same diligence he used to devote to building model aeroplanes when he and Per were children. He still remembers the smell of the glue they used to assemble the tiny parts they'd spread out on the desk in Tomas' boyhood room. He hadn't had the patience for it; he'd frequently left his best friend to worry about the tiny grey pieces of plastic while he turned his attention to his record collection. Tomas' uncle had worked in the music industry and provided his nephew with the latest albums, something Per could only dream about.

'You can have it,' Tomas would tell him, when he saw Per squinting to read every letter on the back of the cover of some single he'd barely glanced at. 'You should take it, I have loads anyway.'

Now he can hear the clatter of china and cutlery being arranged on the table, the creak of a cork reluctantly letting itself be pulled out of a bottle before capitulating with a plop. The eager patter of feet going in and out of the house, brisk steps to fetch something else to put on the table. And the voices. Voices rising and falling, interrupted by laughter, by someone hollering for someone to bring something from the kitchen.

The sounds of a party.

He really should get up and help, but he can't bring himself to abandon his reverie. And now Brandon starts humming 'I Feel Like I'm Fixin' to Die-Rag' and someone else – is that Ingela? – tentatively joins in the verse. She can't quite keep up with the lyrics or Brandon's tempo, but when he gets to the chorus, they all laughingly sing together:

'And it's one, two, three,
What are we fighting for?
Don't ask me, I don't give a damn,
Next stop is Vietnam.'

Per suddenly realises he's opened his eyes and is singing along, too. And then he meets Anne-Marie's eyes, and they mime along together as she dances toward him.

'And it's five, six, seven,
Open up the pearly gates . . .'

Then she's on his lap, pressing her lips against his neck, tickling the sensitive skin.

'You were right,' she mumbles.

'*We* were right; didn't you want this as much as I did?'

He can feel her nodding, feel her smiling against his neck. Yes, she wanted it, too.

That's how it had worked; his idea at first, but a decision made together. To pack up, leave everything and start over.

A different life this time.

13

At the bunker-like police headquarters in Dunker, all but two floors are dark. The only light in the reception on Redehusgate is seeping out from between the closed lift doors.

The Doggerland Police Authority is divided into four main districts: north and south Heimö, Frisel and Noorö. Each district is further divided into local police areas, which handle most of the day-to-day policing. All serious crimes, punishable by a prison sentence of five years or more, are investigated centrally by the Doggerland National Criminal Investigation Department, usually referred to by its abbreviation, CID. The department is located on the third floor, sandwiched between community policing and traffic on the second floor, and technical and IT on the fourth.

The Clinic, as most police officers who've had the dubious pleasure of working in the building call it, was built on land made vacant by the demolition of four blocks of old eighteenth-century wooden houses, which was pushed through despite massive public protests. Today, the six-storey Police Authority colossus looms ominously over Dunker's venerable city hall, which is putting up defiant resistance across the street.

On this particular night, at five past seven, eight people have gathered in the largest conference room on the third floor. Aside from Interim Head Karen Eiken Hornby, the CID is represented by two detective inspectors, Karl Björken and Evald Johannisen, and two constables, Astrid Nielsen and Cornelis Loots. Also present is Head of the Technical Services Unit Sören Larsen and Coroner Kneought Brodal and, via phone, the on-duty prosecutor, Dineke Vegen.

Karen looks at the group that has spread out around the long conference table. A platter of dry sandwiches, a coffee urn and a rickety tower of plastic mugs form a bleak still life under the fluorescent lights. No one looks tempted to dig in.

'OK, I think we're all here now,' she says. 'Welcome and thank you for coming. We're all tired and there's no reason to drag this out, but we do need to take stock at this point. I'd like to start with some basic facts.'

No one speaks; the only sounds are a chair creaking ominously when Evald Johannisen shifts in it, Kneought Brodal's stifled yawn and the rustling of Astrid Nielsen fishing a lozenge out of a bag. Studying her tall, blonde, provocatively fit colleague, Karen instinctively straightens up and sucks her tummy in before clearing her throat and pressing on.

'At 11.55 a.m. today, emergency services contacted the chief inspector. Six minutes earlier, at 11.49, they had received a call from a man by the name of Harald Steen, a resident of Langevik, regarding a woman having fallen over and hurt herself in her kitchen. According to the operator, Steen had been unable to say whether the woman was badly injured, since he could only see her through a window. Or, rather, he'd only been able to see her feet and lower legs.'

Another yawn from Brodal and then one more, this time from Cornelis Loots, who tries to hide his open mouth behind his hand. Karen feels her confidence take a wobble. This isn't about me, it's just been a long day, she reminds herself and carries on.

'Wisely, the operator decided to contact the chief inspector in addition to dispatching an ambulance. At 12.25, constables Inguldsen and Lange arrived at the scene, ahead of the ambulance. After a forced entry, they quickly established that they were dealing with a dead woman, sprawled on the kitchen floor with extensive facial injuries. Harald Steen was still at the house and was able to identify the deceased as Susanne Smeed.'

So far, nothing Karen has said is news to anyone in the room, but the name of their boss's ex-wife still provokes a general creaking of chairs as several people shift uncomfortably.

'And how the fuck did he know it was her? Did the idiots let the old man in?'

The interjection makes everyone turn to Evald Johannisen. Karen studies her colleague's raised eyebrows, hears the dissatisfaction in his voice and knows that Johannisen isn't going to make it easy for her.

'No,' she replies calmly, 'but Susanne Smeed was his closest neighbour, and he knew she lived alone. But sure, you're right, Evald, he *assumed* it was Susanne Smeed.'

'And we do *know* it was Susanne Smeed,' a sharp voice says from the other end of the table. 'Can we move on?'

Kneought Brodal is slumped in his chair with half-closed eyes, his hands folded over his substantial gut.

'Thank you, Kneought,' Karen says, 'we'll get to your report in just a moment. Yes, the reason it's me standing here and not Jounas Smeed is because the deceased woman is Jounas's ex-wife. As a consequence, the Chief of Police has decided that Jounas Smeed will be placed on leave while the investigation is ongoing and that I will act in his place and that as part of my duties, I will also lead this investigation.'

The room is still dead silent. Karen resists the urge to have a sip of water and forges ahead.

'I realise this is a difficult situation for all of us, and to make matters worse, this case is, as you will all be aware, of great interest to the media. It's therefore more important than ever that we have no leaks. Until further notice, Viggo Haugen will be dealing with the press. I will be keeping him and the Head of Media abreast with the investigation.'

'The press is going to be livid,' Karl Björken says with a wry smile. 'They always want to speak directly to whoever's in charge of the investigation; they'll to do everything they can to get around Haugen.'

'Either way, that's how we're going to play this,' Karen says curtly. 'Everything will be channelled through the Head of Media and Viggo Haugen; neither you nor I will answer any questions from the press, until we are told otherwise. No leaks about timings, murder weapons or methods. No comments about Jounas as a person or what his marriage to Susanne was like or anything along those lines. This time, we're going to keep our mouths shut. OK?'

She's surprised by how authoritative she sounds. This is exactly the tone that riles her the most coming from her superiors: pre-emptively scolding.

'Then I think it's time to hear from you, Kneought, before you doze off,' she adds with a wry smile and reaches for her water.

The coroner starts his slideshow; everyone turns to the big screen on one of the walls. There's a collective gasp. The picture shows Susanne Smeed, on her back, her face smashed in and her neck at a sharp angle against the matte black edge of a large cast-iron stove. Through the bloody mess, what remains of her broken teeth forms a grotesque smile.

Karen notices Cornelis Loots's freckly skin turning paler. He quickly looks away and runs his hand through his strawberry blond hair a few times, as though trying to distract himself. Sitting next to him, Karl Björken constitutes a contrast in both appearance and reaction; his raven hair is neatly combed and his dark eyes stare unwaveringly at the screen. Only someone who knows him well would know how to interpret the frantically working muscle in his jaw. Karl Björken is by no means indifferent.

Even Astrid Nielsen looks like she's lost her cool self-control for a split second.

'My God,' she mumbles and reaches for her bag of lozenges.

'I concluded the autopsy about thirty minutes ago,' Kneought Brodal announces. 'I will type up the full report tomorrow, but I can give you the keynote right now. And yes, I'll try to use language even the Doggerland police can understand,' he adds to answer a question no one asked, but which obviously comes up often enough to irk him.

Brodal clicks to the next picture, a close-up of Susanne Smeed's face; Karen forces herself to study it again. She's painfully aware everyone's eyes will soon turn from the picture to her. Looking for some kind of answer she doesn't have, expecting her to provide leadership.

So it's my responsibility to figure out who offed the prick's ex-wife, while he sits at home knocking back glass after glass of whiskey and refuses to cooperate. And I don't even know how to lead myself.

'As I said, it is Susanne we're seeing in the pictures,' she hears Brodal say at the other end of the room, now with a crack in his voice, as though it's about to break. He clears his throat and continues. 'She and I were closely acquainted since back when she was married to Jounas, so I was able to identify her, despite her injuries, but we will be confirming her identity using DNA as well.'

Brodal pulls up a new picture and everyone's eyes are reluctantly drawn to the broken skin and strands of hair black with blood.

'The injuries we see here are the result of three very powerful blows to the head, likely dealt with an iron poker, but I'll leave it to Sören to tell you more about that. The first one came diagonally from behind in a swing that crushed the right ocular bone and nose. It probably struck as the victim was getting up from the kitchen table, or possibly she was able to get up right after that first blow, depending on the height of the perpetrator. At this point, Susanne was still on her feet.'

Brodal clears his throat again, takes a deep breath and presses on.

'The second blow followed immediately after the first. The murderer realised the first wasn't enough and therefore dealt another, which crushed her maxilla with such force the victim was thrown backwards and hit her head on the stove.'

Kneought Brodal pulls up yet another picture. This time a close-up of Susanne Smeed's head.

Like a chicken with its neck snapped, Karen thinks to herself.

'Bloody hell,' Karl Björken says.

'You can say that again,' Brodal counters. 'The immediate cause of death was a massive epidural bleed between her skull and her brain. The blood pushed the brain toward the respiratory hub where the brain meets the spinal cord, which caused the victim to stop breathing. Or, as you might put it, she died of a broken skull.'

There's silence around the table.

'And one more thing.' This time, there's pent-up anger in Brodal's voice.

'The perpetrator ripped one or possibly two rings off Susanne's left pinkie after she died. There are also clear marks around her neck, most likely caused by a necklace being torn off.'

This time, there's no creaking, no rustling, no yawning. Every-one is having the same silent thought: maybe Susanne Smeed was killed over something as pointless as a common-or-garden burglary gone wrong. That should be easier to solve. Futile, for sure, but in the end easier for everyone involved. At length, Karen clears her throat, breaking the silence.

'Can you tell us anything about the perpetrator, Kneought?'

She asks the question without much hope of getting a useful answer. She's already heard both the question and the answer too many times.

'Not much,' the coroner replies. 'Forget about the injuries revealing the exact height or weight of the person who caused them, that only ever happens on TV. What I can say is that it must have required a certain level of upper body strength. The poker itself is fairly heavy, and the blows were powerful.'

'Or rage?' Karl Björken chips in.

'Well, that's for you to find out, I guess. But sure, rage, or fear for that matter, can often allow a person to tap into unexpected strength. Besides, it takes quite a bit of strength, or rage, if you prefer, to rip the rings off a dead person. They look like they fitted relatively snugly.'

Another few seconds of contemplative silence.

'Have you been able to determine the time of death?' Karen asks.

'As I said, the kitchen was extremely warm when I got there. Apparently, the wood-burning stove had been lit and the kitchen door closed. Both the front and kitchen doors were subsequently opened by the constables who were the first at the scene, which let in the cold, causing the temperature to plummet, but then the door was closed again. The point is these changes in temperature make it impossible to pinpoint the precise time of death.'

The coroner pauses for another sip of water.

'But I've managed to narrow it down slightly. According to my assessment, death most likely happened sometime between half past seven and ten. Even more likely between eight and half past nine, but I can't be 100 per cent sure.'

Karen takes a deep breath. Might as well say it and get it out of the way.

'I can personally contribute another piece of the puzzle as far as the timing goes. At about quarter past eight, I drove past Susanne's house and saw her from the road.'

'Quarter past eight? Who in their right mind is out and about at that hour the day after Oistra?'

Evald Johannisen sounds doubtful.

'I'd spent the night at a friend's house in Dunker, but woke up early and drove back home. As I said, I saw Susanne, very much alive, walking back up to her house after a morning swim at about quarter, twenty past eight.'

Karen quickly glances around the table, but no one looks about to question her information. Then she notices Johannisen's raised eyebrows and ironic smile. He can't know something, can he? How close are he and Jounas? She feels her cheeks redden but is saved by Brodal's voice.

'All right, then we know,' he says, a note of impatient tiredness in his voice. 'That tallies with my conclusions. And I don't have much else to add, except that her stomach contents match what was on the table: sugared coffee, yoghurt, muesli consisting of oat, rye, raisins and almonds. The kind of fucking horse pellets my wife insists on buying because it's healthy,' he adds.

'I was thinking you're looking unusually fit,' Karl Björken quips with a wry smile.

Scattered chuckles around the table. The crude jargon the members of an investigative team usually employ to protect themselves against gruesome pictures had been out of their reach this time. Karl Björken's lame attempt at a joke is therefore gratefully received; the mood is lightened further when Brodal finally closes his PowerPoint.

'Any further questions for Kneought tonight? No? Then I think it's time for us to send you home to your wife and that muesli,' Karen says.

'Right,' she says when the door shuts behind the large coroner's back. 'Over to you, Sören. And please keep it brief, if you don't mind,' she adds. 'We're all tired and want to go home.'

Me especially, she thinks. Her morning nap and pure adrenaline has kept her relatively alert until now, but suddenly, she can feel exhaustion in every part of her body. She opens the document Sören Larsen emailed her half an hour earlier and pushes the keyboard and mouse over to him.

'It's all right,' he says, declining the computer with a wave of his hand. 'We don't really need to look at the pictures right now; you can do that tomorrow. What we've been able to ascertain so far can be summed up quickly. As Brodal mentioned, the killer used an old cast-iron poker. It follows that the poker ought to be considered the murder weapon, even though the perpetrator was given a helping hand by the wood-burning stove at the actual moment of death. The poker's hand-made, just under thirty inches long, likely dating from the end of the nineteenth century. No fingerprints have been found on it.'

'Not even Susanne's?' Astrid Nielsen asks.

Why doesn't she look tired? Karen wonders, studying the blonde woman sitting diagonally across from her. Astrid Nielsen looks like she's come straight from an invigorating walk; her cheeks are rosy and her eyes alert. But then again, maybe little Miss Goody-Goody didn't drink copious amounts of wine last night. Karen suppresses a pang of guilt. Astrid's good, really good even, and easy to work with, too. But definitely a goody-goody. Three children and a husband who works for the police's IT unit and always has a neat haircut and a pious smile on his face. Karen strongly suspects he's evangelical; his Noorö dialect certainly supports that theory.

'No, none at all.' Larsen's voice makes Karen snap back to attention. 'The killer probably wiped the poker clean or he could have worn gloves. But if that were the case, there should, as you say, have been other prints. But there was, in fact, a second poker in the house, a considerably lighter, more modern implement, and we did find Susanne's prints on that.'

'Right, so we don't know whether the stove was lit by her or the killer,' Evald Johannisen puts in, disappointedly. 'But why she would be lighting fires at this time of year is beyond me. It must have been at least ten degrees out, and she had a boiler. Right?'

'Yes, that's correct,' Sören Larsen confirms. 'We haven't found anything out of the ordinary in the ashes either, just the remnants of firewood and newspaper. In other words, why someone lit the stove and whether or not it's even connected to the murder is for you to puzzle out.'

Karen remembers Susanne Smeed shivering; wanting to warm up your house quickly after a dip in the Langevik River at the end of September is nothing to wonder at. But that can wait until tomorrow. She motions to Larsen to continue.

'Either way, it's highly likely the perpetrator was the one who tried to set the basket of firewood next to the stove on fire,' he says. 'But the wood was damp, and the basket was actually an old copper tub, so the fire died before it reached the curtains. If it hadn't, we'd be looking at a very different situation.'

Sören Larsen pauses briefly to flip through his notes, then continues.

'Certain signs support the burglary theory,' he says. 'The dresser in the hallway looks like someone rifled through it, her wallet – which we have to assume contained both her bank cards and driving licence – was removed from her handbag. There was no laptop or mobile phone in the house, though we haven't confirmed Susanne Smeed owned either. That being said, the lack of a landline points to her owning a mobile phone. We will, of course, be checking with the big service providers to see if she had a contract.

He pauses briefly to consult his notes again.

'A further clue that could point to burglary would be what Brodal just told us about Susanne's jewellery. But then, there were a few obvious items a burglar should have taken: silver cutlery worth approximately twenty thousand marks and a few other old silver objects, dating back to the eighteenth century, as a matter of fact, so we're likely talking substantial value, though we haven't been able to establish their exact worth yet.'

'Maybe the burglars weren't sophisticated enough,' Evald Johannisen says dourly. 'Young junkies might not watch *Antiques Roadshow*. Any shoeprints?'

'Nothing useful so far, but we've secured the ones that were there. Our colleagues dragged quite a bit of mud and gravel into the hallway and kitchen when they first arrived at the scene, so don't hold your breath. We've found both DNA and finger-prints from people other than Susanne Smeed, but we won't have the results of our database search until tomorrow night at the earliest, or more likely Tuesday morning. What we do have is an early match for recent prints found in the living room, the downstairs bathroom and the kitchen.'

He pauses dramatically, waiting until he has everyone's full attention.

'Those prints belong to Jounas Smeed.'

14

After a ten-minute break, they're back in the conference room. This time, it's a smaller group; left around the table are only the members of the CID, Eiken, Johannisen, Björken, Loots and Nielsen.

Cornelis Loots reaches out and picks up one of the dry sandwiches from the platter before pushing it toward Astrid Nielsen who silently shakes her head. Karen watches as the platter is passed around the table. When it's her turn, she studies the wilted lettuce peeking out from under perfectly square, sweaty slices of cheese with disgust. The ache in her stomach and a nascent headache persuade her to give in. With a sigh, she takes a sandwich from the platter before passing it on.

While they chew, they listen to Karl's account of his and Karen's meeting with Harald Steen and his phone conversation with Steen's carer, Angela Novak. The latter part is new to Karen as well.

'So what he said was right then? I thought that was too much to hope for,' she says.

'It would seem so. Angela Novak confirms she arrived at Steen's much later than usual. But it wasn't because of the oyster festival, as she was very careful to point out. Apparently, she'd been to see some other patient in the village,' Karl says.

'Not patient,' Johannisen breaks in. 'We're supposed to call them clients now, you know. Bloody hell, it won't be long before someone asks us to call the slags clients, mark my fucking words,' he adds around the last piece of his sandwich, while already reaching for another one.

Karl Björken shoots him an exasperated look and continues.

'Well, the thing is that this other . . . client, was a woman of eighty-five who was on the floor of her bedroom when Angela got there. Since the woman was confused and barely conscious, Angela called an ambulance and she obviously had to wait for it to arrive before going over to Harald Steen's.'

He glances down at his notes.

'I've checked with the hospital and Angela Novak's information seems to check out. A Vera Drammstad was picked up at her home at 9.40 a.m. and taken to the A&E at Thystedt Hospital. It was probably just a TIA, but she's still under observation , in case you're interested.'

'So did she see anything? Angela Novak, I mean,' Karen says, stifling a yawn, without really expecting an interesting answer.

She doesn't get one.

'No, nothing, as far as she could recall. But she was on edge from dealing with the old lady and stressed about turning up late at Harald Steen's. Probably knew he'd be on her about it.'

'What a delightful line of work,' Cornelis Loots mutters.

'But both she and the old man did hear a car starting and driving away. According to Angela Novak, it was just before the ten o'clock news started,' Karl continues. 'And she did say something about it sounding like her father's car back in Poland. But the coffee was just about ready and she was helping Steen out of bed, so neither one of them saw the car drive away.'

'So at least in theory, it could be a completely unrelated car. Maybe someone driving by on the road,' Johannisen says, spreading his hands.

'Yes, in theory,' Karl says, clearly forcing himself to remain calm. 'But Harald Steen swears he recognised the sounds it made.'

Evald Johannisen's lips curls into a querulous smirk.

'So the old man's sure about that, yet neither one of them noticed the house next door was on fire while they were sipping their coffee? Isn't that bloody strange?'

'Not really,' Karl snaps. 'According to Brodal, the fire went out on its own fairly quickly and the kitchen window faces away from Steen's house. What made Harald react an hour later wasn't the smoke from that fire, but rather the smoke coming out of the chimney. He thought it was strange for Susanne to have a fire going when she clearly wasn't home. Which is why he went over there in the first place. Are you not paying attention?'

Karl Björken looks up at the ceiling and spreads his arms as though seeking strength from a higher power. Johannisen gears up to retort.

'All right,' Karen cuts in. 'Cornelis and Astrid, have you found anything useful? Also, pass me those dry sandwiches and yeah, the coffee as well.'

'Sadly, no,' Astrid Nielsen replies. 'We talked to every neighbour within five hundred yards of Susanne's house.'

'There can't be many,' Karen mutters while she pumps a thin trickle of coffee out of the urn and into her plastic cup.

'No, outside Langevik proper, the houses are few and far between, but we did find a few other properties, in addition to

94

Harald Steen's, that are close enough the people living in them might have seen something.'

Only if they'd been leaning on their garden fences, staring over at Susanne's house, Karen thinks to herself, knowing full well which properties Astrid's referring to.

'And,' she says, feeling bitterness tug at her taste buds as she washes a bite of sandwich down with lukewarm, sour coffee. 'Nothing?'

'Unfortunately, we only found people at home in one of the houses. Lage and Mari Svenning, a young couple, who according to their own information slept until noon. So they hadn't seen or heard anything.'

'What about the Gudjonssons?' Karen prods.

Cornelis Loots gives her a surprised look.

'Do you know everyone in Langevik?'

'Not everyone. Not anymore.'

'They're on vacation,' Astrid says glumly. 'Apparently, they've gone to Spain for a couple of weeks and will be back next Sunday, according to Johannes Gudjonsson's parents, who we reached by phone. A shame, because I'm told it's a large family. With four children, chances are at least one of the parents would have been up and about on a Sunday morning.'

'How the fuck do people afford it?' Evald Johannisen exclaims grouchily. 'Two adults and four children in a hotel on Costa del Sol, how much do you reckon that sets you back? Besides, shouldn't the kids be in school?' he adds in a tetchy voice.

'Johannes Gudjonsson is head engineer at NoorOyl,' Karen replies, 'and his wife runs an accountancy company, so I think they're good for it. And their children are young. I don't think

95

the oldest one's in school yet and the youngest are twins and only about a year old.'

'So you know them?' Astrid asks.

'Only as far as that,' Karen replies and changes the subject.

There's no reason to tell them that for a few years, her old schoolmate Johannes Gudjonsson used to stop by hers when he was on shore leave from the oilrigs. Their emotionally uninvested but sexually satisfying relationship had ended the day the twins were born. He probably can't find the time anymore, Karen thinks to herself. Or the energy.

Out loud, she says:

'Any news on Susanne's car, Evald?'

Johannisen gives her a bored look.

'You don't think I would have told you if I had something? How about you, have you talked to the boss?'

Karen gives them a brief account of her visit to Jounas Smeed's house. And she tells the truth and nothing but the truth. Just not the whole truth.

Not a word about their night at the Hotel Strand, nothing about Jounas's drinking and unwillingness to cooperate when she spoke to him, or about the fact that he practically threw her out into the rain. Instead, she briefly informs them that Jounas Smeed, having celebrated Oistra the night before, had left his car in the town centre, walked home and fallen asleep on the sofa. And she recounts, just as truthfully, Jounas's story about being woken up by Viggo Haugen calling the next day and that he'd gone to pick up his car to drive over to his daughter's to give her the news of her mother's death.

With a deftness that surprises her, she skirts around the fact that not only Jounas's car but the man himself stayed in town that night and that his walk home hadn't taken place until the next morning.

Silence falls in the conference room once more. No one asks the question out loud: does Jounas have anyone who can corroborate his claims? No one suspects that the only person who could give him an alibi – at least until twenty past seven in the morning – is Karen Eiken Hornby. On the other hand, it makes no difference, she tells herself. The question is what Jounas Smeed did after she left the hotel room.

15

Karen is sitting in her car, staring straight ahead. The street-lamps along Redehusgate twinkle faintly; beyond them, she sees the waxing moon over a dark Holländer Park, and beyond that, cars pass by occasionally on their way to the better lit Odinsgate. The town centre has been wrapped in a sluggish Sunday blanket all day and is now ready for bed. She's bone-weary; her hands rest heavily on the wheel. It's half ten and home's almost an hour's drive away. The taste of two dry sand-wiches and the watery coffee from the urn coats her mouth; she bitterly remembers that morning's promise to start a healthier life. Was that really this morning? It feels like days ago.

She glances down at the passenger seat where the banana and can of Coca-Cola she brought from home are still sitting next to her handbag. The banana has darkened to a brownish black and emits a tart smell as the car grows warmer. She contemplates chucking it out the window, but can't be bothered and leaves it where it is. Instead, she reaches for the Coke can, listens to the hiss when she lifts the tab and drinks a couple of sips of the sweet, lukewarm liquid before putting the can down in the cupholder between the seats with a burp and grabbing the gear-stick. Then she aborts the movement and rummages through her handbag instead. She puts the cigarette between her lips, lights it and takes a deep drag. She reasons that new weeks and new habits always start on a Monday. There's still one hour of Sunday left.

She drives at consistently top speed, turning off the high beams whenever the occasional car on its way to Dunker appears on the sporadically lit road, focusing on staying awake while she goes over the events of the day. Waking up in the hotel room feels remote now, almost unreal, and she has no desire to return to that memory. She has also managed to push the memory of her early morning run-in with Inguldsen and Lange into the hazy backdrop of her mind – probably out of sheer self-preservation – but the rest of her memories from the day are still sharp.

Then she suddenly comes to think of her conversation with Viggo Haugen. During the phone call, all her thoughts had revolved around the fact that Susanne Smeed had been murdered and how on earth she was going to get through the next twenty-four hours without throwing up. Not until now has she had time to ponder why Haugen picked her to lead the investigation. And to take over for Jounas as head of the department. Why not Johannisen or Karl? Granted, they were her juniors, but Haugen could easily have come up with some kind of justification. He'd done so before.

Her previous attempts to make head of the department had certainly not been successful.

Karen's promotion to detective inspector had taken place under Wilhelm Kaster's leadership. It's possible he thought of her as his natural successor once it was time for him to retire. But then, four years before his longed-for last day of employment, he died of a heart attack and all plans for Karen's further advancement perished with him. Instead, Kaster was swiftly succeeded by Olof Kvarnhammar, who seemed bewildered by women in the workplace; the higher they'd managed to climb, the more perplexed he was. And yet, even Olof Kvarnhammar realised he could hardly demote Karen. But there were other methods of exclusion. In the years that followed, she was systematically overlooked when the most interesting cases were assigned, routinely ignored in meetings, constantly picked on because of her lack of street experience. The fact that she had successfully completed her police training, had done six months in the field and held a bachelor's degree in criminology from the London Met meant little compared to the years her colleagues had spent patrolling the streets of Doggerland on sore feet. That she, prompted by a direct question by a journalist, had confirmed that the gender equality within the Dogger police authority left much to be desired, had done nothing to increase her popularity with management. The fact that the quote was twenty years old, given when she was a student at the police academy, hadn't seemed to make any difference. For the crime of shitting where you eat, as Kvarnhammar put it, there is no statute of limitations.

But Karen's biggest mistake, the black mark against her name, was that she'd sold out; she'd quit. Had left the country, even, and spent several years abroad. She couldn't just waltz back in like nothing had happened, pretending she was one of the boys.

When Kvarnhammar passed away, too – in his case from a ruptured aorta – after less than five years at the helm, Karen had sensed a new dawn. While the boys went down the pub to drink to his memory, she'd gone home, sat down at the kitchen table with a large whiskey and written an application for the top job. But then Jounas Smeed had appeared out of nowhere.

By Haugen's reckoning, six years as a uniformed officer, an unfinished law degree and three years as deputy head of the Economic Crime Unit made him the best qualified candidate to take over as head of the CID. Also, as Haugen put it when introducing their new boss, 'even during his years as a patrolman, Smeed had always put his best foot forward' (here he'd paused for polite laughter), and if that wasn't enough, Smeed had shown 'great organisational progressivism and farsightedness' during his years at the Economic Crime Unit and was also able to demonstrate 'proven leadership skills'. Karen had stopped listening when he said 'patrolman'.

She still can't entirely shake the feeling that the main reason for Jounas Smeed's elevation was that he was a member of one of Doggerland's most prominent families. On the other hand, if she's being completely honest, she's never been 100 per cent interested in the top job. The thought of drawing up guidelines, setting priorities and leading the most complex investigations – and proving that she could do all of it a hell of a lot better than Olof Kvarnhammar – had been the reason she'd written that application. But the other aspects of it were less tempting: HR surveys, salary negotiations, regular reporting to the Chief of Police, having to suck up to politicians and, worst of all, having to manage *employee relations*. Her disappointment at not getting the job had quickly been replaced by relief.

And now, she's in the shit anyway.

But only temporarily, she reminds herself and lights another cigarette. The sooner this case is closed, the sooner Jounas Smeed can come back to work and she can have her freedom back.

16

Panting, Karen leans forward with her hands on her knees and gazes out at the sea. A freight ship is slowly gliding along the dark band between sky and sea at the horizon. She slowly straightens up and feels the wild thumping of her heart subside as her breathing returns to normal. Two and a half miles along the forest path that hugs the coast, straight north from Langevik. Just two and a half miles, and yet sweat is streaming down her back and her mouth is dry. It's been a long time since she did any form of exercise, she realises. Too many months and too many cigarettes ago.

For a few minutes, she enjoys the cool wind against her flushed cheeks, but then she shudders when her baggy, sweat-soaked T-shirt is pressed against her body. She pushes her hair out of her face and looks longingly over at the cliffs. A quick glance at her wristwatch: twenty past six. She still has time for a short sit-down on the leeward side of the promontory before she has to jog back. If she's lucky, there might be rainwater in one of the crevices.

She drinks the ice-cold water out of a cupped hand and settles in with her knees pulled up and her back against the rough rock wall. Just sky, sea, cliffs and an unbroken horizon. And yet, she could identify this particular spot among thousands like it. Every part of it is etched into her since childhood. And it was to this place she returned many years later, when her life was abruptly pulled out from under her. Only here could she continue to exist without John and Mathis. It's been eleven years now. She still screams their names at the sea sometimes.

She never thinks of the sea as blue. Down on Frisel and even in Dunker and along the entire west coast up toward Ravenby, the sea is different from here. There, white breakers skip merrily across deep blue seas and white cotton-ball clouds drift across the clear blue sky. There, the rolling hills are green and the trees grow tall and lush. But here, just a few miles north-east of the capital, everything hugs the ground. Here, stunted pine trees creep along the cliffs, seemingly bent double by the wind. Here, any plant that battles its way out of the meagre soil cowers to escape the violent gusts. And for the few days a year when a cloud-free sky colours the sea blue, this landscape feels almost alien to her, unctuous and untrustworthy, as though it were trying to dissemble.

Here, the colour palette is different from the greens that dominate Heimö's fertile inland and from Frisel's yellow sandstone. This place is as rich in variety as either of them, but only a trained eye can discern the colour splendour of a landscape consisting of granite grey cliffs eternally repelling the open sea.

Karen sees it. Her eyes have learnt to distinguish between the different shades, note how the sea changes from silver to tin to lead. She notices the unassuming lustre of creeping willow and bulrush. She sees the hints of violet in the rock crevices and the changes the seasons bring with the thrift of early summer and the purple loosestrife of high summer. And now, when the plants are going to seed along the cliffs and summer is inevitably drawing to a close, she will look further inland, where heather covers the hills. This is where she belongs.

Safe in that knowledge, she gets up and starts jogging back.

17

Langevik, 1970

'Is she ever getting up?! I can't take it anymore!'

Anne-Marie picks up the pillow she's been pressing against her ear and hurls it across the room. Screaming and sobbing, she starts crawling out of bed. Per pulls one of his arms out from under the duvet, reaches out and grabs her arm.

'Calm down, it'll pass,' he mumbles drowsily.

She whips around and stares at him, accusingly, as though he were complicit.

'Pass? When? I'm never going to get used to it.'

Her yelling drowns out the screaming coming from the bedroom next door. Suddenly, the house is dead silent.

'I meant Love's colic will pass,' he says patiently. 'Disa told me just yesterday that he's going to be better any day now. Hear that? He's stopped crying. Tomas is up, I can hear him walking around. Can we go back to sleep now?'

'*Disa told me,*' she mimics back at him. '*Tomas is up.* Can you hear yourself? The only person who's not lifting a finger is Ingela.'

Her voice breaks into falsetto, cutting shrilly through the night, and he thinks to himself that it must carry through the walls, slip through the cracks under the doors. He wonders if Tomas can hear it, maybe Ingela, too. Per Lindgren lets go of his wife's arm and pulls himself up into sitting position. With a soft sigh, he turns on the bedside lamp.

'She's breastfeeding,' he says gently, well aware that every word he says risks adding fuel to the fire. 'It can be very tiring and the boys are only just over a year apart.'

'I'm so glad you know all about what it's like to breastfeed. Because I guess I'm never going to find out. Is that why you're so keen to watch? You don't think I notice?'

He feels a pang of guilt. Not because Anne-Marie's right, but because he can so clearly see how he can use the accusation to turn the tables and take her place as the martyr. Now, he's the wounded one, and he's going to wrench the weapon out of her hands. He does so by not replying. Instead, he turns his head away and stares blankly out the window. It's already light outside and their makeshift blind is unable to keep the June night out. Without looking at his wife, he knows her fury and frustration have already turned into anxiety.

'I'm sorry, Per,' she says. 'I know you would never . . .'

He lets her words fill the room before turning back to her.

'You know we talked about how it might be difficult for you with all the children. That you might not be able to handle it,' he says.

'But I can. I can handle it. It's just that . . .'

Per Lindgren studies his wife with a mix of tenderness and annoyance. Now that's she's stopped yelling, now that her anger has subsided and been replaced by weakness, he can handle the situation. Do what he does best. Comfort her.

'Come here,' he says and lifts up the duvet.

She hesitates, but only for a moment, before snuggling in next to him with her cold back against his warm stomach. He pulls the duvet over them both, up over their heads, and burrows his nose into the back of her neck. Her hair is slightly damp, he realises; he starts to caress her shoulders. Pretends not to hear when she mumbles:

'It's not fair, it's like babies are just shooting out of her, and she's not the slightest bit grateful.'

'Shh,' he says and continues to caress her back. Feels her thin shoulders like bird's wings under his hands. Shudders and is instantly ashamed of his reaction when he realises Anne-Marie is now crying silently.

'She doesn't even seem to care about them. Tomas is practically looking after them by himself, even though they're not his. The only thing Ingela does is breastfeed,' Anne-Marie says and snivels. 'I know you're not looking at her, but why does she have to flaunt it all the time?'

And while his hands pull up Anne-Marie's nightgown and the palms of his hands trace the virtually imperceptible curves of her thin body, he pictures it. Ingela, pushing back her flaming red hair before unbuttoning her blouse with one hand and lifting out a milk-filled breast. Her eyes meeting his as she does so.

And with that image in his mind, Per Lindgren enters his wife.

18

Karen gets off the lift on the third floor, her legs trembling and her hair still damp. The incline on her way back from the cliffs was tough, but after a quick shower, a bowl of porridge and some strong coffee, the feeling of satisfaction still lingers. New week, new habits and at least this time she's starting off well.

Not even the sight of Astrid Nielsen, who probably got up at five and ran twice as far, and who already looks absorbed in her work, can ruin her good mood this morning.

'Good morning,' she says. 'Are we the first ones here?'

'Morning, boss. No, I think Johannisen's probably just getting another coffee.'

Since when does he get in before eight? Karen feels her smile fade. She walks over to her desk in the open-plan office, takes off her jacket and hangs it over the back of her chair. Just as the familiar jingle announces that her computer has started, Evald Johannisen appears behind her, holding a cup of coffee.

'So you're not taking over the boss's office?' he says with feigned surprise.

Before she can reply, there is a ding from the stairwell and Karen spots Karl Björken and Cornelis Loots stepping out of the lift together. They walk in, loudly and intensely discussing what sounds like next weekend's bets on the ponies at Rakne.

The brief interruption is enough to stop her from snapping at Johannisen. Instead, she replies calmly:

'No, Evald, I'm actually hoping this situation will be over so quickly it won't be worth the effort of moving offices. I'd have thought you shared that hope.'

He turns without replying and stalks off toward his desk.

Twenty minutes later, the members of the investigation team take their seats around the conference table with their coffee cups, notepads, laptops and rumpled packets of nicotine gum. The only one missing is Evald Johannisen, who is still out in the hallway, talking on his phone. Karen has, with Cornelis's help, brought in a big whiteboard and rolled it over to the end of the room. While they wait for Johannisen to finish his call, she puts up a few photographs, using round magnets, next to a map of Langevik and the surrounding area. The first picture is a blown-up passport photo of Susanne Smeed. Underneath that, she puts up a photograph showing Susanne dead on her kitchen floor and a third picture showing a blood-smeared cast-iron poker with blonde hairs stuck to it. Next to them, she writes the names Jounas Smeed, Sigrid Smeed, Harald Steen and Angela Novak. At the bottom, she adds – for lack of anything more useful – a series of pictures from Susanne's house and the plot of land it's on.

Not a lot to go on. Nothing at all, really.

'You'll be able to add another picture soon,' says a voice from the door. 'They found the car.'

Evald Johannisen has swapped his habitually sour look for an expression of cautious excitement. Now he enters the room and shuts the door behind him.

'It was in a car park up in Moerbeck,' he says and takes a seat. 'They've cordoned it off and the technicians are on their way.'

'Good. Could you ask them to have an extra close look at the starter to see if it makes any particular kind of noise?'

Johannisen eyebrows shoot up, but he nods and makes a note.

'Do we have a passenger list from the cruise ship?'

'Yes, unfortunately,' Cornelis Loots says gloomily. 'There were 187 passengers on the ship.'

Karl whistles.

'One hundred and eighty-seven? That's going to take a while to go through.'

'Yes, and as far as cruise ships go, it's a small one. Apparently, that's the latest trend, small ship cruising. Compact but ridiculously exclusive.

'Who did you talk to?'

'First the harbour master and then the onboard head of security. He was very helpful, but at the same time pretty amused at the thought of one of his guests being involved in a murder. Apparently, the average age on board is pretty high. Mainly well-to-do American pensioners who have turned taking cruises into a lifestyle, but some Scandinavians, too, and Dutch and Italian people. I'm not entirely sure what it is you want us to do with the list.'

Cornelis Loots shoots Karen a resigned look.

'Well, I assume we'll find out if any of the passengers go missing,' she says. 'We'll have to check if any of them have criminal records. I realise it seems a bit futile, but it has to be done, for formal reasons if nothing else. We'll have to enlist the help of our colleagues in their respective home countries. But I'll put someone else on that. Haugen's promised us all the support we need.'

'That would be a first,' Evald Johannisen mutters grouchily. 'Imagine what a bit of media interest can do.'

Karen hides a smile. Johannisen's right, Viggo Haugen is normally anything but generous with resources, but clearly, in this case, he's willing to splash out.

'Just say the word and I'll make sure you have all the help you need, all available resources are at your beck and call,' he'd told Karen when she had spoken to him on the phone ten minutes earlier. 'And keep me posted on everything that happens, are we clear?'

All available resources. That's not much to boast about in this building. True, the units for economic and environmental crimes have managed to increase their efficiency through a mix of experience and successful recruitment, but there is a very limited supply of experienced murder investigators. Full-blown murder investigations are a rare occurrence on the Dogger Islands. Manslaughter, rape and assault are relatively common, but Karen can personally only recall participating in a handful of murder investigations where the perpetrator was unknown. And one of those cases is still unsolved; they've never been able to prove who killed an elderly couple at the northern tip of Noorö sixteen months ago. The badly indebted son – the only person who stood to gain from his parents' passing – had a watertight alibi. The prevailing opinion among the police is that the son had an accomplice, but there was no evidence to support that theory and eventually, the media turned their attention elsewhere.

This time, there's little chance of their curiosity dwindling of its own accord, Karen thinks. The fact that a very senior police officer – who is also a member of one of the republic's most prominent families – has a connection to the case is going to sustain the journalists' attention until the murder is solved – and perhaps beyond that, depending on the outcome of the investigation. The risk of information leaking to the media is greater than ever and for each person they bring on board, the risk of someone slipping up increases. I don't want the entire building sticking their noses in, she'd thought when the Chief of Police gave her his generous offer.

'We'll start with a small group, and expand as need arises,' she'd told him.

Now, Karen Eiken Hornby turns to those around the table.

'The people involved in this investigation are the people in this room. I'm also going to borrow Inguldsen and Lange to do legwork for us. They're already involved in the case and can help out with some of the more time-consuming tasks. Cornelis, you're going to coordinate their work and liaise with their superiors when we need to borrow them.'

Loots nods.

'I assume you don't need me to emphasise that any and all information leaves this room through me and no one else. And yes,' she adds, 'there's going to be a press conference at twelve noon; Haugen's doing it himself, so I'll be briefing him after this meeting about what we have so far.'

'That won't take long,' Johannisen mutters.

'Yes, I know we don't have a lot to say yet, but Haugen's assessment is that it's important that we demonstrate transparency from the start. Besides, it could lead to valuable tip-offs from the public,' she adds, ignoring her co-workers' sceptical looks. News of the murder had spread online the night before and the morning media have rehashed what little there is to tell ad nauseam. Today's press conference is going to be a meagre feast; Karen's grateful she's not required to attend.

She takes a deep breath and continues.

'Let's move on to today's assignments. Björken and I will be speaking to Susanne's daughter, Sigrid, as soon as I'm done with Haugen. Evald and Astrid, I want you to check out Susanne's workplace. She worked at a nursing home in Odinswalla, if I've understood it correctly.'

'Yes, that's right,' Evald Johannisen confirms. 'Managed to track down the manager on the phone late last night; she said she was going to be there from nine at the latest.'

'Good. We have to talk to everyone who can tell us anything about Susanne Smeed: colleagues, neighbours and relatives. Who was part of her social circle? Did she have a lover? Interests, quarrels, anything that can lead us to a possible motive. And Cornelis, I want you to stay in touch with the technicians and keep me posted on any progress on that front. She must have had a mobile phone at home and probably a laptop, too.'

They all receive their assignments with silent nods and note-taking. Not even Evald Johannisen objects. But a feeling of silent expectation permeates the room. Did I forget something? Karen wonders with a sudden flutter of panic. Am I supposed to say or do something else?'

And at that moment, she realises what they're waiting for.

'I know this is a unique situation, not least for me,' she says and looks from person to person. 'Some of you might be wondering why Viggo Haugen chose me to lead this investigation; I've asked myself that very question.'

Evald Johannisen's chair creaks ominously when he crosses his legs and slowly leans backward. He meets her eyes with raised eyebrows, as though he's interested to hear what's next.

'And . . .?' he drawls. 'Do you have an explanation?'

His words turn her insecurity into irritation; she'll be damned if she backs down.

'I suppose it's to do with me being the most experienced detective inspector here. It's true my CV's light on patrolling; I know some of you have more experience in that area, but in this department, I'm the one with the most experience investigating serious crime and I believe our different backgrounds complement each other. Either way, I hope I can count on your support and cooperation. If not for me, then for Jounas.'

Evald Johannisen looks down at the table, but the others nod.

'Of course,' Astrid says.

'What about Jounas?' Karl Björken asks. 'Who's going to talk to him?'

'I will,' Karen says. 'I'm going to talk to him again, later today. But you and I are going to start with the daughter. And the rest of you, get digging and we'll meet back here at 4 p.m. to take stock. And call me immediately if you come across anything of interest.'

The stairwell of Aspvägen 48 smells like disinfectant, food and recently cleaned-up vomit. The grey stone floor in the lobby is still wet after the morning's cleaning efforts; the cleaner, with whom they cross paths outside the front door, is striding towards a white van with a bucket in one hand and a long mop in the other.

Sigrid Smeed lives on the sixth floor, according to the large name board that covers the greater part of a wall on the ground floor; they take the lift. Karl Björken has already spoken to Susanne Smeed's daughter on the phone to let her know they're coming; her door opens before they have a chance to ring the bell. She must have been listening for the lift, Karen decides, and catches a brief glimpse of a pale face before the young woman turns around without a word and disappears into the flat. Karl and Karen exchange a look while he pulls the door shut behind them. Then they follow Sigrid into the living room.

The room is dark. A sofa draped in a cloth with an oriental pattern faces away from a window whose closed curtains shut out the autumn sun. The room's only light source is a ray of sunlight seeping through a four-inch gap where the maroon curtains don't quite meet. Bookshelves filled with paperbacks, CDs and a remarkable number of vinyl records cover two of the walls. On the third wall is a poster from an Andy

Warhol exhibition at the Louisiana museum in Denmark and a framed newspaper clipping of something that looks like a review from the Frisel Music Festival. Below them, two black guitar cases and a stack of newspapers sit next to a black Marshall amplifier.

Sigrid has parked herself cross-legged in the middle of the sofa, a clear signal she wants to be the only person on it. A packet of cigarettes and a green plastic lighter lie next to a chipped blue tea mug on the low coffee table made of dark, stained wood. The mug is still half full and the sandwich next to it looks untouched.

Without asking permission, Karen takes a seat in a tattered wingback armchair and watches as Karl folds his gangly body onto a low light brown leather pouffe. She contemplates the dust particles hovering in the ray of sunlight, then turns to the black-haired girl on the sofa.

Her face is pale and closed and her mouth tense. Her septum is pierced by a thick gold ring and sinuous green and blue tattoos depicting some kind of serpentine creature wrap around both of her crossed arms. Her shoulder-length hair is tousled, as though she just got out of bed. That its raven colour isn't real is amply demonstrated by her bloodshot eyes, hiding behind blonde eyelashes. Exposed chinks in her tough armour.

How different from the little blonde girl smiling in the photographs in Susanne Smeed's living room. How old can she be, not much more than eighteen or nineteen, surely?

'Hi Sigrid,' Karen says. 'How are you feeling?'

A shrug. Karen braces herself.

'I want to start by saying how sorry I am for you. I understand it must be very difficult to lose your mother. Especially like this.'

115

Sigrid's only reaction is to glance up briefly at the ceiling, as though waiting patiently for her visitors to get to the point. Karen tries again.

'As I'm sure you understand, we are doing everything in our power to find out who killed your mum, which is why we need to ask you some questions. It won't take long . . .'

'What do you want to know?' Sigrid cuts her off in a harsh voice. 'Just fucking spit it out and then you can leave. I'm working tonight, so I need to sleep.'

'You're working?' Karl asks in surprise.

'Why?' Sigrid asks and turns to him. 'You don't think it's appropriate?'

He makes no reply, but glances over at Karen, who takes over again. Some of the softness in her voice is gone when she asks the next question.

'You work at one of the music bars downtown, don't you? What's the name of it?'

'Lucius.'

'On Thybeckgate?'

No answer.

'All right,' Karen says. 'Were you working there on Saturday night?'

'Yes.'

'Until when?'

'I always work until closing.'

'And what time is that?' Karen asks patiently.

Sigrid is now studying her nails. Apparently, she's found something interesting and is scratching at it with her thumbnail. A flake of her black nail polish peels off and falls into her lap.

'Come on,' Karl intercedes, obviously annoyed. 'We'll be out of here sooner if you don't make us drag every answer out of you. When do you close?'

'One,' Sigrid mumbles while biting off a piece of cuticle from her right index finger.

'One,' Karl confirms and makes a note.

'But on Saturday we stayed open until three,' Sigrid adds, holding up her finger to study the result.

Nice one, Karl, Karen thinks. Maybe you've managed to break the ice.

'Did you go straight home after work?'

'No, I didn't. I went to get my bike first,' she adds after a short pause.

Karen suppresses an urge to raise her voice. Karl is doing annoyed today.

'Were you alone, or was someone with you?' she asks as neutrally as she can manage.

'Like was I hooking up with someone, you mean? You think I bring clients home from work like some fucking whore?'

'No, Sigrid,' she says with exaggerated patience in her voice. 'I meant maybe you had a boyfriend with you. Or maybe someone waiting for you at home.'

Something in Sigrid's face changes; a faint twitch at the corner of her mouth, as though she's fighting back tears. She pulls on the sleeves of her knitted jumper, stretching them out to cover her hands, and sits in silence for a moment before turning back to Karen and replying, her voice steady once more.

'No, no one. I was alone.'

'But you don't live here alone, do you?' Karl says and nods in the direction of the guitar cases. 'Are they both yours or do you have a boyfriend?'

A shrug; they wait.

'I don't fucking know,' Sigrid says after a while. 'I have no fucking idea if he's planning on coming back. We had a fight and he left. Haven't seen him since.'

'What's his name?'

'Sam. Samuel Nesbö.'

'And you normally both live here?'

This time there's a nod and a quick wipe with her sleeve under her nose.

'What happened? Can you tell us?'

'I told you, we had a fight.'

'On Saturday?'

'Yes.'

'About what?'

'What's it to you? Do you want me to tell you how things are in bed or what?'

'No, we don't give a shit about that,' Karen says calmly. 'But we do want to know what you were fighting about, and what time it was.'

'He got pissed when I talked to some Dutch guys, OK? We'd played and they came up to me during the break. I don't know what time it was, maybe two?'

'Played?' Karl says in surprise. 'I thought you worked behind the bar.'

Sigrid rolls her eyes and shakes her head with a wan smile at his unfathomable stupidity. For a moment, Karen imagines she

118

can sense the lingering presence of the little girl in the photographs in Susanne Smeed's living room.

'I do,' Sigrid says, and now it's her turn to use an overly patient tone. 'But we have gigs, too, you see. It *is* possible to do more than one thing, isn't it?'

She pauses briefly and then continues.

'So on Saturday, I worked the bar until half eleven and then we played until closing. Two jobs in one night, super weird, right? Are you going to arrest me now?'

Karen can feel the sides of her mouth twitching; she frowns to suppress the smile. She looks down at her lap for a moment before catching Sigrid's gaze and holding it while she asks her next question.

'So you're telling us you and Sam had a fight, and you went home alone after closing. Did you go straight home?'

Karen sees Sigrid's eyes narrow and her upper lip curl up in something that looks like genuine contempt.

'No, I took a detour to Langevik to kill my mum first,' she says slowly and pulls the corners of her mouth up in a provocatively mirthless smile.

Out of the corner of her eye, Karen notes that Karl is gearing up to jump back in.

'You did?' she says calmly, beating him to it. 'You went to Langevik?'

'And why the fuck would I do that?'

'Well, maybe you didn't want to be here alone. Maybe you were upset and wanted to spend the night at your mum's house?'

'Do you know how far that is? It would take hours on a bike.'

119

'If you were on a bike. Maybe you hitched a ride, I'm guessing lots of people were going that way after Oistra. Hardly impossible to find someone willing to drive you, I'd guess.'

'I went home,' Sigrid says tersely. 'Besides, I had no idea she was home. She usually goes away over Oistra. I guess she can't bear being around happy people.'

Karen pricks up her ears. This is new information.

'Where does she normally go?'

Another shrug.

'The usual, I guess. Probably takes the ferry to England or Denmark. She used to go to Mallorca and Greece and whatever, but I doubt she can afford that nowadays.'

'So you didn't know your mum was staying home this year?'

'No, but even if I had known, I wouldn't have gone over there. Mum's, like, the last person I would have wanted to see.'

'How come? Did you and your mother not have a good relationship?' Karl asks.

Sigrid throws him a disdainful look.

'*Did you and your mother not have a good relationship?*' she mocks in an over-the-top impression of Karl. 'We didn't have a relationship, period, if you have to know. I haven't seen her in over a year. Barely talked to her either.'

'And why is that?' Karen says.

Sigrid leans forward and pulls a cigarette out of the packet on the coffee table. Her thin hand trembles slightly when she holds the flame of the lighter up to the cigarette and takes a deep drag.

'She was mad,' she says succinctly and blows out smoke. 'That's why.'

'Mad? In what way?'

'Bitter, always nagging. Hated everyone. Thought she could control me even though I haven't lived at home for over two years. Is that enough?'

'Two years? You must have been very young when you moved out. Was she really OK with that?'

'The day I turned sixteen. I didn't ask permission.'

Another drag; her voice is more relaxed now. Some of the shrill overtone has disappeared.

'And before you moved out? Did you move back and forth after the divorce, or did you live with your mum?' Karen asks and tries to think if her boss has ever mentioned anything about this. No, she concludes, he's never talked about his daughter at work, at least not in front of me. Only mentioned her in passing once or twice.

Sigrid takes another drag; this time she blows little smoke rings and watches as they rise toward the ceiling.

'I moved back and forth. Had to pack up my things every Sunday. And it was hell, in case you were wondering.'

'Moving back and forth? Is that what you meant?'

'No, that the two of them were such fucking pricks. I'm probably the only kid in the world who prayed to God every night that her parents would get a divorce. I guess I figured things would get better if they did, but they got worse; they were always fighting and wanted me to act like some kind of go-between. They're out of their minds, both of them,' she adds and stubs her cigarette out violently on the saucer of the half-empty tea mug.

As though realising she just used the wrong tense about her mother, Sigrid suddenly looks confused.

Karen and Karl both feel a growing sense of unease as this new information sinks in. That Jounas Smeed's marriage had been stormy and that the fighting had continued after the divorce was something they would have preferred not to know, particularly in connection with the investigation into the murder of his ex-wife. And hearing it straight from his daughter fills them both with a feeling of snooping around something they want nothing to do with. Like sniffing someone's dirty laundry.

'One last question,' Karen says. 'Do you have any idea who might want to hurt your mother? Someone she had an issue with?'

Sigrid looks at her with an air of resignation.

'Issue? Aside from Dad, you mean? Well, only, like, every person she ever met.'

'Anyone specific come to mind?'

'I've no idea what she got up to or who she spent time with. Like I said, we've had practically no contact in the past couple of years.'

She falls silent and her eyes well up.

'OK, Sigrid,' Karen says. 'We're done bothering you for today, but we may need to speak to you again.'

She pulls a business card out of her jacket pocket.

'This is my number. If you think of anything, give me a call. Or if you just want to talk,' she adds, without really knowing what she means by that. If she was looking to have a heart to heart, Sigrid Smeed would hardly turn to one of her father's colleagues. And a copper, to boot.

She puts the card down on the table and stands up. When Karl closes the front door behind them, Sigrid is still sitting motionless on the sofa.

She should lock the door, Karen observes.

20

They ride the lift back down in silence. As they exit the building, they notice three boys of about thirteen scurrying away from Karen's car like rats.

'Goddamn kids, why aren't they in school?' Karl exclaims furiously, studying the black felt-tip letters on the windscreen: FUCKING CUNTSTABLES.

'The real question is how they spotted us, given as how we're not even driving a patrol car,' Karen counters.

Karl laughs bitterly while he tries to rub off the text with the sleeve of his jacket.

'Come on, those brats can spot a copper a mile away. I'm guessing it's genetic.'

'Stop that, you're ruining your jacket. And tone down the prejudice, will you?'

She opens the door and turns on the windscreen wipers. Karl has slid into the passenger seat; a faint smell of ethanol spreads through the car as they watch the wiper fluid smear the black letters into grey slush across the windscreen.

'That was rough,' Karl says after minute.

Karen nods silently.

'Are you sure you want to talk to Jounas by yourself? Maybe it would be easier if we both go?'

'Thanks, you're nice to offer, but I think it would be best if I went alone again. We didn't get very far yesterday, he was . . . in shock and not particularly easy to talk to.'

Karl shoots her a look.

'You mean hammered? Well, I certainly wouldn't blame him if he took to the bottle. I know I would if someone beat my ex to death. Even if she was a right witch,' he adds; Karen wonders if he's referring to his own ex-wife or Susanne Smeed.

She decides it makes no difference.

'I guess he wasn't entirely sober,' she replies drily. 'Either way, I'm going to have one more go on my own before we up the ante. After all, it depends on what the others dig up, too. Let's just wait and see where we are at the end of the day.'

She drops Karl off on Redehusgate, outside the station. A car from the public radio station is parked across the street. Between the open back doors of a van adorned with the logo of Doggerland's public television broadcaster, DTV, Karen glimpses a photographer she recognises as the constant companion of TV reporter Jon Bergman. He's leaning a tripod against the van while unloading his camera. The moment Karl opens the passenger door to climb out, Jon Bergman himself appears from behind the DTV van. He immediately spots Karen behind the wheel and sets his course for her.

'Get out of here, right now,' Karen hisses to Karl. 'And not one word to the media, you hear me?'

The moment the car door closes behind Karl, she floors it, heading toward Odinsgate. In the rear-view mirror, she sees Jon Bergman standing forlornly in the middle of the street, looking after her for a few seconds before turning around and hurrying into the station after Karl.

Viggo Haugen's decision to hold a press conference hadn't been open for discussion. But when Karen had briefed him and prosecutor Dineke Vegen about the investigation after the morning meeting, he'd looked concerned.

'So you're seriously telling me no one saw or heard anything? And you have no idea who did this?'

'That's correct; so far, we've found neither witnesses nor motives, but it's still early days. It's not even been twenty-hours since we were called to the scene.'

'And what am I supposed to say at the press conference?'

The chief of police had spread his hands and looked at Dineke Vegen, as though expecting her to back him up in his criticism. But the prosecutor had ignored him and instead made a note in her papers.

'Well, I guess you'll have to tell them everything we do know, except for the method and the murder weapon, obviously,' Karen had replied. 'Who died, where it happened, that we can't rule out murder but that we are not at liberty to divulge further details. The usual crap,' she'd added before being able to stop herself.

Viggo Haugen had given her an annoyed look, and Karen had quickly attempted to take the sting out of her words.

'But I agree it can be a good idea to talk to the media at an early stage. It could generate valuable information from the public.'

What do you know, my tongue's already getting longer and browner? she'd thought to herself, offering a conciliatory smile.

Maybe it is, if not good, then at least necessary, to hold a press conference now, she thinks, watching Jon Bergman's back disappear into the station. That the head of the CID is closely connected to the victim is of course already known to every editor in town. They have to inform the media about what steps they're taking to keep Jounas Smeed safe while the investigation is ongoing. What she said about tips from the public, on the other hand, is a long shot. Previous experience has shown that anyone with truly valuable information usually gets in touch without being urged by the media. The rest, on the other hand, are triggered by appeals for information and will burden both the local phone networks and the country's police stations. Valuable time will be wasted talking to lonely people and nutters about things that have nothing at all to do with Susanne Smeed's death.

Karen turns left onto Odinsgate and then right down Slaktehusgate toward Packartorget Square. About twenty people are scattered on the steps of the National Museum, faces turned toward the sun. It's really too early for lunch and she's not particularly hungry, but she realises she should have something to eat before she pushes on toward Thingwalla. Seeing Jounas Smeed is going to be hard enough under the best of circumstances; with low blood sugar, it could prove a disaster.

  She parks in the square outside the market hall and enters through the large doors, quickly passes through smells of freshly ground coffee, spices and bread and continues toward the fishmonger at the back. Here, crates of smoked herring and prawns jostle for space with piles of different kinds of rough-shelled oysters, troughs full of bright red lobsters, ice beds where anglerfish, cod and mackerel are stacked next to wolfish and haddock. She stops to look at their wide-open eyes and gaping mouths and makes a mental note to buy a nice piece of cod for the weekend. A memory of Susanne Smeed's empty, dead eyes flashes through her mind; she continues toward the food-to-go section.

Ten minutes later she takes a seat on the museum steps with a salmon salad and a bottle of mineral water. She shades her eyes with her hand and looks out across the square where eager fruit and vegetable sellers shout to make themselves heard over the classical music streaming out of the speakers. After much agonising, Dunker Town Council has decided to splurge on another year of lunch music at some of the city's prominent gathering places. The whole thing had started as one of the many events put on for the Capital of Culture year when the city's political parties had competed to come up with creative suggestions for how to increase the availability of any and all forms of culture. No one had thought there would be strident protests when the speakers were taken down at the end of the year; in the end, the council had rolled over and let the public will triumph. Consequently, for two hours every day, classical music still streams out across Packartorget Square. Any attempt to vary or modernise the repertoire has been rebuffed, however; no one is willing to pay for the right to play music when works over seventy years old are free, in accordance with international copyright laws. There are limits.

Karen closes her eyes and listens for a few seconds to something she believes may be Mahler. Even though the sun is considerably lower in the sky now than just a few weeks ago, it still warms her cheeks and forehead. But a new crispness has crept in across the island, like a mild but insistent reminder that this is a temporary reprieve; summer is definitely over, and soon, harsh Atlantic winds will blow in across the Dogger Islands.

127

She opens her bottle, takes a sip of mineral water and digs into the warm smoked salmon. While she chews, her thoughts meander to the meeting that awaits her. Turning up unannounced at Jounas's house again is a gamble, but her plan is to disarm him before he has a chance to put his guard up. He won't like it. At the same time, it can hardly come as a surprise to him that she's back so soon.

Given the statistics, he should actually be bloody grateful she hasn't brought him down to the station yet. In nine cases out of ten when a woman's murdered, the perpetrator's either the husband or the ex-husband. The question is how cooperative Jounas will be this time. And how sober.

21

As Karl Björken passes through the revolving door to the police station, he hears Jon Bergman's all-too familiar voice in the compartment behind him.

'Hey, Björken, do you have a minute? Hey, hold on, will you?'

Without turning around, Karl continues briskly toward the lifts, but the young reporter from DTV's *The World Today* catches up before he can even push the button. I should've taken the stairs, he thinks and glances over at the reception desk, where the on-duty constable is trying to placate the journalists who are impatiently waiting for their visitors' passes to be printed. Dark blue circles under the arms of his uniform shirt reveals that the system's on the blink as usual; the loud opprobrium from the assembled press is peppered with words relating to bureaucracy and police incompetence.

A security guard from Gardia is blocking the door to the main auditorium, his arms outstretched, doing his best to prevent a criminal reporter from *Kvellsposten* from walking in without registering.

Karl glances up at the clock above the reception desk: three minutes to twelve. Viggo Haugen is probably pacing nervously behind the scenes right now, waiting to make his entrance, anxiously wondering why the auditorium is still empty. This is certainly getting off to a stellar start, Karl Björken considers, and turns his back on the debacle. Noon is an idiotic time to hold a press conference, anyway. At least, it is if you don't intend to offer the gaggle of scandal-sniffing reporters anything to ward off their worst lunchtime hunger pangs.

But then this press conference isn't going to offer anything of substance in either a literal or a figurative sense; Viggo Haugen is as tight-fisted as he's hungry for media attention; Karl thanks his lucky stars he's not required to participate in the pointless spectacle.

'Is Jounas Smeed's ex-wife the murder victim? Can you at least confirm that? Come on, we already know it's her; I just need official confirmation.'

Jon Bergman asks the question while glancing over at his photographer, who's crowding the reception desk with the others. Annoyed, Karl pushes the lift button again and looks up at the displays above the doors. One lift seems stuck on the fourth floor while the other is on its way up.

'Has Smeed been suspended? As a family member he has to be considered a suspect, right? Or do you already know who the killer is?'

Jon Bergman tries to get around Karl to catch his eye. He takes a quick breath and continues.

'Do you know what weapon was used? Smeed must have a firearm, right? Come on, Björken, give me something, will you?'

Karl listens absently to the deluge of questions. For once, the details haven't started leaking yet. Out of respect for Jounas, his colleagues seem to have actually kept their mouths shut. With relief, he notes that one of the lifts finally seems to be on its way down.

'Absolutely,' he says with a grin just as the doors ding and slide open.

'What? What do you mean?'

Jon Bergman looks puzzled.

'Hey, I think they're about to start in there now.' Karl nods toward the auditorium where the security guard has stepped aside to let in the horde of impatient journalists and photographers. 'You'd better hurry or you'll miss it,' he says and smiles at the reporter as the lift door slides shut between them.

While the lift works its way up, Karl pulls out his phone and taps out a text to Karen. He presses send just as he steps out of the lift on the third floor.

Smeed is going to have visitors very soon.

Evald Johannisen seems to be staring fixedly at the computer screen, but Karl can tell from his vacant eyes that his thoughts are somewhere else entirely.

'All right, Evald?' he says and slams his fist into the side of his desk. 'Daydreaming, are we?'

Johannisen startles and, for a moment, a look of uncontrolled rage distorts his features. A fraction of a second passes, he has composed himself, smiles widely and leans back casually in his office chair.

'Look who's here; did she let you off your lead or did you break free?'

'Believe it or not, I'm allowed to run free for a bit. Have you seen Loots? I figured I'd check to see if he'd heard back from the technicians.'

Evald Johannisen jerks his head toward the kitchen.

'Probably on a coffee break as usual. Where's the boss lady got to, then?'

'She went over to Smeed's. Like she said she would this morning.'

'Yes, apparently she prefers to see him ... shall we say privately? Very thoughtful of her, outstanding managerial potential, if you ask me.'

Karl Björken studies his colleague and makes a quick assessment. Johannisen is tiresomely disgruntled as usual, but his sarcasm usually has a bit more subtlety to it. The appointment of Karen Eiken Hornby as interim Head of the CID has clearly touched a nerve. Karl has an urge to say something about sour grapes, but decides not to.

He likes Karen; despite her lack of social polish and one or two tiresome idiosyncrasies, she's always done a good job. On the other hand, no one wants to get on the wrong side of Johannisen. Even worse than having to put up with listening to him bashing someone else would be knowing he was criticising you behind your back. Besides, this new power structure is highly temporary and caution should always be the guiding principle when it comes to office politics. Upon Smeed's return, Karen's going to be pushed down the ladder and Johannisen's stock will rise again. He settles on simply shooting Johannisen a crooked smile, which he is free to interpret as he pleases.

'What about you?' he says in an attempt to distract and redirect. 'Weren't you and Astrid going out to Susanne Smeed's workplace today?'

'Yeah, we went, but it didn't turn up much. The manager talked about how devastated she was about what happened, but the people who were there didn't seem to have worked

132

very closely with Susanne. I think we're going to have to have another go.'

'Eiken and I just talked to Jounas's daughter, not much luck there either,' Karl offers. 'It was impossible to get anything useful out of her; she mostly seemed resentful.'

'Yeah, I know, tattoos and nose ring and the rest of the look,' Johannisen grins, looking like he's trying to coax something out from between his teeth with his tongue.

'Oh, so you've met her? I got the impression she doesn't have much contact with Jounas.'

'That's certainly true, but Erlandsen pointed her out to me on the street a few weeks ago and told me that was Smeed's girl. Poor sod! First all that stuff with his wife and then a daughter who looks like a bloody junkie.'

'*All that stuff with the wife*, what do you mean?'

Evald Johannisen has stuck his pinkie deep into his mouth and is now laboriously working on whatever is clearly stuck between his molars.

'Come on, Björken,' he says, 'surely half of Doggerland knows Susanne Smeed made Jounas's life hell for years. And not just his life, if I've understood things right; she apparently made a nuisance of herself in all kinds of areas. No, there's no shortage of enemies or motives there. Are you really that out of the loop, Charlie-boy?'

With revulsion, Karl Björken watches his colleague wipe his index finger on his trousers; he can feel his irritation intensifying.

'Well,' he says, shrugging indifferently in an attempt to take the edge off the news value of Johannisen's statement. 'I knew she was no Mother Teresa, obviously, but I think you're going to have to be more specific if you want the village gossip to yield anything useful.'

Evald Johannisen slowly shakes his head and smacks his lips with a rueful smile.

'Rule number one for coppers: never underestimate village gossip. Nine times out of ten, that's where you'll find the truth. But I'm sure our precious lady detective and her Charlie-boy will be more than able to dig up all the dirt on the boss and his family, rather than having me serve it up on a silver platter.'

As usual, Evald Johannisen delivers his offensive comments with a big smile, always ready to backpedal and claim he was just kidding if need be. But Karl can hear a new edge in Johannisen's voice, something he hasn't heard there before. As though he's punching from below this time and knows it.

'And I'm pretty sure you're professional enough to share anything you know that could help the investigation,' Karl retorts. 'Despite being a prick,' he adds and notes that his voice sounds a smidge harsher than he'd intended.

'Christ, I guess you're not up for a bit of friendly banter, then. Is Charlie-boy offended?'

Yet another smile, but something else crosses his face, too, turning the smile into a pained rictus.

'Not half as offended as you seem to be, Evald. You should at least give Karen a chance. She didn't exactly ask for the promotion and no one here's enjoying poking around Smeed's private affairs.'

Evald Johannisen makes no reply, just stares vacantly into space.

Tired. Karl studies the dark circles under his colleague's eyes. Pale and tired. Bitterness comes at a cost, clearly.

'You know as well as I do we have to treat Jounas as any other potential perpetrator until this case is solved,' he continues. 'And that includes digging up every conceivable motive and unsavoury detail. Karen interviewing him in private instead of dragging him in here is actually a thoughtful concession.'

'So you say . . . I haven't got time to argue with you,' Johannisen declares with a glance at his watch. 'Someone here has to step up and find the killer, so we can have the real head of this department back. Don't you have a job to do too, or are you just here as eye candy for her majesty? Ouch, holy fuck!'

Evald Johannisen's face contorts and he clutches his left upper arm with his right hand. Next, he emits a rattling sound and collapses onto his desk. The smack when his colleague's forehead lands on his keyboard is so loud it makes Karl jump.

22

He's lying in one of the recliners by the pool. His long body is dressed in jeans and a grey lambswool sweater; a baseball cap has been placed like a lid over his face and his bare feet dangle limply over the edge of the chair. Karen hears soft snoring when she approaches and contemplates how to wake him. She tries stomping her feet a little harder than necessary when she climbs the three steps to the wooden deck. Clears her throat. No reaction. Sighing inwardly, she walks up to the recliner and studies the sleeping man. The snoring has stopped now, but aside from long, even breaths that make his stomach slowly rise and fall under the lamb's wool, there's no sign of movement. She clears her throat again, slightly louder this time.

'Are you always like a cat burglar?'

The unexpected voice from under the baseball cap makes Karen jump. Jounas Smeed is still lying motionless, but now she spots a highball glass full of fizzy liquid and a slice of lemon on the deck next to the recliner.

Gin and tonic, she thinks. Great.

Soon, a hand reaches out, fingers fumbling through the air until eventually, they find what they're looking for and close around the glass. Then he lifts up the baseball cap, pushes himself up on his elbow and drains the glass in three long gulps.

'Calm down, Eiken,' he says with a look at Karen's resigned expression. 'Perrier and lemon, nothing else. What do you want?'

'You know what I want. We need to talk.'

'Christ, not my favourite thing to hear from a woman . . .'

'Cut the crap. Would you mind sitting up properly?'

Unexpectedly obedient, he slowly sits up, rubs his eyes with his wrists and belches loudly.

'Sorry. Gas,' he says and strokes his stomach.

'Could we go indoors?' she says, nodding toward the house. 'The press conference is almost over; there will be reporters here any minute. I would feel better talking inside.'

'All right, then we should absolutely head indoors. It's important we are both satisfied,' he drawls and gets to his feet. He stands still for a moment, peering down toward the driveway, and Karen notes that her threat about the imminent arrival of the press has had the desired effect. Now it's time to put the rest of her strategy to the test.

She follows him into the house without a word and sits down in the same place as the night before. Jounas Smeed stops halfway into the room.

'Cup of coffee?' he asks, jerking his head in the direction of the kitchen.

'I want to know how long your little performance is going to go on for,' she says curtly. 'Because I'm getting bloody tired of it.'

He stiffens, but makes no reply.

'Well?' she says, meeting his eyes without blinking. 'Do you want us to have a good talk about what happened? I'd be happy to set aside five minutes for your sleazy comments, so we can get down to business.'

'Fuck me, you're in a nasty mood.'

'Are you surprised?' she says, steadily holding his gaze. 'I come over here to interview you, which you know I have to do, and you do everything to sabotage it. But all right, let's have it all out, so we can move on. Want me to go first?'

'All right, that's enough, Eiken . . .'

Jounas's voice suddenly sounds threatening. Or is that a hint of insecurity she detects?

'This is what happened,' Karen continues. 'We got drunk and made bad decisions. Granted, I have only vague memories of how we got to the hotel, but unfortunately, I remember all the fucking. Really stupid and unnecessary, and definitely not memorable, so would you mind getting over it already?'

'Was it really that bad?' he drawls. 'Because it seemed to me like you were—'

'Since you're asking, yes,' she cuts him off. 'The parts I can remember were incredibly bloody dull, and it's never happening again. And if you refuse to stop referencing it, I imagine it's going to be worse for you than for me.'

She can see him stiffen and his eyes become watchful. He slowly walks over to her and sits down on the edge of the coffee table. His head is a good foot and half above hers and she curses herself inwardly for having sat down. Then he nods slowly and smiles, looking as though he'd been waiting for what she's just said.

'Are you threatening me, Eiken?' he chuckles. 'Are you going to claim it wasn't consensual? That I somehow forced you . . .'

'Come off it,' she snaps and gets up so suddenly he has to lean back to avoid a collision.

She moves away from him and crosses her arms.

'It was completely brainless, but, unfortunately consensual in every way. What I mean is that I'm not the only one best served by putting it behind us.'

'Is that right?'

'Yes, I don't think your career would be helped by news getting out that you have terrible judgement. Checking into hotels and screwing your underlings while intoxicated. I reckon you'd lose some of your cred.'

'You fucking cun—'

He breaks off suddenly.

'No, go on,' she prompts. 'Let it all out! Why don't you rant a bit about feminists needing a good fuck, too, while you're at it; I'm sure that would make you feel better. Don't hold back on my account; I've been listening to that bullshit for almost four years now.'

'I'd tread carefully if I were you,' Jounas says, standing up slowly. 'Don't forget that I'm going to be your boss again the minute this farce is over.'

'I know, but right now, you're not. And unless you have something to hide, you'd better start cooperating. The sooner this investigation is wrapped up, the sooner you can come back to work and start making my life hell. OK?'

Jounas Smeed has walked over to the windows and is gazing out at the garden. Even though she can only see his back, she can sense that she should stop talking, that she's won. Just for now, just this one round, but it's enough.

At length, he turns around and makes as if to speak, but she beats him to it.

'Does the offer of coffee still stand?'

Fifteen minutes later, she puts her cup down on the coffee table.

'Tell me about Susanne,' she says.

'What do you want to know?'

His voice is weary now, but not hostile.

'Everything, I suppose. Start with your marriage. How did you meet?'

He leans back with a heavy sigh.

'May of ninety-eight, at my sister's wedding. They were classmates in high school and stayed in touch afterwards.'

'So you'd met Susanne before that?'

'Sure, a few times with Wenche, but I'm two years older than my sister and moved abroad about a year after they finished school. And when I came back after a few years, Wenche had already met Dag, so they had probably grown apart and didn't see as much of each other. But yes, I'd met her a few times before. Before she sank her claws into me.'

Karen ignores his bitter tone.

'So they kept in touch after high school?' she says. 'Wenche and Susanne, I mean.'

She makes a mental note to go see Wenche Hellevik as soon as possible.

'I guess, on and off. Enough for her to be invited to the wedding, anyway. As I mentioned, that's where we met properly.'

'What was Susanne like back then?'

Jounas Smeed leans back and makes a gesture as if to suggest the question's superfluous.

'Really good-looking, of course. Sexy as hell. But that was then,' he adds.

Karen suppresses a sigh.

140

'Lucky you, but I was more interested in what she was like as a person.'

'Back then? Happy, easy-going, no bitching.'

Smeed's ideal woman, Karen supposes. Sexy, happy and easy-going. Soon he'll be adding grateful and obedient, too.

'So you had a good relationship? At first, I mean.'

Jounas emits a short laugh. A bitter, toneless snort.

'At first? Sure, I suppose you could say that.'

'Enough to get married, anyway.'

'Yes, the following autumn. The usual story.'

'Susanne got pregnant?'

He nods.

'Yep, a few weeks in. Wasted no time, I have to give her that.'

'It takes two, doesn't it?'

'That's what she claimed.'

Karen drops the subject. She can't bear to listen to Jounas's views on whose responsibility it is to make sure there are no unwanted pregnancies.

'And Sigrid is your only child?' she asks even though she knows the answer; wants to maintain the pretence that this is an interview like any other.

'Yes,' he replies curtly. 'She was born in late January.'

Karen quickly glances down at her notepad.

'Which would make her about eight at the time of your divorce.'

Jounas shrugs without commenting.

'We talked to Sigrid and she told us she lived with both you and Susanne until she left home.'

Yet another shrug; Karen wonders if thinking about his daughter is making Jounas copy her body language. Clear questions, she reminds herself, or you won't get any answers.

'She said you and Susanne fought a lot. What were the fights about?'

'What are fights ever about? You have a failed marriage in your past, too . . .'

For a second, Karen is sinking, fumbling for something to hold onto, clawing and clutching, finding a rough handhold. Then she resurfaces.

'We're not talking about me,' she retorts quickly and hears her pulse thumping in her neck, almost drowning out her words. 'Please just answer the question.'

He shoots her a resigned look

'We fought about everything,' he says. 'Absolutely everything.'

Karen studies Jounas, whose eyes seem to have got stuck in the empty air in front of his face. He slowly shakes his head; she waits until he continues.

'We fought about where to live, where to go on holiday and about Sigrid. Which school she should go to, which activities she should do. And about money, of course. And my job, mostly about my job. Or my choice of career, to be specific.'

He looks like he's contemplating what he just said. Then he chuckles.

'Well, being a copper's wife wasn't what Susanne had envisioned when she married into the Smeed family. Of course she was fucking livid.'

Karen tries to recall what she's heard. There must have been a lot of raised eyebrows when Axel Smeed's son had eschewed following in his father's footsteps, embarking instead on a much less lucrative and hardly suitable career as an officer of the law. But her recollection of the local gossip is hazy. She had

142

graduated from the academy the same year he'd enrolled. They hadn't known each other growing up, Jounas and her. She'd grown up in the country, he in central Dunker, different schools, different social circles, different lives, even though they were the same age. They'd probably gone to some of the same parties, though Karen had no memory of it, and their paths had likely crossed in some of the bars that took a relaxed approach to age limits. The town was small enough to virtually guarantee it.

But even though Jounas Smeed hadn't left an impression back then, every islander knew who his father was. Axel Smeed and his brother Ragnar had made the most of the inheritance from their own father. Between Axel's land investments and property exploitation and Ragnar's law firm, the brothers had multiplied the fortune. Ragnar's political involvement and his two terms in parliament had also helped; any obstacles that couldn't be overcome through the skilful use of legal loopholes, could always be circumvented through equally deft use of connections in the realms of justice and politics. Popular belief held that the Smeeds owned a third of Heimö and half of Frisel. Karen remembers what her father used to say: 'What the Smeeds don't own today, they'll steal tomorrow.' And she remembers how smug he'd sounded on the phone when he told her Axel Smeed's son had enrolled in the police academy.

'Apparently, he's going to be a copper, just like you, Karen. Not so fancy, then, after all, the Smeed boy.'

But Susanne could hardly have been surprised by Jounas's choice of career; he must have already graduated from the academy by the time they met. Had she not known that?

Jounas answered the question before she could ask it.

'I didn't enrol until a few years after high school. I started and dropped a number of courses at university before that; I didn't know what I wanted to do. Applying to the academy was probably primarily about rebelling against my dad somehow. Becoming a police officer was as far from his plans for me as I could get.'

'Did it work?'

'I guess so. The old man threatened to disinherit me and all that shit. The problem was I wasn't exactly wild about it myself. I liked the training, but the first years on the job . . .'

'Arresting drunks and attending domestic disturbances,' Karen says. 'No, that wasn't exactly the time of my life either.'

'At least I stuck it out longer than you: almost two years.'

'So I've gathered.'

'But then I left the island.'

Karen is taken aback. She had no idea.

'What did you get up to?'

'The short version?'

Karen nods.

'I travelled around South America and then the US. I worked off the books on various construction sites and in bars in California and spent the last six months in New York. I guess that's where I had a bit of an epiphany and realised the prospect of living hand to mouth forever wasn't all that appealing. So I started considering going home and settling down one way or another. Simply put, I was tired of being broke all the time.'

'And so you decided to be a police officer. Interesting choice . . .'

They smile in a moment of mutual understanding.

'No, first I went crawling back to Daddy. Promised to forget all my former plans; my years at the academy weren't even mentioned. Apparently, my dad was more embarrassed about my flitting around South America and getting high in the US. So instead, I started studying law. After a while, they let me work extra at my uncle's law firm, in exchange for a promise that I would complete my studies and then be at my father's beck and call. Pure nepotism, in other words. And he gave me plenty of dosh and bought me a big flat on Freyagate.'

Jounas gets up suddenly and looks at Karen.

'If you're going to insist on digging through this crap, I'm going to need a stiff drink. I don't imagine there's any point asking if you want one, is there?'

'Sorry, no,' she smiles. 'I can't exactly drink on the job with my boss watching.'

She says it as a tactical politeness. Wants to emphasise that she's aware the present role reversal's temporary. He's finally starting to talk; she doesn't want to risk him clamming up again.

'Nice one, Eiken,' he says.

She thinks she can make out a twitching at the corner of his mouth before he turns around and leaves the room. When he comes back, Karen enviously eyes his foggy glass, in which tiny bubbles are fizzing around two ice cubes and a slice of lemon; this time it's definitely a gin and tonic. She can almost smell the juniper and taste the bitterness on her tongue when Jounas takes a big sip. Salad for lunch and now this. How many weeks of clean living was it she'd promised herself again?

'Go on,' she says encouragingly. 'You were studying law and working extra for your uncle. Was that when you met Susanne?'

'Bingo. I had a couple of years of resigned conformity under my belt, was rapidly approaching thirty and I guess my guard

145

was down. That's when Susanne sunk her claws into Axel Smeed's only son.'

'So you were just a tragic victim . . . First of your dad's whims and then Susanne's?'

Jounas glares at her over the edge of his glass but then carries on.

'I think in fact she considered herself a victim,' he says calmly. 'She was looking for a lawyer and found a police officer. She was bloody disappointed, I can tell you that.'

He smiles, pleased about his Edith Södergran reference, and Karen has to laugh a little. So he knows his Nordic poets, or at least remembers the highlights from school.

'And what expression did that disappointment take?'

'Well, obviously she raised merry hell when I dropped out of uni six months after we got married. I'd been unhappy for a long time and in the end I just couldn't take it anymore.'

Jounas Smeed sips his drink; Karen silently waits for him to continue.

'Dad and Susanne took turns trying to persuade me to think again. For a while, they were united in their struggle, but when the old man started threatening to disinherit me again, she turned on him, too. And then he coldly informed us he was selling the flat on Freyagate and that we would have to move out.'

'Even though you had a baby? Was he that callous or was he trying to scare you?'

'Well, I suppose he was callous in his way, but I get where he was coming from. Why would he help us out financially if I refused to give in to his wishes? Either way, I wasn't prepared to carry on with law just because my father or my wife wanted me to. Besides, I've always suspected my uncle was fairly grateful to be rid of me. It was just never my thing.'

'So you chose to go back to law enforcement instead. Pulled that uniform back on . . .'

'I did. I did six months up in Ravenby and then another couple of months here in Dunker before they announced they were looking for a chief inspector. Advancement didn't take as long back then; every year there was another restructure.'

'But Susanne wasn't happy?'

'Are you joking? One year into our marriage, she'd traded down from a five-bed on Freyagate to a two-bed in Odinswalla. Moreover, I had destroyed any prospect of a dazzling law career and given up my position as the heir of my father's empire. We barely spoke for a whole year.'

'But you stayed married for a long time after that?'

'At least on paper. And at times, it worked OK. I did keep getting promoted and we moved from the two-bed to a terraced house in Sande. Things improved, put simply. The problem is, it was never enough for Susanne. She could never find it in herself to get over what we could've had and that my parents never invited us over. But for some reason, she absolutely didn't want to get divorced. And me, for my part, well . . . I suppose I figured . . .'

It was practical, Karen thought to herself.

'I suppose I figured we should wait to split up until Sigrid was a bit older. In hindsight, though, I wonder if that was the right decision,' he says dejectedly. 'All the fighting took a toll on her, I'm afraid. Well, you've met her,' he adds, as though that answers the question.

'I don't think there's anything wrong with Sigrid,' Karen says cautiously, keenly aware the slightest misstep could make him flare up again. 'She seems a bit angry, but maybe that's only natural.'

'*A bit angry*. Are you sure you met her? Did you see the nose ring? Kid looks like a bloody bull, if you ask me.'

'I'm not asking. What I would like to know more about is Susanne and what happened after the divorce.'

'What do you want to know? She was a greedy, calculating bitch. Isn't that enough?'

Jounas knocks back the last of his G&T, puts the glass down a little bit too hard and checks his watch. Karen studies him, seemingly calm; she's far from done with her questions. If they can't continue to talk here and now, until she has all the answers she needs, she will have to bring him to the station, and she would prefer to avoid that for as long as possible.

'All right,' she says and stares at him fixedly. 'What I hear is that your relationship with Susanne was . . . frosty. And according to Sigrid, the divorce didn't improve matters. May I ask what your fights were about at that point? After the divorce, I mean.'

'Still about money, of course,' he snaps. 'Everything was about money for Susanne. It was all she cared about.'

Karen thinks about Susanne's house, comparing it to the one she's in now. Two bedrooms in Langevik, white laminate bookshelf and Ikea sofa. Neat and tidy, but light years from this ginormous Thingwalla villa with its oriental rugs, valuable art and pool. Apparently, her roving eyes gave her musings away.

'It's called prenup,' Jounas remarks. 'Fair as can be. You take out what you brought in. Nothing else.'

'And she was happy to sign one. Just like that?'

'No, but she didn't have much choice, did she? Nor did I, if we wanted somewhere to live. Which was a necessity with a

148

child on the way. It was Dad's idea from beginning to end: without a prenup no flat, no allowance, no job. Sure, I could have ripped it up later, once I'd cut the ties to the old man anyway. God knows Susanne badgered me about it. But . . . well, I suppose I didn't feel inclined to oblige her. I think it almost drove her over the bloody edge.'

'And when you divorced . . .'

'She got nothing. Zilch, apart from the few things we'd bought during our marriage. What she did get was money every month, a truckload of money, I can tell you that. Voluntary contributions; I'm not completely heartless. At least while we shared custody of Sigrid. The money was really there to make sure Sigrid had a tolerable standard of living when she wasn't with me. But idiot that I am, I never made sure I knew how Susanne spent it.'

'How did she spend it?'

Jounas snorts and spreads his arms, making the ice cubes tinkle against the side of his glass.

'How should I know? Pedicures, clothes and liposuction and whatever else nonsense you women want. And constant travel: Thailand, New York, Spain. I think she even managed to squeeze in Turkey.'

And shoes, Karen notes inwardly.

'What about her house in Langevik, how did she come by that?'

'It was her childhood home. Her mum was dead when we met, but her dad lived there until just before the divorce, when he was put in a hospital. So the house was very conveniently empty, just waiting for Susanne to move in.'

Convenient for both of you. Karen marvels at Jounas's ability to pronounce every word he says about Susanne like an implied or overt accusation. Not even now, when she's dead, can he curb his contempt.

'So her dad was in the hospital. Did he die there?'

Jounas shrugs, looking like he's lost interest.

'Yeah, he allegedly drank quite a bit and I guess his liver eventually gave up. But I know almost nothing about Susanne's parents; she never wanted to talk about them. I suppose they didn't live up to her expectations either.'

'One more question before I go. How come your finger-prints were found at Susanne's house? According to the tech-nicians, there were recent prints from you in several places in her house.'

For a moment, she thinks he might explode. Or implode, more like. She watches her boss's face turn from white to red. Then he bursts out laughing.

'So, Eiken, you've been holding that little morsel back all this time, eh? Don't get your knickers in a twist; it's not half as excit-ing as you're hoping.'

'Would you please just answer the question,' she says wearily.

'Because I was there, of course. A week ago, bit less maybe.'

'How come? Nothing you've told me indicates you wanted to see her.'

'Because she called. Claimed she wanted to discuss Sigrid and that it was important. I was reluctant, obviously, but she insisted we had to be able to talk about our daughter without fighting, that she'd discovered something that had made her worried. And she really did sound worried, so . . .'

He breaks off.

'So you went out there?' Karen says doubtfully.

'Yes,' he bellows. 'But you can't fucking imagine what it's like, that concern for your child can make you put all other things aside.

There's a buzzing in her ears; she's free-falling. The buzzing turns into a loud roar, making Jounas's words sound remote and strange.

'But I can tell you, Eiken, that for Sigrid, I would do considerably worse things than have a conversation with some crazy bitch. Because it turns out she was just as mad as ever. All she had was the usual nagging about how Sigrid should get an education instead of working at a bar, and then something about her boyfriend, who Susanne apparently didn't approve of. According to her, he's into all kinds of dodgy things, stealing and drugs and whatever else she could think of. And suddenly, it was incredibly fucking convenient that I was a police officer. She virtually demanded that I put surveillance on the boy and predictably flew off the handle when I refused to oblige.'

Karen's listening with her head lowered and her eyes closed while the roaring slowly subsides and the sound of Jounas's voice returns.

'. . . so I left and I haven't seen or heard from her since. And I didn't kill her either, though I had both reason and a strong urge to many, many times.'

She's silent for a few more moments, telling herself she mustn't cry, not yet, not until she's out of the house. Then she slowly exhales and stands up on numb legs. She has to get out before she falls apart.

'OK,' she says. 'I'll be on my way, then.'

'Just like that?'

'Just like that. I'll be in touch.'

She only just makes it.

At least he's not dissembling, she concludes, having wiped the mascara from under her eyes with paper napkins and started the car.

He knows nothing about me. He can't have meant it personally.

But he's still a fucking prick, she adds, recalling the spiteful tone Jounas Smeed used to talk about his late ex-wife. Most people avoid speaking ill of the dead; in every investigation Karen's worked on, even the most hardened criminals have always been portrayed as sweet little lambs as soon as they've shuffled off this mortal coil. She actually can't remember anyone expressing such undisguised contempt for a dead relative. Or hatred, actually. Could he have hated her enough to have driven out there one last time to beat her to death? She doesn't think so; if that were the case, he would probably have made sure to downplay his feelings toward Susanne. And she hasn't found a concrete motive. At least not yet.

Unfortunately, I know exactly where that bastard was yesterday morning, she thinks ruefully and turns right on Valhallgate. Jounas Smeed actually has something incredibly rare: a watertight alibi, at least until twenty past seven. But after that? According to his own information, he didn't leave the hotel until half past nine, over two hours later, 'properly bloody hungover'. That last point, she believes. She has to find something to verify his claims, unless she wants to be the one to give him an alibi for part of that time.

He didn't speak to anyone, aside from a homeless person from the beach. Well, he could hardly have found a less credible witness if he'd tried, and probably impossible to track down to boot. And just like when she snuck out of the hotel, the front desk had been unmanned; that neither strengthened nor weakened his claims. If she was lucky, someone had been there, even though Jounas hadn't seen them. She would have to check on that, today. Dear Lord, let someone corroborate his statements, she thinks; if they're true, they can write him off and no one would ever have to know where he spent the night. Or with whom. If he left the hotel when he says he did, he simply couldn't have killed Susanne. On the other hand, an annoying voice in her head interjects: if he left the hotel right after me, he would have had enough time.

Her thoughts are interrupted as she stops at a red light and her phone rings, making her jump. She digs around her handbag with one hand while keeping an eye on the lights. In the hour or so she spent with Jounas, her phone has rung four times; she declined the calls as soon as she saw the number. Jon Bergman. Clearly, the media department has done its job, deflecting attention from her, but Jon has her direct number. Glancing down at the screen, she's convinced it will flash the reporter's name again. Instead, it reads Karl Björken; she picks up immediately.

'Hey, Karl, she says. 'Any news?'

He wastes no time on greetings.

'Johannisen's out,' he says through gritted teeth. 'He's had a heart attack.'

23

Karen looks up at the top shelf in her tool shed with a pang of guilt.

The satisfaction she felt after sealing all seven windows on the ground floor of the main house has been replaced by defeat. The entire first floor still has to be seen to; the house is going to be very draughty this winter unless she tackles it soon. A bit of caulk isn't really enough. Each window should ideally be taken out, each frame scraped clean of old paint, primed, dried and finally painted with blue oil paint.

At least there's a lot of paint, she notes. For some reason, her late father apparently felt a need to keep a store of about ten big buckets, which are still lined up neatly, if reproachfully, on the shelf in front of her. He probably acquired them from someone who'd got their hands on a few pails 'someone's cousin had found somewhere'. Walter Eiken was incapable of passing up an opportunity like that. Always careful not to be directly involved when a shipment of something 'fell off the back of a truck', but always ready to jump in at a later stage in the supply chain. Walter Eiken's Noorö genes never decisively triumphed over what he inherited from his mother's side, which amounted to a modicum of uprightness, the house in Langevik and the fishing rights that came with it. Which was enough to keep him on the right side of the law for the last forty years of his life.

Karen scans the shelves, sawhorse bench, walls and floor again, without finding what she's looking for. If it's not in here either, she must have lent it to someone. The question is to whom.

With an annoyed sigh, she pushes the tool-shed door shut and turns the wooden latch. Slowly, she ambles across the lawn and picks up the rake discarded on the ground.

She pauses, holding the long wooden handle, and looks around her yard, studying each building in turn with the expression of a mother eyeing a delinquent son. So much tenderness and love – so many worries. All the things she should be getting to. The remains of a fallen roof shingle lies in a pile underneath the kitchen window – she knows all too well that once one of the shingles have gone, more will soon. Though she can't see it from here, she knows the north wall of the guesthouse is a sorry sight. And she knows what it ought to look like.

She slowly moves back toward the house, pinches a cluster of berries from the big rowan outside the kitchen window and studies their colour. Not quite time yet, but as soon as the first frost hits, she will make sure to brew a few bottles of bitter. That much she's willing to do. All the other things that – according to the meticulous notes her grandmother left her – are supposed to be harvested this time of year, she's planning to leave to Mother Nature. Common couch and polypody, shepherd's purse, forest lamb mushrooms, searocket and rosehip . . .

She pauses and looks down toward the beach rose bramble next to the guesthouse. Maybe she should pick some of the hips after all. How hard is it really to chuck a few handfuls into a pot and boil them? And dry the rest. Maybe next weekend.

Karen leans the rake against the trunk of the rowan. No point putting it back in the shed before the leaves fall. Besides, it's handy for raking up rowan berries. But that's for another time. Right now, she should be calling around to ask, 'Did you borrow my jigsaw?'

She makes perfunctory use of the boot scraper on the front step before opening the front door and noting with another heavy sigh that the hinges need greasing.

While the coffee maker emits a few final rattles, Karen studies the flat pack on her kitchen table. Of course she's not going to try to hunt down the damn saw tonight. In reality, it's been so long since she saw it, it could be anywhere. Maybe she should just pop by Grenå on the way home from work tomorrow and buy a new one. It's going to be chilly, but until she can install the cat flap, she's going to have to live with leaving the kitchen window ajar.

I should at least open the box and study the construction. Measure out exactly where to put it now and figure out how to install it. Or even go down to the basement and look for the bloody saw there.

The thought is so unappealing she considers calling her mother instead. Surprising her with an extra call in addition to the mandatory one every Saturday morning. Being a better daughter than she's been the past few . . .

Just then, she's struck by an idea, as obvious as it is incomprehensible. Why hasn't she thought of this before? She quickly puts the cat flap package down on the floor, tops up her large coffee mug and adds a splash of milk, sits down at the table and picks up her phone.

156

'What's wrong?'

Eleanor's voice sounds so tense when she picks up Karen is overcome with guilt. Hearing from her is clearly so unexpected it elicits a fear response in her mother.

'No, no,' she reassures her. 'I just wanted to ask if you might know . . .'

She instinctively shies away from her real purpose for calling and casts about for an alternative. Something a good daughter would call her mother to ask about.

'. . . what to do with the rosehips.'

There's a few seconds of silence before Eleanor speaks again.

'The rosehips?' she says in disbelief. 'You want to know what to do with the rosehips?'

'Yes . . . I can't remember if you're supposed to clean them first or boil them with the fuzz and pips.'

'And you're calling your old mother to ask instead of using the internet?'

The voice on the other end sounds so amused Karen regrets calling for a split second. Horrified, she realises she has involuntarily slipped back into her sullen teenage tone.

'Well *excuse me* for asking.'

That makes Eleanor Eiken, who has put over a thousand miles between herself and forty years of household chores, laugh heartily. Then she clears her throat and continues in a more maternal tone.

'You can do either, but if you don't clean them, you'll have to strain it after, of course. Use the chinois strainer that's hanging on the back of the pantry door. The one that doesn't fit in the drawers.'

'OK, thanks. How are things otherwise? How are you and . . . Harry? No new ailments?'

157

Karen thanks her lucky stars she managed to remember his name. They haven't been introduced yet, but it's probably only a matter of time before Eleanor appears on her doorstep with her new friend. There's no doubt her mother has fallen in love in her old age; Karen has listened to her go on about Harry Lampard since the moment he moved into her co-op on Spain's Costa del Sol last year. Now, they seem to be spending all their time together.

'Since Saturday, you mean?' Eleanor laughs. 'No, actually. But why don't you go ahead and tell me why you're really calling? You know, a ewe knows her little lamb . . .'

Karen sighs and sips her coffee.

'Do you remember Susanne Smeed?'

'Susanne? Of course I remember her. Not a nice person, if you ask me. Not one of the people I miss down here. Why do you ask?'

'She died a couple of days ago.'

There's a brief silence.

'What are you saying? She was your age.'

'Three years younger, as a matter of fact.'

'That's terrible, and here I am, speaking ill of the dead. Was it cancer? It took her father, I believe. Or,' Eleanor lowers her voice, 'did she kill herself?'

'Why would you ask that?'

'Well, sometimes things like that run in the family. Susanne's mother was an anxious sort of woman and rumour had it she killed herself. But I don't know that on good authority. The Lindgrens were never really part of the community. Being outsiders and all.'

Karen takes a deep breath.

158

'Susanne was murdered,' she says.

Eleanor Eiken is not a sensationalist, but Karen's announcement draws an audible gasp.

There's a faint tremble in her voice when she continues.

'Was it the Smeed lad?'

Karen's quiet for a few seconds. Then she asks, as neutrally as she is able:

'Why would you think it was him?'

'Well, they were like cat and dog, everyone knew that, whether they wanted to or not. Your father always said it can't be easy to live with a Smeed, but I'm telling you, being married to little Susanne can't have been a walk in the park, either. There was something wrong with that girl, I don't mind telling you, though she may be dead now. I guess I figured Jounas finally had enough.'

'They've been divorced for almost ten years.'

'Yes, you're right; silly me. Then who was it, do you know?'

Karen decides not call her mother out about her feigned confusion.

'Not yet. But it's only a matter of time,' she replies, wishing she could have managed to sound a bit more confident. 'We're mapping out Susanne's life at the moment. That's why I was wondering what you might know. You used to keep track of things in the village.'

'Oh no, sweetheart, I was never a gossip,' Eleanor says primly.

'I just meant that you lived here a long time and knew most of the locals. You must have known Susanne's parents.'

'Well. Everyone knew *about* them, of course. But that's not the same thing as *knowing* them. They were outsiders, as you know and . . . well, you know how that goes.'

'Outsiders? Where were they from?'

'Sweden, of all places. But Susanne's mother was the grand-daughter of Vetle Gråå; you remember him, don't you? No, of course you don't, but I'm sure you've heard about him; he used to own a lot of land. Both forest and pastureland. Well, either way, they inherited the old man's property, so I guess they did belong here in a way. Otherwise they likely wouldn't have been accepted at all, because I never knew how they made their living. It wasn't sheep or fishing anyway.'

'Why did they move here in the first place?'

'Oh dear, well, they lived up on Lothorp Farm for the first few years, if I remember correctly. Not just the Lindgrens, apparently other people moved here, too, looking for a new life. But only the Lindgrens stayed.'

Her words awaken a childhood memory. Rumours about the Lothorp cult had survived among the children of Langevik. In equal parts fascinated and frightened, Karen had listened to the older children's tall tales about what had used to go on up there: secret rituals and child sacrifices to pagan gods. And the most terrifying part: that all the cult members were dead now and haunted the place.

As an adult, she's surprised more than anything. Why would Langevik attract people looking for a new life? Why would any-one move here voluntarily?

'But all of that happened when we were still up on Noorö,' Eleanor says. 'By the time we moved to Langevik, those moon-light farmers had long since given up.'

Karen nods. Even though she always regards herself as a Langevik native, her first years were spent up on the windswept west coast of Noorö, where her father was from. She doesn't

160

have any memories from that time; everything she knows about it is based on what her mother has told her. It wasn't until Walter Eiken, as the oldest son, inherited his grandparents' house in Langevik that his wife saw a chance to escape the hateful island for good. Eleanor Eiken, nee Wood, didn't mind ruining her hand cleaning fish or spending nights mending chewed-up nets, even though she was a doctor's daughter from Ravenby. It was the sanctimonious mix of lawlessness and religiosity on Noorö she had failed to reconcile herself with. Eleanor was neither a criminal nor particularly religious, and she didn't want her daughter to be, either. Putting a decent distance between her and her husband's family would improve Eleanor's quality of life considerably. The mother-in-law in particular would be much improved by distance. And even though the weather on Heimö's east coast was often harsh, it was nothing compared to the north-west coast of Noorö.

She had put all of this to her husband, adding that if he insisted on staying on Noorö, now that they finally had an opportunity to leave, he should also start looking for another wife. And whether it was because Walter Eiken took his wife's ultimatum seriously, or because he was ready to try something new, they had moved to Langevik. It was 1972 and Karen was three. And the commune up on Lothorp Farm survived only in ghost stories told by the local children.

In other words, they had missed the beginning of the Lindgren family's life in Langevik, but surely there was something her mum could tell her about Susanne?

In response to her unspoken question, Eleanor adds:

'To be honest, I don't really remember Susanne as a child. The village was teeming with children, we didn't really have time to pay much attention to all of them. But given how her parents were viewed, I can imagine she had a tough time of it. I'm sure you know more about that than I do. You went to the same school, after all.'

'She was three years younger and lived on the other side of the village, so my memories of her are fairly vague. What about later, what do you remember about her as an adult?'

'Not much, really. She left home early and then she married into the Smeed family. I don't think I saw her once during those years. But there was talk, of course.'

'What did people say?'

'That she'd married up, naturally. Envy, mostly. But as they used to say when I was young: "Marrying rich can prove costly". Well, maybe we should all pay more attention to those old sayings,' Eleanor chuckles. 'Not that Harry's so *very* rich, that's not what I meant. Well, not that we're planning to get married, either, for that matter . . .'

Karen notes that her mum has transitioned into nervous blathering only to then fall abruptly silent, as if suddenly realising her light tone stood in stark contrast to the actual topic at hand.

'And once she got divorced and moved back it was around the same time all the other things happened . . . We had enough on our plates. Well, you know that as well as anyone,' she adds.

Yes, Karen thinks to herself. I know that all too well.

24

When they take their seats in the conference room once more, the mood is sombre.

Speaking to Johannisen's wife on the phone the night before, Karen was told it hadn't been a heart attack but rather a severe case of angina. The doctors had recommended rest and medication. Right now, he's feeling relatively OK, his wife told her. Just like Harald Steen, Karen notes, but Johannisen must be at least twenty years his junior.

When she informed Viggo Haugen about Johannisen's health emergency and impending sick leave half an hour earlier, he'd managed to look even more troubled than usual.

'This couldn't have come at a worse time, but I can reassign people from elsewhere.'

'Thank you, I might take you up on that, but as things stand, it wouldn't be very helpful to have lots of people running around.'

She had steeled herself to resist his attempts to persuade her to expand the group. Instead, she'd been surprised at Haugen's easy-going response.

'Well, you're in charge of the investigation,' he'd said. 'It's your call, Eiken.'

The explanation for it came when Head of Media Johan Stolt came looking for her in the department. Apparently, the press conference had been a disappointing experience for everyone involved. After the initial run-through of the facts and a handful of follow-up questions he'd been unable to answer, the journalists' interest in talking to the chief of police had been non-existent and their complaints about the fact that no one in an operational position was available to them had grown strident. The representatives of the various news outlets had grumblingly left the auditorium, discontentedly tossing their visitor's badges on the reception desk. A press statement would have been just as useful. They'd cancelled lunch meetings and hadn't been told shit.

'I think you're going to have to start preparing yourself for having some level of contact with the media after all,' Johan Stolt had told her with a resigned look on his face.

She'd stared at him sceptically, and not only because his choice of clothing had been a double-breasted, checkered tweed jacket.

'Me? But Haugen was extremely clear about me not speaking to the media under any circumstances.'

'Well, he's changed his mind. I'll be bearing the brunt of it, so we're going to have to stay in close touch about what information we can make public. But if we hold another press conference, you'll be needed. Have you had any media training?'

For now, the chief of police has retreated to lick his wounds after his shambolic press conference, but it's a temporary reprieve. He's going to take me off the case, Karen realises. Unless we get this cleared up sharpish, Viggo Haugen's going to put someone else in charge of the investigation and make me the scapegoat.

She pauses in the door to the conference room and looks around the table where her team and the Head of Media have now taken their seats. She hesitates for a few seconds, then continues past the chair in the middle she chose both the day before and that morning.

My investigation, my responsibility, she tells herself and sits down at the head of the table.

'Is everyone here?' she says and looks out at the group. 'Cornelis, would you mind closing the door?'

Cornelis Loots pushes the door shut and sits down next to Astrid Nielsen. They both offer Karen their undivided attention, while Karl Björken busies himself with mugs and coffee urns. There's a plate of dry sandwiches on the table again today. Boiled ham and peppers this time, she notes, watching with a shudder as Karl pours a stream of the watery coffee into his mug.

She quickly recounts what she was told by Evald Johannisen's wife and hopes none of the relief she feels at not having to deal with him as they move forward shows on her face.

'I will of course make sure to stay in touch with Johannisen's wife; she's promised to keep me posted on his condition, but his surgery isn't until tomorrow, unless there's some acute development.'

'Maybe we should send flowers,' Astrid Nielsen puts in.

Karen sighs inwardly: why didn't she think of that?

'Great idea, let's make that Björn Lange's first task,' she says quickly with a nod to Cornelis, who obediently makes a note. 'Make sure he buys something sizeable and gets a card we can all sign.'

Then she turns to Johan Stolt. They've agreed he will attend today's meeting but only take part as needed, for instance in case of a major breakthrough, thereafter.

'Anything from the press conference the group needs to know?' she asks.

'Not really. The chief of police went over the basic facts and that was pretty much all we had to say. We got the inevitable questions: how did it happen, what weapon was used, is Jounas Smeed a suspect, are there any other suspects . . .'

'And what did you say?' Karl Björken asks.

Johan Stolt heaves a resigned sigh and smiles.

'That unfortunately we can't go into that, for technical reasons, of course. But it's hardly going to stop the journalists from trying to get the answers by other means. I've tried to get hold of Smeed all day to hear if they've turned up at his house, but I haven't been able to reach him. Maybe we should warn his daughter, too, if we haven't already. But we have to tread carefully there,' Stolt adds. 'We can't be giving the impression we're trying to gag people who don't work for the police.'

'I already talked to Jounas,' Karen says, 'and he knows what's what. But I haven't warned the daughter, though she doesn't strike me as chatty; hardly the type to do a tell-all interview.'

'She might need the money . . .'

'Sure, and we can't stop her. But maybe we should warn her, for her own sake, so she's not caught off guard. There's always a risk they lay siege to her building, if they're desperate enough. Would you mind giving her a ring, Karl? As soon as we're done here, if possible?'

He nods mutely.

'All right, enough about that. Since Evald isn't here, maybe you could tell us about your visit to . . .' Karen consults her notes, '. . . the Solgården nursing home,' she says and turns to Astrid Nielsen.

Astrid Nielsen gives a self-assured account of her and Evald Johannisen's meeting with the manager of Solgården, Gunilla Moen, who told them Susanne Smeed had worked at the nursing home as an administrative assistant, with duties such as payroll and handling purchasing invoices, for four years. As far as Gunilla Moen knew, Susanne had been a secretary at an architectural firm before that, but had been laid off when the company moved to the UK. But Gunilla Moen hadn't been 100 per cent sure; she had only worked at Solgården for just over a year and had 'inherited' Susanne Smeed, as she put it.

'Both Evald and I had a strong sense she didn't like Susanne, but it was impossible to get her to say anything overtly negative,' Astrid Nielsen says. 'But, then, she was shocked at learning what had happened, of course, so then it was challenging to get anything useful out of her at all.'

'Did you talk to anyone other than Gunilla Moen?'

'Yes, we spoke to some of the carers, but they didn't seem to have had much direct contact with Susanne. She seemed to have kept to herself; someone even hinted that she thought herself "above" the other employees and had turned up her nose at the idea of socialising with her co-workers. On the other hand, she doesn't seem to have socialised with Gunilla Moen or any other member of the management either.'

We're going to have to go out there again, Karen reasons. Someone she worked with must have something to say about her. Astrid's given them all the facts; everything from employment history to periods of sick leave, but Johannisen's impressions from their visit would have been valuable. He may be a prick, but he's also an experienced detective and a sly old bastard, she thinks as she thanks Astrid. She turns to Cornelis Loots.

'Anything from the technicians?'

'It looks like Harald Steen was right about the car. The starter's in a terrible way, so it may very well be that it was Susanne Smeed's car he and his carer heard.'

'All right,' Karl says. 'So Susanne was killed sometime between about quarter past eight when you, Karen, drove past and saw her, and a couple of minutes to ten when old man Steen heard Susanne's car leave.'

'That tallies with Brodal's estimate,' Karen confirms. 'Anything else?'

She turns back to Cornelis Loots who glances down at his notes and then looks up.

'A few things, actually. We didn't find a computer, but packaging and a receipt for a laptop – an HP – purchased just over three years ago. That may indicate that the killer took it, though three years is a lot for a computer these days.'

'Maybe he didn't realise how old it was,' Astrid suggests.

'Still haven't found a mobile?'

'Nope, but there was a Samsung charger on the hallway table. And here's the best part: using triangulation, they've been able to locate signals from Susanne Smeed's work phone to a place just north of Moerbeck. They just told me.'

Cornelis looks around the table expectantly, but is met with looks of resignation.

'You're from Noorö, aren't you?' Karl Björken asks.

'Yes . . .' he admits hesitantly, as though the answer might get him into trouble.

Cornelis Loots was, indeed, born and raised on the most northerly of the Dogger Islands. But unlike Karl, he only moved to the capital on Heimö six months ago, when he was promoted to detective constable. Getting his wife Lise to agree to the move had required almost three weeks of virtually daily persuasion, negotiation and in the end a promise that Easter, the summer solstice *and* Christmas would be spent with her parents.

'Five years, at most. I won't have our children grow up on Heimö,' she'd told him.

And after just two months in their flat in Gaarda, with a view of the drug peddling at the playground below their kitchen window, Lise had discovered she was pregnant and given him yet another ultimatum.

'We either buy a house somewhere else or I'm moving back home.'

Two rooms upstairs and two on the ground floor on a south-facing plot of land in Sande turned out to eat up the entirety of the pay rise that had accompanied Cornelis's promotion, as well as preclude any attempt at saving, but Lise was content. And every night, when Cornelis sees his very pregnant wife on the sofa, balancing her teacup on her enormous belly, looking pleased, he knows the house was worth every shilling.

Confused, he now looks around at his colleagues.

'There's a big gravel pit a mile or two north of Moerbeck,' Karen explains. 'A deep, water-filled gravel pit,' she adds.

'And,' Karl puts in, 'even if they were to fish the phone out before it dies, I'm not sure what we could get out of it.'

'But we can request the call log from the operator, right?' Astrid says.

Cornelis nods.

'The prosecutor has requisitioned them and TelAB is working on it.'

'Wow, so maybe those lazy sods will actually deign to pull their fingers out within a couple of months,' Karl sneers and throws down his pen so hard it rolls across the table and falls to the floor with a faint jingling sound.

No one around the table says anything; everyone knows Karl is basically correct, though he may be exaggerating somewhat. TelAB is hardly known for their eagerness to cooperate or swift compliance.

'We'll have to keep on them,' Karen says. 'Does anyone else have anything else?'

Headshakes all around.

'All right, then let's call it a day. I have a short meeting with Viggo Haugen and Dineke Vegen tomorrow morning at eight, but it shouldn't take more than half an hour. So we'll meet back here at eight thirty. And call me if you turn up anything before then.'

25

It's completely dark; headlights sweep this way and that across the large car park, looking for free parking bays. The temperature has plummeted during the day and the almost summerlike warmth has been replaced by a cold, steady drizzle. Unprepared islanders who have spent the day shivering in inappropriately light clothes have hurried home to attics and basements to dig out coats and hats.

Beyond the rows of cars loom the bunkerlike buildings of the Grenå Mall, home to two competing superstores, a large DIY shop, a furniture store, plant nurseries and all the major clothing retailers, as well as Karen's reason for making the trip here this evening. Judging from the packed car park, the locals haven't let the cold or last weekend's festivities dampen their appetite for consumerism. That being said, she can't recall a single visit to Grenå, on any day, at any time, that didn't come with long lines, screaming children and clenched teeth behind giant trolleys.

After two crawling laps around the car park, Karen finally spots a Nissan reversing out of one of the bays. With a skill that most likely comes across to the other driver as sheer rudeness, she manages to slip into the desirable spot by slamming on her brakes and reversing fifteen feet. Filled with equal parts dread and bloodlust, Karen Eiken Hornby strides toward the furthest illuminated bunker.

Within thirty minutes, she has managed to heave a big box onto the cargo bed of her Ford Ranger and shuts the tailgate with a bang. She shudders and climbs in behind the wheel with a heavy sigh. Driving home is going to be a slog in this weather: visibility is virtually zero; as soon as she leaves the motorway, she'll be unable to avoid the potholes.

That's all the excuse she needs; she reaches toward the glove compartment. The door is stiff; she gives it a practised whack with the heel of her hand and notes that she remembered right; there's an unopened packet of cigarettes she's forgotten to throw away. Was it last Friday she bought it? It feels like ages ago.

Without much effort, she suppresses a pang of guilt, leans back and inhales the smoke. She sits motionless in the dark for a few minutes, watching headlights track back and forth, as cars look for somewhere to park. A shivering homeless man walks around, begging for trolleys to return so he can collect the coins from them and buy himself some more beer. Most of the shoppers who have just finished unloading their bags seem grateful not to have to bring their trolleys back, but one woman is clearly having none of it. Karen watches their exchange through her windscreen like a silent film, and has no difficulty imagining the curses hurled by the homeless man as he ambles away, shoulders pulled up under his soaking jacket. The woman looks after him until he's far away enough, then gives her trolley a shove that makes it roll away and into a lamp post, jumps into her Mercedes and drives off.

'Fucking bitch,' Karen mutters, taking one last drag before putting the cigarette out and the key in the ignition. Then she pulls a couple of cigarettes out of the packet and carefully places them on the passenger seat.

As she drives up alongside the homeless man, she rolls down her window and waves him over. She hands him a fifty-mark note and the rest of the cigarettes.

'You should get out of the rain, you'll get pneumonia,' she says and shudders when his freezing hand touches hers.

Before she exits the car park, she glances up at the rear-view mirror and sees the top of the big box in the cargo bed over the seatbacks. Viggo Haugen is probably going to fly off the handle when the invoice arrives, but she's willing to take on that fight.

26

Karen is greeted by a familiar mix of warmth, soft voices and a faint smell of mould when she pushes open the door to the Hare and Crow. Langevik's one remaining pub is less crowded than usual. Only about twenty patrons are seated at the tables, but the backbone of the establishment is seated along the bar as usual. By their own estimation, the three regulars guarantee the profit margin that keeps the Hare and Crow afloat. The three familiar backs belong to Egil Jenssen, Jaap Kloes and Odd Marklund, whose by-now fairly ample behinds cover the greater part of their stools. All three of them born and raised in the village, all three of them once active in the fishing industry: Jenssen and Kloes as cod fishermen and Marklund as a manager at the Loke factory where he supervised the peeling and packaging of shrimp.

Karen hesitates for a moment before walking over to the bar. The moment she sits down next to the old men, she's going to be forced to listen to them gripe about how the village is going to the dogs, the closing of yet another shop, the invasion of the cufflink people from Dunker, not to mention Marklund's usual rants about the terrible turn the Loke factory has taken, and the bitter fact that the shrimp are now being shipped to Latvia, Poland and Tunisia to be peeled and put in brine. On the other hand, these three big-bummed gentlemen constitute a bottomless well of information about everyone and everything, and for once, she's come to catch up on the village gossip.

'Hiya, Arild,' she says, slapping the counter. 'Any news on tap today?'

Arild Rasmussen looks up from the till with a sour expression. Clearly, he doesn't appreciate allusions to the pub's meagre selection. That the bars in Dunker serve all kinds of beers these days doesn't impress Rasmussen. The recent explosive expansion of the local microbrewing industry may admittedly have passed the Hare and Crow by completely, but the pub's offerings do reflect the Scandinavian, British and Dutch demography of Doggerland, and Rasmussen feels that's enough. The Hare and Crow's patrons can choose between Carlsberg, Heineken – and Spitfire or Bishop's Finger, but never both at the same time. The rare customer who prefers wine can choose between red and white. These options are presented by Arild Rasmussen in such a brusque tone that any intention to ask inconvenient questions about country of origin or vintage is inevitably nipped in the bud. On the other hand, not a lot of people come to the Hare and Crow to drink wine or eat food, although Arild Rasmussen is actually capable of throwing together a perfectly nice lamb stew.

The recipe's from his wife, Reidun, whose unique blend of schlager singing and salty curses would frequently stream out from the kitchen until eight years ago. The Rasmussens fought non-stop for the thirty-two years they served lamb stew and beer at the Hare and Crow, sometimes so fiercely the sound of 'you evil sow' and 'you useless old goat' from the kitchen had the patrons shifting uncomfortably in their seats and glancing at their watches.

And yet, the locals worried Arild wouldn't be able to run the business on his own after Reidun suffered a stroke one lovely day in May. Was the last pub in the village going to go the way of the now shuttered quayside pub the Anchor?

After Reidun's stroke, the Hare and Crow stayed closed for eleven days, but then one morning, Arild turned the sign over once again and opened his doors. The menu was less ambitious; other than the lamb stew, it consisted primarily of pre-cooked fish croquettes with peas and mashed potatoes and pre-cooked burgers with French fries. It's said Reidun still barks orders from her bed in the flat above the Hare and Crow, where she and Arild live, but no one knows for sure.

Be that as it may, the taps at the Hare and Crow are always clean and the price of a pint is still a shilling lower than in Dunker.

Now, Arild picks up a pint glass and cocks an eyebrow.

'The usual?' he asks, putting his hand on the Spitfire tap.

Karen nods. Instead of bringing her glass to her favourite spot in the back, next to the fireplace, she pulls out one of the stools and hangs her handbag on one of the hooks under the bar. Arild Rasmussen puts down a cardboard coaster with the Shepherd Neame logo on it and puts her pint on top. Karen thanks him with a big smile. There are only two ways of making Arild Rasmussen talk: flattery or getting him to have a glass or two himself.

'You've gone all out,' she says with a nod toward the tables, which are decorated with plaid runners and green glass tealight holders.

'You noticed, did you?' Rasmussen mutters. 'Bought some new things for Oistra,' he adds, trying to hide a pleased grin.

'Looks really nice, proper posh,' Karen tells him and inhales some foam from her glass.

The three regulars have listened to their brief conversation with poorly concealed curiosity. Now Jaap Kloes turns to Karen.

'So, a visit from the town bobby, eh? Or maybe I should say bobette?'

Karen notes that as usual, Kloes manages to squeeze several insults into one sentence. But she's not offended; in here, people big themselves up by doing others down; it's tradition. And once you peel away the jargon, there's not really much malice there.

'Well, I've actually been a detective inspector for quite a few years now,' she says and smiles regretfully. 'But I understand it's hard for you to keep up with all the changes, old man; first women's suffrage and now women police officers and even detectives – what is the world coming to?'

Kloes mutters something under his breath and quickly turns back to his pint while the other men guffaw cruelly.

'Eiken one, Kloes nothing,' Odd Marklund says. 'You're on fine form tonight, Karen lass.'

'Don't get excited, I'm not staying long,' she says. 'A pint or two and some gossip's all I'm after. You won't mind helping me out, will you?'

'You want to know about the Smeed woman, I take it?'

Karen nods and takes another sip. Then she wipes the foam from her top lip with the back of her hand.

'So, what can you tell me about Susanne? I want to know everything.'

It takes roughly thirty minutes for the four men in the bar to add considerably to the picture. The three regulars and the pub owner were unanimous in their assessment: Susanne was a prickly, bitter wretch with a well-developed ability to rub everyone around her up the wrong way. While Karen is irked by the judgemental, condescending tone of the men's descriptions, she has to admit the picture confirms her own impression.

And maybe Susanne had been like that as a child and teenager as well; Karen has nothing but a hazy, very vague memory of her from back in those days. A fair-haired girl who lived on the other side of Langevik. The three-year age difference had been an effective barrier, at least to Karen's mind. When Susanne started first grade, Karen had moved on to middle school and while Susanne was in middle school, Karen had already tasted the joys and challenges of high school: new subjects, new teachers and – most importantly – the boys in the higher grades. All permeated by a thrilling feeling of finally being an adult. She had been preoccupied with her own shortcomings, the awesomeness of other people and wondering whether Graham in the ninth grade liked her or not. She'd had no time for the babies in the lower grades.

Even though she and Susanne had grown up only a mile or two apart, the distance between them had been enormous and, for some reason, it hadn't diminished with age. They knew each other by name, said hi and exchanged a few words whenever they would run into each other as adults, but that was all it had ever been. Until that time four years ago.

Soon after Jounas was appointed the head of the CID, Karen and Susanne had ended up in line next to each other at the plant nursery one day in early April. While the queue inched forward at a snail's pace, it became impossible not to exchange at least a few words. With a firm grip on a trolley full of pansies, Susanne had replied monosyllabically to Karen's attempts at conversation. And then, after a long awkward pause, she had blurted out:

'You should be careful, Karen. Jounas has always gone after women who . . . well, women like you.'

Then she'd turned her trolley around, made an excuse of having forgotten something and walked back in among the shelves of seedlings and potting soil. Karen had paid and driven home with two plum trees and an unsettling feeling she knew what kind of women Susanne was referring to.

The unanimous picture of Susanne Smeed being painted at the Hare and Crow this evening is that although she used to be a 'pretty little thing', over the years, she had become a pariah.

'She complained about absolutely everything,' says Jaap Kloes. 'Buses idling, the road association's accounting, speed bumps by the school, her neighbours' kids. And according to the missus, she was no different at work; neither carers nor managers could bear being around her. The only thing that can be said in her defence is that she kicked both up and down, I guess. A nasty fucking bitch, if you'll pardon my French.'

'Just look at the shit she stirred up about the windmill, for instance,' Egil Jenssen adds. 'We were obviously all against it from the first, but in the end, people accepted there was nothing to be done about it.'

Especially the people who were handsomely compensated for their land and made a small fortune. But Karen says nothing.

'I get that it riled her when they built those turbines,' Kloes continues. 'Her land was right next to them. But she wouldn't bloody let up! Constant nagging, letters to the papers and the council. Did she really expect them to take the blasted things down again once they were built? Just because they bothered her?'

179

'Pretty tragic, actually. One lonely woman waging war on both landowners and the power company; she didn't stand a chance,' Odd Marklund says, shaking his head slowly.

Unlike Jenssen and Kloes, Marklund has a note of pity in his voice when he talks about Susanne. Karen's not surprised. Odd Marklund proved himself to be both courageous and mindful of others when Karen had her first summer job on the shrimp-cleaning line at the Loke factory, where he'd been the manager. Unlike the over-zealous shift manager who, with poorly concealed glee, constantly docked workers' pay for sloppiness, Odd Marklund had approached leftover shell fragments with equanimity.

Which was why Karen hadn't been surprised to learn Marklund had been laid off by the giant fish company a few years later. Norwegian investors had demanded the Dogger factory be streamlined; any part of the process not handled by a machine was a threat to their profit margins. At fifty-six, Odd Marklund had been made redundant.

He knows exactly what fighting against something bigger and infinitely stronger entails. Who could be in a better position to empathise with Susanne Smeed's futile struggle against the wind energy company Pegasus?

And Susanne was hardly the only one fighting; equally incendiary fights had been legion in the past few years. The debate leading up to the parliament's decision twenty years ago to save Doggerland's economy and secure the future growth of the islands by allowing a massive expansion of wind power and the export of electricity to northern Europe had raged for a long time before burning itself out. Over time, resistance, appeals and delays had melted away because the most powerful landowners saw their bank accounts grow as they were compensated for the appropriated land.

The expansion has undeniably come at a cost. The bird life in large parts of the archipelago has seen a dramatic decline, and there are still rumours alleging the power company has people on their payroll tasked with clearing the dead birds from around the turbines. But it's rarely talked about now. And the power company is making obscene profits, but on the other hand, the state's stake has also ensured two decades of economic growth. Given that, most islanders seem willing to overlook the fact that half the profits end up lining the pockets of venture capitalists.

Susanne Smeed was clearly of a different opinion. She seems to have been literally tilting at windmills. And yet, judging by what Karen has just been told, she hadn't even owned the land in question. Karen signals with a nod to Arild Rasmussen that she'd like another pint.

'So you're telling me she was fighting the landowners? I thought Susanne's family owned everything up to the ridge?'

'That and much more. The whole of the ridge plus a sizeable chunk of the forest on the other side,' Arild replies. 'And it would all have been hers if her father hadn't sold it. Per Lindgren managed to sell off every last bit of land he inherited from his wife, hectare by hectare.'

Arild wipes the outside of the glass with a green bar towel and plonks it down in front of Karen.

'Actually, it started before then, while the wife was still alive,' he continues. 'I guess that's how they funded the commune or whatever they called it. A dodgy lot they were, either way, living up on old Gråå's farm.'

Karen recalls what her mother told her and the stories she heard as a child about Lothorp Farm.

'Those crackpots only stayed for about a year, then they dispersed,' Egil Jenssen puts in. 'But the Lindgrens stayed on and sold off their land instead of putting in an honest day's work. Made paintings no one wanted to buy, that's all Lindgren did, until the bitter end. Lord knows how his wife and little Susanne bore it. They had no income and they had to pay for food and clothes somehow, so I suppose that's why they auctioned off the family fortune, bit by bit.

'I bought a strip of forest myself, adjacent to my property. It must have been in seventy-four or possibly seventy-five, if I remember correctly. Bloody good deal, I'll tell you that.'

Clearly cheered up by the memories and the gossip, Jaap Kloes smiles out of the corner of his mouth, raises his glass to the others and drinks deeply with the pleased look of a suckling infant.

'Crazy Swedes,' Kloes continues after putting his glass down and wiping his mouth. 'Remember when they bought geese? Thought they could roam free both day and night. The fox took every last one before the summer was over. But you know what they say: you can season it with Bretons, Friesians and Flemings . . .'

'. . . the Dogger soup still mostly reeks of Scandinavians,' Karen finishes with a weary smile.

Jaap Kloes chuckles delightedly.

'Well, I believe there were both British and Dutch people in that commune,' Egil Jenssen says curtly and turns to Karen. 'I'm surprised they stayed as long as they did. Your father bet a hundred shilling the whole commune would give up before the first winter. That was a lot of money back then.'

'My dad? How come?'

'Not just him, they had a pool going down at the Anchor. Harald Steen was the bookie and there was a lot of bickering about how to distribute the money when it turned out the Lindgrens stayed and the others shoved off. What year was it they came here? Sixty-nine?'

'Seventy,' Kloes says. 'Same year my youngest boy was born. I remember when they arrived in their Peruvian knitted hats, talking a big game about organic agriculture and living off the land and all kinds of nonsense like that. They were going to share everything, they said.'

'Mrs Lindgren almost drove my wife batty with her lectures about pesticide-free produce and plant-based dyes and God knows what,' Jenssen says. 'Probably smoked a bit of the jazz tobacco, too, I'd wager. No, I never understood what they wanted here.'

'The green wave,' Odd Marklund says. 'Quite a lot of people came out here during those years. Went to Frisel, a lot of them. Back to nature, and whatnot. There were farmers down there who made a pretty penny off them; they'd sell them a piece of meagre land at a hiked-up price and buy the whole lot back at a lower price when it turned out life in the countryside wasn't that easy. They couldn't live off what they managed to grow.'

'Well, the Lindgrens certainly didn't have to buy land. The wife, Anne-Marie, I think her name was, inherited old Gråå's property – he was her grandfather, so it was all hers, even though she'd never set foot on the island before then, as far as I'm aware. He was a stingy old bastard, was Vetle Gråå; remember him, Karen? Bent over like a scythe but he did the rounds of his property until the day he died. Two sons he had, one drank himself to death, the other married a Swede, so no wonder the old man was grumpy,' Jaap Kloes says.

'So, Anne-Marie's dad,' Karen says. 'What happened to him?'

'Wasn't he the one who fell off a scaffold at a construction site in Malmö and died?' Odd Marklund says and is met with a triumphant nod.

'Yep. Despite all those wondrous workplace safety laws they have over there. Old Vetle had no time for our brothers in the east after that, Scandinavian though he was.'

Karen shakes her head. Of course she's heard of Vetle Gråå. Her mother had been right in saying his name had survived him. But Karen had never paid any attention to who owned what land or who cheated whom in the endless series of inheritances, emergency auctions and trades her parents discussed at the kitchen table. Everyone in the village, both young and old, had, however, known that old man Gråå's properties in Langevik had been extensive.

'So Susanne's mother was Gråå's grandchild,' she says thoughtfully. 'And yet you're telling me that the only thing left for Susanne to inherit was the house.'

'All that remained of Gråå's property was the garden around the old stone house where Susanne lived, the one the Lindgrens moved down to after the commune failed. That's when they sold the farm up at Lothorp and the land around it. And whatever was left – tracts of land stretching all the way to Kvattle and the forest – was slowly sold off by Per Lindgren over the years; when he popped his clogs, there wasn't so much as a strip of grass left.'

'This commune,' Karen says searchingly, 'how big was it? I mean, how many people lived there?'

184

'Well, I never exactly popped over for a headcount,' Egil Jenssen says. 'The Lindgrens, of course, and another Swedish family. And a Danish lady, I seem to remember. I think my wife talked to her a few times and said she seemed perfectly reasonable. A better sort than the rest of them, she told me.'

'I think there were people from the UK, too, or maybe Ireland; either way, they often spoke English to each other; you'd hear it when they came down to the village. I'm not really sure, but I reckon it was about eight or ten adults, and children, of course. But I don't know any of their names . . .'

Odd Marklund turns inquiringly to his drinking mates who both shake their heads.

'The other Swedish woman was a looker; that I remember,' Jaap Kloes puts in. 'We'd sit down at the Anchor, fantasising about what went on up there when the lights went out. We were all a bit curious what with all that talk about Swedes and free love, you know.'

'Speak for yourself; I certainly never had the time to go snooping around Lothorp Farm in the evenings,' Arild Rasmussen retorts and disappears into the kitchen with a plastic crate full of empty pint glasses.

Karen studies the scruffy old men. What they're talking about happened nearly forty years ago; they must have been in their thirties when the Lindgrens and the other members of the commune arrived. About the same age as them, probably, but from very different worlds. To a thirty-year-old man – on whom fifteen years of North Sea fishing had already taken a toll – people who were prepared to abandon comfortable lives to grow vegetables on a windswept island in the middle of the sea must have appeared out of their minds. For people whose childhoods had consisted of wood-burning stoves and kerosene lamps, an existence without modern conveniences held no romantic appeal. There was no rhyme or reason to voluntarily giving up what others toiled so hard to acquire. Back then, migration flows had mostly gone the other way; why would any sane person trade modern Sweden for Doggerland?

Karen has no trouble imagining the islanders' fantasies about the members of the commune; next to the prematurely aged fishermen's wives in Langevik, the young women must have come across as exotic, to say the least. The women of the village had probably been a great deal less enthusiastic at the sight of tie-dyed, braless freedom. On the other hand, not even the drooling menfolk at the Anchor appeared to have welcomed the newcomers into the fold. Despite their curiosity, they seemed to have viewed the members of the commune with equal measures of schadenfreude and jealousy. And yet, despite this hostility, Per and Anne-Marie Lindgren had stayed. What had made them stick it out?

And now the whole family's gone and no one seems to mourn any of them, she realises with a sense of unease. No one has anything good to say, not even about Susanne, who grew up in Langevik. What must it have been like for her to grow up in the village?

'Do we know anything about how the commune worked? They did keep at it for over a year, after all, living together and sharing everything, you said. Were there no rumours about discord or fighting?'

Kloes shrugs, as though he's lost interest in the subject.

'Well, they did leave, so clearly it got to be too much free love and organic bullshit even for them,' Jenssen says. 'I don't mind

186

telling you I wouldn't share my wife either. Not that anyone wants her,' he adds with a laugh that turns into a roaring coughing fit.

Odd Marklund puts his pint down and meets Karen's gaze.

'A lot of people were exploring different ways to live back then; some were looking for something different and others were probably running away from something. They're not the only ones who've fled both to and from here over the years, are they, Karen?'

He knows, she thinks and looks at her hand clutching the bar, studying the damp handprint it leaves on the dark wood.

'Are you feeling all right, lass?'

Odd Marklund studies her with a look of concern; she gives him a reassuring smile.

'I'm just a bit light-headed. Haven't had anything to eat since lunch, so I think it's high time for me to be heading home now.' She turns to Arild Rasmussen who has returned from the kitchen.

'Just one last question. You said something about Susanne not owning the land above her house anymore, the plot with the windmills. But she was still in a fight with the power company?'

'Well, I guess that was the problem. She didn't know the land had been sold, thought she still owned it. Until surveyors and engineers turned up, uninvited, on what she thought was her land. It was just after she got divorced and moved back, so I guess she didn't have a clear idea of what was what. But then her father died and she found out everything had been sold off a long time ago.'

'No wonder she felt duped,' Karen says. 'What she thought was her land had already been sold, and now it was being sold again and forty-two wind turbines were being built next door.'

'You're wrong there,' Arild Rasmussen cuts her off. 'The owner of the land never sold it. Wily bastard managed to get Pegasus to sign a fifty-year leasehold with profit sharing and the whole to-do. Talk about having your cake and eating it. Lord knows how he pulled it off.'

Rasmussen's voice is now brimming with equal parts contempt and admiration. Karen, for her part, mostly feels awkward about Susanne Smeed's bad fortune.

'That does sound like a good deal,' Karen says drily. 'And who is this "wily bastard" then – do you happen to know that?'

'Axel Smeed's boy Jounas, of course, who else?'

27

'Wait, let me help you!'

'That's OK, I've got it, but if you wouldn't mind holding the door, I'd be very grateful.'

Cornelis Loots does as he's told, walking briskly from the lift to the frosted glass door leading into the CID. Feeling distinctly unhelpful, he then watches while Detective Inspector Karen Eiken Hornby shuffles through the door sideways, her face bright red, panting under the weight of the enormous box she's lugging.

'Goddamn it,' she mutters when her big carrier bag slips off her shoulder.

Cornelis Loots feels like an idiot when he can't think of any other way to assist her than to lift up the bag and walk next to his boss while she lumbers on with her heavy load, tipped back, feet wide apart. When she turns off toward the kitchen, he can't take it anymore. Together, they manage to put the beast of a box down on the floor without any alarming sounds. Karen shoots him a grateful smile and rubs her tender hands.

'Bloody lucky you were here; I would never have got that door open by myself. Are you good at technical stuff, by the way? Would you mind helping me set this up before the others get in?'

She makes a sweeping gesture toward the box; only now does Cornelis realise what the picture on the glossy cardboard is of.

'Christ, that's a monster,' he says. 'How much did something like that set you back?'

Karen shrugs.

'You don't want to know. But Haugen was very clear about giving us all the resources we need.'

'And you don't think he meant in terms of extra staff...?'

'My professional assessment is that we can't carry on with this investigation with that atrocious excuse for coffee as our only fuel.'

Karen waves vaguely at the brown coffee maker on the counter. Someone has put the unwashed glass pot back on the heater; the sour smell of yesterday's coffee suffuses the small kitchenette.

After twenty minutes, Cornelis Loots puts the screwdriver down on the counter and rolls his shirt sleeves back down while he and Karen contemplate their joint achievement. She has watched him hook the machine up to power and water with a mix of respect and surprise. Now she won't have to call the janitor, Kofs, and listen to his whingeing about how this isn't in his job description. She takes a step forward, wipes a fingerprint off the machine's shiny chrome shell and snaps her forefinger against the bent arm of the steam wand, making it spin. Purchasing's going to throw a fit.

'Doesn't something like this need special coffee?'

Thirty days before the invoice arrives ... Smeed might be back by then. She pushes the thought down and smiles broadly at Cornelis. Then she pulls two one-pound bags of whole coffee beans out of her messenger bag.

'You fire that monster up and I'll pop across the street for a bit. I have a quick meeting with Vegen and Haugen starting' – she glances at her watch – 'two minutes ago.'

28

'Seems to me we should be able to strike Smeed off the list of people of interest; I see no reason why he can't come back to work.'

Viggo Haugen quickly covers up the faint tremble in his voice by ending the sentence in a deep, chesty baritone. They've gathered in the prosecutor's office, sitting in the group of armchairs at one end of the room.

Karen sighs inwardly and exchanges a quick look with Dineke Vegen. Vegen's good, a curling at the corner of her mouth signals that she's well aware things are not as simple as the chief of police is trying to make them out to be, but her raised eyebrows reveal that she's going to leave this particular fight to Detective Inspector Eiken. She hasn't seen a reason to step in and take over the investigation yet.

'I understand where you're coming from,' Karen replies, looking straight into Haugen's ice blue eyes. 'Of course it would be great if we could clear Jounas right now, but there are still too many unanswered questions.'

Viggo Haugen opens his mouth to interrupt but shuts it again when Karen pushes on with feigned conviction.

'Like you, I have a very hard time picturing Jounas killing Susanne, but that's not enough. He still doesn't have an alibi for the time of the murder and there are, unfortunately, a few circumstances that might be seen as incriminating. He has been to Susanne's house recently – six days before the murder according to his own information – and their relationship can be described as complicated, and that's putting it mildly.'

'Well, no wonder; that's hardly a solid lead. If everyone who had a "complicated" relationship with their ex-wives were automatically considered suspect . . .'

Viggo Haugen makes quotation marks in the air and spreads his hands.

'Karen's right,' Dineke Vegen's voice puts an end to his little performance.

Haugen fall silent with a surprised frown on his face.

'Once the casefile is made public,' the prosecutor continues, 'you can be sure it will be picked apart by every journalist in this country; there mustn't be anything to suggest we let Jounas's position influence the investigation. On the contrary, we have to take special care to get to the bottom of anything that could be used against Smeed.'

Viggo Haugen clears his throat, his mind racing. Unlike Karen, Dineke Vegen radiates the kind of female authority he actually respects. More education and elegance and less . . . surly bitch. He turns to the prosecutor with a smile.

'Naturally, I didn't mean that we should . . .'

'Not least for Jounas's own sake,' Karen puts in. 'Unless he's completely cleared of all suspicion, it's going to be hell for him to come back. And believe me, I'm going to do everything I can to clear him,' she adds.

Viggo Haugen replies instantly with a sidelong glance at Dineke Vegen.

'I would suggest you focus on finding the actual killer instead. I think that's what would serve Jounas best.'

'That's what I meant,' Karen mutters softly. 'I didn't express myself clearly.'

'Well, that's hardly the first time. Anyway, I hear you and I'll let Jounas know as soon as we're done here.'

Dineke Vegen raises her well-groomed eyebrows again.

'About his continued sabbatical, I mean. Nothing else. All right then, it's decided,' he announces and gets to his feet.

Karen throws Dineke Vegen another glance and receives a hint of a small smile in return.

29

'Never in my wildest dreams did I imagine we'd ever have to put up with their kind here. Poor old Gråå would turn in his grave if he could see what they're doing to his farm.'

The woman at the till in the hardware shop firmly, almost angrily, punches in the price of three hundred wood screws while she speaks, then looks up at her customer, seeking agreement.

Anne-Marie Lindgren is standing between shelves lined with paint cans and wood oil and kerosene. She was bending down to pick up paintbrushes but has frozen mid-movement, hunched over, as though ashamed.

Do they know she's there? Do they want her to overhear or did they just miss her coming in? Her cheeks flush; the words feel like a slap in the face.

Now she hears a muttered reply from the customer, then the voice of the worked-up clerk cuts through the room again.

'Have you seen what they're like? Dress like junkies the lot of them, long dresses and long hair. Eighty shillings, please. And little children they have, too, a bunch. God knows how they take care of them. Are they going to go to school here, in the village, when that day comes? Play with our kids? If you ask me, they shouldn't let people like that procreate. Yes, I know that sounds harsh . . .'

Apparently, the man buying the screws says something, because the clerk's irate voice is lowered somewhat.

'Yes, Arthur says the same thing,' she sighs. 'Six months at most, he says. Twenty shillings change and your receipt, there you are. Well, it's one thing in the spring and summer, but when the autumn storms sweep in, they'll give up and move back home, mark my words. That's what Arthur says, but I don't know.'

More mumbling from the customer before the clerk takes over again.

'Really, you don't say. Well, we'll have to hope for the best. Thank you for your business!'

Anne-Marie straightens up without a word, turns around and quickly walks out of the shop. Feels their eyes on her back when the doorbell shrilly announces that the door has been opened. They're probably going to think I stole something, she thinks. Add new accusations to the already long list. And they're going to win in the end. We're not going to be able to live here; I'm not going to be able to bear it.

After jogging home, aware of the censuring looks she gets from everyone she meets, she enters the main house out of breath, trying to blink away burning tears. She doesn't want to tell the others, doesn't want them to brush it aside and suggest she's being too sensitive, that she has to not care what other people think. She doesn't want to worry them; they're always so worried about her.

Per is sitting at the kitchen table with Theo, and Disa is standing by the hob, dyeing sheets in a large pot. She lifts out a section of

195

the fabric with her ladle and studies the yellow colour. The smell of beans, onion and spices is rising with the steam from another pot, fogging up the kitchen windows. Brandon is slumped on the bench, with his guitar hugged to his chest as usual; five-year-old Mette is helping him strum the strings. And now Ingela is coming down the stairs with baby Orian on her arm.

'Look,' he shouts, his little fingers clutching a long piece of string with rattling mussel shells that's tied around his neck. 'My necklace!'

No one heard Anne-Marie enter, but Per still turns around instinctively, as though he can feel her presence. His smile morphs into a look of concern when he sees her flushed cheeks and teary eyes, which they all notice. They make a fuss, lead her over to the table, pull out a chair, give her a cup and fill it with tea and honey. And she assures them she just got winded going up the hill, the road from the village is steep; she's just feeling unusually tired, maybe she's caught the cold some of the children had last week. She realises Per is watching her with eyes that can't hide his flaring hope. That meaningless, hopeless hope that she might be pregnant.

No, she tells them nothing. Not about what she overheard when she went down to the village to buy paintbrushes to paint the window frames with. And not about her sudden realisation that the idyll that currently reigns on Lothorp Farm is going to be shattered. The threat feels so palpable, sending shivers down her back, like a first gust of air, finding its way into the house, an omen of impending storms. She can't tell from which direction it's coming, doesn't know how close it is. Just that it's something much worse than a gossipy old hardware store bitch.

30

The moment she puts her hand on the door handle, she's overcome with doubt. Is this really such a good idea? Maybe they're going to think she's trying to ingratiate herself, that she's trying to buy popularity with a stupid coffee machine.

Instead of going straight in, Karen pauses in the hallway for a few seconds, her mind racing. Maybe they're right. Isn't it in fact a kind of bribe? A desperate way of getting the group on her side?

At least Evald Johannisen isn't here, she reminds herself and squares her shoulders. The mere thought of the cutting barbs he'd probably throw her way makes her wince. Maybe the others would have agreed with him.

'Fuck,' she says so loudly it echoes down the stairwell.

And the blasted thing has to be paid for; there's bound to be more a lot more sour faces in thirty days' time. Twenty-nine, she corrects herself and pushes the door open.

The smell of coffee hits her before she crosses the threshold.

The door to the conference room at the end of the hallway is standing ajar; she can hear the faint sound of voices coming from inside. She quickly walks through the empty office landscape to her desk and pulls a folder out of her top drawer. Then she continues, with determined, slightly angry steps, toward the conference room and opens the door.

Ungrateful bastards.

Karen sinks into her seat, her cheeks on fire, while the spontaneous round of applause subsides and a plate full of cinnamon buns is pushed toward her.

'Damn fine initiative, Eiken,' Karl says. 'But I'm assuming they're going to give you all kinds of hell for it.'

'Cross that bridge when I get to it,' she replies and gives him a crooked smile while she sinks her teeth into one of the giant buns.

'Shall we shtart?' she slurs and licks a few grains of pearl sugar off her index finger.

She quickly relates what she found out from the old men at the Hare and Crow and ends with the words:

'So I think it's safe to assume Susanne Smeed rubbed a lot of people up the wrong way and was hardly considered a ray of sunshine by the locals And her managers and co-workers seem in agreement.'

'And her daughter,' Karl Björken adds. 'And presumably Jounas wasn't particularly complimentary either?'

'That's correct. So far, no one has described her in positive terms, and that's putting it mildly. The question is whether she managed to piss anyone off enough for them to kill her. Might she even have been involved in some kind of blackmail? Surly and unpleasant, that much we know, but was she the snooping type? Anyone?'

Everyone is silent, looking pensive.

'More like inquisitive,' Astrid Nielsen says. 'At least judging from her boss and the handful of colleagues Johannisen and I managed to track down. Susanne Smeed seems to have been the type that notes other people's mistakes and relishes pointing them out. A bit of a tattletale, too.'

'Cornelis and Astrid, I'm going to have you go back out to Solgården today to dig up anything you can. I'm going to go see Wenche Hellevik – Smeed, as was. She's Jounas's sister and one of the few friends Susanne seems to have had,' she adds after looking up and being met with quizzical looks. 'Maybe she can give us a more detailed picture. But I need someone to go with me. Karl, do you have time?'

He nods and Karen turns back to Cornelis Loots.

'Do you have anything to tell us about the technical investigation or anything else you're in charge of?'

'I spoke to Larsen this morning; they're working on DNA and fingerprints now and will likely have a result before the end of the day. Well, in addition to the prints that have already been identified as Jounas Smeed's,' he adds, looking uncomfortable. 'And we're still waiting to hear from Susanne's bank and the cruise ship.'

'Right, how's that going? How far have you got?'

'We've sent out inquiries to the home countries of each of the passengers, which includes all the Scandinavian countries, the US, the Netherlands and Italy. Germany, too, actually; one of the Danes turned out to hold German citizenship,' Cornelis Loots says, reading from his papers.

'And . . .?'

'So far, no reports of serious crimes, as defined by a minimum of one year in the nick. Granted, the sentencing scale varies between the different countries, but looking at anyone who has ever been incarcerated, we're talking to two people. Namely . . .'

Cornelis flips through his papers.

'A Swedish businessman, Erik Björnlund, who spent eighteen months behind bars for insider trading and an American, Brett Close, who did six years, for manslaughter, actually. But when we looked into that, it turned out to be a case of drink driving where a three-year-old girl was killed. And either way, Brett Close is seventy-two years old and that all happened back in the mid-seventies. Since then, he's been clean as a whistle and according to the head of security on the ship, he and his wife are both deeply religious. Episcopalians, I think he said.'

'Well, we've seen God-fearing men commit terrible crimes before,' Karen says sagely. 'Don't forget that pastor on Noorö who offed his wife and four children to save them from further sinning. But I see your point, Brett Close doesn't exactly feel like a red-hot lead. Anything else?'

'No, that's all we have so far, but we haven't heard back from everywhere and the Italians haven't responded at all. I'm calling them again after this.'

Karen sighs. The chance of finding something useful via the cruise ship had always been a long shot and it certainly wasn't looking promising. Once Loots and Nielsen had had replies from every country, they would likely be able to drop that line of inquiry and focus on something else.

The question is what. The first twenty-four hours of an investigation are always critical; statistically, the chances of solving the case weaken by the hour. They are now going on for three days without a suspect or even a clear motive. Eighty per cent of crimes involving lethal violence are, according to the numbers, cleared up in the first three days.

But regardless of whether they're dealing with murder in cold blood or manslaughter in a moment of passion, this case is looking increasingly unlikely to be included in that 80 per cent. After a run-through during which nothing of substance was presented, a customary speculation session regarding likely courses of events and possible motives and the handing out of assignments, Karen ends the meeting, asking Karl Björken to hang around. She tells him that she has an errand to run that morning and agrees to meet up in the car park at one.

Twenty minutes later, she steps through the revolving doors of Hotel Strand.

31

Karen looks at the young receptionist and sighs inwardly. Truls Isaksen is a regular guy of about twenty-five who eyes her with that air of required politeness and deeply felt superiority that is so common among young people in the service industry. His dark hair is neatly pulled back into a discreet ponytail and small, vertical slits in his earlobes reveal that they're usually adorned somehow when he's not at work.

As soon as Karen has introduced herself and told him what she's there for, his little smirk is erased and his eyebrows are lowered to a more relaxed height. Granted, his work requires him to treat the hotel's guest with a certain level of politeness, but no one said anything about kissing police arse.

They've gone back to the staff kitchen behind the reception desk and Truls has, after pouring himself a cup of coffee, asked if she wants one, too. She doesn't. While demolishing half a packet of chocolate biscuits, he pulls out a packet of cigarettes and starts impatiently turning it over in his hand. Apparently, he assumes their conversation will be over quickly so he can step out into the small backyard and have a well-deserved smoke. Karen contemplates offering to go with him and continue their conversation outside. And maybe she would have if she'd been in a better mood, or if Truls had been more welcoming. Instead, she pretends not to notice the cigarettes he has now placed on the table in front of him, proceeding instead to play with a red plastic lighter.

Thus their conversation begins; Karen asks questions without letting him provoke or wind her up and Truls Isaksen answers increasingly tersely and uninterestedly. She can feel her mood turn even fouler.

No, he has no idea when the guest in room 507 checked out on Sunday morning; the room had been paid for in advance and he could have dropped the key off at the front desk at any time. The hotel doesn't make a habit of spying on its guests. No, he's not at the front desk every second of his shift; he has a right to both eat and go to the bathroom. And yes, he is entitled to grab a few quick cigarette breaks, too, when things are quiet. Besides, there's a bell people can ring if they need assistance. And yes, he must have been the one who checked the guest into room 507, no one else would have been working at half past midnight. No, he has no clear recollection of the person in question. No, that's not strange, considering that spontaneous check-ins are fairly coming during Oistra; he'd probably served half a dozen unannounced guests that particular Saturday night. And we all know what they're here for.

'Horny old men and women skulking over by the lift, trying to keep out of sight,' Truls Isaksen says with an air of jaded experience. 'It actually happens on regular weekends, too, but it's worse during Oistra; lots of drunk middle-aged people panting for some action.'

Karen squirms inwardly as she listens to the young man's highly accurate description. Outwardly, she shows no hint of her thoughts; the ability to keep her face impassive is a skill she's practised during countless interviews. Even so, what Truls Isaksen says next makes her flinch.

'But weren't you here yourself? I feel like I've seen you before.'

The young receptionist's sudden epiphany makes Karen study him incredulously. How is it possible that this guy – who neither saw nor heard anything, who can't remember guests or times and who probably snored his way through half his shift – recognises her of all people? Now he's eyeing her with an interest that is as unexpected as it is unwelcome.

'Aren't you the one who scarpered at the crack of bloody dawn on Sunday morning? At like seven? I was coming back from the bog and I saw you slink out the doors . . .'

Karen watches him, her eyebrows raised again; maybe he interprets it as surprise or indignation at his inability to distinguish between officers of the law and hotel guests. Or maybe he doesn't give a toss. Either way, the flash of interest in Truls Isaksen's eyes is extinguished and he leans back with a heavy sigh, as though his sudden recollection has sucked all the energy out of him. His next words send a wave of relief through her.

'Whatever, I guess it was someone else. Come to think of it, she looked more like a dumb, drunk slapper than a copper. Though she did remind me of you. No offence, obviously.'

Karen clears her throat and smiles stiffly.

'Just one more question, then I'll let you get on with your smoking,' she says with a nod to the packet of cigarettes. 'You're telling me there's no way of ascertaining when a guest leaves the hotel so long as the room is prepaid and no one at the front desk notes down what time a key card is returned? Are there no cameras?'

'Only in the car park. If the bloke had a car . . .'

Truls Isaksen looks like he regrets his words the moment they come out. Is she going to make him show her where the

CCTV tapes are now, too? Fuck that, some things have to be up to his manager.

'Unfortunately, he didn't,' Karen tells him. 'At least not parked here at the hotel.'

She stands up and holds out her hand.

'OK then, thank you for your time.'

Truls Isaksen shakes her hand while pulling out a cigarette with his other one. Then he turns and quickly walks out of the kitchen, disappearing down a hallway that seems to lead to the back door. Apparently, he has no intention of walking Karen out. She watches him go. The door to the backyard remains open for a second; she catches a glimpse of a woman standing on the small paved patio, puffing away on a cigarette. She's clearly cold in her thin blue cleaning coat and orthopaedic sandals; it looks like she's hugging herself to stay warm. Then the door closes and Karen turns to walk the other way toward the hotel lobby. Just then, she hears Truls Isaksen's voice.

'Oi, you . . .'

He's standing in the doorway, exhaling a thin cloud of smoke with a contented look on his face, waving Karen over.

'I realised Rosita might know something,' he says.

'Rosita?'

'Yeah, she was cleaning here on Sunday morning.'

Then he steps aside, making the woman in the light blue housecoat visible once more.

32

Rosita Alvarez gives a clear account of her daily duties and how she always keeps meticulous notes about which rooms have been cleaned or if she's noticed anything out of the ordinary, such as stolen towels or a need for additional cleaning efforts. Karen listens attentively without interrupting.

'People throw up,' Rosita says succinctly. 'Not always in the toilet. It gets on the floor and people don't clean up after themselves. One guest had vomited all over the bathtub, but that time I went to the manager and told her I wanted extra time. We only have fifteen minutes per room if they're leavers.'

'Leavers?'

'Yes, people who are checking out. Then we have stayers, people who stay for more than one night; I only have seven minutes to do their rooms.'

Karen doesn't ask whether the cleaning of room 507 had required an additional effort, doesn't want to know. Instead, she listens with mounting horror to Rosita's account of a normal day at work for a hotel cleaner. Rosita Alvarez matter-of-factly tells her about stolen towels that she has report to avoid getting in trouble herself, about real, imagined and made-up thefts where the cleaners are always the go-to suspects, various kinds of stained sheets, groping guests, insults and the constant time pressure. And she tells her how she likes to start work as early as possible so she can get home to her husband and thirteen-year-old son in Moerbeck.

'I always start on the top floor and work my way down. The second round I do the other way around and then for the third one, I start at the top again. Three or four rounds is usually enough.'

'Yes, please, why not,' Karen says and accepts a cigarette from the packet Rosita holds out to her with an encouraging nod. 'So you have to keep coming back to floors you've already covered?'

'Yes, someone's always sleeping in; some people have breakfast in their rooms and some hang the do-not-disturb sign on their doors. So then you have to wait.'

'You wouldn't happen to remember what it was like on Sunday morning? Because I need to know when the guest in room 507 checked out.'

'Don't be crazy,' Rosita says and takes one last firm drag. 'We have fifty-one rooms; I can't keep track of it all.'

She leans across a garden table and stubs out her cigarette against an upside-down terracotta pot serving as an ashtray.

'But I can have a look in the book,' she adds, smiling broadly at Karen's disappointed expression. 'I always write down the times, so I can keep track of which rooms I've done. I'm not so young anymore, after all,' she says, tapping her knuckle against her forehead. 'You can come with me after you're done with your cigarette . . .'

'Do you save all your logs?' Karen asks and quickly stubs out her half-smoked cigarette while sending up a silent hallelujah to the heavens.

'Not forever, but for a month at least,' Rosita replies and holds the door open. 'In case there are any complaints from the guests after the fact. Or from management, for that matter,' she adds with a grim look while she brushes a few flakes of ash off her housecoat.

If only everyone was like Rosita Alvarez, Karen considers as she approaches the car park across from the police station. She and Karl agreed to meet there so they can go see Jounas's sister, Wenche Hellevik, together. A glance at her watch tells her she's seven minutes early. She carefully sits down on the dusty newspaper box outside the corner shop at the intersection of Kirkegate and Redehusgate and gazes over at the station entrance.

With a smile, she thinks back to her meeting with Rosita Alvarez, the extraordinary cleaner at Hotel Strand. Karen thinks the woman deserves a medal.

The do-not-disturb sign had been on the door of room 507 when Rosita checked the fifth-floor hallway that morning at a few minutes past nine. While she waited, she had busied herself with rooms 501 and 503, whose guests had already left the hotel. When she was done, half an hour later, the sign had been taken down and Rosita Alvarez had cleaned room 507 between 9.35 and 9.50, according to her notes.

Karen goes over the timing one more time. Jounas's own claim that he left the hotel around half nine seems to tally. Theoretically he could, of course, have left the hotel just after Rosita saw the do-not-disturb sign a few minutes past nine; there was still a thirty-minute gap while she cleaned the other rooms. According to Kneought Brodal, Susanne died no later than 10 a.m., and more likely before 9.30. Say Jounas left the hotel just after nine, she ponders. If so, he would have been eminently able to make it out to Langevik before ten and could have killed Susanne within the time frame specified by Brodal.

But first he would have had to walk over to the car park by city hall and retrieve his car; another five minutes at least. Just over forty-five minutes left. Well, she has covered that same distance in half an hour once or twice when she's been in a real hurry, but not without severely breaking the speed limits. If he floored it, he should have been able to make it, but why would Jounas risk getting caught? He'd had no reason to race over there.

Goddamnit, she thinks, that's not good enough.

Karen looks away from the station entrance, turning her face toward the autumn sun and closing her eyes. She's so close to being able to rule her boss out. Haltingly close, but not quite there. There's still a theoretical possibility. The minutes and seconds point to him having had the time, but what about a motive? What would the trigger have been? Could something have happened, that morning at the hotel, after I left? she ponders. A phone call, a text, an email; something that woke Jounas up and made him furious? Or frightened?

'Catching rays, are we? Your car or mine?'

Karl's voice startles her. Mine, obviously, she thinks, but stifles the impulse. She always feels uncomfortable in the passenger seat, but today she should leave the driving to Karl.

'Why don't we take yours,' she says. 'I need to think.'

33

The motorway out of Dunker towards Ravenby cuts straight across the Sörland plain. Mile after mile of meagre fields and deciduous forest, broken up by vast heaths of heather. In the far west, where the road turns north, the horizon comes into view; even this far inland, you can sense that the island's western side drops precipitously into the sea. These days, few people still believe in the legend of Frendur the giant, who in a fit of rage split Heimö asunder with his sword, sparing the eastern half while letting the western one, where his adulterous wife and false-hearted brother lived in sin together, sink into the Atlantic Ocean. But just like the Earth can seem flat and the sky look like a blue glass dome on a fine summer's day, Heimö's coast really does look like it was created by a massive sword blow dealt by someone in a towering fury.

Karl drives fast but well, and just over an hour later, they've covered almost seventy miles, turned off onto route 20 and are now following the signs for Helleviksnäs. It's turning overcast again, Karen thinks to herself and leans forward to peer up at the grey clouds scudding in from the west, stacking up above them.

'Is it just a coincidence?' Karl asks with a glance at the GPS. 'That their surname is Hellevik and they live in Helleviksnäs, I mean.'

'Wouldn't have thought so,' Karen says. 'I seem to recall that Wenche's husband's family is rather large; they probably owned the village once upon a time. But I guess that's not entirely uncommon.'

'Maybe not here, but down on Frisel it's virtually unheard of. No one there owns anything beyond their tiny plot of land. If that, even.'

'No, you Friselians aren't exactly known for your ambition. Nor for your hard work,' she adds, shooting Karl a teasing look.

Karl snorts with feigned indignation. He's heard it before; the further north you live in the Dogger archipelago, the more likely you are to be considered hardworking and honest. The residents of Noorö – with their predominantly Norwegian and Swedish heritage – are still described as industrious, quiet and God-fearing, while their cousins on the southernmost island – where the population has more extensive Danish and Dutch roots – are said to be frivolous and leave their nets in the water for too long. In between is Heimö with its unholy mix of British, Scandinavian and continental European heritage. People came here from different parts of the world and for different reasons. It's probably true that a long time ago, Heimö served as a safe haven for people who found themselves compelled to leave their homelands for whatever reason, but hardly to the extent the stories try to make out. Yet, although the thieves, murderers and other criminals have never actually been as numerous as some would claim, the main island is, according to the natives of Noorö and Frisel, mostly populated by fish poachers, land owners, shipping magnates and others of their ilk, who don't mind enriching themselves at the expense of others. And Dunker, the capital, is, naturally, the worst.

'Makes sense,' Karl Björken mutters. 'Far be it from Axel Smeed's daughter to marry down. If you've grown up with a silver spoon in your mouth, you obviously can't just fall for a pauper. I bet they're swimming in money.'

'I guess we can always ask,' Karen replies sarcastically.

But they only have to turn in through the gates to the Helleviks' property to know that though the family may not be literally swimming in money, they definitely are in a figurative sense. The tennis court to the right of the driveway has both a clubhouse and two rows of raised seats and the kidney-shaped swimming pool beyond it is the largest private pool Karen's ever seen. She hears Karl mutter something about Scrooge McDuck when he spots the twenty-foot diving board. They continue toward the impressive mansion and park next to the copper green fountain adorning the driveway. Karl kills the engine and leans forward to glance up at the façade through the windscreen.

'Do you think we're allowed to park here? Or are we expected to use the servants' entrance?'

Before Karen can reply, a tall woman appears around the corner of the house, stopping at the foot of the magnificent flight of steps leading up to the front door. She's trailing two wet Yorkshire terriers, who are overcome with excitement at seeing the visitors. Yapping and jumping with joy, they dash back and forth between their owner's feet and Karl's car. Behind them, Karen glimpses something that looks like an equally wet but much calmer Irish setter. It trots up and sits down next to the woman, who automatically puts a hand on its chestnut head.

Karl and Karen open their doors as one and climb out of the car.

34

'Welcome!' Wenche Hellevik calls out. 'All right, all right, settle down!'

She doesn't move forward to greet them, but her smile is warm; Karl and Karen walk toward her outstretched hand as quickly as they can. Karen discreetly studies Jounas Smeed's sister. Her white-blonde hair is pulled back into a French twist as stern as her clothes: a dark green jacket over a white turtleneck, a fitted, green-checkered skirt below her knee, discreet pearl earrings and faintly pink mother-of-pearl nails. The only thing detracting from her curated look is a pair of newly hosed-down wellies, from which her legs grow like dainty flower stalks.

They shake hands and introduce themselves.

'I thought I heard a car. We only just got back from a little walk and had to rinse off in the mud room. No, I've told you, no jumping! Can I offer you a cup of coffee? Or tea, perhaps? You must be exhausted from the drive. No, bad dog!'

That last part is said in an unexpectedly powerful voice to the Irish setter, who doesn't seem to understand why this would be a bad time to shake the water out of his fur. Wenche Hellevik leads them up the wide stone steps and in through the richly ornamental oak doors. Because of the stark contrast between the autumn sun outside and the gloom inside, it takes Karen a couple of seconds to realise the gigantic hallway is covered in plastic sheets and cardboard. Two men in white are standing among the jumble of ladders, paint tins and Polyfilla tubes, rollers and brushes. They're discussing something with a third, unusually tall, man in a blue suit. All three look worried and one of them is pointing at the ceiling.

'You'll have to excuse the mess; we've had a leak from one of the upstairs bathrooms and are going to have to renovate the entire hallway. Darling, the police are here, come say hi before you leave!'

The conversation with the painters is quickly wrapped up and the tall man joins them, shaking first Karen's and then Karl's hand with a polite smile.

'Magnus Hellevik,' he introduces himself. 'I believe my wife told me you're here about this awful business with Susanne.'

'Yes, that's right, we need to talk to as many people who knew her as possible,' Karen replies.

'I don't know if talking to me would be of any use; I'm at your disposal, of course, but I would have to ask you to start with me. I have an urgent errand up in Ravenby and should really have left long before now, but we're having some issues here, as you can see.'

Magnus Hellevik gestures toward the paint and ladders while studying Karl and Karen in turn, as though pondering who's more senior, even though they just introduced themselves.

'Did you now Susanne well?' Karen asks.

'Not at all. We did socialise a bit as a family while she and Jounas were married, but I haven't seen her since. And it's been years since they parted ways.'

Karen nods.

'Then we won't add to your stress,' she says with a smile. 'At least not today. We're primarily looking to talk to Wenche, but we'll be in touch if we have any questions for you.'

Magnus Hellevik looks relieved and excuses himself with a smile and a quick peck on his wife's cheek.

'Shall we?'

Wenche gestures toward a pair of sliding doors on the right, before taking the lead and pulling them open with a rumbling sound.

'Do have a seat; I'll be right back. Did you say tea or coffee?'

A few minutes later, she returns with a tray laden with three cups, a small tea urn and a plate of lemon muffins. She sits down at one end of a bone-white sofa and turns toward her guests, who have made themselves comfortable in floral chintz armchairs.

'Help yourselves, and then tell me what I can do for you. Milk?'

She's nothing like her brother, Karen thinks. Same nose and build, perhaps, but, thankfully, that seems to be where the similarities end. So far, there's no trace of either bitterness or arrogance on Jounas's sister's face. She meets Karl's eyes and nods for him to go ahead.

'Would you mind telling us about how you and Susanne met? I understand you went to school together?'

'Yes, that's right, but not until sixth form college. Susanne lived in Langevik and spent her first nine years there, but college was a cherished opportunity for her to move away from home.'

'Oh?' Karen says. 'So she didn't commute to Dunker, like everyone else?'

For a split second, she's hurled back in time thirty years, to the bumpy yellow Leyland bus she took to school every day for three years. She recalls the constant nausea, caused either by reading her homework on the bus or the cigarettes at the bus stop.

'No, and that's actually how we became friends,' Wenche continues. 'Dad owned a block of rental flats on Nygate and he let me have a small one-bed on the condition that I pay the rent myself. He was very particular about things like that.'

She takes a sip of her tea and slowly puts her cup down before continuing.

'I had my student grant and worked extra on the weekends, but since I wanted to go to parties and buy clothes, it was hard to make ends meet, so after a couple of months, I put up a flyer to find a flatmate. Susanne must have been the first person to see the flyer and I imagine she tore it down immediately. Anyway, she contacted me during a break that same day and . . . well, she moved in a couple of days later.'

'And you became friends. Were you close?'

Karl reaches for a muffin and Karen notes that the resentful look he had on his face when they first arrived has softened. Probably placated by the bit about her father not paying her rent, forcing her to work extra. Also, Wenche Hellevik actually seemed fairly down to earth, despite the pool and the tennis court.

'Close? I guess you could say that. It's so easy to make close friends when you're young. Before you develop a fixed personality, if you know what I mean. Later in life, we're more or less fully formed when it comes to our views on all kinds of things, but in our late teens, I believe the things that loomed large in our world were boys, clothes, music and unfair teachers.'

Karen nods in agreement. Those are the subjects she remembers talking endlessly about on that bumpy bus.

'And young people are so terribly conformist, even though they *think* they're so incredibly radical. Most just want to fit in, at any cost. But, to answer your question, yes, we were as close as any two teenage girls would be. Besties, I guess they'd call it.'

'Could you tell us what Susanne was like? What did you think of her as a person?'

Wenche Hellevik gets an absent look in her eyes as she searches her recollection.

'Anxious,' she says at length. 'Decent and helpful and always very eager to please and fit in. Fairly bright, actually, but she wasn't particularly interested in studying, seemed more focused on developing her social network.'

'Was she popular?'

'Susanne was very good-looking; she had no trouble finding boys. But she wasn't as liked among the girls and never put any effort into finding girlfriends, other than me. For some reason, she seemed to look up to me in particular; she copied the things I did, got a haircut when I did, bleached her hair like me. Well, I'm a natural blonde, of course,' Wenche Hellevik quickly corrects herself, 'but you know what I mean. She just imitated me, bought similar clothes and things like that, as much as her finances allowed.'

'And how did you feel about that?'

Wenche Hellevik shrugs her shoulders; Karen catches a glimpse of both Jounas and Sigrid in the gesture.

'I was probably annoyed from time to time, but it wasn't a big deal. I guess I was a bit flattered, too. If anything, it seemed to me she was impressed by my family and a tad ashamed about her own background. She wanted to leave her old life behind.'

'Did she tell you anything about her family?'

'Very little at first, but over time I got a clear impression of a less than blissful childhood. Not so much that she was treated poorly at home, more like she – how do I put it? – I guess I got the feeling she didn't respect her parents. They were eccentric, I guess, and being different must have been very hard back then, especially in a small place like Langevik.'

'Oh? In what way were they eccentric?' Karl asks.

He manages to look genuinely surprised, as though he has no idea, even though Karen filled him in on what her mum and the old men at the Hare and Crow told her about the Lothorp Farm commune on their way over. She makes a mental note to tell the lab to hurry up and release the photo album she and Karl had found in Susanne's bedroom.

'They were what people would've called hippies, I imagine,' Wenche Hellevik says hesitantly. 'Her parents moved here from Sweden and if I understood her right, they lived in some kind of commune during their first years on the island.'

'Did she tell you anything else about those years?'

'No, she was so little then, I'm not sure how much she knew about the commune. But there were a lot of other things that were hard for her afterwards.'

'Such as?'

'Well, for example, neither of her parents had a proper job, which I know Susanne found embarrassing. Her peers in the village were mainly the children of fishermen and pilots and other so-called upstanding professionals, while Susanne's dad just stood around in their garden, painting pictures.'

That matches what Jaap Kloes and the others said, Karen notes. If Susanne's most fervent wish was to fit in, it can't have been easy to be a Lindgren.

'And her mum died far too young,' Wenche continues, 'so I feel bad saying this, but I know Susanne was ashamed of her.'

'Ashamed? How come?'

Apparently, Karl sounds too eager, because Wenche Hellevik's voice is dry and faintly sarcastic when she replies.

'I'm afraid I don't have any juicy scandals for you. I think it was simply because Susanne's mother was the kind of person who attracted attention and didn't give a damn about convention; she dressed differently from the other mothers, did yoga and healing and things like that. And Susanne probably wanted the kind of mother everyone else had. Not one people talked about. But that's really all I know,' she adds.

Her smile is apologetic, but the authority in her voice signals firmly that Wenche Hellevik has nothing more to say about Susanne's childhood. Karen decides to change the subject.

'From what I'm told, the Lindgrens supported themselves by selling off their land,' she says. 'Apparently, they'd inherited extensive property from one of Susanne's mother's relatives.'

'Yes, I'm aware of that, but Susanne didn't know anything about that back then, I'm sure she didn't. She probably thought they lived off old Grââ's savings. But he had nothing in the bank, I've since learnt; his entire wealth was tied up in land.'

She pauses for a sip of tea before continuing.

'She obviously knew she had roots on the island, and that her mother had inherited from her grandfather who had a lot of property. But that the inheritance was sold off piece by piece to pay their way, that she didn't find out until much later. I actually don't think it became clear to her until her father passed away. I didn't find out for many years, when my brother mentioned it to me in conjunction with his divorce.'

'So Jounas knew before Susanne . . .?'

Wenche Hellevik looks uncomfortable.

'I think so. Because Dad bought large tracts of the Lindgrens' land. I'm ashamed to say he didn't pay a fair price for it either. Susanne's father was no businessman and probably figured he could trust a relative by marriage. And when he died, Jounas inherited the land.'

'Jounas inherited, you say. What about you?'

'Of course, but the inheritance was divided; Jounas got most of the land and I took over Dad's companies. As a police officer, Jounas has neither the time nor the inclination to run the businesses, whereas Magnus and I do.'

Karen ponders the implications of what Wenche just told them. That means old Axel Smeed must have continued to buy land from his daughter-in-law's father while Susanne and Jounas were married. Systematically buying up Susanne's inheritance so he could give it to his son. Had Jounas, contrary to Wenche's claims, known this all along? Or had Axel gone behind his son's back, too?

As though she can read Karen's mind, Wenche catches her gaze and holds it.

'Dad was a hard man,' she says. 'He couldn't stand "tinkers, people from Frisel and other scum", as he put it, and he always assumed his children would walk in his footsteps and share his values. Jounas was the one who rebelled, not me. It was hard on

Dad when his only son enrolled in the police academy instead of going into the family business he'd built. And when Jounas married Susanne, with her background and eccentric family, I think he gave up on him. Instead, he transferred all his hopes to the next generation. Magnus and I never had children; Sigrid is his only grandchild.'

'So he wasn't looking out for his son so much as his grand-daughter,' Karen says thoughtfully.

'Exactly, I think he realised the land would, in case of a divorce, be safer in Jounas's hands than in Susanne's. She was a gold-digger, he'd say, and the daughter of Swedish rabble who didn't understand the value of money. I think he assumed they would get divorced and prepared accordingly. And he was right.'

And they did have a prenup; Axel Smeed had made sure of it. It had been his condition for helping his son and pregnant daughter-in-law with accommodation, according to Jounas. It all fits with Axel Smeed's reputation; harsh and willing to go to any length to make a good deal. He hadn't even flinched at going behind his daughter-in-law's back, buying her future inheritance for a pittance and handing it to his disappointment of a son for safekeeping, to make sure it would eventually end up where he wanted. In Sigrid's possession, his only grandchild, his heir.

An image of Sigrid, bristling on the sofa, tattooed and pierced, flashes before Karen's eyes. Hardly the picture of an heiress of the entire Smeed fortune. Probably not the grand-child Axel Smeed would've wished for. And hardly the daughter either Jounas or Susanne had hoped for when they signed her up for riding and ballet lessons.

I wonder what it feels like to be such a disappointment?

'Do you see Sigrid at all?' she asks.

'Not for a long time now. She basically cut all ties with her parents the moment she moved out. All ties to her family in general, really.'

'And why was that?'

Wenche Hellevik hesitates for a few moments.

'My brother's not always easy to deal with,' she says finally. 'He can be callous and unyielding; he certainly was to Susanne. And she was bitter and combative. It was constant conflict and they used Sigrid as a go-between, pushing her to take sides. In the end, she saw no other way than to distance herself from both of them, running away from the whole situation.'

Just like Susanne did, Karen notes. They both left their parents' house as soon as they were able. At least they had that in common.

'Jumping ahead a little,' Karl says. 'Did you and Susanne remain friends?'

'Yes and no,' Wenche Hellevik says with something like relief in her voice, as though she's only too happy to change the subject. 'We didn't fall out or anything like that, but I went to the US to study and we simply lost touch. We did see each other sometimes when I was back for breaks, but it became increasingly obvious we were growing apart.'

'How's that?'

'Well, for me, higher education was always a given, while Susanne went to work straight out of high school. She just took the first thing that came along, with no real direction, I suppose. She actually even had a few gigs as a model, since she was both beautiful and tall.'

222

'Really,' Karen says with surprise. 'A model?'

'Well, they weren't big jobs, but a few fashion shoots and some advertisements, I think. Not enough to live on, unfortunately, but she clung to the dream; maybe that's why she never bothered to get an education. But Doggerland's not exactly overflowing with modelling gigs, so she had to take various other jobs to make ends meet.'

'And when you moved back for good, did you continue seeing her?' Karl asks.

'From time to time, especially when neither one of us had a boyfriend. There were a few years in our mid-twenties when we hung out in various clubs and went to parties. It was fun, sure, but to be honest, I always felt she wanted to be seen more than I did. And then I met Magnus and had less time for both Susanne and my other friends, infatuated as I was. She was pretty upset, as I recall.'

'How did that manifest itself?'

Once more, Wenche looks absent, as though she's being transported back in time.

'I think that's when my impression of Susanne began to change in earnest,' she says contemplatively. 'She made me feel uneasy, almost guilty, every time we met up; talked a lot about how I had everything and she had nothing. There were some harsh words said about how I acted like she wasn't good enough anymore. Her modelling jobs had dried up almost completely at that point as well; she probably felt all the doors were closing for her while I kept moving forward.'

'Did you stop seeing each other?'

'No, I did feel a bit guilty about allowing Magnus to monopolise my time, so I made sure to invite her to parties and to go for a drink with her from time to time. I guess I was eager to prove to Susanne that I didn't think myself above her. And a year or so later, Magnus proposed and of course we invited her to the wedding. Jounas might have told you our wedding was actually where he met Susanne?'

'Yes,' Karen replies, 'he did tell us that. And apparently she accidentally became pregnant just a few months into the relationship.'

Wenche emits a snorting laugh that seems out of step with her otherwise kind and restrained nature. After a moment, she stands up and smooths out some invisible wrinkles in her skirt.

'Accidentally,' she says drily. 'I'm not so sure about that.'

She walks over to a sideboard where bottles and crystal decanters jostle for space. She turns to Karen and Karl, eyebrows raised; they shake their heads.

'Well, I for one feel a need for a stiff drink.'

She pours a couple of fingers from one of the bottles and takes a sip before returning to the bone-white sofa. By the time she sits back down, her warm smile has returned. She takes another small sip and puts the glass down on the coffee table.

'So you don't think Susanne's pregnancy was an accident?' Karen picks the conversation back up.

'I don't think anyone did. You'll have to excuse me if I seem upset, but the fact is it felt like . . . well, like some kind of violation, as though she deliberately insinuated herself into our family.'

'So you don't believe she and Jounas were genuinely in love?'

Wenche Hellevik shrugs again and sighs.

'Jounas was attracted to her, naturally, but I hardly think he would have agreed to marry her under any other circumstances. And as far as Susanne's concerned, I'm inclined to agree with my father; I believe it was primarily our family's fortune and status that attracted her. She may have been in love with Jounas, but there was never any real chemistry between them. Never any visible spark, no spontaneous kisses, no loving looks. And yet, she somehow seemed content with the situation. Never missed an opportunity to talk about how we were going to be sisters.'

'And after the wedding; how would you describe their marriage?'

'I think the first two years were relatively harmonious, not least thanks to little Sigrid, whom they both loved, of course. But when Jounas quit law school and returned to the police authority, things fell apart. Dad was livid, Susanne somewhat hysterical and Jounas stubborn and unreasonable. It affected us all, almost tore the family apart. Nothing was ever the same after that. We saw each other on high holidays and birthdays, of course, but aside from those occasions, Jounas and Susanne were isolated from the rest of the family. Dad withdrew all financial support and they had to leave their posh flat on Freyagate. I think I only visited them once in their two-bed in Odinswalla; Susanne was a completely different person then.'

'In what respect?' Karen asks.

'Bitter, disappointed. Those tendencies had always been there, but now it was like they'd taken over completely, making her dejected in a way I'd never seen before. I almost felt sorry for her. And to be frank, Jounas behaved like a right prick.

I understand he wanted to go his own way and not march to the beat of Dad's drum and whatever, but he didn't think of anyone else, didn't consult anyone, not even his wife. Ironically, his behaviour made it clear he and Dad were peas in a pod; completely ruthless and willing to do whatever it takes to get their way.'

Back in the car, Karen and Karl are both deep in thought. At length, Karl breaks the silence.

'You don't think . . . I mean, how sure can we really be he was at home when Susanne was killed?'

'Not sure enough.'

'What do you mean?'

Karen takes a deep breath and exhales slowly.

'All right,' she says, 'but I want this to stay between us. Jounas spent the night at the Strand after Oistra.'

Karl turns to face her so suddenly the car lurks.

'What the fuck, Eiken, why didn't you say so before? You told the team he went home.'

'I know exactly what I said, and you're right. He really did walk home, but not until the next morning.'

'You lied to us.'

'I didn't tell you the whole truth, but I was very careful not to lie to you outright.'

'Oh, I see, not outright. That's decent of you . . . really.'

Karl's voice is dripping with sarcasm; she shoots him a quick glance. He's staring at the road, but his clenched jaw is a clear sign he's angry.

'Listen to me, Karl,' she says. 'I didn't want to tell the whole team our boss spent the night in a hotel with a woman. But I checked when he left with the hotel. He would have had at most forty-five minutes to walk over to city hall to pick up his car, drive to Langevik and kill Susanne. How probable does that sound to you?'

'Not particularly.'

They sit in silence for another couple of miles. Karl is once more the person to break the silence.

'But not impossible,' he adds.

35

Karen is standing by the window, looking down at the car park diagonally opposite. The large trees in Holländar Park are swaying in the wind, and more and more yellow leaves are joining the conkers on the ground. It's almost seven and completely dark, but the light of the street lamps reveals the pavement is slick with rain.

'I don't believe it,' Karen mutters, leaning closer to the glass.

That moment, a tiny white snowflake lands on the window and slides downward as it rapidly melts. Yes, it's undeniable: sleet. In early October. A month early, at least, even by Doggerland standards.

She can just make out her Ranger on the left side of the car park; it occurs to her that it's time to start parking in the shelter of the underground police garage. The unpleasantness of climbing into a freezing car is soon going to outweigh the unpleasantness of the subterranean environment with its fluorescent lights. And it's free for employees, too.

It's getting late, she thinks, I should head home before the weather takes a turn for the worse.

But she stays where she is. The slushy motorway is about as tempting as her dark, silent home. What she wants to do is hit the nearest bar, enjoy the warmth of strange bodies, listen to the din of their voices and get drunk. She wants to stay in town and get to work early tomorrow morning. Or, in a more likely scenario, get an extra hour of sleep.

I don't actually have to go home. The kitchen window's open a crack and there's plenty of food and water for the cat; he'll be fine for one night. Karen immediately realises she shouldn't be leaving the window open in this weather and that she really ought to go home and install that bloody cat flap. She pushes down a pang of guilt and pulls out her phone. Scrolls down the call list to one of her most frequently dialled numbers.

The voice that picks up sounds happily surprised.

'Hiya, love! So, you're alive?'

'Only just barely, I reckon. Are you still in town?'

'Sorry. I'm in the car, almost home. Where are you?'

'Still at work, but I was thinking of calling it a day and was hoping for company.'

'You could have called sooner,' Marike replies. 'I don't think I'm up for driving all the way back in this weather. They're talking about freezing rain. In October, insane!'

'Really? Well, that makes me even less keen to drive home. Would it be OK if I stayed over in the studio?'

'Go ahead, you have the keys. I'm sure it's nice and warm; the kilns have been on since yesterday; I only just turned them off when I left. What about Saturday?'

Two seconds of desperate fumbling through her memory bank before finding something. In a moment of weakness, she invited some friends over to celebrate her last birthday on the right side of fifty.

'Fuck, I'd completely forgotten.'

'Forgotten?'

'I've been busy. You've read the papers, right?'

229

'You know I only read the arts section. But seriously, not even I could miss that some poor woman's been murdered in Langevik. Are you on the case?'

'Not just on it, I'm in charge of the investigation.'

Marike whistles.

'Perfect. Then we want to hear all the juicy details on Saturday.'

Karen doesn't answer straight away.

'I honestly don't know if I'll have time. And it's hardly something to celebrate. But next year . . .'

'Then consider it a wake. You promised to make your *kricklings*.'

'I was drunk. Promises made during Oistra don't count.'

'Speaking of which, Kore said you pulled after I left. Who's the bloke?'

'No one. It didn't amount to anything.'

A tad too quickly, a smidge too harsh to sound convincing.

'Oh really, is that right . . .'

'Whatever, I'm not in the mood to talk about it.'

'So one of your usual tossers. Have you ever considered sleeping with someone you actually like?'

Before Karen can respond, Marike continues:

'Anyway, my exit's coming up, so I have to go. We'll talk more about this some other time. But if you're serious about changing your mind about Saturday, you should probably call Eirik and Kore; they've been looking forward to it.'

Karen does some quick calculations: she can boil mussels in her sleep and wine she can pick up after work. Unless there's a break in the case, she should be able to pull it off. Besides, she could use some company.

'No, you're right,' she says, 'of course you should come. But I won't have time to clean and you're going to have to bring some bread from town; there's no decent bakery in Langevik anymore. And if something happens and I have to go back to work, you're on your own.'

Forty-nine, she thinks after ending the call. When the fuck did that happen?

36

Twenty minutes later, Karen's pushed her way through the noisy
bar section of Restaurant Kloster and taken a seat at a table for
two. After a quick glance at the blackboard, she waves the waiter
over and orders cod with melted butter and horseradish.

'And a half bottle of the house red,' she adds.

She looks around the room. Over by the bar, above a wall of
bodies, arms keep shooting up, trying to catch the bartender's
attention and get in one last order before happy hour ends. The
restaurant section, on the other hand, is barely half full; she
observes the other patrons under the guise of studying the décor.

Kloster is only a stone's throw from the Dunker City Theatre; several of her fellow diners are probably heading over there
when they're done: possibly the middle-aged couple who are just
now being served dessert; definitely the four dressed-up women
of about sixty-five who are ordering another bottle of white with
their bill and laughing uproariously. Maybe the thirty-some-
thing couple at the next table as well, though that's less likely.
The woman is talking intently about something while the man
chews his entrecote and throws longing glances at the bar. From
time to time, he emits preoccupied but practised grunts. Karen
is overcome with the same feeling she gets when she sees a bored
parent pushing his or her child on the swings in the park on a
Sunday morning with an absent-minded smile, looking like

they're thinking: when is the little brat going to get tired of this? Or a dog owner on an evening walk, patiently waiting for his or her dog to finish sniffing around and do its business.

Is the woman really so oblivious to her companion's lack of interest, or does she not care? Is she happy being treated like a dog?

Steam rises from the freshly boiled potato when the waiter puts her plate and a small copper jug full of melted butter down on her table. The cod looks enticing; shiny and just the right level of saltiness, it obediently flakes when Karen touches it with her fork. She can feel the burn of the horseradish behind her eyelids and smiles to herself as she chews. She's grown comfortable eating out by herself over the years; she ignores both the fascinated and the pitying looks from the increasingly raucous bar. When the woman from the next table shoots her a vague look of condolence, Karen raises her glass in a toast and smiles back so cheerfully the woman immediately lowers her eyes and whispers something to her husband. He quickly turns his head to get the measure of their neighbour, looking Karen up and down before turning back to his food, continuing to chew with a bored look on his face. Here we are, two women, feeling sorry for each other, Karen relects.

She thinks about Karl. His anger at her failure to be completely up front regarding Jounas's whereabouts on the night before the murder has abated, but a certain distance has opened up between them. A note of politeness lingered in his voice the rest of the day, like a little punishment. And during their evening meeting, he was ominously quiet.

Karl Björken is her closest confidant at work. He's the one she turns to when she needs to talk things over or discuss ideas or wants to go for a pint after hours. Granted, he's never openly objected to the laddish jargon that has come to characterise the CID in recent years, but he's also never participated. If I lose his trust, Karen thinks, work is going to become a nightmare.

Halfway through her cod, Karen freezes. She has glimpsed a familiar profile by the bar; panicking, she turns her face away and casts about for a way out. But it's already too late; he's spotted her. Jon Bergman is walking over with determined steps and a big smile. In normal circumstances, she would have been happy to see him; now she has to make him go away.

'Hey, Karen. You alone? May I join you?'

'Absolutely not,' she replies with emphasis.

He's already put a hand on the chair across from hers to pull it out but freezes mid-movement, his face incredulous. Karen puts her cutlery down on her plate and leans back.

'You know I can't talk to you while there's an ongoing investigation.'

'Fair dos,' he replies. 'But go on, tell me something, would you? Is Smeed still a suspect?'

'Who told you he was a suspect?'

'Well, when a woman's murdered, it's usually the husband or the ex-husband. So long as there's no other obvious perpetrator, of course. But maybe there is . . .?'

Karen heaves a deep sigh.

'Please, Jon, there's absolutely no chance I'm going to let anything slip. Would you please let me finish my dinner in peace?'

'So there's something that could slip? Is that what I should take from this?'

234

'What you should take from this is that I want to eat my cod before it gets cold and that I want to do it all by myself.'

Jon Bergman ignores her gesture toward her plate, takes a sip of his beer and puts his glass down on the table.

'To think you used to be so open and free with your opinions once upon a time.'

'Maybe a bit too open.'

She wants to take it back the moment she says it, knows Jon Bergman is going to pounce.

'Aha, so you've been gagged; you can lead the investigation, but you can't talk about it. That's why that sorry sod Haugen did the so-called "press conference".'

Jon Bergman puts quotation marks around the words with his fingers, making Karen think how much she hates it when people do that. Then she thinks that the rest of her cod will definitely have gone cold by now. She signals to the waiter that she wants to pay.

Granted, Jon Bergman is a TV reporter and not a newspaper journalist, so she runs no risk of being misquoted in tomorrow's paper, but she's lost her appetite. She knows it's just a matter of time before he drags up what happened over four years ago. A short but intense summer fling, a couple of weeks when they barely got out of bed and a few more months after that when they still met up sporadically, before it all petered out. A pleasant interlude she rarely thinks about, since she and Jon move in different circles and rarely run into each other these days. Although it was a long time ago, her credibility would be severely damaged if their brief romance were ever to become a topic of conversation around the police station water coolers. There have been too many leaks to the media;

the question of who might be letting things slip is the subject of constant speculation.

Having wine with Jon Bergman during an ongoing investigation is out of the question. Give him an inch and he'll never let go. She bends down and pulls her wallet out of her handbag.

'Well, if you won't leave, I will,' she says. 'I'm in a hurry anyway,' she adds to take some of the edge out of her words.

'Bloody hell, relax, will you,' Jon Bergman says. 'You could give me something, for old times' sake . . .'

Karen hands the waiter her card without responding. He punches some buttons on the card reader, puts it on the table in front of Karen and glances down at her plate.

'I hope there wasn't a problem with your food?' he says, studying the leftover cod sitting in its lake of butter.

'Not at all,' Karen replies, 'I'm just in a hurry.'

She stands up and shoots the waiter a quick smile. Jon Bergman has taken a step back and watches while Karen pulls on her coat.

'I didn't mean to ruin your dinner. Let me at least buy you a drink at the bar? Or maybe somewhere else?'

'I really don't have time.'

He's hard on her heels as she strides toward the exit.

'You have my number,' he hollers when she pushes the door open. 'Call me!'

She stops mid-movement, turns around and smiles.

'All right, Jon, I promise. If I ever lose all judgement again, you'll be my first call. But it won't be until after the investigation is done.'

37

Would you rather leave the guilt... she says as she is going anyway. She asks to be excused, since she reached out in the morning

The lingering heat from the kilns envelops her as soon as she steps through the door. For a moment, she had considered driving back to Langevik after all, since her night out came to such an abrupt end, but then she realised she had in fact managed to drink most of the red wine. Her guilt at driving home hungover and likely still technically intoxicated last Sunday morning is still hanging over her like a dark cloud. It's true a lot of islanders routinely drive with considerable quantities of alcohol in them; the laws are toothless, the fines are low so long as there's no accident and there are few roadside checks anyway. But Karen Eiken Hornby has promised herself: never more than one glass. The keys to Marike's studio in Dunker's Old Harbour are part of that promise.

She dumps her coat and handbag on a bench in the shop part and walks into the rectangular room at the back of the building, where Marike's precious clay is turned into art. The special blue-ish-green clay that tempted the sculptor to leave Copenhagen and buy land on Heimö. A swampy inland plot where nothing grows and she can't build anything. A plot that isn't even beautiful, but under the surface of which lurks tonnes of what Marike considers the equivalent of gold.

The plot is how Karen and Marike first got to know each other. The seller of the land was Karen's cousin Torbjörn; she'd been visiting one Saturday morning almost seven years ago when a tall woman with a very determined look in her eyes had turned up unannounced on Torbjörn's porch.

The woman had brought a map of the area on which she'd outlined a plot of land with red felt-tip pen, which – she had announced in virtually incomprehensible Danish – she wanted to buy at any cost. Those had been her words, *at any cost*, and they had, once he'd managed to decipher them, lit a rapacious spark in Torbjörn's eyes.

The negotiation had been a joke. Once his initial surprise at there being interest in the uncultivatable south-west corner of his property had subsided, Torbjörn had seized on the chance to pad his wallet. And it had soon become perfectly clear the Danish woman knew nothing about Doggerian property prices or the conditions required for building the house she was planning. Moreover, the communication difficulties, caused primarily by the incomprehensible Danish way of counting and the Doggerian currency system – both unfathomable to outsiders – had eventually forced them to switch to English, despite their Scandinavian kinship.

At first, Karen had listened to her cousin's deft profiteering with amusement, but in the end, she'd been unable to stay quiet. Defying Torbjörn's furious glances, she'd stressed the negligible value of the plot and pointed out that building anything on it was absolutely out of the question. Then she'd suggested including the adjacent strip of land overlooking the Portland River, which was traditionally counted as belonging to the plot under discussion anyway, in the sale; the Danish woman could build her house there and get a really decent view into the bargain, at least in one direction.

Her interference had cost her six months of frosty relations with her cousin, but had led to a lasting friendship with Marike Estrup.

Now she lifts up a corner of the plastic sheet covering one of the big troughs in the studio and pinches off of a piece of clay, rolling it between her thumb and forefinger, testing the plasticity while she studies the finished sculptures lined up along the long window wall. She's witnessed every step of the laborious process; Marike, dressed in waders, digging up clay in the field behind her house, rinsing it several times, patiently letting it dry and eventually beating it soft with her strong arms before driving it to her Dunker studio. There, the transformation begins. Karen is fascinated by the power and determination of her creative process; shapes seem to appear out of nowhere, colours change in the intense heat. She has experienced the excitement of opening the kiln doors, watched Marike's anxious eyes as they scrutinise the results of her efforts.

And yet, it's still hard for her to wrap her head around the fact that the sculptures exhibited in prestigious galleries all over the world originally sprang from the sticky lump she's rolling between her fingers.

Then reality catches up with her and she concludes that the murder of Susanne Smeed is her own sticky lump, which may never take shape. The conversation with Wenche Hellevik has added detail to the image of Susanne Smeed; growing up in Langevik can't have been easy for a girl from a family who stood out like peacocks among a flock of herring gulls. That probably at least partially explained Susanne's desperate need to fit in, to belong, to force her way into a family so different from the one she was born into. And then the bitterness when it fell apart.

About the divorce and being forced back to the village, only to realise the land she should have inherited had been sold and now belonged to the man she hated the most: Jounas Smeed. She wouldn't have been surprised to hear Susanne bashed his head in with a poker. But the other way around? No, she can't see that Jounas would have had a motive. And yet, the theoretical possibility, the exasperating mathematical possibility that he could have done it. And who else?

The accounts given by Cornelis Loots and Astrid Nielsen in the late-afternoon meeting had been commendably clear and detailed. They'd spoken to both Susanne's closest co-workers, the carers and cleaners, and to the manager of Solgården, Gunilla Moen, again. About half of the interviewees had no opinion of Susanne Smeed whatsoever, knew her by name only and had little to no contact with her personally. The other half stated without exception that Susanne – who was in charge of invoicing and processing payroll and leave applications – had been meticulous and well organised as far as her own work was concerned, but had lacked any capacity for flexibility and helpfulness; not even in charitable cases had she been prepared to go so much as an inch beyond her duty to help someone in a difficult situation. An application for leave that ended up on Susanne's desk after the cut-off date was never granted, even if temps were queuing up to cover the shifts. Salary advances had been categorically refused, without exception. At the same time, she'd had an annoying habit of sticking her nose in, pointing out other people's shortcomings and questioning information about overtime worked or a need for new work clothes. In brief, Susanne Smeed had been 'a fucking busybody', as one of the cleaners put it.

No one had been able to tell them anything useful about Susanne's private life. It was unclear why, according to Nielsen and Loots. Ostensibly, either because there was nothing of interest to tell, or because no one at Solgården had been interested in finding out what Susanne did outside of work. Most knew she was divorced and lived in Langevik; her older colleagues also knew who she had been married to and that there was a daughter. A few were aware that Susanne liked to holiday abroad, but that the trips had become less frequent over time; it had been a long while now since she had returned to work with a tan from the Mediterranean or Thailand.

'I think she had trouble making ends meet, which is hardly a shock given the salaries here,' Gunilla Moen had told them.

A few more titbits had emerged. Susanne had applied for but not got the job as assistant manager just over a year before, even though she had covered for Gunilla Moen on occasion. The reason was, according to Moen, the inability to cooperate and lack of flexibility several of her co-workers had spoken of. Since then, Susanne Smeed had isolated herself, always had her lunch alone, eschewed any staff gathering that wasn't mandatory, arrived promptly at eight and left at five on the dot. Not one minute past, not one minute to.

But last spring, following a management decision to prohibit the private use of work phones, Susanne had come out of her self-imposed isolation and thrown an unexpected fit of rage. Four people had witnessed her screaming at Gunilla Moen that 'she had a thing or two she could tell people about this place' and that they should 'watch their step'. Both Gunilla Moen and everyone else claimed to have no idea what she was referring to. Some guessed Susanne's outburst had been caused

241

by a drinking problem, others that she was simply a 'typical menopausal bitch'.

Susanne had never acted out or mentioned the affair again, but her embarrassing outburst had exacerbated the tension with her colleagues. In the end, someone had reported the whole situation as an HR issue and Susanne had been summoned to a meeting with Eira's central head of human resources to discuss a possible transfer to one of the other eight nursing homes the company ran. Susanne had refused and been allowed to continue at Solgården under caution.

Over the past few months, Susanne had missed enough work to make Gunilla Moen contact HR again, but no steps had been taken yet. The Monday before she was killed, Susanne had called in sick. This time, she hadn't even given a reason, just left a message on the answering machine. She hadn't been back to work since.

The police's IT department had concluded its investigation of Susanne's work computer; their report was thin. Around the same time as Solgården had decided to prohibit the private use of work phones, Susanne's private use of her work laptop had ceased completely as well. And before then, it had mostly been emails about online ordering of clothes and beauty products, a few verbose complaints addressed to the wind energy company, appeals of a number of late fees for various bills and sporadic, and more often than not unanswered, emails to her daughter.

There was one exception: one email of a private nature had been received, but never replied to. Someone called Disa Brinckmann had sent an email to Susanne.smeed@solgården.dg at the end of May. It seemed to be written in some kind of mix of Swedish and Danish. Karen had passed the printout around the table.

> Dear Susanne!
> You probably don't remember me, it's been many years since we last saw each other, you were very little. But your parents may have mentioned me. For a few years, we lived together in a commune in Langevik. I have some information that may be important to you and would therefore like to get in touch with you as soon as possible.
> Regards,
> Disa Brinckmann
> Phone #: +46 40 682 33 26

The email had been sent from dbrinckmann@gmail.com, but no reply had been sent, at least not from Susanne's work email.

'She could have replied from a private account, of course, if she had one,' Karl had suggested. 'Or she could have called. Have we checked the number?'

'It's registered to an address in Malmö,' Karen had told them. 'In the south of Sweden,' she'd then added.

'Thanks, I know where Malmö is.'

'I've tried to call,' Karen had continued, ignoring Karl, who was clearly still feeling sore. 'But I've had no answer and there's no voicemail, so I wasn't able to leave a message. We'll keep trying, naturally, but given how anti-social Susanne was and how she felt about her parents' way of life, I reckon there's little chance this Disa Brinckmann was ever successful in her attempts at making contact.'

The meeting had concluded on a note of resignation. A faint but unmistakeable whiff of defeat had crept into the room for the first time, like a fart everyone can smell but no one acknowledges. With a voice ringing with utterly unfounded conviction, Karen had tried to turn the dejected mood around: Disa Brinckmann might give them new leads and they would of course look into whether Susanne might in fact have known something damaging about Gunilla Moen, Solgården or its owners. Then she'd stressed it was still early days, the investigation was only three days old. But everyone knew three days was exactly the amount of time that shouldn't pass without progress. No one had said it, and maybe she was imagining things, but hadn't it been there, unspoken: 'If Smeed had been here, we would have had more to go on at this point'.

Karen puts the small lump of clay back in its trough and rubs the dampness off on her jeans. Then she walks into the kitchenette next to the studio and opens the fridge. Marike doesn't disappoint. Granted, on the top shelf there's only half a block of cheese, a couple of bananas, an out-of-date carton of milk, a few rolls of film and a jar of olives, but on the lower shelf, the olive trappings are lined up neatly: three bottles of gin and one of vermouth, which according to Marike belong to the staples category. Karen opens the freezer compartment and takes out one of the martini glasses that Marike always keeps in the freezer 'just in case'.

After fetching her bag from the bench in the shop, she returns to the studio and sits down on the sofa with a brimming glass. The first sip brings with it a sudden urge to smoke and she realises that this time she won't be able to break her promise; she gave away her last cigarettes to a homeless man at the Grenå Mall. For half a minute, she toys with the idea of heading out again, walking up to Varvsgate, where the closest corner shop can be found, but she dismisses the idea after a look out the window. Instead, she opens her bag and pulls out a heavy plastic bag, leans back with her legs crossed and places the bag in her lap. She carefully pushes open the Ziploc bag's small plastic runner and pulls out the thick photo album she and Karl found in Susanne Smeed's dresser, which has finally been released by the technicians.

She studies the album, gingerly stroking its surface; the binding is deftly painted to make it look like leather, but the tattered corners expose frayed cardboard. Then she opens the album, releasing a familiar smell of dust and old glue.

38

In her own home, she might have three or four photo albums from various time periods; this one album seems to hold all of the Lindgrens' family photographs. Perhaps the most important pictures were collected in one place before they left Sweden. The oldest are sepia-toned studio portraits from the previous century and probably show either Anne-Marie's or Per's ancestors. Karen reads the Swedish names neatly printed underneath each picture along with a year: Augusta and Gustav, 1901; Göta and Albin, 1904; in both cases the women are wearing black dresses, have their hair pulled back into tight buns and are standing behind their husbands, who are sitting stiffly in their Sunday suits on wooden chairs. Name and year, but no explanation as to the relationships between the people in the pictures.

The next few pages contain an exposé of the Lindgrens' friends and relatives through the successive decades of the twentieth century; with each passing decade, the motifs become less obviously connected to special occasions and more everyday in character: a suited and booted man, Rudolf apparently, is proudly leaning against a Model T Ford; a laughing, big-chested woman in a floral 1930s dress and white shoes in a garden is apparently called Anna-Greta and the year is 1933. Another photograph, probably taken at the same time, shows a young man, Lars-Erik, in his student cap with his arm around the same woman on the front steps of a yellow wooden house. Mother and son, Karen thinks to herself.

The following year, someone called Ulla is doing gymnastics on a beam and the next picture shows young boys Karl-Artur and Eskil who in 1935, along with a few other, unnamed, children, practised diving from a jetty. Two polyphotos from the Second World War show young men wearing uniforms and grave expressions. A few women in their forties look cold at a wintry train station: one of them is waving at the camera while the others look like they're serving soup to uniformed men queuing in a neat line. Katrineholm 1943, is written in cursive under the picture.

Among the other ancestors is also a very small photograph with a background that looks familiar: it looks like it was taken down by one of the fishing sheds in Langevik and shows an old couple sitting on wooden chairs, mending nets: Vetle and Alma Gråå, 1947.

To her surprise, Karen feels moved. Several of the pictures could just as well have come from her own family albums; the sudden sense of ongoing connection and of the meaningless of this transient existence makes her throat feel tight. Long lines of women, men and children, looking serious or happy, who witnessed bygone decades, and are now likely all dead. Generation upon generation, striving to survive and to perpetuate humanity – and maybe to achieve a degree of happiness. All these ancestors whose woes and joys can now only be vaguely glimpsed in a handful of faded photographs. People who meant everything to someone once, yet are forgotten within a few passing generations.

Some of us even sooner than that, Karen muses and empties her glass.

The urge to smoke washes over her again and on a sudden impulse she gets up, walks into the kitchenette and opens the cupboard above the buffet. Marike still smokes sometimes. Like Karen, she frequently commits to quitting but gives in far too easily whenever the going gets tough; Karen had noticed her puffing away during Oistra, while complaining about her failed glaze.

Karen scans the shelves full of cups, glasses, plates and bowls. Feels around wherever her eyes can't reach and there, at the far back, behind a large red clay bowl, her fingers graze a familiar shape. Triumphant, feeling only the faintest pang of guilt, she pulls out half a packet of Camels.

After mixing herself another dry martini, opening two windows and pulling on a cardigan, Karen sinks back down onto the sofa and fires off a text to Marike, informing her about her plan to finish off her emergency stash of cigarettes. Then she picks the heavy photo album back up and resumes her study of the photographs. Lars-Erik could be Per's father. Which of the photographs, if any, show Anne-Marie's relatives is harder to say. No surnames or kinship bonds are given; she turns the pages with waning curiosity, looking at the endless line of anonymous faces and staged poses.

Now the cautious optimism of the post-war years is beaming up at her. The pictures are still black and white, but as the forties turn into the fifties, the settings begin to look more modern: children playing in suburban fountains, three young girls with slim waists and tall hair pouting their lips seductively, a young man with jeans and a leather jacket squatting next to a moped. Per 1957, it says under the moped. A couple of death announcements: the big-chested Anna Greta Lindgren apparently died at the age of sevent-four in 1955, mourned and missed by 'husband, children and grandchildren'. Two more graduation pictures: in the first, a girl with a neat up-do and a timid smile: Anne-Marie, 1959. In the photograph next to her is an equally neat-looking young man with tidy blond hair and a handful of scars bearing witness to healed acne on his high cheekbones.

Karen lights another cigarette, sips her dry martini and turns the page again. Now she's reached the sixties; the Lindgrens' memories are depicted in a riot of colour with that characteristic yellow cast like a film over the pictures. By now, cameras are ubiquitous; a new-found spontaneity brings life to the pictures but the quality suffers. The focus is often on something in front of, behind or even to the side of the pose, and disembodied arms and legs peek out from the edges. And, possibly due to the same lack of care, names and dates are no longer noted. There can be no doubt it's the sixties, however. Granted, most of the older people still wear clothes that were modern ten or twenty years previously, but the fashion ideals of the new decade are all the more noticeable among the younger generation. And two people keep appearing in the pictures: a couple who look to be in their late twenties. Karen recognises them from their graduation pictures. Clearly very much in love, Anne-Marie and Per pose in various situations, she in miniskirts and he in tight suit trousers, sometimes alone, but usually together with a group of friends. One member of the group is clearly eager to immortalise every get-together: parties, dinners, vacations. There's an increasing number of pregnant women in the pictures and then small children. A young couple lift a little boy by the hands so that he dangles laughingly between them; a young woman with long hair breastfeeds her child on a blanket in the grass. Even though her face is partly hidden, it's clear she's smiling.

Karen looks away from the photo album and closes her eyes. Had she smiled in that oblivious, blissful way? Back then, before the colic, flu, chickenpox and ear infections tainted the ecstatic rush with an edge of ever-present anxiety. Back then, before scattered pieces of Lego cut into bare feet, before the terrible twos made getting dressed a battle. Back then, before their house became filled with the sound of her nagging. The constant hectoring about mittens and scarves, homework and TV and for-God's-sake-don't-eat-the-cereal-straight-out-of-the-box and John-could-you-teach-him-to-put-the-seat-up-next-time and make-sure-his-seatbelt-is-buckled-you-know-he-unbuckles-himself-the-second-you're-not-watching.

Had she studied the little bundle in her arms with a melancholic, almost sad smile, too, as though she could sense what was to come? What was actually going to happen if she let her guard down for so much as a goddamn second. If, for a moment, she told herself not to worry so much. If she didn't have time to steer clear of danger.

Mechanically, without really noticing the tears streaming down her face, she wipes them with the back of her hand and stops the snot running with a quick sniff. Her hand is only shaking a little bit when she holds the lighter up to another Camel; when she picks up her glass, it's steady once more. It's over for now. Still as frequent, she reflects, but of shorter duration. It's getting better.

A deep breath, then she lets her eyes return to Susanne's collection of photographs, turning the page and studying the pictures with new detachment. She matter-of-factly notes that the fashion – now that the late sixties have consumed the Lindgrens – apparently prescribes wide bellbottoms, tight shirts, long, tie-dyed dresses and centre-parted hair. Picture after picture of laughing young people against a Kodak-blue sky.

Did any of these people come with the Lindgrens to Doggerland? Are some of them the same people the old men at the Hare and Crow talked about in such a derogatory way? She quickly turns the pages and then, there it is; the picture that finally connects Per and Anne-Marie Lindgren's life in Sweden with their new existence in a commune on these remote islands.

A group picture by the railing of a car ferry. Karen immediately recognises the green logo of the company in the background: the stylised fish above a wavy line still adorns the ships trafficking the Dunker-Esbjerg route.

Three women, two men, three children. A girl of about five is holding one of the women's hands and smiling at the camera. Another woman carries an infant in a long shawl wound around her body; one of the men is holding a pram. The child in the pram looks to be about one. Their long hair is whipping in the wind and the women's skirts are tangled around their legs.

They must have asked a fellow passenger to take the picture, or there was one more person in their group. Karen studies their excited faces and shudders. Some of them would be back in Sweden less than two years later and the ones who stayed in Langevik are now all dead.

There's a single picture glued to the next page. Above it, someone has printed two-inch letters and numbers with an orange felt-tip pen: Langevik 1970. Colourful drawings of flowers and peace signs frame the photograph. The photograph itself is a group picture. Eight adults – four women, four men – have squeezed into two rows on a flight of stone steps leading up to the green double doors of the main house. A handful of children are sitting on the lawn in front of the steps.

Their names are neatly printed underneath the picture: apparently, Disa, Tomas, Ingela and Theo are in the top row.

Karen leans forward to study the woman on the far left. Disa Brinckmann. So that's what she looks like. Or, rather, that's what she looked like almost fifty years ago. She must be well into her seventies by now. Karen looks at the people on the lower step and reads their names: Per, Anne-Marie, Janet and Brandon.

Per and Anne-Marie Lindgren, Susanne Smeed's parents, she thinks, studying their smiling faces with a feeling of unease. The picture was taken before Susanne was born; thankfully, neither of her parents could know how her life would end.

The name on the bottom line read: Orian, Mette and Love. Orian looks like a boy of about one. Mette, who appears to be about five, is sitting with her legs crossed, holding Love in her arms: it's impossible to say if Love's a boy or a girl.

Three of the women, two of the men and all three of the children look like they're the same people from the ferry; the other faces are new. And no surnames, of course, Karen notes with disappointment.

The handful of pictures that follow were never glued in, just inserted between the last few pages. A few views of Langevik harbour and some from Lothorp Farm: the main house, the two

252

guesthouses, outbuildings, the chicken coop and something that looks like a newly-dug potato patch. A picture of a bare-chested, long-haired young man with round glasses, sitting on the roof, brandishing a hammer. Karen compares it to the group picture and decides it's probably the man named Brandon.

She picks up the next photograph. The slightly blurred picture shows a woman, possibly a tad older than the others, standing by the hob, stirring something in a big pot. Her long ash-blonde hair is gathered in a thick plait that hangs down one of her shoulders. She's wearing a floor-length dress and is turning toward the camera with a bashful smile, without letting go of the wooden spoon. She turns back to the group picture again: yes, that's Disa.

Another photograph: a woman with hennaed hair and a belly like a balloon under her long tie-dyed dress, looking tired with both hands on her back. It must be the woman from the ferry, the one who was carrying an infant in a wrap, Karen decides and turns back to the group picture again. Ingela: at least one of the children must be hers and now she's apparently pregnant again; no wonder she looks tired.

The very last picture shows two women sitting on the porch. Still, after more than forty years, Karen can sense the tension. Anne-Marie's sitting with her head in her hand, her face half turned away, red-headed Ingela has raised one of her hands, as if to ward off the photographer.

A different life, Karen supposes, that's probably all they wanted. A new age, new ideals, a new country.

They had probably, just like everyone else, been searching for a better life, community and happiness, however they conceived of those things. And they had travelled far, put everything on the line to find what they were looking for. They'd had the courage and the will to create the existence they wanted. Yet even so, their dream had died after just a year or two.

Something clearly went awry up there on Lothorp Farm. The question is what. Suddenly, getting hold of Disa Brinckmann feels urgent.

39

Langevik, 1970

Guilt squeezes his chest, radiating down into his gut. Per Lindgren bends over and breathes in shallow gasps to ease the cramping. After a while, he straightens up and continues down the path without wiping away the tears streaming down his cheeks. How could he? How fucking could he?

But he knows the answer; the summer's been three months of continuous foreplay. Ingela's laughing mouth and full red lips, so unlike Anne-Marie's sad smile. Ingela, who with hands black with soil from the potato patch pours a scoop of water from the barrel by the wall over her head and down her back. His eyes on the shapely curves outlined underneath the wet fabric of her tank top. Ingela's carefree joy, so unlike Anne-Marie's constant anxiety.

Ingela's eyes when she looks at him. Her hands, which stroke his back in passing every time she walks by, her thigh against his under the table, her tongue teasingly licking wine from her top lip while her eyes hold his.

And him. Always attuned to where Ingela is. His eyes constantly seeking hers, wanting validation and getting it every time. He, who laughingly tousled Anne-Marie's hair that time a few weeks ago when she confronted him yet again with her accusations. Why is he looking at Ingela that way? Does he think she's blind? Has he slept with her? Tomas' wife. His best friend's wife. Answer honestly: has he?

'Oh, Ammi,' he'd told her, with a surprised chuckle, so convincing he'd realised how easy it would be for him to betray her. Using her pet name and a voice so soft her anger had melted into tears. 'Are you jealous?'

'Just tell me the truth,' she'd said.

Instead, he'd denied it and turned her accusations around. No, there was nothing between him and Ingela, of course not; you're imagining things. And even if there was something, Anne-Marie had no right to throw it in his face. They'd agreed they didn't own each other. Wasn't that exactly the kind of petty bourgeoisie value they wanted to rise above in the commune?

'Why can't you just tell me the truth?' she'd pleaded again.

And he'd said something about her smothering him. In the end, she'd backed down, given up, said she believed him. But he'd seen the anxiety in her eyes and had promised himself to stop looking at Ingela's breasts and lips. She was Tomas' wife, for God's sake, his best friend's wife. And he loved Anne-Marie. He really did.

I do, he thinks, gazing out at the sea. I love her. Anne-Marie can never find out; I'd lose her. I'd lose Tomas, too. At that thought, unreasonable fury flares up inside him. Why is he being judged so harshly? Brandon, the horny bastard, certainly ogles Ingela too when Janet's not looking. And who knows what he got up to with Theo's sister when she came to visit a couple of weeks ago.

And hadn't Tomas himself been the most eager advocate of free love, of not owning other people, of love having no limits?

Hadn't he taken Ingela back after they'd been apart for almost three years, when she'd come crawling home, looking for security? Loved her again, even though she'd had children with someone else? Said that all children are everyone's children? Cared for Ingela's kids as though they were his own, feeding them, carrying them, changing their nappies and whatever else?

That's what they'd agreed: we're going to share everything, possessions, food, drink, work, joy and sorrow. Community, freedom and honesty were supposed to be the guiding principles of life on the farm. And love. The rest would work itself out.

The problem was none of them was being particularly honest. Not Brandon, cheating on Janet, not Theo hiding the best weed in his mattress. Not even Anne-Marie, who'd said she believed him when her eyes revealed she didn't.

And least of all he himself. Like a coward, a thief in the night, he'd seized the opportunity when Tomas had to go back to Sweden.

My best friend leaves his family on my farm to bury his mother, and I go and fuck his wife, Per thinks, wallowing in shame. Not just once, either; they'd continued after Tomas got back, gigglingly, furtively, relishing their secret, exchanging looks over the dinner table when no one was looking.

Surely no one had been looking?

Never again, he promises himself. Never again, he says out loud.

No one needs to know the child Ingela's expecting isn't Tomas'. This time either.

It's your child, Per, she'd told him. I know it is.

He's certainly not going to confess to Anne-Marie or Tomas. Why should he be honest when no one else is? And Ingela

257

mustn't tell them either. It would break Anne-Marie and she knows it.

And Tomas. Maybe this time he wouldn't be so quick to forgive, Per had told her. If they tell them, everything's going to fall apart, he'd said. The farm, their friendships, his and Anne-Marie's relationship. Everything would be wrecked, everything they were trying to build would be ruined if they told the truth.

In the end, Ingela had promised to keep shtum. She'd actually promised.

The problem is that she's so bloody . . . unpredictable.

Per turns around and starts walking back toward the farm. I have to talk to her again, he thinks to himself. Now, before it's too late.

40

'Who the fuck goes hiking in Spain? Is this some kind of Swedish idiocy?'

Karen leans back in her chair with such force it rolls backward and crashes into Johannisen's empty desk.

No one's picking up at Disa Brinckmann's address in Malmö, but Astrid Nielsen has discovered that a Mette Brinckmann-Grahn, daughter of Disa Brinckmann, lives in Lomma outside Malmö with her twenty-three-year-old son Jesper. And when Karen calls, the son actually picked up.

The southern Swedish dialect had been difficult to interpret, but she'd managed to gather that Jesper Grahn knew nothing about his grandmother's attempts to contact a woman called Susanne Smeed in Doggerland. In fact, Jesper Grahn seemed largely uninterested in his grandmother's affairs. Possibly, he offered, she might be in Spain.

'Some fucking Jesus hike or whatever it is they get up to,' he'd said with heavy diphthongs. 'But you'd have to ask my mum; she'll be home in an hour.'

And when Karen was in fact able to reach Mette Brinckmann-Grahn just over an hour later, she had confirmed her son's information. Disa Brinckmann had gone to Santiago de Compostela and would probably be back in about ten or twelve days.

'Mum's big on the spiritual stuff. I think it's her third time doing that trail now, so it's not an organised trip. She's usually gone for a couple or at most three weeks. But I think she said she has tickets to a concert here in Malmö next weekend, so she should be home by then.'

'OK, does your mother have a mobile phone? We haven't been able to find a number.'

'She does, but it's registered to me because I pay for it. I gave it to her for Christmas. It's right here, in the kitchen. I gave her a ride to the airport and she asked me to look after it.'

'How come?'

'She didn't want to bring it on her hike, given as how the point of it is silence and reflection. She was afraid of losing it, too. I asked her how I was supposed to get hold of her if something happened if she didn't bring it, but she said the phone ringing would ruin the experience. There's just no point nagging her. Do you want the number anyway? Like I said, she should be home soon.'

Karen had sighed inwardly, written the number down and changed the subject.

'Is it true you and your mother lived in a commune in the early seventies?'

There had been a long pause and when Mette Brinckmann-Grahn finally replied, there was a cold edge to her voice.

Her guard's up now, Karen had thought to herself.

'Yes, that's correct, but that's over forty years ago. We moved back home again before I started school. What is this about?'

Karen had briefly told her that one Susanne Smeed had been found dead and that the Doggerland police had certain indications pointing to Disa trying to get in touch with her a few months earlier. As part of the investigation, they were simply asking anyone who had been in contact with Susanne in recent months a couple of routine questions.

'Do you have any idea why your mother wanted to get hold of Susanne?'

This time, the answer had been immediate.

'No idea.'

Karen waited silently on the other end, and Mette Brinckmann-Grahn had at length expanded on her answer.

'I assume she wanted to get in touch with someone from back then and figured Susanne might be able to help. Mum's a bit . . . how to put it? She's still very stuck in the seventies, in a way. But you're going to have to ask her when she gets back.'

They'd ended the call after Mette had promised to make sure her mother contacted Karen as soon as she was back, or sooner, if Disa happened to call her from Spain.

Karen closes her eyes and thinks about Jesper Grahn's words. 'Jesus hike.'

She chuckles. Well, that's one way of putting it. She's read about the pilgrimages to Santiago de Compostela and seen amazing pictures from the various trails, but has never felt tempted. What little faith she had as a child – her father's family had made a few half-hearted attempts to bring her into the fold during the summer weeks she'd spend with her cousins on Noorö – had withered and died a Tuesday in December eleven years ago.

Pilgrimages and sore feet are not high on Karen Eiken Hornby's list. And how on earth does a woman who must be over seventy find the energy to traipse around dusty Spanish byways for weeks on end?

'And how on earth can a person be back on their feet just days after a heart attack,' she mutters in exasperation, scowling at Johannisen's desk before rolling back to her own.

Evald Johannisen has made it known through his wife that he's being discharged tomorrow and that if all goes well, he'll be back at work in just a couple of weeks.

'Angina,' Karl corrects her. 'It wasn't a heart attack. My dad's on nitroglycerine and calcium suppressants, too . . .'

'Fine, but he's a bloody dentist, not a detective,' she cuts in testily. 'Johannisen should take this as his cue to retire. He was hardly in top shape before he collapsed; how does he imagine he's going to hold up now?'

'The question is how you're going to hold up. You seem under pressure, and that's putting it mildly,' Karl says calmly. 'Have you had lunch?'

'Not hungry,' she dismisses his question. 'And it's hardly a big shock I'm under pressure; we're not getting anywhere.'

'It's been five days,' Karl says and gets to his feet. 'A lot could still happen, as you said yourself in the team meeting yesterday.'

'I lied,' she said grimly.

'Yes, it's been made clear to me you do that sometimes.'

'I thought we were done with that,' she snaps.

Karl's probably right. A slight light-headedness suggests her blood sugar has dropped to her ankles.

'Dial it down a notch, Eiken.'

'I'm sorry. I'm just so sick of not getting anywhere. Every lead's a dead end. Someone killed Susanne Smeed and we have no idea who or why.'

'Well, she wasn't exactly Miss Popular, so it's hardly impossible to imagine someone having a motive.'

262

'I'm not Miss Popular either, but you don't see anyone bashing my head in.'

'Not yet . . .' Karl retorts with a grin. 'I bet Johannisen would like to. I would, too, sometimes.'

'I just know Haugen's going to put someone else in charge of the investigation unless we come up with something that at least resembles a theory soon. Besides, I feel like the team's fading.'

'Well, either way, I'm hungry and was going to head down to Magasinet. Do you want to come? They have properly nice sprat on the menu at the moment . . .'

She gets to her feet with a sigh and takes her jacket off the back of her chair.

It's almost half one and the worst of the lunch rush is over. Karen takes a sip of her beer and gazes out at the harbour.

The big fishing vessels are docked in Ravenby these days, but stern trawlers and chubby gillnetters are still moored in long lines alongside the oyster fishermen's light aluminium craft. A group of divers are standing in a huddle on the edge of the pier; seemingly deep in discussion, gesticulating wildly. Probably complaining about the competition from the oyster banks down on Frisel, as usual. Further away, a hunched man is pushing a shopping trolley, looking for empty drink cans. Karen recognises him from the morning after Oistra, when she was standing up by the promenade wall and saw him snoozing on the beach.

So much has happened since she woke up in a hotel bed next to her boss that she's not really had time to wallow in her regret and abject shame. Now, recalling it, she shudders in dismay and quickly turns to Karl.

'Oh yes, that's the ticket,' he says, sounding pleased, when the waitress brings their food and a breadbasket.

Her stomach pinches when the smells reach her; crispy fried sprats, garlic butter, lemon and parsley. And steaming-hot sourdough bread. The garlic is a recent addition; older people still eat their sprat with melted lard, a dash of vinegar and chopped ramsoms, when that's in season. She relishes the gentle crunch when her fork sinks into the first fish; she smiles at Karl.

'You were right,' she says. 'I am hungry.'

They eat in silence until Karl mops up the last remnants of his melted butter with a piece of bread. He takes a few sips of his beer, then leans back and studies Karen, belching discreetly behind his hand.

'Do you really think it might be Jounas?' he says. 'I think everyone's dying to know if you think he did it, or if you're just yanking his chain.'

'Yanking his chain? It wasn't my bloody decision to put him on leave; even Haugen could see it had to be done.'

'I know,' Karl replies calmly. 'But you've been interviewing Smeed without anyone else present; you're the only one who can really assess whether his account of his whereabouts last Sunday holds water. And you don't really think it does, if I've understood things right.'

'I wish I did. Believe me, I didn't ask to be in this position.'

'So you're not angling to be head of the CID? Admit part of you likes the idea, Eiken.'

She meets his gaze without returning his smile.

'I don't want it like this,' she replies. 'Either Jounas comes back and makes my life hell, or he doesn't and I don't get the permanent promotion anyway.'

'Why wouldn't you? Because you waste money on outra-geously expensive coffee machines?'

'Because if Jounas Smeed doesn't come back, it's because I helped nail him for murder. The Smeeds have a lot of pull among the top brass. You realise Jounas's uncle is married to Haugen's sister, right?'

'Are you saying that's why he got the job?'

'Not the only reason. Jounas is a good detective. Arrogant and unpleasant, but bloody clever, you know that. And the boys like him. Johannisen would lick his boots if he asked him to.'

'OK, then what doesn't add up? Go over the timings again.'

'I've checked with the hotel where Jounas was staying and they confirm he left the room no earlier than five past nine. That's when the cleaner noted the do-not-disturb sign was still on the door.'

She sips her beer and continues.

'His car was parked by city hall; walking there would have taken him no more than six to seven minutes. That would give him forty-five minutes to drive to Langevik and kill Susanne. According to Brodal, she might have been murdered as late as 10 a.m., though it was probably earlier. As you know, he can't be more specific than that. I've personally driven from Dunker to Langevik in just under thirty minutes. Normally, it takes forty.'

'So ten minutes. That's the window.'

'Yep.'

'What does Haugen say?'

'He's annoyed, but luckily, Prosecutor Vegen's an astute woman. She realises we can't rule Smeed out so long as that window remains.'

'And what does Jounas have to say about it?'

'That he left the hotel at half past nine and walked straight home. No one at the hotel saw him leave, which may very well be true. The bloke at the front desk isn't exactly the type to be glued to his post.'

'What about before nine, have you considered that? According to Brodal, the murder could have taken place as early as eight. Jounas could've left the hotel early and gone to Langevik and back. If it was as easy as you say to sneak past the bloke at reception, that would've been possible. Have you talked to the woman who was with him?'

Karen, who has just raised her drink to her lips, freezes mid-movement, so abruptly the beer sloshes against the side of the glass, splashing the back of her hand. She makes a desperate attempt to mask her reaction with a cough. Karl studies her, eyebrows raised. A moment passes, she can see the penny drop.

'No way,' he says. 'No fucking way.'

'What do you mean?' she asks and puts her glass back down, avoiding his eyes.

Her voice is steady, but her cheeks are flushed and she knows he can tell. It took Karl a fraction of a second to see through her. He's a clever detective, too.

Now he's watching her without speaking; she steels herself in anticipation of the inevitable deluge of sarcasm. He's not going to tell on her, the whole department won't find out, but Karl knowing is enough. Karen Eiken Hornby slept with the boss.

He doesn't push her to confess, knowing full well he's right.

'And when did you leave the Strand?' is all he says.

'Twenty past seven,' she replies quietly.

'So that kills that theory,' Karl says sourly. 'Want another? I certainly need one.'

He waves the waitress over and orders two more pints after noting Karen's nod in response to his question.

'All right then,' he says and turns back to Karen. 'Regrets?'

'What do you think.'

'Well, I'm not going to ask what it was like. I assume your memories are somewhat foggy.'

'Well, you know, Oistra,' she says, and tries to smile, but fails. 'Just please promise you won't . . .'

'Oh, it goes without saying, I'm going straight to Haugen to tell on you. Then I'm going to call Jounas and ask if you're any good in bed. Who do you think I am?'

'Thanks. Sorry.'

Another attempt at a smile; it turns into a twitch in one of her cheek. She gratefully focuses on the fresh pint the waitress puts down on the table in front of her. They drink in silence until Karl speaks again.

'Well,' he says, 'if I had five marks for every bad shag I've had, I'd be a rich man. But seriously, Eiken, you and Smeed . . . I wouldn't have believed it. You must have had a magnificent hangover last Sunday.'

As he says it, he seems to have another epiphany.

'And then Haugen calls and tells you Smeed's wife's been beaten to death.'

'Ex-wife,' Karen corrects him.

Karl Björken leans forward with a hint of schadenfreude in his wry smile.

'Well, well, well. So that's why you were so set on inter-viewing him by yourself. I'm so bloody gullible: *She's being considerate*, I told Johannisen.'

Karen looks down at the table and says nothing.

'It must have been hell, Eiken. Serves you right.'

It's almost three by the time they get back to the station. Karen is focusing all her strength on keeping her intense feelings of shame at bay by reviewing the written reports sent to her over the course of the day. Replies have come in from all relevant countries regarding the cruise ship passengers' potential criminal records. Only one person has been added to the list of people with a prison sentence in their past. An Italian man guilty of repeat-edly flashing children at schools and playgrounds. After his most recent arrest, he served eight months in open prison before being allowed to return to his wife and children in their house outside Palermo. These days, however, he suffers from severe rheuma-tism and is more or less confined to a wheelchair, according to Cornelis Loots' notes.

A couple of hours later, Karen glances at her watch and real-ises the afternoon meeting is starting in six minutes. Despondent, she gets up and walks over to the coffee machine. Something gnaws at her while she watches the black coffee spout into the mug. Something that's right there, but slinks away when she tries to grasp it. A vague feeling she's seen or heard something but failed to follow up on it. Something potentially pivotal.

41

'We're pretty much dealing with just five recurring ingoing and outgoing numbers. Gunilla Moen's direct line, the direct line to the head of HR, Solgården's switchboard, Jounas Smeed's mobile and Sigrid Smeed's mobile. And a smattering of calls to and from various sales people and suppliers as well, of course. And one logged call from a Swedish number and three from an unlisted pay-as-you-go number.'

Cornelis Loots' big, freckled hands flip through the stapled-together A4 sheets detailing the past six months' calls to and from Susanne Smeed's work phone. Even Karl Björken had been forced to admit TelAB had proven unusually expeditious when their report arrived a couple of hours earlier.

Cornelis Loots puts the papers aside on the table and looks up at his colleagues, who are all looking back at him expectantly.

'And,' he says slowly, as though relishing being the centre of attention for once, 'that pay-as-you-go SIM card was purchased in Sweden. In Malmö, to be precise.'

'I see. By Disa Brinckmann, I'd bet,' Karl says and leans back with a sigh.

Karen has nabbed the call list from Cornelis. Now she flips through her own notes, stops and then shakes her head.

'Nope, it's not Disa Brinckmann's phone,' she says. 'But the listed number's hers. So clearly, she did get hold of Susanne in the end. They spoke for almost an hour on 21 June.'

'Then who the fuck's the other caller? Another person who also lives in Malmö; what are the odds of that? Nah, I'd bet anything that pay-as-you-go number belongs to Brinckmann as well.'

'Since Susanne wasn't allowed to use her work phone for private calls, she must've had a private mobile, too,' Astrid Nielsen puts in. 'I bet anything juicy would be on that one.'

'I agree, it must have been more than a regular alibi phone,' Karl puts in.

Karen looks at Karl with raised eyebrows.

'An "alibi phone"?'

'Yeah, to keep up appearances at work. You don't have to use it for anything other than porn surfing and making black-mail calls.'

'Do you have one? To keep up appearances, I mean?'

'Of course not; I'm always on duty.' Karl grins. 'The state's going to have to pay for the few private calls I make.'

'Well, I do have a personal phone,' Astrid says. 'We have some kind of family contract that lets you have several numbers.'

Of course, Karen concludes with a sigh. Mr and Mrs Goody-Goody always make the right decisions: they go running and eat healthily and have family phone contracts. They probably go to church, too. Just then, it strikes her that Astrid's looking unusually pale. A strand of hair has slipped out of her ponytail; she wearily pushes it out of her face.

'Either way, Susanne had a total of three incoming phone calls from the pay-as-you-go number to her work phone,'

Cornelis Loots continues patiently. 'Two calls at the end of June, the first lasting almost half an hour and the second just over two minutes. Then nothing for almost three months, which is when another call is logged from the same number, but that one seems to have gone straight to voicemail.

Cornelis pauses for effect before pressing on.

'That call came in on the twenty-seventh of September at 10.15 a.m.,' he says.

'The twenty-seventh. But that was last Friday!'

The room is dead silent for exactly four seconds. Someone called Susanne two days before she was murdered. Four seconds of silence before Cornelis Loots clears his throat once more.

'TelAB has also helped us identify the location from which the call was made and it looks like it was relayed by a mast in central Copenhagen.'

'Then it's definitely not Disa Brinckmann. She went to Spain on the' – Karen flips through her notes – 'twenty-seventh, actually. She would hardly have had time to pop over to Copenhagen on the same day she flew to Bilbao.'

Astrid Nielsen has been sitting quietly, fiddling with her phone. Now she reaches for the water jug while popping a blister pack of paracetamol with her other hand. She really does look tired. Karen pushes the jug closer to Astrid. I should probably talk to her, ask her how she's doing. Astrid discreetly puts the pill in her mouth and swallows it down with two quick sips of water.

'There would have been enough time,' she says. 'The train from Malmö to Copenhagen takes just over half an hour. And there are a lot more flights from Kastrup Airport in Copenhagen

271

than from Malmö Airport. It may well have been the easiest way for Disa to get to Bilbao.'

'Provided she's actually in Spain,' Karl put in. 'She may have come here instead. We have all the passenger lists from the twenty-seventh, right? Maybe there was a Disa Brinckmann on a flight from Kastrup to Dunker.'

Cornelis nods and gets up.

'I'll check right now.'

The conference room is humming with something Karen hasn't felt in days. Hope. Maybe they've finally found a lead worth pursuing.

Hope has quickly shrivelled up and died.

'There was no Disa Brinckmann on any flight to Dunker on the twenty-seventh,' Cornelis Loots announces when he returns to the conference room, with an almost apologetic look on his face.

'She might have come earlier, we're going to have to check a few more dates.'

'No point, I'm afraid,' Cornelis Loots says. 'According to SAS, there was a Disa Brinckmann on the 9.40 a.m. flight from Malmö to Bilbao on the twenty-seventh of September.

Silence envelops the room once more.

'So the old lady was verifiably on her way to Spain when the call was made,' Karl says dully, putting into words what they've all figured out already. 'All right, so it can't possibly have been Disa Brinckmann. Then who the fuck was it?'

42

Karen turns off the motorway at the Grenå Mall exit. It's almost half past six but at Tema the queues are still long. The Friday afternoon crowds at the supermarkets have become so intolerable in recent years that more and more people have started doing their big shops on Thursdays. And now, the race to buy food for the weekend has brought the crowds forward even further, to Wednesday nights. At this rate, Karen ponders grimly with a glance at her ticket for the alcohol counter, we're all going to have to do our weekend shops on Sunday night.

The islanders' discipline when it comes to buying alcohol is strict and their efficiency level high. At the deli counter, people are allowed to dither, wavering between pâtés and serrano ham; at the fishmongers', a certain level of pickiness and contemplation is expected. At the alcohol counter, on the other hand, you're supposed to know what you want, place your order quickly and clearly, swipe your card, take your receipt and collect your purchases at the pick-up counter a few minutes later. A kind of assembly line principle that makes the ticket numbers tick by quickly. A bottle of wine or beer can be picked up from a corner shop, with their limited selection, but more large-scale purchases are always made at a Tema or Freja supermarket. Karen intends to make a large-scale purchase. The food she's planning for Saturday may be simple, but there will be plenty to drink. Besides, she needs to restock her stores anyway.

Within twenty minutes, she's pushing her clinking trolley across the car park's pitted tarmac.

After loading two boxes of wine, a tray of beer cans, two bottles of gin, a bottle of whiskey and a carrier bag containing onions, garlic, butter and cream into her car, she bites off a large piece of the chocolate bar she'd picked up at the tills and spins around to return her trolley.

She goes over her plan: she has time to swing by the harbour to pick up mussels on Friday and Marike has promised to bring freshly baked bread from town, but she should probably serve some kind of dessert, too. Why hasn't she thought of that? The idea of going back in again for more food is off-putting to say the least.

A young man in a red Tema smock has detached a long line of parked shopping trolleys and started dragging them toward the entrance. Apple pie, she decides, I have a tonne of apples at home, that'll do.

'Hey, do you want this one, too?'

The young man stops and turns around, but doesn't look like he appreciates the interruption. He accepts Karen's trolley with a sigh and pushes it into the end of the train. He has to really put his back into it to get the long line of trolleys moving again; Karen's eyes linger on the hunched figure while her mind keeps running through her Saturday plans. A classic apple and cinnamon pie, perhaps, or maybe a tarte Tatin . . .

Then she stiffens. She quickly pulls out her phone and scrolls through her contacts.

Jounas Smeed picks up after five rings.

'Why, hello again, Eiken, what can I do for you this time?'

His words are impeccably friendly, but his tone reveals that he's not happy to hear from her. She ignores that and gets right to the point, not bothering with a greeting.

'That man you ran into on Sunday morning. He asked you for cigarettes, you said. Do you remember anything else about him?'

'Oh, give it a rest, will you. No, as I already told you. Do you have any idea how many drunks are staggering around this town? Haugen did tell me you were pretty much at a standstill, but have you really not found anything better to look into?'

'You really can't remember anything?' she wheedles. 'Anything at all. Try.'

'You mean aside from the reek of sweat and old booze? Please, Karen, you're really not good-looking enough to be *this* dumb.'

He chuckles, clearly pleased with his double insult, and she struggles with an urge to hang up. It would be so easy to just forget the whole thing. It's certainly not for Jounas's sake she decides to make one more attempt.

'You said you ran into him on the promenade. Did you maybe see which direction he was coming from?'

'How the fuck should I know? He was standing at the end of the street, swaying, at the top of the hill above the turn-off to the beach. What are you getting at?'

There's a change in Jounas's voice; a faint hint of curiosity coming through the feigned indifference. She hesitates before asking, doesn't want to nudge him in any particular direction. This is a brittle straw she's grasping.

'Well, like, did he have anything with him?'

An exasperated sigh indicates that whatever interest had been budding in Jounas Smeed has now withered again just as quickly.

'I don't bloody know if he had something with him. I think he had one of those big shopping trolleys some of them steal from supermarkets, but I didn't ask to see what he kept in it. Seriously, Eiken . . .'

Without another word, she ends the call.

43

Spinnhusgate looks deserted when Karen slowly turns at city hall park and continues up Valhallagate toward the parking garage behind the old market hall. She's hunching forward over the wheel slightly, peering out the side windows to the monotonous accompaniment of the windscreen wipers, which sweep the drizzle off the glass every four seconds. As she draws level with the garage, she spots what she's looking for. She quickly pulls over, leans across the passenger seat and rolls the window down. The woman, who's just about to duck under the yellow boom blocking the exit, stops at the sound of a car braking and whips around. She instinctively pushes her bosom out and puckers her lips invitingly. A split second later, she realises who's in the car and gives up the act.

'Hiya, Gro,' Karen calls out, 'would you like to hop in and warm yourself for a minute? There's something I want to ask you.'

Gro Aske hesitates for a moment, then totters over to the edge of the kerb in her high-heeled boots. Then she bends down and shoots off a crooked smile that reveals a missing canine in her upper jaw.

'God, you sound exactly like a punter.'

Her bleached hair has dark roots and is damp with rain; her short, white, faux-fur jacket is probably a lousy choice for the weather.

'You wouldn't happen to have anything to drink?' Gro Aske says hopefully after climbing in and blowing warm air into her cupped hands. 'I could use something to warm me up.'

At least she had the good sense to leave the miniskirt at home today, Karen muses, eyeing the skinny jeans wrapped around Gro Aske's stick-thin thighs.

'Sorry,' she replies. 'But how about a cigarette instead?' she adds and pulls a new packet out of her jacket pocket.

She remembers the boxes of wine, beer and whiskey in the flatbed. If you only knew what I have in the back . . . Then she winces at the rattling that rises out of Gro Aske's lungs as she takes a first drag and lets out a spluttering curse. Karen has seen Gro walk the streets for almost ten years, and yet it's only now, up close, that she realises how haggard the other woman really looks; emaciated, her eyes hollow, her skin grey. She's probably not even thirty, trying not to show how awkward she feels.

'Isn't it time to call it quits soon?' she asks.

'With the smoking, you mean?' Gro retorts with a sarcastic smile.

'You know what I mean.'

'And do what?'

'I don't know, wake up without anxiety for once, maybe. Stop worrying about how to pay for that shit. Maybe see your daughter again. You'd probably get a place at Lindvallen right away if you applied.'

'I know. I think about it every morning, actually, as soon as I get my first hit, but then every night, there I am, out looking for more. Well, you know how it is . . .'

Do I? Karen wonders.

What does she really know about these women and young girls in their obscenely short skirts and freezing legs, bending down to talk through car windows? What does she know about sleepless mothers who are haunted by visions of freezing drug dens and forks stuck in fuse boxes and who live in fear of that inevitable call informing them of a deadly overdose? What does she really know about what it takes to break out of that?

Is her own inability to get her life back on track really as different from Gro's as she likes to imagine?

Karen decides to go straight to the point.

'I need your help,' she says. 'You know most of the homeless people in this town, right?'

Gro pouts to indicate that she might and studies the glowing end of her cigarette without replying.

'There's this man who pulls a big shopping trolley around,' Karen continues.

'A lot of them do. They call them bum buggies.'

Karen lets out an involuntary chuckle.

'This bloke hangs around the promenade a lot, I think, collecting empties.'

Gro takes a deep drag, holds the smoke in her lungs for a few second then exhales with a loud puff.

'I don't grass. You know that.'

'I know, and I'm not trying to nail him for anything. If that were the case, I wouldn't have come to you.'

'Then what the fuck is it about?'

'He might be able to give a person an alibi, that's all. I promise, Gro.'

'And you don't have anything to drink?'

Karen puts her hand on the ignition key.

'Are you going to help me out or not? If not, I'm going to have to keep looking.'

Gro Aske takes one last deep drag, opens the door and flicks the butt out onto the pavement. But then she closes it again.

'You're probably talking about the new guy,' she says. 'Leo Friis, I think. He keeps to himself, mostly, but sometimes he hangs out in the park with the other old gits for a bit. Though I hardly think he'll be there in this weather.'

Leo Friis. Karen knows there's something familiar about that name. He's probably been nicked for public intoxication more than once.

'What else? Do you know where I can find him?'

'And you're telling me he hasn't done anything?'

'I promise. Cross my heart.'

Karen holds out the cigarettes, wiggling the packet invitingly; Gro reaches out with a frozen hand.

'Apparently he's a bit nuts about confined spaces. Have you checked down at the New Harbour, under the loading docks?'

44

The call comes just as she's turning off the motorway toward Dunker. Karen turns the eight o'clock news down and pushes in her earbud.

Her attempts to locate Leo Friis the night before were futile. Having circled the storage buildings and loading docks at a crawl, headlights sweeping like searchlights, for twenty minutes, she gave up. The old harbour with the misleading name the New Harbour was small by today's standards, but difficult to search. If Leo Friis was holed up in one of its countless nooks and crannies, chances were he'd see her long before she could spot him. And if he, like all other homeless people, was able to smell a copper from a mile away, he'd be unlikely to make his presence known.

By contrast, her sudden impulse to call Sara Inguldsen's mobile had been a success. No, she'd said, she was home at the moment, just about to go to bed, in fact, but she and Björn were on duty from half past five tomorrow morning. Of course they were happy to keep their eyes peeled for a homeless man pulling a shopping trolley in the area around the old New Harbour.

'Don't nick him,' Karen had reminded her one last time before ending the call. 'Keep your distance and let me know where he is; I'll speak to him.'

And lo and behold, this morning, Sara Inguldsen had called to inform her they'd spotted someone fitting Friis's description trudging up the slope from the quayside toward Gammelgårdsvägen.

It takes her six minutes to locate him. Leo Friis is shuffling up the gentle incline of Gammelgårdsvägen toward the town centre, his shoulders hunched under a grey woollen blanket. Karen drives past and stops further up the street. Then she climbs out of the car, pulls out a packet of cigarettes and pretends to be looking for something in her handbag. Bloody lucky I haven't managed to quit, she quips to herself; maybe I should claim the smokes as a work expense.

'I'm sorry,' she says as Leo Friis approaches. 'You wouldn't happen to have a light?'

He stops and looks around, befuddled, as if to make sure she's talking to him.

'Oh, wait, here it is,' she says, embarrassed at her poor acting skills. 'Want one?'

She holds the packet out; Leo Friis seems to hesitate. He's bloody well not the kind of man who gets stopped by random women offering cigarettes, unless there's some devilry afoot.

'What do you want?' he says curtly.

'Leo Friis?'

'And who the fuck are you?'

'Karen Eiken,' she says, extending her hand.

He doesn't take it. Torn between the sound impulse to walk away and the urge to smoke that's afflicted him since last night, he keeps his eyes fixed on the packet of cigarettes in Karen's hand. She tries again.

'I'm a police detective and – no, come on, calm down, you haven't done anything wrong, I just want to ask you something.'

'I've nothing to say.'

Leo Friis moves to get the heavy trolley rolling; she quickly takes in its contents: carrier bags full of empty cans and bottles, something that looks like a rolled-up sleeping bag, a pair of winter boots and a handful of unidentifiable bundles. Without blocking him outright, Karen steps to one side so he has to at least walk around her.

'Not even if you could help prove someone's innocence?' she says.

Leo Friis doesn't reply.

'Do you want breakfast? That café over there's open,' she says quickly like a telemarketer. 'My treat, coffee and a couple of sandwiches. And cigarettes after. I'll give you the whole pack.'

She nods toward the café across the street and notes that Leo Friis follows her gaze.

'You seriously think they'd let me in? Forget it.'

'They'll let you in if I tell them to.'

He eats with gusto and frequent quick glances at his trolley outside. Thankfully, he left the blanket outside, too, and Karen noticed he ran his fingers through his hair as if to neaten himself up before entering. The confident way in which she placed her guest at a window table and then ordered a large pot of coffee, a glass of milk, two cheese sandwiches and one with sliced lamb had persuaded the girl at the till to refrain from commenting. Karen can't do anything about her suspicious glances, but Leo Friis seems oblivious, or maybe he simply doesn't care. Luckily, the place is half empty and the few customers who come in choose tables as far away from the odd couple by the window as possible.

She lets Leo eat in silence, studying him from behind her coffee cup. From afar, she'd figured him for about sixty, maybe older. Now, seeing him close up, she realises he can't be much more than forty. His hands are calloused and have assumed a reddish-purple colour, probably the result of too many nights sleeping rough. Half his face is hidden behind a beard, but around the eyes, his skin is relatively unwrinkled. A faint smell of sweat and mould wafts her way every time he turns his head to make sure his precious belongings are still safely parked outside the window.

'The morning after Oistra,' she says at length, after he's washed down the last mouthful of the lamb sandwich with a big gulp of milk. 'You slept on the beach that night, didn't you?'

'Is that against the law now?'

'Not that I know. I think you were the person I saw when I was standing across from Hotel Strand just after seven, looking down at the beach. Is that correct?'

Leo Friis meets her eyes above the rim of his coffee cup for a second. He takes a sip and nods briefly.

'Not impossible. I've been sleeping there all summer. This bloody cold only blew in a couple of days ago.'

'Yes, I remember it was a warm morning and I thought to myself that the man on the beach wouldn't be feeling great when he woke up. To be honest, I wasn't exactly feeling great myself,' she adds.

Leo Friis makes no comment on the relative balminess of the morning or the fact that the woman across the table is revealing personal facts about how she was feeling for some unknown reason.

284

'Anyway, I believe you'd woken up after a couple of hours and climbed the slope to the promenade. I'd like to know if that's correct and if so, whether you remember running into anyone there? Someone you tried to bum a cigarette off.'

He looks utterly unmoved. Stares into space vacantly, as though he didn't hear the question. This is a long shot, obviously, she thinks to herself, or more like a shot off the post. How could she even for a moment have imagined that a man who lives his life like Leo Friis would be able to remember where he was or who he talked to five days ago? He's probably lucky if he remembers what he did an hour ago.

'And if I do . . .' he says slowly.

'What, do you or don't you?'

'Look, I'm not completely out of it. Not yet. Yeah, I remember chatting to a bloke.'

'Are you sure. What did he look like, do you recall?'

'No, just a regular bloke. Some suit guy wandering about at the wrong time of day. But aside from the get-up, he looked worse for wear, I can tell you that. Didn't look in much of a better state than me.'

'Suit, you say?'

'Yes, but I can't tell you what brand. Arm*aaa*ni, maybe, or Hugo-*Nazi*-Boss.'

Leo Friis pronounces the names in a nasal voice and Karen's surprised he knows the names of any fashion designers. On the other hand, why not? Something tells her it wasn't too long ago Leo fell off the face of the Earth. His addiction hasn't left enough scars yet.

'All right,' she says with a smile. 'Why don't we skip that detail, then. What I'd like to know is whether you have any idea what time it might have been. I mean, I realise you might not know exactly, but . . .'

'Twenty to ten,' he cuts her off.

Karen stares at him cautiously.

'Twenty to ten? And you're sure, just like that?'

'Yes, I'm sure. Just like that. Think about it, officer.'

Something in his voice makes her swallow her next question and instead do as she's told. She thinks about it. What could make a man who has slept his buzz off on the beach and woken up, probably sweaty and hungover, remember exactly what time it was? A split second later, the answer presents itself.

'The corner shop,' she says. 'They open at ten on Sundays.'

'Bingo! Four cans of lager and a small packet of cigarettes. A packet of sausages as well, actually. I was unusually rich that morning; the beach was covered in empties, all I had to do was pick them up. The problem was that when I woke up, nothing was open yet.'

Leo reaches for the coffee pot and pours himself another cup before continuing.

'I kept a close eye on the church tower clock the whole time while I filled my trolley. And when that bloke turned up, I remember I'd just thought to myself I had another twenty minutes to go before I could buy cigarettes, but I wanted one so bloody badly I might have clocked him if he hadn't let me bum one.'

45

'Brilliant! I'm calling Jounas right now to tell him the good news. Well done, Eiken, really well done!'

Viggo Haugen beams at her and makes as if to get up from his visitor's chair in Prosecutor Dineke Vegen's office. Then he stops himself and sinks back onto the plush seat. He turns to Karen again, tilts his head a little and gives her a sympathetic smile.

'I suppose this means Jounas Smeed will be able resume his duties immediately. You have done well filling in for him, Eiken, but there's really nothing to stop Smeed from taking over the investigation now. You did realise your promotion was temporary, right?'

Karen looks at him in surprise. Clearly, she will no longer have to fill in as interim head of department, but she could never have imagined Smeed would be taking over the investigation.

Dineke Vegen clears her throat.

'Hold on a second, Viggo,' she says. 'This is good news, that we can rule Jounas out, I mean, but I don't think it would be appropriate for him to head up the investigation.'

Viggo Haugen leans forward, poised to object, but a wave of her hand makes him close his mouth.

'Even though Jounas is no longer under suspicion, he has a very close personal connection to the victim. If I've understood things right, you still don't have a suspect or even a theory about possible motives?'

Karen nods reluctantly. Unfortunately, Dineke Vegen has understood things right, as she is all too aware. Viggo Haugen seizes the moment.

'But that's exactly why we need Smeed,' he says, sounding annoyed. 'Well, no offence, Eiken, but it's been five days without any progress.'

'No, Viggo, that's exactly why Jounas *shouldn't* have anything to do with the case,' Dineke Vegen explains patiently. 'We have to conduct more interviews, widen the circle. He can hardly be expected to interview his own relatives: his daughter, for instance.'

'His daughter,' Viggo Haugen sneers. 'You've already talked to her, haven't you? And her boyfriend too, unless I misread this morning's report.'

'Yes, that's correct; Karl Björken managed to track down Samuel Nesbö late last night; his statement corroborates Sigrid's account of the late gig and the fight the two of them had. Which doesn't in itself mean either one of them has an alibi for Sunday morning, only that she didn't lie about what happened Saturday night. Or they're both lying,' Karen adds and notes out of the corner of her eye that Viggo Haugen is scowling at her.

'Either way, we can't write off the daughter or the boyfriend,' Dineke Vegen concludes.

Viggo Haugen refuses to give up.

'And what motive could they possibly have had? Susanne didn't leave any money to speak of. And that house . . .'

'That's hardly relevant to the issue at hand,' the prosecutor interrupts, now with a hard edge to her voice. 'Let me put this

very clearly: It is out of the question for Jounas to come anywhere near this case. You know I prefer not to meddle with
police investigations, even though as a prosecutor I have every
right to step in and take over. I won't hesitate to do so this time,
if it becomes necessary.'

'Well, now, hopefully things won't get to that point. We usually see eye to eye, don't we?'

Karen studiously avoids looking at the chief of police. A man
in his position shouldn't have to be admonished by a superior
in front of an employee. Haugen has, in a remarkably unprofessional manner, created a situation that's embarrassing for
all three of them. He's going to take it out on me, she reasons.
Sooner or later.

'I suggest Karen keeps going with the team she's assembled
and continues to report to the two of us. Jounas will resume his
work as head of the CID, but will stay very far away from this
particular case. Are we clear?'

Haugen is at least partly right, Karen accepts, as she collapses
into her office chair. Someone else should probably take over the
investigation. Not Smeed, obviously, but someone else, someone who has the necessary drive. She for her part feels utterly
spent. There was a time when she would have approached a case
like this like a terrier that's discovered a meaty bone. A time
when her professional ambitions had included notions of rising
to become management, of being able to shape the long-term
work of the police. She knows better by now.

The mere thought of Jounas Smeed coming back to work is
paralysing. The fact that she's going to retain ultimate responsibility for the investigation and bypass him entirely by reporting

directly his bosses – the chief of police and prosecutor – is hardly going to make things between her and Jounas less tense. His absence has provided temporary respite, a small bubble of air in which she could breathe and even feel a bit of enthusiasm come creeping back into her work. Now that bubble has burst. What happened between them at the Strand is always going to hang over her. Any respect Jounas might have had for her before will certainly have been erased, but her worst fear is that he will let it slip, that the others will find out. Can she really stay here with that kind of sword of Damocles hanging over her?

No, I'm definitely not the right person to lead this investigation, she sighs inwardly. The prosecutor might be able to inspire the team and find new angles. Or Karl, at least he's still hungry. As she thinks that, Karl appears next to her.

'What did they say?'

'Jounas is coming back but he won't take part in the investigation. Haugen was going to call him straight away.'

Karl nods.

'As expected then. Though I'll admit I thought Haugen would go to bat for Jounas taking over the case, now that he's officially ruled out.'

Karen hesitates. Should she tell him what happened or let Karl believe Viggo Haugen made a sound decision of his own volition?

'No, we're going to keep going like we have been,' she says. 'Same team.'

'Good. Besides, now you can forget all about' – he looks around the open-plan office before continuing more softly – 'that night in the hotel since someone else is vouching for Jounas, right? So why do you look so damn defeated?'

She slowly swivels around in her chair and looks Karl Björken in the eye.

'Because I have no earthly idea where to go next.'

Just then, the phone rings.

It's Kneought Brodal, who informs her the DNA results are in and that they confirm the deceased is, indeed, Susanne Smeed.

'Since the victim's identity has now been verified and there's no doubt whatsoever about the cause of death, I'm going to release the body to the relatives for burial,' he says in a matter-of-fact tone that doesn't reveal that he knew Susanne personally.

The relatives. Karen pictures Sigrid; Susanne had no other relatives. How is Sigrid supposed to arrange a funeral? There's hardly going to be a wake; Karen doubts Sigrid's going to care about tradition. But the funeral itself is probably difficult enough to organise. Hopefully, she's smart enough to let her father help. Jounas may be a prick and clearly has nothing but contempt for his ex-wife, but he would be there for his daughter if she would just ask, wouldn't he? Either way, it's urgent, if they want to follow the seven-day rule: in Doggerland, a dead person is supposed to be in the ground within a week. Down on Frisel, it's still five days, though the younger generation is adopting more Scandinavian customs. Or Norwegian and Danish ones, to be precise. To eliminate the risk of having things degenerate to a Swedish level – where dead people can stay in the freezer for up to two months – new legislation has recently been introduced. If a person's loved ones are unable to sort out burial within five working days and two weekends, the authorities are now required to step in and the burial will take place in their absence.

Susanne's funeral will likely be on Saturday. Karen knows she'll have to ask Karl to attend, if she can't make it herself. Even though of course it's nothing like on telly, where the murderer furtively lurks in the bushes at the cemetery, it could be important to go. Someone of interest could turn up; some old friend of Susanne's they've missed.

46

Twenty to four that Friday afternoon, the investigation team is revitalised.

They've been pawing the ground like greyhounds at the starting line for a whole working week, while time has relentlessly kept passing. And gradually, the yapping in the starting box has subsided. One by one, the critical points have come and gone: the first twenty-four hours during which 90 per cent of clumsy, desperate perpetrators are, as a rule, identified; the three days during which slightly wilier perpetrators are usually able to stay one step ahead of the police. Now, on the sixth day of the investigation, the hope of DNA or other technical evidence shedding crucial light on the case has been extinguished, as well. Everything they have is spread out on the table. No one's hoping for a new, vital witness statement, for a gift from the gods anymore. Nothing of what little their investigation has uncovered looks like it might lead anywhere. Except possibly Disa Brinckmann. They have made initial contact with the Spanish police, but judging from the lukewarm reception, she is likely to have gone back home by the time one of their continental colleagues can be bothered to locate her. The question is how a seventy-year-old woman could possibly be connected to the murder. That she didn't commit it herself is beyond doubt; the hope is she might have something to tell them about Susanne. Something they don't already know.

That's where they are when Cornelis Loots waves Karen over.

A reported burglary of a summer cottage outside Thorsvik on northern Heimö has escaped everyone's notice. Cornelis alights on it through sheer happenstance when he searches the internal database for all crimes reported in the past three weeks. The house, located just east of the ferry port, was burgled on Saturday 21 September, a week before the murder of Susanne Smeed; the Ravenby Police subsequently reclassified the incident as burglary and attempted arson. It's the reclassification that makes him take notice.

The perpetrator's attempt to set the house on fire had been interrupted by a neighbour who had smelled smoke and made his way to the property boundary to see which of his idiot summer cottage neighbours was lighting fires in this weather. But instead of a cottage owner burning debris in their garden, he'd seen a young man exit his neighbour's house with a backpack slung over one shoulder, glancing back over the other, as if to make sure the fire he'd just started was catching.

The neighbour, a man by the name of Hadar Forrs, had, though reluctantly, done the right thing. Instead of following the pyrotechnically inclined young man, who according to Forrs disappeared on a yellow motorcycle, he'd called emergency services and then managed to put out the fire, by resourcefully breaking a window and inserting the garden hose, before the fire fighters arrived.

The owner of the house, David Sandler, who had decided to spend one final weekend in his summer cottage to harvest an unusually rich crop of chanterelles, had been on his way to the shops in Thorsvik town centre to pick up butter and cream when the burglary took place. Having been gone no more than thirty minutes, he returned to find his kitchen floor flooded and his house filled with an acrid smoke from the torched kitchen curtains that would take weeks to air out. His newly purchased laptop and his father's old Rolex, which had been sitting on the bedside table, were gone, and he was now in his cantankerous neighbour's debt, to boot. David Sandler hadn't been best pleased, that much was crystal clear from the report.

'On the other hand, he might have had his head bashed in with a poker if he'd been home,' Karl Björken remarks, speaking out loud what everyone's thinking.

Karen has called an extra meeting; the information about the burglary seems to have made the whole team sense a shift in their fortune. Now they're all sitting bolt upright, their eyes on her, ready to take notes.

'We don't want to get our hopes up, but this does mean we're going to refocus on finding more potential connections. Let's all work on going over every last detail of every single reported burglary. We'll start with today's reports and move backward from there. I'll put together a list of search terms to help guide our work.'

Normally, assigning them this kind of grunt work would have prompted groans and sighs, but this time, Karen barely has time to end the meeting before everyone's dashing to their desks to log into the database.

Astrid waves the others over after ninety minutes. At first, no one understands what's prompted her reaction. Yet another burglary, this time up on Noorö, just north of the ferry port sometime between 17 and 20 September; the owner was away. But there had been no attempt to set fire to the house. Among the stolen items were, aside from two laptops and a – likely grossly exaggerated – amount of gold jewellery. There are a lot of burglaries on Noorö and few are ever solved. There's nothing remarkable about this report either. Aside from one small detail.

On the list of stolen items is a yellow Honda, model CRF 1000L Africa Twin.

Once again, Karl Björken is the one who states the obvious:

'Same bloke. He made off with the bike on Noorö and used it for the heist in Thorsvik. Are there cameras on the ferry?'

Like an invisible gas, impossible to contain, a notion begins to spread through the team; maybe the murder of Susanne Smeed was simply a burglary gone awry. Maybe the bloke who set fire to the house in Thorsvik did the same thing in Langevik the following week. Maybe he'd scoped out his targets and knew Susanne was usually out of town during Oistra. Maybe he killed her in sheer desperation when it turned out she was home. Maybe they now know how and why Susanne Smeed was murdered. If so, it's only a matter of time before they catch the man who did it.

One person who's definitely convinced the tide is turning is Viggo Haugen. That much is clear to Karen when she leaves his office half an hour later.

'Wonderful news,' he repeats, slapping his desk.

The last thing she hears before closing the door behind her is the sound of him picking up the receiver to make a call.

47

The air conditioning in the conference room turns off at 8 p.m.; Karen feels her shoulders drop as the whirring sound dies down. The brown paper cup of whiskey she has swiped from Jounas Smeed's office feels like a small but remarkably effective revenge on this, her last day as interim head of the CID. On Monday, Smeed will resume his duties after a week's gardening leave.

Any second now, she's going to get up and fetch the two carrier bags full of mussels she's managed to shove into the fridge in the kitchenette. It had, once again, slipped her mind that she'd invited people over when she received a text from Eirik a few hours earlier, asking if she wanted them to bring anything tomorrow. 'Nothing. Just relax!' she'd replied, before frantically racing down to the harbour before the shops closed for the day. Then she'd returned to the office.

She's the only one left; she's put her feet up on her desk and is studying the big board by the wall from a distance. Along the top are pictures of Susanne Smeed. On the left, a relatively recent portrait picture provided by Eira Care Homes; all their employees are required to wear photo ID; it had taken Gunilla Moen less than four minutes to provide them with a printout. To the right of a grave-looking Susanne looking straight into the camera is a selection of pictures showing her beaten to death in her kitchen, alongside photographs of the kitchen itself from different angles.

Underneath the neatly lined-up pictures, Karl has drawn a vertical timeline listing the few facts they've been able to verify.

Friday 20 Sept. 4.30 p.m. Susanne leaves her place of work, Solgården.

Monday 23 Sept. 7.45 a.m. Susanne calls in sick to work.

Friday 27 Sept. 7.15 a.m. Incoming phone call to Susanne's work phone, from Copenhagen.

Saturday 28 Sept. No data.

Sunday 29 Sept. 8.30 a.m. – 10 a.m. possible window for murder, according to Kneought Brodal.

Sunday 29 Sept. Approx. 9.45 a.m. Angela Novak arrives at Harald Steen's house.

Sunday 29 Sept. Approx. 9.55 a.m. – 10 a.m. Harald and Angela hear a car drive away from Susanne's house.

Sunday 29 Sept. 11.49 a.m. Harald Steen calls emergency services.

Sunday 29 Sept. 12.25 p.m. Sara Inguldsen and Björn Lange arrive at the house.

For the sake of doing things by the book, they've also listed the names of anyone who had a less than cursory relationship with Susanne: Jounas Smeed, her daughter Sigrid and her boyfriend Samuel Nesbö, Wenche and Magnus Hellevik, Gunilla Moen. There is a question mark after Disa Brinckmann's name. Other than that, the board is empty, which is probably why someone's pushed it further away from the table.

And now, they can cross two of those names off the list of suspects.

New information brought by Karl Björken earlier in the evening had revealed that Sigrid Smeed had not been entirely honest in her interview. In this case, however, telling the truth would have served her better.

After some persistent door knocking in Sigrid Smeed's apartment building in Gaarda, Karl had finally managed to talk to a – still very upset – next-door neighbour, who had been woken up just before eight on Sunday morning by commotion in the stairwell. According to the neighbour, a man in his fifties, whose breath reeked of alcohol and smoked fish, Samuel Nesbö had come home at that point, only to discover the chain was on the door.

Sigrid's boyfriend – the neighbour had recognised him through his peephole – had rung the doorbell very persistently before proceeding to first call and then shout for Sigrid to open the door.

Eventually, she'd apparently let him in, because after that, they had, according to the neighbour, yelled and screamed at each other inside the flat until the boyfriend had left again in a rage about an hour later.

'Did it seem like they were getting physical?' Karl had asked, quietly wondering to himself why no one had called the police. On the other hand, he knew exactly why: domestic disturbances were an everyday occurrence in Gaarda and the calling the authorities was to be avoided at all costs.

'I don't bloody know, but I know she was alive when he left, because she was bawling at the top of her lungs.'

Karen had certainly never considered Susanne's daughter a likely suspect, but now both she and her boyfriend could be definitively ruled out. There were two straws to grasp at: the successful identification of the driver of the yellow Honda and getting hold of Disa Brinckmann. Maybe one of them would lead to something, but nothing would happen before Smeed was back at work. A week without tangible progress; he's not going to let me forget that, she thinks grimly to herself as she gazes out the rain streaked window. People have already tired of discussing the sudden change in weather, from the late-summer heat of Oistra to the premature arrival of freezing temperatures and this never-ending drizzle. The meteorologists have no words of comfort to give: more low-pressure systems are impatiently queuing up out over the Atlantic, waiting to sweep in across Doggerland and unleash their fury on the islands.

Karen studies the kaleidoscope of greys on the window pane while she goes over the case file in her mind. She knows it by heart by now so there's no reason to consult the black binders.

In her mind, she flips to the section on Susanne's personal life, where the word 'conflict' is found in the description of virtually every relationship she had: several conflicts with Jounas, both during and after their marriage, primarily regarding money and land. A conflict with the daughter caused by Susanne's endless fights with her father and Susanne's disappointment at her tulle-wearing ballerina turning into a young woman with a pierced nose and tattooed arms. A conflict with her employer regarding the private use of work phones and an unsuccessful job application. A conflict with wind-power company Pegasus regarding land rights and disruptive noise from the turbine park built close to her house. A conflict with Wenche Hellevik caused by Susanne feeling snubbed and neglected.

No known conflict with Samuel Nesbö had been uncovered, though it could be assumed that Sigrid's frosty relationship with her mother meant her boyfriend had no warm feelings for Susanne either. Whether there had been any kind of conflict between Susanne Smeed and Disa Brinckmann was still unknown.

In the margin were footnotes outlining a series of more minor conflicts with co-workers, bus companies and various suppliers of goods and services, all of whom Susanne had been unhappy with for one reason or another. Susanne Smeed seemed to have had a problem with practically everyone she ever came into contact with.

With me, as well. Karen recalls their awkward meeting at the tills of the plant nursery. Susanne had definitely had it in for Karen Eiken Hornby, long before there was any reason for it. And now she would never know what had happened in room 507 at the Hotel Strand.

The question is whether any of it is serious enough for someone to want Susanne dead. Had she made life so miserable for someone he or she had lost control? Or had she known something that constituted a threat to someone? Without any evidence to back it up, Karen has the distinct feeling Susanne had been exactly the type to stoop that low. Had Susanne Smeed engaged in blackmail?

On the other hand, she thinks to herself, sipping her whiskey, all this pondering is patently pointless. Judging by Viggo Haugen's excited voice a few hours earlier, the murder of Susanne Smeed has been solved.

'Not even you can deny this puts everything in a whole new light,' he'd said. 'A highly plausible explanation for this sad affair.'

Oh well, why not? Karen takes another sip; be that as it may, the Noorö and Thorsvik break-ins had in all likelihood been committed by the same bloke. For some reason he'd decided to up the ante by attempting to set the second house on fire. It's not at all impossible to imagine him continuing his crime spree in Langevik. Maybe Susanne surprised him or maybe he felt a need to dial up the thrill level even further. From burglary, via arson to murder. A classic case of desensitisation, particularly common among criminals with psychopathic tendencies. But that kind of escalation usually takes a lot longer than a week.

'All right, have a good weekend.'

The voice from the doorway makes Karen jump so high the last drops of whiskey slosh up over the edge of the paper cup.

'You're still here? I thought I was the last one,' she mumbles, wiping her hand on her jeans.

'I didn't mean to startle you,' Astrid Nielsen replies and starts zipping up her parka.

She really does look tired, Karen notes again with a pang of guilt. Following up on the new burglary lead entails going over CCTV footage from all ferry routes and running an expanded search for any crime connected to the two burglaries. Given the local police's unwillingness to use the new internal database PIR, which according to IT still suffers from 'teething problems', almost eleven months after being introduced, that means calling all local stations to make sure nothing is missed. Astrid Nielsen has been tasked with keeping a running tally of the results.

'I hope it's not my slave-driving tendencies that are keeping you away from your husband and children this late on a Friday night,' Karen says with a smile.

Astrid hesitates for a moment, then seems to steel herself.

'No, it's not your fault. The children are with my parents and Ingemar is . . . well, I might as well tell you, you're going to find out anyway. Ingemar and I are getting divorced.'

Karen takes her feet off her desk and leans forward.

'Come in,' she says. 'Why don't you have a seat?'

Astrid seems to hesitate again, but then slowly unzips her parka. She sinks down onto a chair without a word; Karen can see her lips quivering.

'Tell me what happened,' she says.

And over the next thirty minutes, Karen learns that Astrid Nielsen isn't as suffocatingly wholesome nor her husband as angelic as she'd thought.

48

Not every seat is filled, but Karen's still surprised at how many people have made heir way to Langevik Church this Saturday morning for Susanne Smeed's funeral.

Sigrid and Jounas are in the front pew with Wenche and Magnus Hellevik. As though out of respect for the loved ones, the row immediately behind them is empty, but elsewhere, Karen spots Gunilla Moen and another woman, presumably one of Susanne's co-workers at Solgården. Several townspeople are in attendance; even Harald Steen has come, as have Odd Marklund, Jaap Kloes and Egil Jenssen and his wife. Who has come to pay their respects and who is driven primarily by morbid curiosity is anyone's guess. Karen has slipped into a pew in the back; neither Sigrid nor Jounas seems to have spotted her. Wenche Hellevik, on the other hand, has given her a nod of recognition and a small smile.

Sigrid looked pale and determined when she walked into the church ahead of her father. While the priest speaks, she's sitting with her head bowed; Karen notices that Jounas tries to say something to his daughter, but she resolutely turns her head away.

It's the usual hymns and the priest keeps things brief, saying only what's absolutely necessary. But at the sound of earth hitting the coffin lid, Karen hears a muffled sob from the front. Sigrid has disappeared from view; it takes Karen a few seconds to realise Susanne's daughter has bent over double.

Jounas Smeed is shifting uncomfortably in his seat and Wenche Hellevik puts a hand on Sigrid's back, but removes it again just as quickly.

The whole thing is over in thirty minutes. When Karen, among the last to leave the church, steps out through the front doors, she notices that Jounas and Sigrid have already reached the car park, while Wenche and her husband have lingered in front of the church, talking to the priest. Jounas and Sigrid are clearly arguing about something. He opens the door of his car and looks like he's trying to persuade her to get in, but she shakes her head. He gestures toward the car, annoyed this time, but she stubbornly stays where she is, arms crossed. Then she abruptly turns around and starts walking towards the cemetery while Jounas calls after her.

Soon after, Jounas is in the car, pulling the door shut with a bang so loud everyone turns to look; Wenche Hellevik glances over anxiously. She then quickly concludes her conversation with the priest and hurries toward the car park with her husband on her heels.

But before they can make it there, Jounas roars out of the car park in a shower of gravel.

For a few seconds, Wenche seems indecisive, looking from Jounas's car to her niece cutting across the cemetery in the opposite direction. Then she shakes her head in exasperation, says something to her husband and they get into their car. Calmly, without any theatrics, Magnus Hellevik backs his metallic blue Volvo out and drives away from the church.

The last thing Karen sees before she gets into her own car is Sigrid's slight figure disappearing behind a tangle of yew trees.

49

The rattling of mussels pouring out of the bucket into the metal sink makes Rufus beat a swift retreat from the kitchen to the living room sofa, but he'll be back. Slowly, like a surgeon before a crucial operation, she pulls on latex gloves and studies the shiny black shells. Then she picks up the shucking knife and gets to work. Eleven-odd pounds of mussels need to be cleaned of dirt and beards; it's going to take a while, but her guests won't be arriving for another couple of hours. It's going to be eight or nine people: Kore and Eirik and Marike, of course; Aylin had been unsure if they would be able to find a babysitter at first, but had then let her know both she and Bo were coming. Too bad, Karen had thought to herself. Bo will definitely not be best pleased when he realises he's spending the evening with a gaggle of women and two gay men. Out of concern for Aylin and the general atmosphere, rather than Bo's enjoyment, she'd therefore also invited her cousin Torbjörn and his wife Veronica. That is bound to lift Bo's spirits considerably. As a prominent lawyer with nascent political ambitions, he already has an extensive social network, but he and Veronica belong to the same party and Bo has big plans. It's for Aylin, she tells herself.

If she wants to see her friend, she simply has to invite her husband, too, and make sure he's happy. So long as Marike keeps her mouth shut, everything's going to be fine. According to her, Aylin's husband's a 'bloody prick' with a 'pathological need for control'.

'I'll bet you anything he beats her. Why is she always wearing long sleeves?' she'd said last summer.

Karen had actually asked. Stopped by their house when she was sure Bo wouldn't be there. And after two cups of coffee, she had finally voiced her concerns and had been rewarded with a hearty laugh. Granted, Bo had his failings, but he didn't hit her. Of course not.

The memory still stings.

Her phone dings on the kitchen table; Karen dries her hands. It's a text from Astrid:

Too tired to come this evening. Had a sleepless night and have a lot to deal with. But thank you for inviting me and happy birthday!

Her spontaneous decision to invite her colleague had been driven in equal parts by surprise and sympathy. Little Miss Goody-Goody and her neat and tidy IT husband are getting divorced and the reason is infidelity. Astrid had found out by chance, she'd told her. A classic trope, the accidentally opened letter addressed to her husband, a glance at the bank statement it contained and the sudden realisation that made the world stop and her body to turn to ice. Two restaurant meals and a hotel night. In Paris.

Astrid had been presented with incontrovertible proof Ingemar hadn't gone to London with his friends for a Premier League game that weekend.

He'd confessed immediately. The previous football trip had been a lie, too, but the ones before that had all been genuine. He'd emphasised that last point with grave sincerity, as though that would absolve him somehow.

'But is it serious between him and this other woman?' Karen had asked, wishing instantly that she hadn't.

'You think it matters? Am I supposed to wait until he's done sowing his wild oats and comes crawling back to home and hearth?'

No, Karen hadn't thought so, though over the years the concept of eternal fidelity has come to seem increasingly untenable to her. Is it really so impossible to forgive and forget? One little slip is hardly the worst thing that can happen to a family. A lorry that suddenly veers out of its lane, on the other hand, certainly can be.

Out loud, she'd said:

'No, of course not. How long have you known?'

'Since Tuesday night. The plan was to have Ingemar's mother take the children this weekend so we could talk, but I don't want to. I just booked a room at Rival. I just wish I had a bottle of booze with me so I could stay in my room, but I guess I'm going to have to go down to the hotel bar. Actually, I think I'm going to pull someone to get even.'

For a moment, Karen had considered fetching the whiskey bottle from Jounas's office and giving it to Astrid, but then she'd decided against it. Sitting alone in a hotel room was probably the last thing she needed. Not that the hotel bar at Rival was much better, but at least it was less lonely; picking someone up there certainly wouldn't be much of a challenge.

And then it had just slipped out:

'You know, if you can bear to put off the pulling, I'd love to have you over to mine instead.'

Astrid hadn't said yes or no to the invitation. She might be going up to her sister's in Ravenby, even though she was a pain; Karen had told her to feel free to come over if she felt like it.

She's probably right not to come, Karen muses, carefully tapping an open mussel with the knife. She probably has more important things to deal with today; thinking about how to tell the children, for instance. And Ingemar's parents on Noorö, who according to Astrid are very sternly religious. Apparently, I wasn't completely wide of the mark there, Karen had thought, though their orthodox views of the sanctity of marriage had clearly skipped a generation in the Nielsen family.

She straightens up and looks out the kitchen window. The morning's drizzle has stopped; an earful of waxwings has seized the chance to invade the rowan tree. In about an hour, every last red berry will be gone, but the sight is worth a winter without rowanberry jelly. Motionless, she studies their silky backs. Then the stillness is shattered by a predatory chatter coming from Rufus, who has jumped up on the kitchen counter and is now longingly eyeing the birds.

'Oh no, sweetheart. Have a mussel instead.'

Together, they watch the waxwings feast for a while, then Rufus gets bored and jumps down and Karen resumes cleaning mussels. Lulled by the rhythmic sounds of tapping and scraping, her mind wanders once more. They're going to have to eat in the kitchen, even though fitting nine people around the table will be a challenge. Granted, the veranda is roofed and the temperature has inched up a few degrees, but it's still too cold to eat outside. This is why I should have converted the boathouse, like everyone else, Karen tells herself. Maybe I should bite the bullet, after all. Get to it next spring so it's done by the summer.

Her reverie is interrupted by three sharp honks of a car horn.

Then the waxwings take flight and Marike's car bounces in through the gate and pulls up next to her own in the driveway. Karen opens the front door without taking off her latex gloves and studies Marike's ample behind as she reaches into the back seat to pull out carrier bags and a flower bouquet. Then she turns around with a big smile and starts belting out the Danish birthday song.

Karen listens patiently to the rather tone-deaf performance, then accepts the yellow roses and a hug.

'Thank you, that's lovely. Just one verse today? No, no, that's plenty!' she adds quickly.

'Ungrateful wretch. Hi, love!'

The last part is addressed to the cat, who has followed Karen onto the porch and is now rubbing himself against Marike's wellies. Then she picks up the heavy bags she's brought and pushes past Karen into the kitchen.

'Straight from the oven,' she announces and pulls out three large sourdough loaves. 'Or at least baked this morning, according to the guy at Bakker. And check this out, also straight from the oven.'

Marike has carefully placed the other bag on the table and now extracts from it a large ceramic plate in shades of blue and green. The colours blend into each other, seemingly in multiple layers; the thick glaze creates a three-dimensional depth that gives the illusion of peering down into a shallow sea cove.

Karen is speechless. Without a word, she puts her arms around Marike and hugs her for a long time.

'All right, that's enough now. Do you have any wine?'

310

50

An hour and a half later, Karen Eiken Hornby's standing in her boathouse, taking in the transformation. A word in passing about boathouses converted into extra living space had been enough to spur Marike into action. A phone call to Kore and Eirik, who were just about to get in the car, but who didn't mind going by the studio. A quick search through the house and the storage shed, while Karen fried onions, garlic and carrots, poured in wine and cream and finally let a large chunk of sheep's cheese melt into the mixture. And while she was busy cutting up apples and sautéing them in butter and sugar, taking the puff pastry out of the fridge and covering an oven tray with baking paper, Marike had, with the assistance of Kore and Eirik who had now joined them, dragged down two old doors, four trestles and two sheets to the shore. By means of a box heater plugged into an extension cord snaking all the way from the grounded outlet in the guesthouse, across the gravel road and into the boathouse, they've managed to push the temperature up at least ten degrees.

The long table they've set up along one wall probably isn't stable enough to dance on, and the people sitting with their backs against the giant rowboat are going to have to watch out so they don't fall in the water. But the warm glow of every candle and lantern they could find hides the fishing spears, shovels, pitchforks, broken nets, yellow oilskins and even the rusty old iron bed in two parts her father once dragged home, but which his wife refused to allow into the main house.

Blankets have been placed on garden chairs, a few of Karen's kitchen chairs and a bench they unearthed in the shed. Two white sheets cover the table and someone – Karen assumes Eirik – has crafted a centrepiece out of chicken wire, juniper and whatever rowanberries the waxwings hadn't managed to gobble down, which runs the length of the table between plates and glasses.

'Happy birthday,' Kore says with a smile when he sees her surprise. 'Being friends with a couple of resourceful gays and a manic Danish lady doesn't seem so bad now, does it?'

A mood of contentment permeates the boathouse. This is a night I should make sure to remember, Karen resolves, studying each person around the table in turn. Kore's slumped next to her, talking to Marike; they look like they've been gossiping about something that has made them both burst out laughing. Maybe Kore let slip some salacious detail from yesterday's recording session at KGB Productions, which he co-owns together with two Swedish blokes, and to which artists from all over Europe make pilgrimage to record their music, for reasons that have always been obscure to Karen. At least there's no immediate danger of Marike picking a fight with Bo while she's talking to Kore.

Bo and Torbjörn have, has predicted, sought out each other's unchallenging company; her cousin is studying something Bo seems to be drawing with his fork on the tablecloth. Torbjörn nods attentively and reaches for one of the wine bottles to top up their glasses. At the other end of the table, Eirik is looking serious, deep in discussion with Aylin, who looks troubled and is absentmindedly picking apart a piece of bread. Maybe the solemn look on her face is caused by the fact that she's the only one who's sober – of course Aylin's the designated driver. Or maybe it's because she's married to a prick. At least Bo seems to have left his fiery temper at home tonight, and so far he's refrained from making demeaning comments about his wife.

In a little bit, she's going to make coffee and reheat the apple pie.

'Forget it, you're not lifting a finger,' Kore says and pulls her back down onto her chair.

Instead, Karen turns to Veronica, who has been watching the others in silence. She too has clearly been assigned driving duty and is sipping her wines slowly. They're unlikely to get caught; the fastest way home for Torbjörn and Veronica is the narrow road across the Langevik Ridge, on which no one has seen a police car in the past thirty years, but Veronica is on the parliamentary committee for public health and can ill afford to risk it. Now she meets Karen's eyes and raises her glass.

'Cheers, Karen, just one year until the big day! Time really does fly. I'm dreading it already, and I have a few years to go yet.'

'Well, this time next year, all that'll be left for me to do is to drag myself down to the watering hole to die,' Karen says with a wry smile and takes two gulps of wine. 'How are things in parliament, any progress on the new care guarantee?'

She immediately regrets asking. The Progress Party's election promise to provide care for everyone over eighty, free dental care for everyone under eighteen and rehab and guaranteed

313

accommodation for anyone willing to sign a so-called drug-free contract, did give them the votes they need to enter a power-sharing agreement with the Liberals, but making good on them has proven difficult. Two years after the election, the papers are still full of stories of old people being refused a place in a nursing home and the number of addicts willing to submit to the conditions stipulated for rehab has been embarrassingly low. To make matters worse, the morning news claims things are getting worse rather than better.

Veronica Brenner replies like the politician she is.

'Thank you for asking, I think parents in this country appreciate being protected from extortionate dentist bills for their teenagers,' she says with a smile.

Probably, Karen concludes. The newspapers have reported that dentists have become increasingly likely to recommend braces since the law changed. Soon, every last snaggle tooth will have been eradicated in Doggerland. It's a shame, though, that neither of the two more worthwhile reforms has yielded much in the way of results.

Out loud, Karen says:

'Of course, and I suppose these things always take time.'

'Speaking of time,' Veronica replies, 'how's the murder investigation coming? Are you making any progress at all?'

Without waiting for a reply, she continues.

'I heard Jounas Smeed's going back to work on Monday. That must be a relief for you?'

'Where did you hear that?'

For a second, Veronica Brenner looks puzzled.

'Well . . .' she says slowly, as though considering whether any part of her answer might be damaging.

'I think Annika Haugen must've mentioned it,' she says, 'Viggo's wife. She and I have been friends since we were in the party's youth organisation, as you know. Yes, I must've heard from her that Jounas was going to be back in charge, so to speak.'

'Yes, Jounas is coming back on Monday,' Karen tells her. 'But naturally he won't be involved in the investigation of the murder of his ex-wife. The team and I will carry on like before.'

Veronica chuckles.

'Well, maybe not like before, I hope. Isn't it high time you found out who killed poor Susanne?'

'Did you know her?'

'I wouldn't say that, but we'd run into each other in various situations while she was married to Jounas.'

'How about in recent years, did you see her at all after they got divorced?'

Veronica looks surprised.

'No . . .' she replies, as though it were a strange question to ask. 'No, I don't think I ever did. I saw her out and about, of course, and maybe we exchanged a few words, at least at first, right after the divorce, but not in recent years. Though I always said hi,' she adds.

How gracious of you, Karen simmers. She's never been close with her only cousin on her mother's side, even though she and Torbjörn have always lived relatively near one another. Growing up, they'd see each other at family get-togethers, wedding and funerals and such, but no more than that.

As an adult, she's made a few sporadic attempts at bridging the divide; popped by for a cuppa and invited him and Veronica over a couple of times. And she has really done her best to ignore his arrogant view of the world and his apparently insatiable desire to make even more money. Because there's something about her bluntly straightforward cousin she likes, despite it all. Maybe it's that he never tries to act like something he's not. Torbjörn admits to his prejudices and his greed. And unlike his wife, he's not particularly interested in social climbing. Nor does he hold a grudge; six months had followed after Karen helped the newly arrived Marike to buy her clay plot at a decent price, but since then, he's never brought it up or acted surly.

Veronica is a different sort. Unlike her husband, Veronica Brenner makes an effort to veil her insults and always delivers them with a small smile. She's never said a word about the fact that they could have made twice as much off the sale of the clay plot if it hadn't been for Karen, but even though they've lived next door to Marike Estrup for almost seven years now, she still calls the five feet eleven, internationally renowned artist Marita Estrup, Marike Ernstrup or, simply – when talking to Karen – 'your Danish friend'.

Maybe there's something about Karen's facial expression that makes Veronica continue.

'I obviously would have said hello to Susanne last Saturday, too, but I don't think she saw me. And then . . . well . . .'

'Pardon?' Karen says and puts her wineglass down. 'You saw Susanne?'

'Yes, I actually saw her the day before she was murdered,' Veronica replies. 'I thought about that when I heard what happened, that it was the last time, I mean. Frightening, actually, that you never know when you're going to be seeing someone for the last time.'

'Exactly when and where was this?'

A disapproving wrinkle pulls Veronica's eyebrows into a frown at Karen's demanding tone, but she replies without objection.

'In the car park by the ferry terminal, on Saturday morning. Alice had come over on the early morning ferry from Esbjerg and wanted to be picked up. She's studying in Copenhagen, as you know, but she wanted to come home for Oistra. And Mum obliged, of course, even though it was seven in the morning and a lie-in would have been a treat for someone who works sixty-hour weeks.'

Veronica says that last part loudly and shoots a significant look at her husband, who keeps talking to Bo, seemingly oblivious.

'Do you know if she was meeting someone or if she'd come back on the same ferry?'

She asks, even though she's fairly sure she knows the answer. True, Susanne had called in sick to work and could very well have used that as cover to travel somewhere, but her name hadn't been on any of the passenger lists they'd checked.

'No, I didn't give it any thought,' Veronica replies. 'I only glimpsed her head above the car and realised she must've been parked just a few bays over. But she wouldn't have used the unattended car park if she'd been over to Denmark. As a police officer, you must know people who make that mistake can expect to be missing some hubcaps when they get back.'

Karen decides he's probably right. Since the parking garage by the terminal was built, the free car park on the eastern side of the pier is mostly used for pick-ups and drop-offs and by harbour workers. But if Susanne hadn't arrived on the ferry, she must have been there to meet someone. Likely the same person who called her at 7.15 a.m., to let her know they'd arrived.

'And you didn't see if there was anyone with her?'

Veronica hesitates.

'I'm not sure. I mean, I didn't see anyone else, but I remember thinking it sounded like she was talking to someone.'

51

The sound of the empty bottles landing in the recycling station's green igloo hurts her ears; Karen winces when the last wine bottle crashes into the pile of glass. She went easy on the drink last night, but the party did go on till morning. In fact, they weren't in bed until half past three, and Eirik, an unbearable morning person, had by means of breakfast and the smell of fresh coffee managed to get everyone up by half nine.

She'd rejected the others' offers to help clean up; Marike, Eirik and Kore's had done more than enough last night, and none of them looked in a shape to tidy. Besides, Karen was looking forward to having her house to herself and catching another few hours of sleep.

'Go home,' she'd told her hungover friends, studying them across the breakfast table. 'Order pizza and spend the day on the sofa; I'll do the dishes tonight.'

But when the last car door had slammed shut, she'd returned to the kitchen instead and set to work, feeling surprisingly energetic. She'd finished the washing-up in half an hour flat and tidying up the boathouse had taken about as long again. She'd left the tables and garden chairs, but dragged the kitchen chairs back up to the house. After collecting Kore and Eirik's sheets from the guesthouse and throwing them in the washing machine, she'd gathered up all the empty bottles and a couple of weeks' worth of old newspapers, shoved it all into her car and driven up to the recycling point at the end of the road. That's what they still called it in the village: the end of the road. To everyone else, it was the start of Langevik Road.

Now she folds up the last paper carrier bag, pushes it into the paper recycling receptacle and gets back into the car. Tiredness is creeping up on her again and she feels warm and sticky after lugging chairs and bottles around. And this blasted drizzle! She looks up at the leaden sky. After a brief reprieve yesterday, the rain had picked up again while they were in the boathouse; they'd had to dash back and forth to the main house to fetch coffee and more wine and go to the bathroom crouched under a tarp.

A pint at the Hare and Crow would be just the ticket. She can probably get her hands on an evening paper at the bar, too; this time of year, the old men usually start arriving around noon with *Kvellsposten* under their arms. Outside, things are bleak and grim, but inside, there's the two things that top Karen's list at the moment: light and company. Arild Rasmussen won't be the only publican rubbing his hands in glee at the sound of marks and shillings rustling and jingling into tills over the next few months as the card readers beep and more orders are shouted.

Karen checks her watch – almost half one. She turns the key in the ignition, checks the mirror and turns the car around.

She slows down after a while, leaning across the passenger seat for a better look. A sudden feeling of déjà vu comes over her and for a moment, she's confused by what she's seeing. But this time, the hunched-over figure climbing the grassy slope isn't Susanne Smeed. There's someone else in her house. Someone who's hard at work dragging things out and dumping them in a pile in the garden.

Karen pulls over. She was present when Karl called Susanne's daughter to inform her that the crime scene investigation had been concluded and the police no longer needed access to the house. But for some reason, she hadn't thought Sigrid would come out here. She watches the slender girl sit down on the front steps, seemingly unable to continue her hauling. There doesn't seem to be anyone with her; Karen waits a few more minutes before putting her hand on the gear stick. Then she removes it again; something about the desolate figure makes it impossible to drive away. Cursing inwardly, she pulls the key out of the ignition and opens the car door.

Sigrid is resting her head on her arms and doesn't notice her visitor until Karen is only feet away. She looks up and makes as if to stand, but immediately slumps back down.

'Hi, Sigrid, it's just me, Karen.'

Sigrid nods, but says nothing. Her face is ashen and her eyes glassy. Grief, Karen thinks. That's what it looks like. She briskly walks up and sits down next to the lonely girl. Sigrid slowly turns to face her, then she coughs and turns away again. The racking sound makes it clear to Karen that the state of Sigrid's eyes is not entirely caused by crying. Sigrid has a fever.

'Sweetheart, are you OK?'

At least she had the good sense to put on a raincoat, Karen notes, studying Sigrid's long wet hair that's sticking to her forehead and cheeks. She gently pushes it back and puts a hand on Sigrid's forehead.

'Sigrid, you're ill. You can't sit out here.'

With a firm arm around Sigrid's thin torso, she pulls her up and leads her in through the open door. Instead of taking her to the kitchen, she continues into the living room and deposits Sigrid on the sofa. There's going to be ugly stains, she realises, seeing the trickles of water meandering down Sigrid's raincoat and being absorbed by the pale upholstery.

'How long have you had a fever?'

'Just today, I think.'

Her voice is weak and carries no trace of the defiance she exhibited when Karl and Karen met her in her flat in Gaarda.

'Have you taken anything for it?'

Sigrid coughs and shakes her head.

'Wait here.'

Karen climbs the stairs to the first floor in four strides. Hopefully, Susanne has something other than sleeping pills in her bathroom cabinet.

Within moments, she watches Sigrid obediently putting a Tylenol in her mouth and accepting the glass of water Karen holds out to her. She winces as she swallows the pill.

'Sore throat?'

Sigrid nods.

'How long have you been here?'

'Since yesterday. I was going to go through . . . I have to take care of . . .'

Her voice breaks and she can't finish the sentence. Instead, she lies down on her side with her head on the armrest and her feet on the floor, her wellies still on. Karen watches the damp from her hair soak into a pink cushion.

Karen takes a seat in one of the armchairs across from the sofa and studies the pitiful figure. Sigrid must have walked here from the funeral service; this was where she was going when she left Jounas in the car park and cut across the cemetery. Karen quickly runs down her list of options. She can't just leave Sigrid here, she's much too ill to be alone. But she absolutely doesn't want to stay in Susanne's house, looking after her troublesome brat. Even disregarding how creepy it would feel, it would likely be an ethical misstep for the lead investigator to spend the night in the victim's house, whether or not the technical investigation has been completed. Calling Jounas and asking him to come look after his daughter is unappealing for a couple of reasons: Sigrid doesn't seem to want anything to do with her father and Karen can't bear the thought of having to speak with him. She doesn't have the boyfriend, Samuel Nesbö's, phone number, if they're even still involved, and she doesn't know any other friends of Sigrid's. She makes equally short work of dismissing every possible excuse she can think of: Sigrid will probably be fine on her own so long as I help her get into bed; I can always pop by tomorrow to look in on her; Yes, she's ill, but hardly dying; If I hadn't happened to drive by, she would've been on her own anyway.

Why did I bloody pull over?

Then she gets up.

'Sigrid, you can't stay here, you're going to have to come back to mine.'

The response, whatever it was supposed to be, is drowned out by a coughing fit.

'Can you get up and walk with me to my car? It's up on the road.'

To her surprise, Sigrid slowly pushes up into sitting position and nods.

'I saw your bag in the hallway, is there anything else you'd like to bring?'

Sigrid mutely shakes her head.

The house keys are on the hallway table and after a quick check to make sure the hob and the coffee maker are switched off, Karen turns the lights out and locks the front door behind them. She glances over at the front yard. A pile of clothes lies discarded on the muddy lawn, alongside cushions, curtains and floral bed-sheets. Next to the pile is a large cardboard moving box, sodden with rain. Karen recognises some of Susanne's ornaments; a lamp base and a handful of picture frames stick out of the box, which is on the verge of collapse. She briefly considers looking for a tarp to cover everything with; nosy neighbours might be tempted to look through the pile, but when another coughing fit makes Sigrid double over, she dismisses the idea. The most important thing now is to get the girl dry and tucked into bed.

Karen is standing in the doorway to her guest room, watching the sleeping girl. Her hair is still damp; her attempts to blow-dry it while Sigrid reluctantly drank some warm rosehip soup were only partially successful. There was no time to change the sheets, Sigrid is sleeping in Marike's sheets, at least for one night. The thermometer had read 39.8, after nothing but a few mouthfuls of rosehip soup but with paracetamol in her system. Karen's going to have to check again in a few hours, but right now there's probably nothing more she can do. She closes the door to the little bedroom as quietly as she can, then changes her mind and opens it a crack before going downstairs.

52

The weather has alternated between drizzle and downpour for two weeks now. The ground is sodden and the smaller roads are beginning to take on an increasingly brown shade as mud slowly spreads from flooding ditches. People have wrapped themselves in windproof cocoons of unfashionable but practical jackets and coats.

A months-long battle against the elements is commencing under swaying streetlamps, in deserted playgrounds and in silent, empty parks. Strong winds and sleet are going whip the land, from the mountain ridges of Noorö to the vast heathlands of Frisel. Storms will rise and subside, ripping up laboriously built fences and walls which will then be repaired without protest by men with stiff, frozen hands. Trees will snap, ships will be forced into ports and fishermen will wait for their next chance to head out with a mix of impatience and dread.

Women will be torn between relief at the ships being forced to lie at anchor and financial concerns when no fish are caught. Heavy shopping bags will be carried against the wind with inward cursing at rising prices and mortgages payments and muttered prayers for the money to last until the next payday.

But something else will emerge from the darkness, too. Black windows in the blocks of flats will be lit by electric wreaths, stars and half-moons. Balcony railings will be wrapped with pine branches and fairy lights and tea-light holders will be dug out of attics and taken off shop shelves, smoke detectors will get new batteries, wood-fired stoves will creak in the heat and birch wood will crackle on the hearths.

Karen set her alarm for six but wakes up thirty minutes before it goes off. The sound of footsteps has penetrated the deep layers of her sleep, finally piercing her awareness with a pinprick of fear. Moments later, there's the sound of a rumbling cough from the next room and her memory kicks into gear. Sigrid. Karen hurries over to the guestroom, stops in the doorway and looks at Sigrid, who's sitting on the edge of the bed.

'Good morning. How are you feeling?'

'What am I doing here? Is this your house?'

'Yes, you're in my house in Langevik, just about a mile from your mum's. You don't remember me bringing you here yesterday?'

Sigrid shakes her head and winces with pain.

'You were very sick. *Are* very sick,' Karen adds and frowns when another coughing fit racks the slight body in front of her.

'I have a vague memory of being in a car,' Sigrid croaks once the coughing subsides. 'And rosehip soup; I hate rosehip soup.'

'All right, no more rosehip soup.'

'Do you have any painkillers? My head hurts like hell.'

'It's probably the fever. Have you checked your temperature this morning?'

Another headshake, gentler this time. Karen nods toward the bedside table, where the thermometer's waiting.

'Go ahead; I'll get you something to drink.'

Karen leaves Sigrid safely tucked into bed and climbs into her car. In the past hour, Sigrid's temperature has fallen to 39.2 and will be lowered further by the Tylenol she took, along with a cup of herbal tea and a sandwich she left untouched.

'Call anytime you want,' Karen had told her, jotting her mobile number down on a piece of paper she placed next to the teacup. 'Your backpack's here, next to the bed. Grab whatever you want in the kitchen, but the most important thing is that you stay in bed and rest.

Sigrid had dozed off before she'd finished the sentence.

At exactly 7.20 a.m., Karen steps out of the lift on the third floor of the Dunker police station; considerably earlier than she would usually get to work. It feels imperative to be early this particular morning. She wants to be able to look up at her boss, who will most likely – true to form – stroll in around nine, with an air of faint surprise. Even though she usually comes in around nine, too. Jounas Smeed is coming back to work after a week's suspension.

Two minutes later, she lets out a curse and throws her handbag down on her desk.

53

He's already at his desk. Through the glass door, Karen can see he's made himself coffee and is now studying something on his computer screen with a look of deep concentration. By all appearances, Jounas Smeed has been at work for some time already and doesn't seem to have noticed her arrival. With more inward cursing, she hangs her coat up on the hook behind her desk.

Just do it, she tells herself. He's not going to go away, much as you might wish he would. With a sigh, she walks over to her boss's office. She pauses for a few seconds outside the door. Three quick raps on the doorframe, another few seconds of waiting before Jounas Smeed, with studied slowness turns to her and only then takes his eyes off the screen.

He gives her the same slightly surprised look she'd planned to give him and then nods vaguely. Karen reads it as an invitation to open the door and come in.

'Morning, Eiken, have a seat.'

She does as she's told.

'So, welcome back,' she says.

He nods at his screen without replying. Then he says:

'Have you checked PIR?'

'You mean this morning? No, I only just got here.'

'The station sergeant called me around five this morning. It's been a busy night.'

Even though Karen can hear how unprofessional she sounds, her first reaction is to gripe about the station sergeant contacting Smeed instead of her:

'Called you? Why? You weren't officially back on the job until this morning.'

Smeed chuckles and spreads his hands.

'All right, down, girl. I guess he'd heard I was coming back and figured it made more sense to contact me directly. Think of it as a lie-in.'

Lie-in, she thinks bitterly. I've been up since half five, looking after your sick daughter; I'd like to see if she'd let you do the same. That thought cheers her up a little.

'What happened?' she asks.

'Two young women have been brutally assaulted and raped in Moerbeck: one on Saturday night in a shrubbery lining the pedestrian path from the town centre bus stop and the other in a bike room in the basement of Karpvägen 122 last night.'

'Bloody hell. But still, it's a bit odd for the station sergeant to wake you up over two cases of rape.'

As she says it, Karen realises why the head of the CID was contacted. Jounas Smeed reads her face and nods in confirmation.

'Murder,' he corrects her. 'The girl on Karpvägen died in the ambulance from her injuries.'

He leans back and picks up a mug adorned with the Thingwalla Football Club logo.

'Nice,' he says after taking a sip. 'I assume there's an invoice on its way that you'd like me to pay.'

'I felt it was a good investment. If you have a different assessment, I can always take the machine home and pay for it myself.'

'Speaking of assessments,' Jounas says, without comment-ing on her offer, 'we will, as I'm sure you understand, have to rethink the allocation of our resources in the light of what's hap-pened up in Moerbeck. I've already put together the team I want on this case and called them in. Both Cornelis Loots and Astrid Nielsen will be joining me; it's always good to have a woman detective in cases like these. Anyway, I'm sure you understand this will have a significant impact on your investigation; we're just going to have to share the resources.'

So you're not taking Karl, Karen thinks, hiding her surprise. After herself and Evald Johannisen, Karl is their most experienced detective. I suppose you don't want anyone challenging your opin-ions. Especially now that Johannisen's not here to lick your boots.

Out loud, she says:

'I'm glad I get to keep Karl. And how do you see this working? My investigation has only just got started.'

'Well, you've had a week. No offence, but your results haven't exactly been stellar so far, despite every available resource being at your disposal. And, as I said, I'm sure you understand we have to review our priorities. Especially with Evald gone, though I spoke with him and he will, I'm happy to say, be back soon, at which point we'll reassess again.'

If you stick me with Johannisen, I quit.

'All right,' she says quickly. 'But what does Haugen say about this? I'm reporting directly to him and Vegen, not you.'

'I guess you'll have to ask him. He was going to call you this morning, or so he said when I spoke to him a while ago.'

The call from Viggo Haugen comes eleven minutes later. The chief of police says nothing unexpected, only what Karen has

330

already realised and, if she's being honest, thinks is right. They need to reallocate their resources and this time Prosecutor Dineke Vegen and Viggo Haugen are in complete agreement. They need to focus on Moerbeck.

'Besides, you said yourself it looks like those burglaries are connected to the murder of Susanne Smeed,' Viggo Haugen adds, probably unaware of the relief in his voice.

The media's criticism of the police and their failure to make progress in the Susanne Smeed case had intensified after Haugen's shambolic press conference. The fact that all information is being channelled through the Head of Media has done nothing to soothe tempers and Haugen has been hung out to dry in several news outlets. Now everyone's attention will be redirected, and this time, Jounas Smeed will be in charge of the investigation. Viggo Haugen can relax.

'I said there *might* be a connection,' Karen says, 'But it's certainly not a given. And even if that were the case, that doesn't mean the perpetrator has been identified, much less arrested.'

'True, but now that we know the likely course of events, you're going to have to focus on that lead. I'm sure he'll be in custody soon enough. It goes without saying you still have access to any extra resources you might need once you're ready to make an arrest. Or if you identify an alternative perpetrator, I guess. Either way, if there's a break in the case, you can request assistance. For now, we have to reprioritise,' Haugen says, stressing each syllable.

Karen does understand that. They're short-staffed and prioritising the rapes is the right call, especially since it's likely the rapist will strike again. Truth be told, she would give a lot to be able to drop anything that has to do with the Smeeds, burglaries and stolen motorcycles, and instead dedicate all her time to nailing the bastard terrorising Moerbeck.

Both she and Karl attend the first meetings about the rapes. Everyone at the CID is supposed to stay abreast of all major investigations at all times. And even though there's nothing to indicate it at this early stage, connections between cases can never be ruled out, nor can the possibility that some of the people who will be interviewed in connection with one case might have information about another. The internal information flow in criminal circles is considerably more comprehensive than the one in PIR, and faster. The police have been able to use that to their advantage more than once.

The news has them all feeling shaken. The room is dead silent while Kneought Brodal runs through the details. A broken bottle was used in both cases; the victims' faces and chests were slashed and then the perpetrator inserted the broken bottles into their vaginas. The bloody remains of a 350 ml bottle of Groth's Old Stone Selection was found at the scene where a passing dog owner came across Sabrine Broe, wandering about aimlessly at four in the morning, bleeding and terrified. She was then admitted to Thysted Hospital, traumatised but alive.

Loa Marklund was not as lucky. At half past seven on Sunday morning, a neighbour of hers at Karpvägen 122 and his eight-year-old son, both carrying fishing rods, had taken the lift down to the basement. They were going to fetch their bikes for one last fishing trip to Lake Svartsjön before the end of the season. When the shocked father called emergency services, it had, according to the coroner, been over six hours since someone shoved a broken bottle of Budweiser into

Loa's vagina and twisted it back and forth. The girl had still been alive when the ambulance arrived, despite catastrophic blood loss. By the time they reached Thysted Hospital, she had passed away.

'Semen?' someone asks quietly; Kneought Brodal shakes his head.

'The question is if there was any intercourse at all. Signs indicate the perpetrator was content with letting the bottles do the job for him. A disturbed son of a bitch. Impotent, too, if you ask me.'

Karen studies the members of her former team while the horrifying details of the Moerbeck assaults sink in. Just like when they were first shown the pictures of Susanne, a paralysing silence envelops the room. Then the mood changes, as though some collective spirit were slowly getting to its feet, shaking itself and letting out a deep growl. Their hunting instinct has been awakened again, but this time it's a different victim and their attention is focused on a different game. Hopefully, this case will be solved faster than hers.

54

Karen grabs the mouse and pauses the playback. Then she leans back in her chair and closes her eyes. Behind her eyelids, the pictures keep flashing by; a seemingly endless stream of vehicles jouncing on board in one frame and rolling off in the other.

The car ferry from Noorö to Thorsvik runs every ten minutes between 6 a.m. and 11.50 p.m. and every twenty minutes after midnight. The puffing yellow boat drags itself back and forth across the sound, whether someone's on it or not. A growing number of people eager to lower taxes have repeatedly suggested an on-demand solution, at least at night, but have been met with strident protests and so far, the Noorö locals have been able to ward off any threat of cutbacks.

Although the number of night-time passengers hardly justifies the frequent timetable, the stream of cars during other times of day is relatively constant. Big cars, small cars, white cars, dark cars; the footage is black and white and offers only an endless greyscale. Volvo dominates along with BMW, Ford and SUVs of all makes. Bus number 78 rides the ferry every thirty minutes and there are private vehicles, commercial vans, two tractors, trucks with the Ravenby abattoir logo, NoorOyl's personnel carriers from the northern harbour, filled with exhausted men and women coming off three-week shifts on one of the oil platforms, bicycles, mopeds, an ATV.

And the occasional motorcycle. Unfortunately, no Honda CRF 1000L Africa Twin. She has a printed picture of the model on her desk for reference.

Karen's eyes register everyone who drives onto the ferry in Noorö Harbour and, after a few seconds of fast-forwarding, disembarks in Thorsvik. There are two cameras on the ferry, pointed in opposite directions. Both angles are shown in parallel on the screen; she shifts her attention from one during loading to the other during unloading. But after two departures and one missed moped, she realises she's going to have to study each separately. A motorcycle is easily obscured by cars, lorries or the bus.

The break-in on Noorö had happened sometimes between half past seven in the morning on Tuesday 16 September and quarter to five on the afternoon of Friday 19 September. Three and a half days, hundreds of ferry departures when a young man on a stolen motorcycle might have been caught on film by one of the onboard CCTV cameras.

She opens her eyes and glances to her right. Karl Björken, who's at the desk next to hers, has just put his phone down and now clicks out the tip of a ballpoint pen and crosses something off a piece of paper with a look of dejection. Another local station with nothing to report, it seems.

'Want to swap?' she says. 'I can't bear to look at any more of this.'

'What are you whingeing about?' Björken says with a wry smile. 'It can't be much more than what, a hundred departures a day?'

'A hundred and twenty-two,' she replies dully.

'How far in are you?'

'I just checked the 9.40 a.m. on 18 September. No Africa Twin on that one either. Not one single goddamn motorcycle since a Kawasaki drove on board at twenty past seven. How are you getting on?'

'What do you think? If by some miracle I were to find anything, I wouldn't keep it to myself. But I was actually thinking of heading home soon; Arne and Frode both have a temperature and Sara's refusing to sleep in her own bed. Ingrid is threatening me with divorce if I'm not home by six. *And I'm* not *taking the children*,' Karl says, imitating his wife.

'Well, then you'd better hurry,' Karen says with a smile. 'Aren't you supposed to be going on paternity leave soon, by the way?'

'From the first of November. And no, it has nothing to do with the marten hunting season.'

So Karl's going on leave in less than a month's time. Right, she decides, another reason Smeed didn't want him on his team.

'I suppose we'd better solve this before then,' Karl says and turns his computer off. 'Otherwise, you're likely to be stuck with Johannisen. Which, on the bright side, would probably lead to him having an actual heart attack.'

'Or me. I just want to get through the rest of the Wednesday departures, then I'm off, too,' she says and stretches.

Just as Karl Björken opens the front door to his semi-detached in Sande and is greeted by the sound of three crying children, Karen freezes in front of her screen and straightens up from her slumped position. She quickly rewinds the film a few seconds and watches the sequence again.

'So,' she says slowly. 'That's what you look like.'

55

Sigrid is sitting at the kitchen table when Karen comes home. On the table in front of her, the cat is licking a bowl that looks like it once contained yoghurt and muesli. I wonder in which cupboard she found that? Karen hasn't had muesli in years. Then images from Susanne Smeed's interrupted breakfast flash before her inner eye. She quickly shakes off her sudden unease.

'So, you're up,' she says. 'How are you feeling?'

Sigrid looks up with something that might be a smile. Karen is taken aback by the transformation; it's the first time she's seen Sigrid when she's not hissing like a cat or drooping with fever. She's still pale and her eyes are glossy, but her cheeks no longer have the rosiness of fever and she's put her hair up in a ponytail.

'Better, thank you. Is this OK?' she asks, nodding at the plate.

'You mean the yoghurt or Rufus? Don't worry,' she adds with a smile, 'he usually does whatever he wants whether I'm here or not.'

She puts the bag on the kitchen counter and watches Sigrid out of the corner of her eye as she gently puts Rufus down on the floor.

'I brought some Indian food from town. It's probably cold by now, but I was going to reheat it in the microwave. Are you full or do you have room for some proper food?'

Karen takes a plate from the drying rack and carefully lifts two aluminium containers out of the paper bag.

'I don't think I can. But thanks,' Sigrid adds.

She sits quietly for a while, watching as Karen dumps out a portion of curry masala on a plate and pops it into the microwave.

'I guess I should go home,' she says and starts getting up. 'Or at least head back to Mum's house.'

Karen pauses mid-movement, her hand on the timer dial.

'How come? You should stay until you're feeling better. Speaking of which, have you checked your temperature since this morning?'

'Half an hour ago. Thirty-eight point six.'

'Sigrid, I don't know what crap it is you've gone and contracted, but you clearly have some kind of respiratory infection. Exactly, see?' she adds and pauses while another rumbling coughing racks Sigrid's thin frame.

'What I'm saying is, you're very welcome to stay here until you're better. What about work, have you called them?'

'I texted them this morning.'

'And your boyfriend, Samuel?'

'My ex,' Sigrid corrects her.

'Right, so you're still apart. Fine, but then I don't know why you're in such a hurry to get out of here.'

There's a ding; Karen takes her plate out.

'Are you sure?' she says, with a nod toward the plate.

'I'm sure.'

She opens the pantry door and takes out a bottle.

'Well, I'm having a glass, but I'm definitely not giving you one.'

'I'm actually eighteen.'

'Great, then you can have a glass when you're feeling better. So you'll stay?'

This time, the smile on Sigrid's wan face is unmistakeable.

She's fallen asleep on the sofa with a blanket over her. She hadn't wanted to go to bed upstairs; she'd seemed to prefer to stay with Karen, who after having her dinner had settled into an armchair with a crossword puzzle. A faint rattling can be heard from the sofa and from time to time, Sigrid coughs in her sleep. Karen lowers the paper and studies her.

The same age, she thinks. Born the same year, though he was a few months younger. He would have been eighteen in December, too. Hanging out in bars, getting himself a fake ID to buy beer down the pub. He would probably have answered her questions tersely, too, trying to hide the smiles he didn't want to share. Her son. Mathis.

Maybe he would have run into Sigrid at some point when she and John took him to Doggerland on vacation. They could have met at one of the places in Dunker on a summer night; maybe he would've gone to the bar where she works. Listened to her band playing.

Stop it.

She turns back to her crossword.

But she can't stop the thoughts from coming. Maybe she and John would've moved here at some point when they were older, like they talked about sometimes. Though she doubts it.

She'd loved London, had her life there and only rarely yearned for the island, in short, sharp bouts of homesickness.

Then her whole body ached with what was missing. The sea. It had been so far away.

'We've got a view of the bloody Thames,' John had protested. He'd only said that once.

'Let's go to the coast,' he'd suggested another time when she was overcome with longing. 'We'll pack everything up and head over to my sister's in Margate. That's the proper ocean.'

'Margate. Come on, John.'

She'd never been able to explain. But it had always passed. She had liked London, had loved the city from when she first shared a flat in Clapham with Scott, Elina and Ulrich. Even though they'd had to seal the windows with hers and Elina's tights during the cold winter months. Had loved the pubs, department stores and parks. Had loved the London Met where she'd studied the horrors people inflict on one another. Had loved listening in court. Had loved John and then Mathis. Yes, she really had loved the city that had given her both a husband and a son. The city that had given her a life.

And yet, she'd left it without a second's pause one day in December almost eleven years ago.

Karen gives up and puts the crossword puzzle down. Is that why I want her to stay? she ponders, studying Sigrid on the sofa. Because her line continues where Mathis's ended? Because she helps me imagine a future for him? Because she helps me remember?

56

An alert has gone out via PIR. She sent it out herself through the internal reporting platform the moment she found the right film sequence from the Noorö ferry. The images of the young man from the 11.20 departure on 18 September were reasonably clear and the motorcycle's licence plate matched the stolen one. The problem was that the helmet had a visor that hid his face. For some reason, the bloke got off the motorcycle, walked over to the railing and leaned over it. But the shot was partially blocked by a van; despite scrutinising each frame several times, she'd been unable to confirm whether he was throwing something overboard or simply wanted to stretch his legs and breathe some fresh air. And he kept the helmet on the whole time.

Comparing his size to fixed points on the ferry, Karen had been able to determine that he was about five feet eight and looked gangly, borderline skinny, in his faded jeans and thin jacket. But that was too vague a description. Consequently, the motorcycle was the focus of the internal alert she'd sent out. Granted, there were other ones of the same model, but the colour was unusual. The problem there was that the colour didn't show in the black-and-white CCTV screenshots she'd posted. But maybe the picture of a yellow Honda Africa Twin she'd found online and posted in PIR alongside the alert would make one of her colleagues react. Or not.

*

'Sooner or later, the bloke's going to make a mistake and we'll nick him,' Karl says the following morning, blowing on his coffee while bending down to look at Karen's screen. 'Crikey, he looks young, how old do you reckon he is, sixteen, seventeen?'

'Yes, he really does look pretty young. Do you really think he could be the one who killed Susanne? If you're being really honest, Charlie boy?'

Karl frowns, his dark eyebrows curving. Partly because of the hated nickname, partly because just like Karen, he doubts it. There's something about the fury with which Susanne was murdered that doesn't tally with the burglar theory. The connection may seem incontrovertible to Haugen and at least perfectly plausible to the prosecutor. But he's far from convinced.

The call from a colleague at the Grunder station comes in just after lunch, within three minutes of Karen leaving an annoyed message on the station's answering machine, saying she wants to be contacted immediately. They've sent out messages to all local stations and all but three have got back to them about potential petty crimes that might be linked to the investigation. Her frustration at no one picking up in Grunder, where the station is manned around the clock, probably made her tone confirm the local officers' view of the 'bullies at headquarters'.

When the call comes, Karen leans back and listens with politely concealed impatience to Sergeant Grant Hogan's explanations about understaffing and toilet breaks, his inevitable griping about PIR and a few convoluted accounts of minor crimes committed in the north-east corner of Heimö during the summer months. Determined as she is not to widen the chasm between central and local police, Karen throws in an 'mm' at

342

the right places while thinking to herself that she should call to check on Sigrid. But a couple of minutes later, Grant Hogan says something that makes her prick up her ears and take her feet off the desk. She waves Karl over and puts her phone down on the desk between them.

'I'm going to put you on speaker now, Grant, Karl Björken will be listening in. Would you mind repeating that last part, please?'

They listen without interrupting; Karen signals to Karl not to try to rush Grant Hogan's circuitous retelling. And between all the irrelevant tangents, something emerges that makes Karl wonder whether Viggo Haugen isn't right for once.

A partially burnt-out house in Ramsviken in the Grunder police district, just two miles north of Langevik. It had happened two days before Oistra; the couple who owned the house had been vacationing in London. Grant Hogan goes on and on about 'theatre plays and shopping', 'newly retired', 'missing laptops and jewellery', 'remote location with wonderful views', 'rising house prices', 'the fire seems to have originated in the kitchen curtains', 'shocked when they got back', 'insurance will cover it' . . . and finally, 'no witnesses'.

Karl looks up and meets Karen's eyes as their colleague on the other end of the line takes a deep breath before continuing.

'I was actually about to call you. Not about the fire, but I was talking to the leader of one of the shooting teams. Yngve Lingvall's his name; he and I go way back. I actually hunt a bit myself, when work allows, of course. That's why he called me in the middle of a hunt, otherwise I don't think he would've bothered.'

'Called about what?' Karl impatiently drums his fingers against the desk but stops after a look from Karen.

'Well, yesterday, one of the guys on the shooting team discovered a wrecked motorcycle in a ravine two miles south of here. Apparently, the bloke's interested in bikes, so he wanted to collect it for his own use, but Yngve felt they should call us first. He's a good man, Yngve is. So, I drove out there and had a look and they were right. It's in the quarry by Kalvmotet, just a mile or two north-west of the station here in Grunder, as a matter of fact.'

'What colour is it?' Karl asks. 'I mean the motorcycle,' he adds, to make sure he doesn't have to hear about the colour of the Grunder police station.

'Yellow, I think, but it's a good way down and properly filthy. And, not that I know my way around motorcycles, but the bloke who found it claims it's a Honda, model Africa Twin. I just saw the alert in PIR and was about to call you, just had to nip to the bog first.'

Karen mimes for Karl to go get coffee and lets Grant Hogan prattle on for a while. After all, her colleague has demonstrated a certain degree of alertness, even if he did end up prioritising his morning bathroom visit. And now Grant's antennae are up. Wasn't there a fire in the Langevik case, too? At least that's what he heard from his son-in-law who's a volunteer firefighter. Signs of burglary, they were saying, too, though the details are apparently hush-hush ... No, he obviously understands why they can't say much. At the end of the day, the most important thing is obviously that they do everything they can to nail the bastard who killed Smeed's wife. Even if she happened to be his ex-wife. They attended the police academy at the same time.

'Smeed and me, I mean, not the wife,' Grant Hogan clarifies.

Karen ends the call with a feeling of resignation. She silently accepts the coffee Karl hands her. Even she has to accept that it's starting to look more like a connection than a coincidence. Common or garden burglaries, committed while the home owners were away. Had the same thing happened in Langevik? Had something that was supposed to be a regular break-in for some reason gone catastrophically wrong? A lone offender who focuses on laptops and jewellery, things that are easily slipped into a backpack. Karen was considering the possibility even before her conversation with Grant Hogan and is now obliged to reluctantly admit the theory does seem to have merit. She doesn't need to consult a map to see the pattern; the timings are right and the locations of the burglaries shows the perpetrator moving from Noorö down along Heimö's northern coast, via the ferry port in Thorsvik, during a week-long spree. It's not hard to imagine him continuing down into Langevik after getting rid of the motorcycle.

'We're going to have to contact the media and put a call out for information from anyone who might have picked up a hitchhiker on the southbound road out of Grunder,' she says. 'The bloke can't very well have walked the whole way. Because there's still nothing about stolen cars in the area, is there?'

'No, I just checked.'

'But why would he have singled out Susanne Smeed's house?'

'Well, why not?' Karl replies and blows on his coffee. 'Susanne's daughter did say she usually went abroad during Oistra. Maybe the burglar knew that for some reason and freaked out when it turned out she was home after all. I don't know what method he used to scout out his targets, but there's a million different ways.'

'But how could he think she was away? According to Harald Steen, there was smoke coming out of the chimney,' Karen counters.

'True, but when Steen saw the smoke, she was already dead. It might have been the killer who lit the stove, not Susanne.'

'And why would he do something so stupid? If he was looking to burn the house down, he would hardly have taken the roundabout route of firing up an old wood-burning stove. If that's what he was after, it would have been faster and easier to torch the curtains, like he did up in Thorsvik.'

Karl shrugs.

'Besides, Susanne's car was in the driveway. That, if anything, should have tipped him off about her being home, no?'

'Not necessarily,' Karl retorts. 'People often leave their cars at home when they go on vacation, if they can find someone to give them a ride to the airport or ferry. Besides, the car might have been the pivotal draw; he clearly needed a new mode of transportation. He might have broken into the house just to find the car keys.'

'Assuming the person who lived there would still be asleep. Bloody risky, if you ask me. He can't have had any idea how many people lived there.'

'Unless he scouted it out, like I said.'

She listens to the arguments, weighs them one by one and together. She's still far from convinced, but apparently Karl has decided to defend the simple solution Viggo Haugen and others are clinging to so desperately.

'Don't forget Susanne was still at the kitchen table,' she says. 'Are you telling me the guy broke in so quietly he managed to surprise her while she was having her morning coffee? That he crossed the yard without her seeing him through the window?'

'Or maybe he came up from the back. I reckon he was trying to avoid prying eyes; Harald Steen's windows face the driveway, after all.'

'True,' she admits. 'But still. I don't think anyone could miss a burglar breaking in while they're having coffee in the kitchen.'

'The radio was on. And loud, according to Sören Larsen.'

Karen shakes her head mutely and sips her coffee. She would certainly notice if someone broke into her house, even if both the radio and the TV were on.

Wouldn't she?

'Maybe she let him in willingly,' Karl says after a long pause.

'Why on earth would she do that?'

'I don't know, maybe he came up with a convincing story. Broadband repairman or whatever . . .'

'On the morning after Oistra? You can do better than that . . .'

'Or maybe he invented an emergency. It would hardly be the first time a thief used that old trick to get into someone's home.'

'Oh come off it, Charlie-boy, we're talking about Susanne Smeed. If anyone was going to close their door on a person in need, it would have been her.'

'Or maybe he just threatened his way in with some kind of weapon,' Karl presses on, ignoring both the nickname and Karen's objections.

'And then she just sat down at her kitchen table?'

'Well, for what it's worth, that's what I would do if someone pulled a weapon on me,' Karl replies. 'Wouldn't you?'

57

There can be no longer be any doubt autumn has taken an iron grip on the Dogger Islands. The blustering weather has announced that everyone's in for a hell of a ride. The drizzle has been replaced with violent gusts sweeping in from the west, a portent of the coming winter. The meteorologists have issued a warning; over the next twenty-four hours, severe winds are expected along the coasts.

By the time Karen exits the motorway toward Langevik, the storm has reached full force. Rain covers the windscreen and the wipers are unable to keep up with the inundation. She drives slowly, hunched over, peering out, parrying with the wheel whenever the wind buffets the car. If the temperature drops below freezing tonight, tomorrow's going to be hell. She feels the tyres slip in the mud sliding down the steep slopes.

She should really head straight home before the roads become completely impassable. Granted, Sigrid's doing much better, but she's far from well. On the other hand, going by Harald Steen's needn't take more than thirty minutes. She will have to drink a cup of coffee, of course, and spend some time making polite chitchat before she can bring up her real reason for visiting. The whole thing is a long shot; when she last saw Steen, he'd shown clear signs of dementia. He'd managed to convey accurate information at his last interview – Angela

Novak had verified everything he'd told them – but it had taken him a long time to recall the events of that same morning. And now she's going to ask him to cast his mind back more than forty years.

She has grudgingly begun to concede, to herself, that Karl's theories may very well prove correct, albeit there are still details that don't seem to add up. But stranger things have undeniably happened than a series of break-ins, all committed by the same offender, who for some reason escalated from burglary via attempted arson to murder. Or at least manslaughter.

The most recent piece of the puzzle, provided by Grant Hogan in Grunder, has at least been enough to persuade both the chief of police and the prosecutor that all resources need to be focused on locating the man on the motorcycle. Haugen, who is sensing the possibility of a swift conclusion to the investigation, would likely pull her off the case immediately if he knew where she was going now and why.

Another gust of wind pushes at the car and she feels the tyres spin in the mud. I really should go straight home, she thinks and turns into Harald Steen's driveway.

'Do help yourself, pet. They're not home-made, I'm afraid, but it's all I have to offer.'

They've sat down in Harald Steen's kitchen, and with a pang of guilt, Karen lets the old man serve her coffee from a thermos and one of the two cinnamon buns Angela Novak put on a plate and covered with clingfilm as an evening treat for Harald.

'She really does take good care of you, from the looks of it,' Karen says, biting into the soft bun.

'Oh really? Yes, I suppose you could say that. But then that's what they pay her for. Pay her handsomely, compared to what I used to make in my day. Four hundred and twenty marks and forty shillings a month had to be enough for me and the wife to get by on.'

'Has she been with you long? Angela, I mean.'

'Oh, no more than a year. Or maybe two at most. It's my damn heart, it doesn't pump like it's supposed to, they say, that's why I get light-headed. If not for that, I'd be fine on my own, even though Harry's lost all faith in me. He's the one who insisted I bring that woman in. Contacted social services without asking me first.'

Karen can't help but think Harald Steen's son has probably been chastised about this intervention more than once. She tries a different tack.

'So it's like you have your own housekeeper, Harald. Well, you certainly deserve one. I wouldn't say no to a bit of ground service myself.'

She accompanies the flattery with her sweetest smile. She has to get the old man in a good mood.

'Is that right? Housekeeper . . .'

Harald Steen hides a pleased smile behind the rim of his coffee cup and pensively slurps away while this new perspective sinks in. Apparently enlivened, he eventually puts his cup down on its saucer with a determined clatter.

'So, out with it now; surely a lady officer like yourself didn't stop by just for a cup of coffee?'

'Lady officer.' Shuddering, Karen shakes off the phrase and bends down to pick up her handbag from the floor. The whole thing is a long shot and she might as well get it over with.

350

'I actually wanted to ask you something. I thought if anyone could help me, it would be you. I'd bet you know everything that's happened in Langevik.'

Karen quickly glances down at the photograph she's pulled out of her handbag. Nineteen seventy, smiling young women and men lined up on a flight of stone steps and three children on the lawn below. Then she turns the picture around and places it in front of Harald Steen.

'Do you have any idea who the people in this picture are, Harald?'

She watches patiently while he slowly reaches for a case on the table, unfolds the arms and places his spectacles on his nose. Without picking it up, he studies the photograph with a furrowed brow. Then he chuckles. A dry, mirthless chuckle followed by a deep sigh.

'Oh dearie me,' he says. 'Where did you find this?'

'It's from Susanne's photo album. From what I gather, the people in the picture lived in the commune her parents started here. The problem is there are no full names in the album, just first names. I've written them on the back.'

Harald Steen continues to contemplate the photograph, without speaking or turning the picture over or even picking it up off the table. Karen studies his face, which shows no sign of recognition, with a sinking feeling. It's almost fifty years ago, she thinks, and he probably can't even remember what he had for breakfast this morning.

Harald Steen suddenly pushes the picture away, removes his glasses and leans back in his wooden chair.

'And what good would their names be to you, if I may be so bold as to ask?'

'Probably no good at all,' she replies truthfully. 'I'm simply trying to get a sense of Susanne's life and figured there might be a small chance she stayed in touch with some of the people who lived here back then. Maybe one of the children.'

Harald Steen snorts derisively.

'I find that hard to believe; I don't even think she stayed in touch with her own daughter. She could barely be bothered to put two words together to me either, even though we were neighbours. Susanne was a difficult person, let me tell you. Not quite right up here, if you ask me.'

Harald Steen taps the side of his head and Karen masks a disappointed sigh with another smile.

'Well, as I said, it was a shot in the dark. I talked to Jaap Kloes, Egil Jensen and Odd Marklund down at the Hare and Crow the other day, and none of them could remember any names, so you're in good company. But then, it's almost half a century ago now, so I hadn't expected anything else.'

This time, the snort Harald Steen lets out is offended and so powerful a droplet of liquid flies from his nostril onto the crocheted tablecloth.

'Kloes and Jensen! When have they ever known anything of value? Hanging about the pub, boasting, that's what they've been doing all their lives. If they have any callouses on their hands, they're not from manning the oars, mark my words. Marklund's a better sort, but how he can bear being around those other two clowns, I'll never know. *Good company*, you should be ashamed of yourself.'

He clutches the handle of his cup hard and Karen notices that his hand trembles as he raises it to his lips. Just don't have a heart attack, she thinks. I don't have the time or the energy. *What* did I come here for?

Then Harald Steen slams his cup down.

'So,' he says, 'you asked them first and then you come to see old man Steen when they were of no help. Suddenly, I'm good enough.'

Karen replies instinctively, like a chastised twelve-year-old.

'They just happened to be there when I went in for a pint. Otherwise I would obviously have come to you first,' she adds, hoping her words will pour oil on his troubled feelings.

Harald Steen leans forward without replying. Then he presses a yellowed fingernail against the couple at the edge of the upper step in the photograph.

'Disa Brinckmann, Tomas and Ingela Ekman and Theo Rep,' he says, slowly moving his finger along the line of people in the picture.

He moves his index finger down to the lower row and declares loudly:

'Janet and Brandon Connor, Per and Anne-Marie Lindgren.'

After the last name, he leans back in his chair again and pushes his glasses up to his forehead. This time with crossed arms and a smile expressing both vexation and triumph.

'I don't remember the children's names; you'll have to forgive me,' he mutters. 'And Susanne was nothing more than a glint in her father's eye at that point. She was born the following year, if memory serves.'

Karen stares mutely at the old man on the other side of the table. Old man Steen may not recall what he had for breakfast, but there can be no doubt he's sure about this. How is it even possible to remember the names of people who were distant neighbours for a short time over forty years ago? She wouldn't be able to. Karen's hope had been that Harald Steen might be able to recall one of the many names, or maybe something else that could indirectly lead her to the information she was after. Now he's named all eight adults in the picture with no hint of hesitation.

'How is it possible?' she says again. Out loud, this time.

Harald Steen calmly looks her in the eye and reaches for his coffee cup.

'I was the one holding the camera.'

58

Normally, driving home from Harald Steen's house would take ten minutes, at most. This evening, it takes thirty-two. While the car crawls through the mud, Karen's thoughts are occupied with what Steen just told her.

'I know the people in the village looked askance at the young folks up at Lothorp, but I certainly saw no harm in them. And I wasn't the only one who took a detour up there to have a gander at the beauties.'

At this point, Harald had winked conspiratorially, but it had still taken a minute for the penny to drop and for Karen to realise the draw had been bra-less allure and provincial fantasies about Swedish sin.

'And how did they like you lurking in the bushes?'

'Oh no, lass, unlike the others, I walked right in and introduced myself. Was offered tea, because they didn't drink coffee, oh no, so it's true, they were a little odd. Well, and then they asked if I would mind taking their picture and one thing led to another.'

And then Harald Steen had told her he'd given them some good advice, sharing what he knew about the farm from Gråå, what the soil up there would accept and what it would spit back out. He'd gone by the farm once a week or so after that, to help them start their potato patch and get some other vegetables growing. A kind of friendship had developed between them; granted, Steen was a bit older than the rest of them, but he'd hardly been an old man in the early seventies, Karen reminded herself.

The car comes to a complete stop on the slight incline north of the harbour. The tyres spin in the mud and she realises she's going to have to find something to put under them for friction. She opens the door with a sigh and climbs out. The rain lashes her face while she folds down the tailgate and with stiff fingers opens the green plastic box she keeps in the Ranger's cargo bed. She spends a second pondering which tool to use, then pulls out the saw. Freezing muck seeps in over the edge of her boots when she steps into the ditch to reach the juniper bushes on the other side.

Harald Steen's words echo in her mind as she saws through the tough wood, cursing loudly.

'I have no idea where the others went off to, but Anne-Marie died in eighty-six and Per lived alone here for years until he ended up in the hospital, too. We'd meet up occasionally for a game of cards for a few years, but both he and I found it increasingly difficult to move about. The bottle claimed him, they say, and that makes sense. Well, and Brandon and Janet who live up in Joms, of course.'

'You mean Joms here on Heimö? They still live on the island?'

Karen had been well aware of how shrilly eager she sounded.

'Calm down, lass, you'll give yourself a heart attack. Well, they were still there last summer, because I ran into them at the market in Dunker after a visit to the dentist. Hellishly expensive, it was, but a person has to be able to chew their porridge.'

When Karen finally opens the front door of the last grey stone house north of Langevik and steps across the threshold with boots covered in grey mud, her mind is busy pondering how to get to Joms the next day if the deluge continues through the night. How to get out of Langevik at all, in fact.

That's why the smell emanating from the kitchen escapes her notice at first. Only after she's unlaced her boots and pulled off her sodden socks does she realise she's not going to have to root through the freezer for something to pop in the microwave. Sigrid is standing by the kitchen counter with a colander in her hand.

'It's spaghetti Bolognese, because it's really the only thing I know how to make. I put the pasta in when I heard the car, so it should be ready in ten minutes.'

Karen feels warmth spread through her body despite the rain-soaked clothes clinging to her.

'You have no idea how great spaghetti Bolognese sounds to me right now. I'm just going to have a quick shower. How are you feeling, anyway? You look a lot better.'

'I'm just a bit tired, but almost no fever, so I think I can have some wine. Do you want me to open a bottle?'

'One glass, that's all you're getting.'

'Have you decided what to do with the house?' Karen asks between mouthfuls after they sit down at the table a little while later. 'It's yours now.'

Sigrid shrugs. Karen is starting to get used to that.

'Sell it, I guess. If I can find a buyer.'

'I don't think that'll be a problem. It's a nice house and Langevik has become popular in recent years. So you'd prefer to stay up in Gaarda?'

'No, I can't stay there. We're subletting from Sam's brother, so it's his. He called today to remind me I have to get my things out. Apparently, he's been sleeping on a friend's sofa since he left and figures it should be me doing that. I'm going to call around tomorrow and see what I can sort out.'

'So you're not considering moving into your mum's house? *Your* house,' she corrects herself.

'It wouldn't work. How would I get to and from work without a car? And before you say anything, no, I'm not going to ask my dad for money.'

'You don't have a licence?'

'I do, but no car, like I just said.'

'Well, but you do, actually; they found your mum's car. There's something wrong with the starter, apparently, but we can get that fixed before you go back to work.'

'Are you serious?'

Sigrid lights up, but then looks doubtful again. Mercurial, Karen decides.

'I don't know if I want to live there. I kind of get a bad vibe from the last time I did. And now I can't go into the kitchen even though they cleaned it all up. You saw it, didn't you?'

Karen nods mutely while searching for the right words. Sigrid's eyes signal both an urge to know and a plea not to have to hear it. For a moment, she looks very lost. Then she gets up quickly and walks over to the kitchen counter. Pretends to clean something up, clears her throat and continues.

'Besides, all those things she bought make me gag,' she continues. 'Cushions everywhere and at least a hundred pairs of shoes.'

Karen studies the slim girl. Hears her efforts to bring her voice under control, to control the unfathomable.

'It's OK to be sad, Sigrid,' she says.

'She's got stuff bloody everywhere. Did you know she has a home gym in her bedroom? And a machine to steam her face and another for foot rubs, at least I think that's what it's for . . . I can't bear to live in the middle of all that crap.'

Karen nods and thinks about the heaps of ornaments Sigrid dumped on the lawn. So that was why she'd gone to her mother's house, because she knew Samuel was going to kick her out of the flat. She'd probably figured she was going to have to stay in the house for a while at least. Karen studies Sigrid, who has got up again to clear the table. She's proud, refuses to ask her dad for anything, even though he's wealthy and would probably fly into action if she'd just let him. I wonder why she's so angry with him. And why she was so angry with her mother?

'How about this? You can stay here for a few weeks while we work on getting the house in order. We'll throw away anything you don't want to keep, repaint and make it yours. That way, you can take your time figuring out if you want to live there or if you want to sell it and buy something else.'

Sigrid seems to consider the offer.

'I won't have money for rent until next week after I go back to work.'

'This dinner was worth a week's rent to me.'

Sigrid eyes Karen suspiciously.

'Why are you being so nice? Mum always said terrible things about you. She said you used to live in England but that your husband kicked you out and that's why you had to move back.'

'She said that, did she?'

Sigrid looks hesitant, then braces herself.

'She said you were the kind of woman who went after other people's husbands, since you'd lost your own.'

Karen reaches for the bottle and tops herself up with a trembling hand.

'She was half right,' she says, noting that she sounds completely unperturbed.

Sigrid says nothing, pondering Karen's reply. When she finally speaks, Karen flinches as though she's been slapped.

'You have a son, don't you?'

59

The rain has stopped. The pale moon, peeking out through a rift in the clouds, illuminates her bedroom and makes the big linden tree outside the window cast shadows across the walls.

Karen realises sleep is still a long way off.

Everything had come pouring out of her tonight. Everything she has kept carefully bottled up inside during the long years of pent-up grief. The whole truth, which previously only her mother knew, everything her closest friends guess at but have learnt not to ask about. She had unleashed a flood of words, heedless of the fact that her interlocutor was an eighteen-year-old girl, who was dismayed at the reaction to her simple question.

Everything that had been set in motion when two police officers and a doctor had given her the unfathomable news and Karen Eiken Hornby had ceased living. Had ceased existing while words like 'massive collision', 'M25', 'Waltham Abbey' and 'one lorry and five cars', sliced through her.

Both Mathis and John had died, they'd told her. They didn't suffer, they'd said. She knew it wasn't true.

Death had been instantaneous, the police officers had whispered to the nurses; the lorry had sliced the car open like a can of sardines. Four people had died and another six were badly injured.

That the woman in the car was unharmed was a miracle, the doctor had said, before immediately correcting himself. Physically unharmed; she still hadn't said a word since they cut her out of the wreck.

Then the doctor had turned to Karen. Was there anyone they could call? She hadn't replied. They must have called their old friends, Allison and Keith, who had turned up, pale, in shock, their eyes red.

She has no clear memory of the first twenty-four hours, only fragments; hushed voices and crying. Valium. Sleep. Worried eyes whenever she woke up.

And then another day. A brand-new morning had broken, as though nothing had happened. As though the world had failed to realise that everything was over.

A brand-new day. And the morgue.

Two bodies, two fallen soldiers with their arms along their sides; one tall, one short, hidden under sheets. They must have called her mother, too. Mum, who'd been standing there when Karen turned around and left John and Mathis in the tiled cold. Mum, who'd sat quietly in the back seat of the police car that drove them from the morgue to the house and squeezed Karen's hand so tightly she could feel it. Mum, who'd found the keys in Karen's handbag, opened the door and made her go inside. Mum, who'd been there every second of the unbearable series of days that followed, one after the other.

Mum, who'd set her own grief aside during the day and let it out at night when she thought Karen couldn't hear her pacing downstairs, from the kitchen to the living room and back again. Hours of sobbing over everything she'd lost, too. John, whom she'd learnt to love. And Mathis, her only child's only child.

Her mum's grief had been given no space, no recipient. And yet, she'd continued to exist when Karen had been unable. With trembling hands, in broken English, she'd seen to everything.

Church. Coffins. Emptiness.

Every minute spent in the house had been unbearable; it was their house, not hers. Without them, it was nothing but a prison of memories. London. Every street a reminder, every neighbour looking for something appropriate to say, every child she saw, every song, every TV programme. Everything was a reminder of the life she'd had. The road forward lay in ruins; nothing tomorrow, nothing next week, not next Christmas, not next summer, not in a few years, never when Mathis is older. No life; there was nothing to look forward to.

Only by looking to her past had she found an ice floe to cling to. She had to go home. Back home.

Sigrid had been still and pale while the words tumbled out of Karen; the whole stinking truth about how her life had ended that day. All the things she'd sworn she'd never talk about she'd deposited in the lap of a young girl.

'I'm sorry,' Sigrid had said. 'I didn't mean to pry, but I saw the picture in your bedroom when I was looking for more Tylenol.'

Karen holds her breath and listens for sounds from Sigrid's room, but can only hear her own pulse. She turns her head to the bedside table and looks at the photograph that prompted Sigrid's question. *You have a son, don't you?*

John and Karen on a beach on Crete, with a tanned, laughing Mathis with a head full of sand between them. John had stubbornly refused to ask someone to take their picture; instead, he'd positioned the camera on a beach chair and used the timer. There had been countless failed attempts before he'd managed to both get all three of them in focus and make it back into the shot on time. Mathis had fallen over himself laughing at his dad's clumsiness and Karen had laughed at her son's trilling laughter and John had laughed at the two of them.

In the end, the picture had come out well, they'd decided, and then they'd headed over to the beach café to eat squid. Their last summer. The last picture of the three of them together.

Her body feels strangely heavy; her arms and legs like lead against the mattress, but her mind is racing. Why hadn't she put the photograph away, like she normally does whenever she has company? Is Sigrid going to tell her father? And is Jounas going to tell everyone else? Is the truth going to spread like ripples of pity around her now? Is she going to have to smile consolingly at everyone who now knows and feels compelled to condole with her? Will her colleagues talk about her and fall silent when she enters the room? Are other people going to discuss her grief? Discuss John. Mathis.

She has worked so hard to keep that from happening. Because it was the only way she knew how to carry on. A past that no longer existed. And a present. Nothing in between. She isolated herself in the house that had been her mother's and was now hers. Weeks of drawn curtains and untouched bowls of soup. Then weeks of furious walking up and down the shoreline; hours of vacant staring at the horizon and the constant pull of the cliff edge.

In the end, her mother had stepped in.

'I've spoken to Wilhelm Kaste,' she'd told her. 'They're hiring a detective sergeant and he's promised to meet with you on Thursday at ten. I'll drive you.'

For some reason, she hadn't even tried to protest. And there, in Wilhelm Kaste's office, the rest of her life had begun.

'Your mother has told me what happened and I want to take this opportunity to tell you how sorry I am for your loss. No one else knows and I won't mention it again, unless you want to talk about it. If you want the job, it's yours; not because I feel sorry for you and not because I've known your mother since we were children, but because you're the most qualified applicant. Or most over-qualified, I should say, but detective sergeant's the only opening we have at the moment. Do you want the job?'

She'd said yes and the day she started, Kaste had called her into his office.

'Since several people here will have access to your file, I've taken the liberty of changing some of the details. This is just the local archive, mind, more senior managers will of course still be able to access the correct information if they put their minds to it, but I sincerely doubt anyone will. As far as people here know, you're divorced after a brief marriage in the UK. No children,' he'd added and cleared his throat. 'Your mother tells me that's how you want it, but I need to hear it from you.'

'That's how I want it,' she'd told him.

And that's how it had been. A truth too painful to talk about, a guilt so overwhelming it had to be suppressed for her to be able to carry on.

Light is seeping out under the guestroom door when Karen gives it a gentle knock. Sigrid is lying on the bed with her backpack next to her, fully dressed, her eyes swollen from crying. She quickly sits up when Karen opens the door.

'I'll be out of here first thing tomorrow,' she says.

Karen sits down at the edge of the bed and puts her hand on Sigrid's.

'Don't leave. This isn't your fault, Sigrid.'

'I shouldn't have asked. If I'd known, I would never have said anything.'

'It's not your fault, Sigrid,' Karen repeats. 'It's just that I've never told anyone about this. It's been my way of surviving.'

'I get that. You don't have to talk to me either.'

'But I did. I just dumped it all on you. I'm so sorry about that.'

They sit in silence while Karen strokes Sigrid's hand with her thumb.

'But there's one thing I didn't tell you.'

And then she says it out loud.

'It was my fault. I was driving.'

60

Even though it's been almost eight hours since the rain stopped, the minor roads are still in a bad state. Traffic is flowing along Thorsbyleden again but the road under the railway viaduct in Västerport has had to close until the water has had a chance to subside.

Karen drives with her eyes firmly fixed on the road, listening through the hands-free to what the police chief inspector has to say about the traffic conditions this morning. According to his information, getting to Joms should be OK, so long as she's careful and doesn't try to drive through flooded sections of roadway.

'They've had to tow nineteen cars so far this morning,' Thorstein Klockare says with a voice tinged with a ghoulish kind of resignation. 'But the inland and lowlands are worst hit. How's the situation in Langevik, by the way?'

Karen adjusts her earbud.

'It was properly slippery last night, but most of it was fine this morning. Do you know what the forecast is? I didn't have time to check the weather before I left.'

'No more rain today, they say, but low-pressure systems are queued up over the North Sea.'

'So, the usual.'

'Same as ever,' Thorstein Klockare confirms.

They end the call and Karen glances over at the GPS. Assuming the police chief inspector is correct, she should be in Joms in half an hour.

Karen pulls over at the end of the paved road. She leans forward and peers out through the windscreen at the house and the narrow gravel road leading up to it. Then she kills the engine, opens the door and climbs out. True, the road looks passable from here, but she can feel how sodden the ground is under her wellies. Chances are the top layer of gravel will give way if she tries to drive up the hill. No need to add to the towers' workload this morning. Instead, she starts walking up the steep hill.

Janet Connor had sounded drowsy when she answered the phone half an hour ago. Or like she'd just been woken up, actually, though she had assured Karen she and Brandon were both up. Of course Karen could stop by, though Janet had no idea what she and Brandon could possibly do to be of assistance.

Now she opens the door before Karen has reached the porch.

'Welcome,' she calls out in a voice that is now wide-awake, 'would you like some tea or coffee?'

Janet Connor's tall, slender body is wrapped in a long kimono that makes her look regal. Her grey hair is held back by a thin green scarf she's artfully wrapped around her head, but on her feet are grey rag socks, which detract somewhat from her majestic air. She looks about seventy, but despite her grey hair, she gives a youthful impression as she smiles at Karen from the door.

Behind Janet, Karen can glimpse a man of the same age. He seems slightly winded and looks like he's adjusting his fly. Karen tries not to think about what she interrupted as she climbs the front steps.

'Either, thank you,' she says with a smile. 'Karen Eiken Hornby,' she adds and holds out her hand. 'You're very kind to invite me on such short notice. I hope I'm not disturbing your morning routine too much,' she adds, regretting it instantly when she notices Brandon and Janet Connor exchanging a quick look.

'Not at all! Come in!'

The kitchen is warm like an incubator and smells strongly of cumin, linseed oil paint and freshly baked bread. I'd bet this room's seen a lentil stew or two, Karen muses and takes her jacket off while glancing over at Brandon. If she'd any preconceived notions about what an old commune member from the seventies should look like, he confirms them and then some. Brandon Connor is, just like his wife, remarkably tall, probably over six feet three. He looks to be in good shape, though she notes his shoulders are slightly hunched when he gets milk and cheese out of the fridge. His thin, wide trousers might be pyjama bottoms, but something tells her they, like his washed-out Frank Zappa T-shirt, could just as easily be Brandon's regular clothes. Like Janet, he's wearing some kind of rag socks, but while hers are knitted from regular grey wool, probably on the island, Brandon's look like they were made by a Peruvian lady with a passion for zany colours. His sparse hair is gathered in a thin ponytail and his chin adorned with a long, narrow beard.

'There's walnuts in the bread,' he says. 'I hope you're not allergic?'

'Not that I know,' Karen replies. 'It looks amazing, did you bake it yourselves?'

369

Brandon looks up from his breadknife with an expression of genuine surprise.

'Yes . . .' he says slowly. 'We're not going to waste our money on the crap they sell down at Kvik. Do you?'

'Sometimes,' she admits. 'Or I buy bread from one of the bakeries,' she adds in an attempt to redeem herself a little.

After some small talk about baking and the quality of the island's supermarket chains, Karen directs the conversation toward the reason she's there.

'I assume you've heard about the murder in Langevik. And I believe you must be aware of your connection to Susanne Smeed?' she adds with a querying look.

'Sure,' Brandon says, 'the murder's been pretty much impossible to miss. But we don't read the evening papers and the morning papers didn't publish the name until a few days after the fact, so it was a while before we realised it was their girl. Per and Anne-Marie's, I mean.'

'That's right. Susanne Smeed was born Lindgren. And that is, as I'm sure you've guessed, the reason I'm here. Am I right to think you lived with Per and Anne-Marie Lindgren and some others in a commune during a period in the early seventies?'

'We did. From March 1970 to the end of February 1971, to be precise. Almost exactly a year.'

'Have you lived on the island since then?'

'Not the entire time. We moved to Copenhagen at first – everyone did back then – but we only stayed for a couple of months before we relocated to Sweden. We lived in another commune there, in Huddinge outside Stockholm, for a couple of years. We didn't move back here until . . . when was it, do you remember?'

Brandon consults his wife with a look.

'May of seventy-six,' she says. 'Since then, we've stayed put.'

'Did you stay in touch with Per and Anne-Marie after you moved back? Or with anyone else from your time at Lothorp Farm?'

'Only with Theo Rep. At least if you mean regular contact. Everyone scattered and with no mobile phones or Facebook, it wasn't easy. We did run into Per and Anne-Marie in Dunker, of course, after we moved back.'

'But you didn't socialise?'

'It was my impression they didn't want to. At least she didn't,' Janet says. 'Anne-Marie was a bit . . . how do I put it? Fragile, perhaps.'

'Don't pussyfoot around; she was weird,' Brandon breaks in brusquely; Janet gives him something that looks like a cautionary look.

'In what way was she weird?'

'Pardon me,' Janet says, 'but I don't understand what all this has to do with Susanne's murder. Both Anne-Marie and Per have been dead for years.'

Karen hesitates for a moment. Then she decides to tell them the truth.

'To be honest, I'm not sure myself. The thing is that we're trying to form a picture of Susanne's life and what kind of person she was. It's a kind of jigsaw puzzle, in which the first piece seems to be found up at Lothorp Farm. What can you tell me about your time there? How did you end up there in the first place?'

Mr and Mrs Connor exchange another look, as though trying to reach some kind of unspoken agreement.

'Well,' Brandon says at length. 'I suppose it started with me deciding Uncle Sam could do without my help in 'Nam.'

'Brandon was a deserter,' Janet explains.

'Oh, so you're American?' Karen says, surprised.

For some reason, she has assumed both he and Janet are from the UK. Both speak fluent Doggerian and it's hard to tell an American accent from a British one.

'What about you? Where did you grow up?'

'Southampton,' Janet replies. 'We met on the Isle of Wight on 31 August 1969. I was there against my parents' express wishes.'

'I was there illegally, had come over from Amsterdam on a private boat, with Theo and a bunch of hippies. Since I'd missed Woodstock a few weeks before, for obvious reasons, we decided to go to the Isle of Wight Festival instead. Not as epic, but I did get to see Dylan and I met Janet, so I shouldn't complain.'

Brandon reaches for the teapot and inquiringly cocks an eyebrow at Karen, who shakes her head. She feels torn; on the one hand, she wants to spend the whole day here, eating walnut bread and listening to stories from a bygone era when she herself was in nappies. On the other hand, she has to stay rational and move things along.

'And then you came here the following year.'

'Yes, Theo had met Disa somewhere I can't remember, and she knew Tomas and Ingela already. I think they met when Disa was studying midwifery in Copenhagen. Tomas was half Danish on his mother's side. And he and Per were childhood friends. Well, either way, word got around that Anne-Marie had inherited a place on Doggerland and that they were considering starting a commune.'

'And am I right in thinking there were children in the picture, too? From the start, I mean?'

'Yes, Ingela had two boys just a couple of years apart, Orian and Love. And Disa had girl of five, I think. Her name was Mette.'

'Do you have children?'

'Yes, a son, but we had him much later. Dylan's a stock trader in London,' Brandon says with a look of dejection that reveals he would have wished his son had pursued a different career. 'We did what we could,' he adds with a crooked smile.

'And Susanne was only born the year after?'

'Yes, but that was after we moved away, so we don't know anything about all that.'

Karen's eyebrows shoot up.

'All that?'

Janet puts a hand on her husband's arm.

'What Brandon means to say is that things turned sour at the farm and we felt it was time to move on. We'd heard a lot of exciting things were happening in Copenhagen, so we decided to go there.'

Janet is talking quickly; Karen half listens while she explains that they joined the squatters in the former military area of Christiania but that they'd only lasted a few months before deciding to head to Sweden. And she senses an inward oath from the other woman when she realises Karen's going to keep the focus on Lothorp Farm.

'Turned sour, you said? Why was that?'

Janet gets up, looking annoyed.

'That's private,' she says. 'I really don't see how that could be relevant.'

'You're probably right, but I'd like to be the judge of that, if you don't mind,' Karen replies levelly. 'It happened almost fifty years ago and the Lindgrens have all passed away, so at least whatever you tell me can't hurt any of them.'

'He was unfaithful,' Brandon says tersely. 'Per and Ingela had an affair while Tomas was away. Per was devastated that he had betrayed both his wife and his best friend and Anne-Marie lost her mind.'

Janet Connor has returned to the table with a topped-up teapot and sits down with a heavy sigh.

'She didn't lose her mind, Brandon. She slipped into what would these days likely be described as a deep depression. No wonder, really; Lothorp Farm belonged to her and she probably felt both used and betrayed by all of us.'

'When did this happen?'

'Late that summer, the same year we moved in. It was wonderful until then, but everything changed when Anne-Marie fell ill.'

'August, maybe September 1970, it must have been while Anne-Marie was pregnant with Susanne,' Karen thinks. 'Finding out your husband cheated while you were expecting could knock anyone off balance. Especially if you have to share a home with the other woman. The home you own.'

'It's like Brandon said, things turned sour and none of us knew how to handle Anne-Marie's depression or Per's desperate attempts to make her better. And besides, I'm sure several of us felt it wasn't such a big deal at the end of the day. A lot of people viewed fidelity as a bourgeoise invention.'

'How did Tomas and Ingela react?'

'Ingela always had a fairly uncomplicated approach to life. Well, I suppose we'd all come to the farm with naïve expectations of sharing everything and liberating ourselves from bourgeoise conventions, but when it came down to it, none of us was able to handle it. Not even Ingela. She felt bad about Anne-Marie being sick, but I don't think she ever thought she and Per had done anything wrong.'

'I think Tomas handled it best, even though Per was his best friend,' Brandon says. 'He was really the one person there who practised what he preached. Live and let live, what's mine is yours, you know. He and Ingela were the most hard-core hippies, if you know what I mean. They were all in, while the rest of us ... well ...'

Brandon trails off and reaches for his teacup.

'They clung on for longer than the rest us, certainly,' Janet takes over. 'I think they stayed for a few more months before deciding to move to Sweden. Them and Disa. But we haven't had any real contact with any of them since.'

'Nor with Per and Anne-Marie, even though you all lived on Heimö?'

'Like I said, we would run into each other in Dunker sometimes and I'm sure we talked about visiting Langevik at some point, but it never happened. Again, they weren't happy memories.'

'Do you know what happened to Ingela and Tomas after they moved?'

'They parted ways. She kept doing the hippie thing, but he did a one-eighty and pulled on a suit and tie. Took over his father's company eventually. And just like that, Tomas Ekman, the dyed-in-the-wool hippie, had turned into a die-hard capitalist. Sadly, he passed away just a few months ago.'

'He did? How did you find out? I thought you said you weren't in touch?'

'Our son Dylan told us when he came home last summer. He'd heard it at work. Tomas was apparently well-known in the business world and Dylan was obviously aware we knew each other when we were young. He found Tomas Ekman considerably more impressive than his old dad,' Brandon says with a wry smile. 'Sometimes the apple falls a long way from the tree.'

'And what about Ingela, is she still alive?'

'No idea,' Janet replies curtly. 'Like I said, we're not in touch.'

'And Disa?'

'I'm sorry, but all of this is a closed chapter to us.'

And as though to underline that they have nothing more to say, Janet gets up and starts clearing the table.

Karen knows she's going to have to give up, as she merges onto the motorway with her course set for the Dunker police headquarters. It's time to forget about that old hippie commune and start focusing on the burglary connection instead.

A faint, haze sunlight has broken through the overcast sky and the road is already dry in spots. After a glance at her watch, Karen speeds up and does her best to shake a feeling Brandon and Janet Connor didn't tell her the whole truth.

61

She straightens up her stack of documents, leans forward and turns the audio recorder on.

'Interview with Linus Kvanne regarding suspected burglary, attempted arson and murder, alternatively manslaughter. Also present are, aside from Linus Kvanne, lawyer Gary Brataas and Detective Inspectors Karl Björken and Karen Eiken Hornby.'

'I haven't fucking murdered anybody. I'm not going to be framed for something I didn't do.'

His voice is unexpectedly deep, in stark contrast to his boyishly slender build. Karen thinks about the images from the ferry's CCTV camera; both she and Karl had guessed sixteen, seventeen years old. But Linus Kvanne has already had time to both turn twenty-four and serve out three sentences at Kabare Prison. The first one for manslaughter.

The incident in which Lars Hayden, a twenty-eight-year-old junkie known by the police, had lost his life six years ago had been described as an act of heroism by Linus Kvanne's lawyer. A New Year's Eve party that had gone off the rails early on had come to a definitive end when Kvanne discovered his then-girlfriend in one of the bedrooms. Hayden had been lying on top of her with his trousers down and a knife pressed against her throat. The court deemed that the first time Linus Kvanne stabbed Lars Hayden could be considered self-defence, as he was trying to disarm Hayden. It was the following four times that had been considered 'excessive force'. But Kvanne's youth and lack of prior offences had been considered mitigating circumstances. After serving five of the nine months he'd been sentenced to, Kvanne had been released for good behaviour; a unanimous parole board had assessed the risk of re-offending as low.

Since then, Linus Kvanne has worked on refining his brand, doing a couple of brief stints in the nick for possession and one for fairly large-scale police theft. His most recent stay at Kabare only ended in July.

He looks relaxed, slouched in his chair with one foot casually resting on the knee of the other leg.

Gary Brataas puts a soothing hand on his client's arm.

'Of course not. Let's just listen calmly to what the police have to say. I'm looking forward to it,' he says and smiles out of the corner of his mouth.

'All right, Linus,' Karen says. 'You were arrested today at 10.45. a.m. in your flat on Tallvägen in Lemdal. At the time of your arrest, your flat was searched and aside from a substantial amount of narcotics, the police also found several items reported stolen in a number of break-ins on Noorö and Heimö. Can you explain that?'

Linus Kvanne pretends to stifle a yawn, stretches and folds his hands behind his head.

'Explanation? As to why the fuzz broke down my front door and stormed in while I was sleeping, you mean? Don't have one.'

Karen shoots Karl a quick glance. He has puffed up his cheeks, his eyebrows raised inquiringly, and now he lets the air out in a sigh that clearly illustrates what they're both thinking: I see, you're one of those; this is going to take a while.

Karen repeats the question, ignoring Kvanne's attempts to rile her.

'I mean, how do you explain the stolen items found in your living room and under your bed?'

Linus Kvanne shrugs and smiles so widely the chewing tobacco under his top lip threatens to fall onto his lap.

'Well, I guess someone must've planted it there. Seems like the most likely explanation, no?'

'And who would that be, do you think?'

This time, Linus Kvanne laughs and spreads his hands.

'I don't know. A lot of people come and go. My home is open to one and all.'

'You know what I think?' Karen says calmly. 'I think you stole those things in a series of burglaries. I think that up on Noorö, you also stole an Africa Twin model motorcycle and that you used that to go to Thorsvik and from there to Grunder.'

'Is that right, darlin'?'

'And after the break-in in Grunder, you got rid of the motor-cycle, probably deliberately because you were worried there might be an alert out for it, or maybe you actually just crashed. Which one was it?'

Linus Kvanne shakes his head slowly, trying to catch Karl Björken's eyes, hoping for some male understanding.

'I've no idea what she's on about. Do you have anything to say before I walk out of here?'

'Sorry, kid,' Karl replies evenly. 'We have pictures of you and the bike on the ferry from Noorö. We also know you were bragging about it at The Cave last night.'

Kvanne quickly puts his arms down and leans across the table.

379

'Who the fuck told you that?'

'My client is not obliged to . . .'

Gary Brataas is cut off by Karen.

'Isn't bragging about your crimes just a bit daft?' she says. 'Especially when you're drunk and in a crowded public place. There's always a risk someone might rat you out. But,' she adds, 'maybe you are in fact a bit daft, Linus. What do you reckon, are you?'

He quickly pushes his face forward until its inches from Karen's.

'Fucking cunt.'

If he'd chosen a different word, she wouldn't have had to deal with that little droplet of spit. Without letting on how revolted she is, Karen waits until Linus Kvanne withdraws and leans back in his chair once more before wiping away the saliva that landed on her lower lip and chin.

Her voice is completely calm when she presses on.

'Was that why you decided to burn the houses down? Got a bit anxious, realising you might have left clues behind, despite wearing gloves? A hair or a flake of skin the technicians could use to tie you to the scene? Well, that's actually good thinking, isn't it?'

Karen turns to Karl, who's nodding pensively.

'Pretty smart, yeah,' he agrees. 'It's just a shame he didn't stay to make sure the fire caught properly before he scarpered. After all, now the technicians have all the time in the world to comb the houses for his DNA. Since we know what to look for now.'

Karen nods agreement while studying Linus Kvanne, who's now drumming his fingers on his armrests. His smile has been replaced by a clenched jaw; his tongue darts in under his top lip to squeeze out some extra nicotine.

'The question is why he then went one step further,' Karen continues without taking her eyes off Kvanne.

'Bloody stupid,' Karl adds. 'I mean, we'd never have the resources to send a bunch of technicians out if it were a regular break-in, but now that it's murder, it's a different story. I'm told all three houses are riddled with technicians now.'

At this point, Gary Brataas breaks in, refusing to be silenced any longer.

'If you have any evidence against my client with regards to the alleged murder or manslaughter, I suggest you share it and drop this am-dram performance.'

'So that was a wildly successful interview,' Karl says twenty minutes later in the lift back up to the CID.

He looks tired, Karen observes, watching him dig through his trouser pockets.

'Don't get me wrong, if we were investigating nothing but a handful of break-ins, the interview would have been a roaring success,' he adds and pops a piece of nicotine gum in his mouth.

Against his lawyer's advice, Linus Kvanne had confessed to four burglaries: one on Noorö, one outside Thorsvik, one unreported break-in in a summer cottage in Haven and finally, the one in Grunder. But he strongly denied any involvement in the murder of Susanne Smeed throughout the interview.

'I've never even fucking been to Langevik,' he'd told them.

The problem is, they believe him.

62

'Want to come out for a smoke?'

Kore holds up a packet of cigarettes and jerks his head in the direction of the door. Karen nods.

'Eirik would kill me,' Kore says in a stifled voice, then exhales with a contented groan. 'I wouldn't be surprised if he could smell the smoke all the way from Germany,' he adds and takes another drag.

They've sat down at a table in the outdoor serving area of Repet Bar and Restaurant, where a surprising number of intrepid souls are defying the autumn chill with the help of heaters and blankets. Kore wouldn't mind staying out all night; Eirik has gone off to some new florist fair in Frankfurt and his boyfriend is seizing the opportunity to indulge in beer and cigarettes.

They're an odd couple, Karen notes, studying the silver skull ring on her friend's tattooed hand. She'd known her old schoolfriend Eirik was gay long before that night twenty-two years ago, when he had finally confided in her, then swore her to silence. No one else could know, especially not his father, it would be the death of him.

So she had kept shtum, watching with dismay as Eirik fought to live up to the world's expectations. As he did harm to himself by pretending to be 'one of the lads', in school, on the football field, with his family. As he spent more and more weekends in London, Copenhagen, Amsterdam and Stockholm. Anywhere; so long as it was far from his parents, team mates and the boys down the pub, Eirik had dared to be himself. During her own time in England, Karen had been able to study his double life from up close. John had eventually taken to calling the guestroom behind the kitchen Eirik's room. He'd never understood Eirik's need to hide who he was. Why couldn't he just be honest, it's the nineties now for God's sake, even in Doggerland? It's no big deal nowadays, he'd said. Karen and Eirik had exchanged looks; a Brit could never understand.

And when Eirik finally stepped out of the closet, it hadn't been an expression of confidence so much as of frustration and anger. That day in December, almost eleven years ago, when a call from Karen's mother had broken down all his walls. John was dead. Mathis was dead. Karen had stopped living. That day, Eirik had been seized by a sudden epiphany about the fragility of life, which he'd been unable to ignore. That day, Eirik From had let himself fall apart and had screamed at his father and the whole world that they could go to hell. And he shouldn't count on getting any fucking grandchildren.

He'd been there when Karen moved back home. She'd only realised that much later. Through thick layers of grief, her mum's and Eirik's anxious voices had drifted up from the kitchen to her bedroom. She'd heard his awkward attempts at consoling her mother, had heard him burst into tears, collect himself and try again. And again. And she'd thought to herself it was a good thing her mum and Eirik at least had each other. Now that she no longer existed.

It was only after several months, as she emerged from her room, rigid with grief, that she'd noticed something different about her friend. His transformation had begun.

These days, Eirik lives up to every gay stereotype there is; he's well-dressed, well-groomed and slightly effeminate in his mannerisms and way of speaking. That he's also a trained florist and owns a nationwide chain of flower shops only serves to cement the impression. Eirik has definitely come out of the closet.

Over the years that followed, he would introduce his boyfriends to her, one after the other; most looked remarkably like Eirik, and they rarely lasted long enough for her to commit their names to memory. Then Kore came along.

Maybe it was the fact that he was the complete opposite of Eirik that had made Karen understand instantly, once the first shock had subsided, that Kore's name was worth remembering. Two men could hardly be less alike in appearance, temperament, interests, social circles. Kore, a music producer sporting a black mohawk, tattooed arms and gold rings in both ears. And Eirik, a florist who favoured freshly ironed dress shirts and shiny patent-leather shoes. If Eirik was the thesis, Kore was his antithesis. Or possibly the other way around. Six years later, they're still together.

Now, Kore runs a hand through his hair without noticing that the column of ash at the end of his cigarette breaks off, sprinkling his dyed black mane with white flakes.

'I feel like a roast chicken,' Karen says, touching her burning cheek. 'How can people stand sitting under these heaters?'

She gestures toward the narrow street where glazed outdoor serving areas are lined up along the old brick buildings. Buildings that once housed the ropewalk, the old lanoline factory, the textile mill and a number of other industries that have long since closed down or moved to modern facilities. Now, the old industrial area has been turned into a neighbourhood filled with restaurants, designer shops, cafés and bars. Innovative restaurateurs have done their best to come up with solutions that both keep nicotine addicts happy and comply with new legislation. Any bar owner who wants to stay in business knows it's crucial to provide a place for smokers to enjoy their vice behind plexiglass and under heaters.

'Last packet for me,' Kore says, raising his cigarette. 'I'm picking Eirik up at the airport at half eight tomorrow morning and he's worse than a bloodhound. Hey, what the . . .'

Karen jumps when Kore whistles piercingly. The sound reverberates between the glass walls, but doesn't seem able to escape the incubator they're in. Kore jumps up and waves his non-cigarette arm violently.

'Friis, bloody hell, come here!'

A moment later, Kore has extricated himself from the serving area, dashed across the street and thrown his arms around a man. Karen watches as they exchange a few words. Then Kore points toward the table where she's still sitting and the man turns around. Karen recognises him with a start. It's Leo Friis, who now, visibly hesitant, allows himself to be ushered toward Repet by Kore. This time, he has no shopping trolley with him and the grey blanket is nowhere to be seen. He still looks mangy, however, and Karen can see the uncertainty in his eyes as he glances up at the restaurant. The noise inside has reached ear-splitting levels and is streaming out through the open doors. The sound makes Leo freeze mid-step.

'It's all right, we're outside,' Kore says reassuringly and manages to drag him into the outdoor serving area. 'This is Karen. Karen, this is the man, the myth, the legend, Leo Friis.'

For a frozen moment, their eyes meet. She does a split second calculation; should she tell Kore they've met or pretend they're strangers? She decides to leave the question open and holds her hand out.

'Hi, Leo. Have a seat.'

Leo shakes her hand and nods briefly.

'Hi, Karen.'

Nothing in their greeting suggests they've met before, much less Leo has been the subject of a witness interview. Kore looks completely unperturbed by his friend's ragged appearance. Karen is suddenly unsure; does he even know Leo's homeless and spends his nights under the loading docks down in the New Harbour? At the same time, Kore seems a bit more hyper than usual.

'What would you like? My treat,' he says and waves a waitress over. 'Same again for you, Karen?'

After ordering, he turns back to Leo.

'Bloody hell, Leo, it's good to see you. How long have you been back for?'

'Just since the start of the summer. Since mid-May, I think.'

'What the fuck, you've been home all summer without getting in touch? What have you been up to? How are you doing?'

'Maybe this would work better if you asked one question at a time?' Karen says calmly and makes room on the table for the waitress's heavy tray.

Leo shoots her a look.

'Sorry, sorry, I sound like my mother,' Kore says. 'I'm just so bloody happy to see you,' he adds and raises his glass. '*Gottjer*, guys, cheers!'

'*Gottjer*,' Karen and Leo say in unison.

They raise their glasses to eye level, lower them again and drink as one.

'Karen and I have actually met,' Leo says after putting his glass down and wiping the froth from his beard with the back of his hand. 'Had breakfast together.'

Kore's eyes dart back and forth between them, his nervous chatter briefly giving way to speechlessness.

'You two? What, you *know* each other?' he demands in disbelief.

'We met once. I interviewed Leo as a witness in connection with a case I'm working on.'

Kore opens his eyes wide in a way that suggests to Karen he's far from as unconcerned about his friend as he's making out to be.

'But you're working on the Langevik murder, aren't you? Hell, did you *see* it, Leo?'

Karen raises her hands in a cautionary gesture when Kore's voice makes the people at the next table turn to look at them. She answers for Leo.

'If only. No, but Leo was able to give someone an alibi for the time of the murder.'

'That's bloody exciting. Who?'

Kore's worry has given way to unadulterated curiosity.

'Oh, come off it. Do you really think I'm going to answer that? But it was valuable information and it spared us a lot of work.'

She smiles at Leo, who raises his glass again and drinks. He doesn't return the smile, but some of the tension in his eyes and body language seems to have eased. Kore looks calmer, too, as he turns back to Leo, now using a normal, almost gentle tone.

'I heard you had a rough go of it after you quit. You know how people talk. But I haven't heard a word for a year. I almost figured you'd gone off grid.'

For the first time, there's a hint of a smile behind Leo's beard.

'That's exactly what I did. Until you outed me.'

'Seriously?' Kore looks around the tables around them and leans forward.

'No one seems to recognise you,' he says quietly. 'And seriously, in that get-up, no wonder. No offence, but you look like shit.'

This time, Leo laughs. A quick chuckle, hard around the edges. A laugh that shows he's aware of his deterioration and accepts it.

A knot grows in the pit of Karen's stomach when it begins to dawn on her who Leo Friis really is.

63

Sigrid drives maddeningly slowly and carefully. What else can you expect, Karen thinks to herself and leans back in the passenger seat. An inexperienced driver with a copper sitting next to her in a car that's seen better days. At least the garage fixed the starter; when Sigrid picked her up at Repslagar Square ten minutes ago the car sounded no worse than any other Toyota its age.

'Did you manage to get everything from the flat?' Karen asks, adjusting her seatbelt, which is cutting into her throat.

'Everything I want to keep,' Sigrid says, jerking her head toward the back seat, where paper bags full of clothes jostle for space with a couple of blue canvas bags. 'There's more in the boot,' she adds, checking the rear-view mirror before turning on the indicator. 'Did you have a good time? Smells like you did. How much did you have to drink?'

Karen slowly turns her head and studies Sigrid with a mocking smile.

'Three pints, Mummy,' she says. 'Yes, seeing Kore's always lovely. And you're very kind to pick me up. The sofa in Marike's studio has its limitations as far as comfort's concerned.'

'He was pretty good-looking. The one in the leather jacket, I mean.'

Sigrid's trying to sound casual. She's not successful.

'He is. His boyfriend is too,' Karen replies drily. 'And nice.'

'Shit. That's a shame.'

'Eirik and I are friends from school; I know Kore through him.'

'What about the other bloke? Have you known him for a hundred years, too?'

'I don't know him at all. But apparently Kore and he are old friends.'

'He looked a bit . . . tattered. Manky, kind of.'

Karen makes no reply.

'Do you know who The Clamp are?' she says after a while.

Sigrid looks at her in surprise.

'Of course I know who they are. Or were, to be precise. Why do you ask?'

'We were talking about them earlier, is all. Apparently, they were pretty big.'

'Sure, but they broke up several years ago. Tragic, according to some people, but I don't know. You have to quit while you're ahead.'

Karen takes in Sigrid's sage view and gives her an amused look.

'So how do you know when you're ahead?'

'You never do until it's too late; which is when you realise you should have quit sooner. I mean, they were all right, but not exactly my thing.'

'What exactly is your thing? Hip-hop? Boys dressed like pre-schoolers with oversized jewellery . . .?'

Sigrid shoots her a look.

'Come on, what are you, a hundred? You don't like rap?'

'Sure. I saw John Cooper Clarke in London in eighty-four. Me and a friend cut class for two days, took the ferry over; Mum was furious.'

'And who the fuck is John Cooper Clarke?'

'Fancy Cuba but it cost me less to Maj*ooo*rca.'

Sigrid shoots her another incredulous glance.

'What are you on about?'

'Forget it. It was a long time ago.'

'Craving,' Sigrid exclaims suddenly. 'A kind of mix of rap and jazz and African music, but it's a hell of a lot more than that. Art and theatre and . . . well, everything. It has no boundaries, sort of.'

'Craving? As in . . . craving?'

'Yeah. Like a whole concept. That's the point, to not limit yourself or wait for something to come to you. Everything right now. Get it?'

Karen doesn't.

They sit in silence as mile after mile of tarmac rolls by beneath the car. Karen closes her eyes and lets her mind wander. It's nice to have company, to just sit next to someone in silence. Even if Sigrid doesn't know who John Cooper Clarke is. She'd love him; Karen should dig up some old albums. It's nice not to be alone in the house, too – at least for a while. She's promised Sigrid she can stay in the guest room while she renovates the house she just inherited.

They've agreed not to discuss the investigation. Sigrid won't ask, Karen won't say more than Sigrid can read for herself in the papers.

It is strange, though, that she never asks anything, Karen muses. Doesn't she care who killed her mum? Or is she simply an obedient detective's daughter, trained not to ask questions? And what made her so relentlessly furious with her parents? She's not going to ask; if Sigrid wants to talk, she's going to have to bring it up.

Her thoughts turn sleepily to Kore. And Leo Friis. She left them at the restaurant when Sigrid honked from the other side of the street. They'd agreed she'd pick Karen up around nine, and she'd honked so punctually Karen suspects she watched them from the car for a while before making herself known.

She'd had no chance to speak to Kore alone. Karen had a thousand questions to ask him about Leo Friis, but unlike Kore, she hadn't wanted to come across as too curious. She'd gathered he'd been the guitarist in The Clamp. She vaguely remembered some of their songs, but for some reason she'd always assumed they were either British or American. They'd been popular during a time in her life when all her strength had been required just to get out of bed in the morning.

Over the years, she's come to understand that for some reason Doggerland, or at least Dunker, has become some kind of hub for the music industry, the home of countless successful songwriters and producers, but she's never kept up with it. Kore looked through her music collection six years ago, then concluded with a sigh there wasn't much to interest even vinyl collectors.

Then he'd inundated her with playlists. The hateful heirs of the pretentious mix tapes guys had bombarded her with during her dating years.

'There's this song you just have to listen to' is a sentence that still makes Karen instinctively cover her ears.

Kore's playlists had contained songs recorded in his own studio at KGB Productions and other things he thought she might like. And sure, she listens to them sometimes, though not nearly as often as Kore imagines. On the contrary, she often seeks out silence. Advertisement jingles, music in every scene of every film, the constant background music playing in shops, at restaurants and in bars wearies her.

But the KGB parties are usually a good time; through Kore, she's met artists that would likely have most people fumbling around for their autograph pad. Leo Friis is, so far as she can remember, not one of them. On the other hand, he probably looked pretty different just a few years ago. At least judging by the fact that no one seems to recognise the rock star hiding inside the bearded tramp. The only looks he got from the other patrons, both at the café the other day and tonight at Repet, were disapproving ones.

Is he going to go straight from Repet's heated outdoor serving area to one of the loading docks tonight? Karen wonders. How long can he keep sleeping rough? The temperature is still hovering around zero, but it's a matter of days before the frost kills whatever's still alive in her garden. And probably a few of the poor sods sleeping under the stars rather than in one of the shelters.

'He keeps to himself,' Gro Aske had told her. 'A bit nuts when it comes to confined spaces.'

I wonder if he's on something or if he's just had a meltdown, Karen ponders but is snatched out of her disjointed reverie when Sigrid turns off the main road and the first pothole on Langeviksvej jolts the car.

'You won't tell Dad about me living with you, will you?'

She straightens up in her seat and shoots Sigrid a quick look.

'No, not if you don't want me to. You're an adult. But I do think it might be good for you to talk to him. Especially now that your mum—'

'Do you want to talk to him?' Sigrid cuts in. 'Is my dad a person you feel good talking to?'

Her voice is harsh and scornful, and Karen remembers her first interview with Sigrid up in Gaarda. The rapport they've built up over the past few days is still fragile, that wall can probably be put back up very quickly. Sigrid certainly seems poised to pull out brick and trowel.

'No,' Karen replies frankly. 'He's not.'

But I have to talk to him. Tomorrow. The order had come just before she left work: the prosecutor's office in city hall at nine tomorrow morning. Chief of Police Viggo Haugen had sent it to both Jounas Smeed and her.

She knows exactly what the meeting's going to be about.

64

'I saw you last night at Repet.'

The meeting with Viggo Haugen is over. The expected things were said and nothing else. Jounas and Karen have taken the lift down and walked through the culvert under Redehusgate to avoid having to dash across the car park in the rain. Now they're standing in the police station garage, waiting for the lift that will take them up to the CID.

When she makes no reply, Jounas Smeed continues:

'I was walking past and saw you in the outdoor serving area in fairly dubious company, if you don't mind me saying.'

Still without answering, she gives the lift button, which is already lit, an annoyed push.

'Well, I suppose your gay friends are fine, but the other one looked like hell,' he goes on, unconcerned. 'No kidding, he reminded me of the blokes who hang out behind the market hall. I actually almost thought I recognised him.'

'You should have.'

Jounas Smeed looks nonplussed and she decides not to tell him Leo's the homeless man who provided him with an alibi.

'Given as how you have such an eye for people,' she says instead in a voice dripping with honey. 'You can tell a person's character straight away.'

'Cut it out, Eiken. You're an officer of the law; do you really think it's appropriate for you to be out on town with people like him?'

'What can I say, I've traded up. Since Oistra, I mean.'

Jounas Smeed is quiet for a second or two, seemingly holding his breath. Then he lets the air out in a heavy sigh and smacks his tongue reprovingly.

'Karen, Karen. Always so angry. Always so defensive. It's getting to be a problem, you know.'

'Maybe I have my reasons.'

Finally, the lift dings. Karen steps into it and silently watches the shiny steel doors slide shut.

'I understand you're disappointed they're suspending the investigation, but you can hardly blame me for that. At the end of the day, it's the prosecutor's decision and she and Haugen agree; we have our guy, he's been arrested.'

'We have *a* guy, who has confessed to four burglaries and two counts of attempted arson. He wasn't the one who killed Susanne.'

'And how can you be so damn sure?'

'Well, we'll never know now, will we?'

The message had been clear: the murder of Susanne Smeed is considered solved. All attempts at finding alternative motives and perpetrators are to cease.

'No, I suppose we won't,' Smeed replies. 'But on the other hand, you didn't come up with a single concrete theory in the time you had.'

'A whole week, you mean?'

'Regardless, at least we finally nicked Kvanne, and no thanks to you, by the way. If not for that tip-off, he'd probably had time to break in and set fire to a few more houses by now. Maybe killed some other poor sod unlucky enough to be home.'

The lift dings again and they get out. As Karen reaches out to open the frosted glass door with the police logo and worn letters announcing the domain of the CID, Jounas Smeed puts his hand on the doorframe, blocking her from entering.

'You know what the deal is, Eiken,' he says. 'Björken joins the Moerbeck case for the next few weeks before he shoves off home to change nappies. You will discontinue all active work on the Langevik case and instead focus on putting together the final report on Kvanne. And you will keep your thoughts to yourself in there. Not a word.'

65

Karen Eiken Hornby really has kept her thoughts to herself. For two whole days she's resisted the temptation to speak her mind. She hasn't said one critical word about the decision.

'The prosecutor really thinks she can make the charges stick?' Karl had asked.

'It looks that way.'

Or maybe she doesn't give a toss, Karen had thought to herself. Other cases were piling up: assaults, drugs, prostitution. And Moerbeck. Despite concerted efforts, no suspect has been arrested. Quite the reverse, in fact; the number of raped and assaulted women has gone from two to three, the most recent attack taking place in the early hours of the previous day. Still only one death, but the latest victim, a twenty-seven-year-old mother of two on her way home from the nightshift at Thysted Hospital is in intensive care, the same department where she'd been working just hours before.

On account of a sore throat and a rising temperature, Greta Hansen had finished her shift early at half past four in the morning and been sent home to Atlasvägen in Odinswalla in a taxi by the head nurse. Annoyed at having to drive a visibly sick customer on his very last day of work before leaving this rainy hellhole for three well-deserved weeks in Thailand, the taxi driver had burned rubber as soon as Greta had climbed out and shut the door. Her husband, Finn Hansen, an editor at newspaper *Nya Dagbladet*, had been sound asleep in their newly renovated and beautifully decorated third-floor flat, unaware that a man was just then shoving a broken bottle into his wife in a shrubbery right next to the building.

The news that the perpetrator has ventured out of socially disadvantaged Moerbeck, expanding his hunting grounds to middle-class Odinswalla has stirred the media into a frenzy.

The condemnation of the police at yesterday's press conference had been unanimous; the police had clearly deployed the promised uniformed and plainclothes officers in the wrong places. Hadn't they considered the possibility of the perpetrator changing his hunting grounds? Were the police able to guarantee the public's safety? What did they have to say to the city's frightened women? Was Haugen himself happy with the police's efforts so far? Had he considered resigning? What did the Minister of Home Affairs have to say?

Colleagues are snapping at each other; everyone looks pale and determined, the overtime logged is making HR edgy. Dunker's police headquarters is seething with frustration that another woman has been attacked, that they don't have the resources to keep a police presence on every goddamn street, that the bastard's still on the loose. And on top of all that, the constant fear that it might happen again. Maybe tonight.

The news that an arrest has finally been made in the Langevik case barely makes the papers, but any hint that they might have the wrong guy would set off a media storm. Linus Kvanne simply has to be found guilty. Besides, it's a crass reality that neither the Dogger Police Authority nor the Prosecution Service has the resources for more than one high-profile case at a time.

The truth is Haugen probably welcomed the Moerbeck case as a chance to redeem himself. Exactly what they needed; a clear-cut case, a competent head investigator and some old-fashioned police work. Order would soon be restored.

Karen decides he's probably not as confident anymore.

But she says nothing. Karen Eiken Hornby is well versed in the art of keeping her thoughts to herself.

That doesn't stop her, however, from looking over at her boss's office two hours later before reaching for her phone.

'No, Mum's not back yet,' Mette Brinckmann-Grahn tells her, now with a hint of irritation in her voice. 'How many times are you going to ask?'

'And you still haven't heard from her?'

Mette Brinckmann-Grahn heaves a sigh.

'Like I told you, she called from Bilbao the day before yesterday and said she'd be back as soon as she could find a cheap flight. But, really, I already explained all of this to your colleague.'

Karen curses her lack of Swedish. She must have heard her wrong.

'What do you mean? Who did you explain it to?'

'The other police officer who called this morning. Mum's mobile was ringing and ringing and in the end, I answered; figured it might be important. But she just asked the same questions you are. Wanted to get in touch with Mum and know when she'd be back. Don't you police people talk to each other?'

For a split second, the world is spinning. A female colleague? Could Astrid Nielsen have tried to reach Disa without telling her? No, she's been transferred to Smeed's case now and won't have time for anything else. And Astrid would definitely have informed Karen if for some unknown reason she'd done something like that.

'This other woman you spoke to, did she really say she worked for the police? I mean, explicitly?'

Mette is quiet for a moment and then says with a tone of genuine surprise:

'No, now that you mention it, maybe she didn't. But she introduced herself and sounded very formal. And she sounded a lot like you.'

'Like me? What do you mean?'

'Well, she had those thick *l*s and *r*s you have. And the same questions, like I said. I probably just assumed she worked for the police.'

Mette Brinckmann-Grahn falls silent again. Then she says:

'Come to think of it, she might just as well have been British. Or American maybe. Which makes sense with her name, too. Anne Crosby, she said it was.'

'Anne Crosby. And you're sure about that?'

'Of course, I have it written down here with her number and everything. I promised I'd call her as soon as I heard from Mum.'

Karen closes her eyes before asking the next question.

'And did you? Did you call Anne Crosby and tell her your mum's on her way home?'

'Of course! I considered calling you as well, but then I thought one phone call to the police was enough. I figured this Anne Crosby could fill you in. I told her she should.'

Mette Brinckmann only now seems to realise her mistake.

'Well, I thought . . . I just assumed that . . . Either way, it doesn't matter,' she adds in a defiant tone. 'Mum's not back yet anyway.'

66

Who the fuck is Anne Crosby? Karen wonders as she gives up after eight rings and throws her phone down on her desk.

Mette Brinckmann-Grahn had, very obligingly and without protest, read out Anne Crosby's phone number, digit by digit, in both Swedish and English to ensure there was no miscommunication. Karen had dialled the number the moment she hung up. Ten beeps, no answer, no voicemail. After five minutes, she makes another attempt and eight more beeps without a result.

Now she reaches for her mouse and watches as the anxiety-inducing perpetual motion of the screensaver is replaced with the Dogger police logo. It takes her two quick searches to establish that there's no one by the name of Anne Crosby in the Dogger Republic, but that the number of women called Anne Crosby globally seems infinite. A third search, this time for the phone number. No hits. Probably a pay-as-you-go SIM, she concludes dejectedly.

She stands up to call Karl Björken over, but changes her mind and sinks back into her office chair. Quickly, and with a strange feeling her boss is watching, she opens the Susanne Smeed case file, finds Cornelis Loots' summary of the technical investigation and scrolls down to the IT department's findings. Forty-five seconds later, she's looked from the screen to her mobile phone and back again enough times.

One more attempt, another eight signals without a result. Annoyed, she dials the Connors' phone number instead and is greeted by Brandon Connor's voice after four rings:

'Janet and I have better things to do than answering the phone at the moment. Leave a message and we'll call you back.'

She does as she's told.

Another glance over at Smeed; he's on the phone with someone; judging from his facial expression, it's not good news.

Smeed and Haugen can go fuck themselves, she thinks, grabs her jacket and walks over to Karl Björken.

'Lunch? My treat.'

Fifteen minutes later, Karl places his knife against the potato he's stabbed on his fork and removes the thin peel with the help of his thumb. They've gone to one of Dunker's finer lunch establishments, on Parkvej up in Norrebro. Over a mile of reassuring safety distance from the station. This is going to hurt her wallet, Karen realises.

'Last *kelpis* of the year,' Karl says, reverently admiring the unremarkable root. 'Expensive, but worth every shilling, if you ask me.'

'The first of the year are better,' Karen retorts, wriggling out of her jacket. 'But either way, they don't taste like they used to. It's all industrialised nowadays; giant lorries full of some green algae mush they spray on the fields. I wish you could have tasted the ones my grandfather grew up on Noorö. Nothing but bladderwrack, straight in the cliff crevices.

'Any *kelpis* is better than none,' Karl says, fishing another potato out of the bowl and placing it next to a hunk of turbot as thick as a finger. 'Can't blame me for seizing the

404

opportunity when someone else is paying. Can I ask why the sudden generosity, by the way? Did you get lucky at the track or something?'

'I figured it was the quickest way to get you alone,' she says dourly. 'You're hardly the type to ask questions when someone waves their chequebook around, are you?'

Karl smiles smugly and shoves half a potato topped with a sizeable piece of turbot and melted butter into his mouth.

'Smeed wouldn't be best pleased if he found out I'm taking a long lunch,' he says between bites. 'I'm supposed to be working on his case, not sitting here with you. I was just reading up on that shit when you came thundering over. It's bloody grim reading, I can tell you that.'

'Good, then you need a break. A friendly lunch, just two colleagues talking. What could he have against that?'

'Come off it, Eiken; you would never buy me lunch unless you were after something. Just tell me what this is about.'

Karen quickly looks around the full room and leans forward.

'I called Mette Brinckmann-Grahn again,' she says.

'I thought you were supposed to focus on Kvanne? Keep your thoughts to yourself and not cause trouble.'

Karen continues without comment:

'I just wanted to check if she'd heard from her mother. Disa said she was going to be back this week.'

'All right. So had she? Heard from her mother, I mean?'

'Yes, apparently she's finally on her way home. But she told me I wasn't the only person trying to reach Disa Brinckmann.'

'I should certainly hope the Dogger Police Authority isn't the old woman's only point of contact with the world.'

Karen ignores his sarcastic tone.

'Apparently, another woman called about the same thing. She introduced herself as Anne Crosby and left her number. The daughter was under the impression she worked for the Dogger police. She didn't claim to, but apparently didn't correct the daughter's misapprehension either. Mette Brinckmann-Grahn was fairly annoyed about having to explain the same thing to several police officers, she said.'

'Your food's getting cold,' Karl says, nodding at the untouched lamb cutlets on Karen's plate.

She dutifully cuts off a piece and pops it into her mouth. Chews and waits for Karl to lob back the ball she's served at him.

'All right,' he says after a while. 'Anne Crosby, you say. And who's that?'

'Yeah, I'm wondering the same thing. I've tried to call, but no one picks up.'

'Exciting. Really. A woman we don't know has called someone who probably has nothing to do with the investigation.'

Karl Björken shoots her a sceptical look over his glass as he sips his beer. Without taking her eyes off his, Karen bends to the side, fumbles around in her handbag on the floor and pulls out a piece of paper. Without a word, she unfolds it and places it next to Karl's plate.

'Well,' he says, after skimming the information on it. 'It made no difference in the Smeed case, but you have to give it to him, Cornelis Loots is meticulous. I hope he's as thorough with the Moerbeck information. We're going to need it if we want any chance of catching that bastard.'

Karl turns his attention back to his plate.

Without comment, Karen puts her phone down on the other side of his plate. The screen shows the most recently dialled number.

Karl Björken has stopped chewing. Then he leans back in his chair and meets her eyes.

'Damn,' he says. 'So the mystery of the unknown pay-as-you-go SIM has been solved. What are you going to do now?'

'Don't know. But I have to follow up somehow. First, this Anne Crosby calls Susanne twice in June and again on 27 September. Just two days before she was killed. And now she's trying to reach Disa Brinckmann. Her trying to contact two people connected to the case can hardly be a coincidence.'

'Or maybe that's exactly what it is,' Karl counters calmly. 'Sheer coincidence, I mean.'

Karen gives him a doubtful look.

'Or, more to the point,' he adds, 'Disa Brinckmann isn't really connected to the case. Just a name that came up.'

'A name that came up during the mapping of the victim's background.'

'Which is why the same person reaching out to both Susanne and Disa is in all likelihood immaterial. This Anne Crosby probably just knows both of them. All cases are full of coincidences that have no bearing on the case itself.'

'If that's true, it's a bloody strange coincidence. Disa and Susanne didn't know each other, after all. Susanne had barely been born when Disa left the island.'

'Fine, but Disa knew her parents. This Anne Crosby is probably linked to the commune in one way or another; knew one of the members or maybe even lived there herself for a while, what do I know? Lots of people must have come and gone. Have you asked Brandon and Janet Connor?'

'Not yet, but I left a message on their machine. Now I'm considering sending a text to Anne Crosby's mobile. Asking her to contact me.'

'Well, why not? Apparently, Disa's daughter already informed her the police were trying to get in touch with Disa anyway. And I'll give you that it's a bit strange Anne Crosby didn't clear up that little misunderstanding straight away. On the other hand, maybe she had no idea what Mette was talking about; that south-Swedish dialect is bloody incomprehensible.'

'So you think I should text her? Even though I've been ordered to focus on Kvanne?'

Karen puts her thumb on the send button.

'What are you asking me for? You already made your mind up.'

There's a beep as the message is sent. Karen turns her phone around to let Karl read the short text saying the Doggerland police are trying to reach Anne Crosby, urging her to contact the Dunker CID immediately on this number. He slowly shakes his head.

'Smeed's going to go ballistic when he realises you're still working on this.'

'But he won't find out. Will he?'

'Not from me, no. I'm perfectly happy to allow you the great pleasure of telling him yourself. If Anne Crosby gets back to you, you're going to have to, I guess. On the other hand, she's only going to call if she *doesn't* have anything to do with the murder.'

67

Langevik, 1971

'It's no use; if we can't get the breastfeeding to work, she's not going to make it.'

Disa puts down the bottle with the hateful formula, wipes her forehead with her wrist and puts the baby against her shoulder.

It had become clear to her after the first day that a mix of milk, flour and a dollop of butter wasn't going to do the trick. Not in this case. And she'd seen the looks they'd given her, seen the flicker of doubt when she told Per to go to the pharmacy in Dunker to purchase formula. Nestlé. The very name was an affront, the exploitation of the third world, the shameless racket. It was a prime symbol of capitalist predation. But he'd gone and he'd purchased. And now they'd sold their souls to the devil and they had nothing to show for it.

Three days now. Disa's eyes and stomach ache with worry and sleep deprivation. Three days and Ingela still won't get out of bed. Just lies there with her eyes closed, even when she's awake. And the others are tiptoeing around with their awkwardness, their lack of experience, their utter helplessness.

Rage unexpectedly flares up inside Disa. They're like children, the lot of them. Stupid children in grown-up bodies.

They've put all their faith in her, assumed she's going to take care of everything, solve all their problems. Disa, the calm one, the safe one. The one with the ancient knowledge; the old remedies, the old treatments. Disa, earth mother, midwife. And why would you need a hospital anyway for something as natural as childbirth?

She'd been able to make out two heartbeats by week nineteen. That Tomas couldn't be the father had been clear to her even earlier. Maybe even before Ingela herself had faced the truth. Disa had seen Ingela and Per, figured out what Tomas pretended not to know. She knows when the children must have been conceived and that Tomas had been nowhere near Langevik.

'You have to tell him,' she'd said. 'Both Tomas and Per have a right to know. And Anne-Marie,' she'd added, realising this would change everything.

And in the end, Per had told his wife the cruel truth. That he'd been unfaithful. That the children Ingela was expecting were his. That he was going to be a father, while Anne-Marie would likely remain childless. Maybe they'd all known it then, when they heard her heartrending sobs from the first floor, known that this was the beginning of the end. Realised it long before the screaming and yelling turned into icy silence. Or had it only dawned on them in the weeks that followed, when their concern for Anne-Marie had slowly morphed into exasperation?

Maybe that was when the unwelcome insight that the idea of sharing everything was beautiful in theory but hideous in practice had crept up on them. When they all secretly found Anne-Marie's reaction easier to relate to than Tomas' indifference. When their admiration for his ability to forgive and forget slowly turned into contempt. Why wasn't he furious? Could he really forgive Ingela and Per? Was he – the thought was as forbidden as it was impossible to suppress – was he not a real man?

One after the other, they'd abandoned their shared dream. Theo had gone back to Amsterdam just a few weeks after the idyll was shattered. Brandon and Janet had stuck it out a while longer. Endured Anne-Marie's grief and Per's remorse-fuelled red-wine orgies. Endured Tomas' incomprehensible serenity in the face of everything falling apart around him. Endured the sight of Ingela's growing belly, like a constant reminder nothing was going to get better. This time, the problem wouldn't go away eventually.

In the end, Brandon had found Janet down by the harbour one freezing February morning, sitting alone on a bollard.

'I'm leaving tomorrow,' she'd told him. 'Are you coming with me?'

'Where to?' he'd asked.

'Anywhere.'

And so, they'd given up, too, and left the commune.

But Disa had stayed. Ever dutiful, she was going to stick it out until after the children were finally born; she'd promised them she would. Then, she'd promised herself, she was going to leave this nightmare, too.

When labour finally began, hope had returned like some kind of innate reflex. Maybe things will get better once the children are here. When life fills the house once more. Ingela had followed her instructions mechanically: breathe, don't push yet, wait, wait . . . Now!

And Tomas had sat by her side the whole time. Tomas, not Per. Maybe that was his revenge, after all. The one small show of strength he allowed himself; shutting Per out. He, Tomas, was going to be one to see the children born, even though they weren't his.

And it had happened surprisingly quickly; the first child was out only a couple of hours after the first contraction. Healthy and strong, the little girl had cried after a gentle rub with a towel. Then Disa had realised something was wrong. Ingela had suddenly run out of strength and slipped into an apathic state. It had been almost an hour before everything was finally over and the other girl was out. Exhausted and limp, half the size of her sister. Disa had heard of such things during her training; that sometimes one twin steals so much of the nutrition in the womb the other is stunted. And sure, she'd read about mothers who were unable to bond with their children, women who instead of the joy of motherhood experienced deep depression. She'd heard and read, but never encountered it.

Three days now. Three days of worry. About the child who won't eat, about Ingela who doesn't seem to care about either of the children. And for the first time since deciding to become a midwife, Disa Brinckmann wishes she was in a hospital.

'This won't do,' she says again. 'We need help.'

She looks up at the others. Tomas' eyes are despondent. Per's are anxiously darting back and forth. And Anne-Marie, who's holding the other baby girl in her arms. Disa studies her and wonders for a moment if she even realises the child's not hers. Anne-Marie seemed to revive the moment Ingela slipped into apathy. She has looked after the healthy girl, rocked her, fed her, soothed her and watched over her as though she were her own flesh and blood. Now she looks uncomprehendingly at Disa before turning her attention back to the child, pressing her closer as she watches her little mouth suck on the bottle's rubber nipple.

'She does eat. When I feed her,' she says.

'Melody does, yes, but Happy's not putting on nearly enough weight. I can't be responsible for this anymore, we need to take her to a doctor. Ingela needs help, too. You all know something's wrong, she doesn't even have the strength to hold her babies.'

Per stand up so quickly his chair topples backward with a crash.

'They're my children,' he says. 'You can't just take them.'

Silence engulfs the kitchen. Endless seconds, anxious breathing, impossible thoughts. Then Disa leans across the table.

'It's up to you, Tomas: either I take both Ingela and Happy to the hospital in Dunker, or we're getting on the ferry back to Sweden tonight.'

Anne-Marie gets up without a word, puts the bottle down on the table and leaves the room with Melody in her arms.

Tomas watches her go and then turns to Disa.

'Let's go home,' he says quietly.

68

Karen exits the Hare and Crow, her face set. She gets into her car and leans her forehead against the steering wheel. She's been wrong.

So goddamn incredibly wrong.

The past twenty-four hours have been filled with paperwork, phone calls to the prosecutor's office and constant glances at her phone. Anne Crosby hasn't got back to her. Nor has Disa Brinckmann.

She has conducted another fruitless interview with Linus Kvanne, who stood by his assertions. Yes, he confesses to all four burglaries. Yes, he tried to set fire to the houses in Thorsvik and Grunder, but he doesn't get what the big deal is. No one was home; he knew that when he started the fires. Fine, but then the laws need to be changed!

And no, he didn't kill Susanne Smeed; he's never in his life even set foot in godforsaken bloody Langevik or whatever it's called.

The last part was only refuted thirty minutes after Karen left the interview room. Sören Larsen had called from the lab at quarter to four that afternoon, apologising vaguely for the amount of work involved in the Moerbeck investigation delaying the results Karen had been waiting for.

She'd listened without comment when he continued.

'Kvanne's mobile phone was connected to one of the masts in Langevik for almost eleven hours, from 10.31 p.m. to 9.24 a.m.,' Larsen had told her, not bothering to hide his glee. 'That poor sod must have spent all of Oistra in that godforsaken hole. You live in Langevik, what on earth is there for a person to get up to there?'

'Not much,' Karen had replied. 'Not much at all, unfortunately.'

'Sure, he was here,' Arild Rasmussen had confirmed when she showed him Linus Kvanne's mug shot a few hours later at the Hare and Crow.

'He was sitting in the corner over there, talking on his phone all night. Stayed inside even though it was a warm night and everyone else was outside. Drunk as a skunk, he got, too; I had to personally throw him out around three. No, I mean twelve, obviously . . .'

'I don't care how long you stayed open, Arild. But the timings could be important.'

'All right, he was the last one to leave, just after three. It was quarter past by the time I got up to the flat.'

'Do you know where he went after that?'

'No idea. He asked if I had a room, but as you know, I don't anymore. I assume he slept in his car.'

'He had a car? Are you saying you saw it?'

Arild Rasmussen has to ponder that for a second.

'No, I guess I didn't, but he must have had one. How in heaven's name would he have got here otherwise?'

Yes, that is the question, she thinks now, with her head against the wheel. How had Linus Kvanne made it almost twenty

415

miles from the quarry where the stolen motorcycle had been found, to the Hare and Crow in Langevik? He had very likely had a car when he left Langevik: a Toyota with a quarrelsome starter engine.

I've never in my life even set foot in Langevik. The little prick had lied to her face and she'd believed him. Karen groans loudly.

I'm going to have to check every single call he made and talk to everyone who was here that night, she resolves and lifts her head back up. Someone must've seen which way he went after the pub closed.

Goddamn Sören, if only he'd let her know a bit sooner. But as she thinks that, she realises there's no point shifting the blame to someone else. Her own stubbornness and refusal to accept irrefutable facts has led to this situation. Thirty-six precious hours, which she could have spent scrutinising Linus Kvanne instead of sniffing around an old hippie commune from the seventies.

With another heavy sigh, she buckles her seatbelt, turns the key and starts the car.

69

Once more, heavenly smells greet her as she steps through the front door of her old stone house. Sigrid comes trotting down the stairs with a towel wrapped around her hair.

'God, that feels good,' she says. 'I hope I didn't get dye all over the bathroom. Did you know they sell hair dye in the hardware shop?'

She bends over, lets the towel unfurl and rubs her wet raven hair.

Karen eyes the stained towel wearily.

'Oh dear,' Sigrid exclaims. 'But I can give you one of Mum's instead; she has like a thousand.'

'Don't worry about it. What's for dinner? It smells amazing.'

'Coq au vin. Sort of, anyway. I stole a bottle from the pantry. Did you know there's a farmer up by the road to Grene who sells organically raised chicken?'

Karen lets out an amused snort.

'Are you talking about Johar Iversen? I don't think he knows how to spell non-toxic. Even maggots won't go near his kale.'

Sigrid looks disappointed.

'Only organic feed and free-range chickens, that's what he told me. I bought eggs, too.'

'Sure,' Karen says, 'they're free-range, all right. Old Johar's chickens run loose across the roads up there. I've probably run over at least three myself. Don't get upset, I'm exaggerating,' she adds when she notices Sigrid's horrified expression. 'I just had a bad day at work.'

'Is it to do with Mum? I know we're not supposed to talk about it, but it said in the papers you've arrested a suspect.'

Karen hesitates. Sigrid's staying with her is predicated on careful mutual avoidance of two subjects: her mother. And her father.

'OK, yes, it's true. And a lot of things point to it being the right guy, I can tell you that much. But before we're 100 per cent sure, I'm not going to discuss who he is or why he's in detention.'

I just hope you don't know him, she suddenly thinks. Granted, Linus Kvanne is a few years older than Sigrid and they don't look like they travel in the same circles, but he lives in Gaarda, just a few blocks from Samuel Nesbö's flat.

Sigrid's version of coq au vin is stripped down, to say the least. Chicken and wine. Instead of bothering with things like bacon, chestnut mushrooms and shallots, she has added a can of haricot beans and thrown in a couple of cloves of garlic near the end for good measure. It tastes surprisingly good once Karen has sprinkled on some salt and pepper. Most importantly, someone else cooked it. I would probably be happy eating hay, so long as someone else served it. She mops up the last of the sauce with a piece of bread.

'If you put the coffee on, I'll do the washing up,' she says, getting to her feet.

Just then, her phone rings.

Karen wipes her fingers on her jeans, steps out into the hallway and pulls her phone out of her jacket pocket. Without checking the number, she answers in the curt tone of someone expecting a salesman on the other end.

'Eiken.'

'This is Brandon Connor. I think we need to talk.'

70

The smell of cumin is as prominent as last time, the kitchen as homey, the table as inviting. Outwardly, both Janet and Brandon look as relaxed as before, but this time, the kitchen is suffused with a palpable tension. Karen notices the couple exchanging nervous glances while they set out the teapot and cups.

She shouldn't have come here, should have explained on the phone that the police are no longer interested in what happened in their commune half a century ago. This time, she wastes no time on small talk.

'You have something to tell me?'

Another exchanged look, as though they're checking in with each other one last time. Then Janet nods for Brandon to start.

'We weren't entirely frank with you before,' he says. 'But we've decided to break our promise and tell you what we know.'

'Promise, to whom?'

'To Disa. She's kept shtum about everything all these years, until Tomas died.'

'So you did stay in touch with Disa Brinckmann after all.'

Brandon nods.

'On and off, you might say. But yes, we stayed in touch. She was here only last summer. That's when she told us everything. Couldn't bear keeping it to herself any longer, she said.'

Karen waits without speaking while Brandon sips his tea, looking like he's pondering how to proceed. Then he puts his cup down, takes a deep breath and continues.

'So this happened after Janet and I left the farm. I'm only telling you what Disa told us. We don't know anything else.'

Karen nods.

'As you know, Disa was a midwife and Ingela became pregnant again during our time at Lothorp Farm,' Brandon says. 'Disa was the one who helped her give birth. Going to a hospital was out of the question, for several reasons.'

'Such as?'

'Well, partly because everyone in the commune had strong feelings about women giving birth at home, without drugs that could harm the baby. But also because we weren't part of the community; none of us was born here, none of us had roots on the island. Well, except for Anne-Marie, but since she'd grown up in Sweden and had never even met her grandfather, she was considered an outsider, too. We had no contact with the authorities and I honestly don't even know if they would have helped Ingela if she'd gone to the hospital.'

They would have, Karen knows. No one would have turned away a woman in labour, not even back then. Out loud, she says:

'Then she must have helped with Anne-Marie's birth as well, I assume? Susanne was born in April of seventy-one; they must have been pregnant at roughly the same time, right?'

'Anne-Marie was never pregnant,' Brandon says quietly. 'Susanne was Ingela's child.'

He leans back in his chair with a heavy sigh and gestures for Janet to take over. She strokes her husband's cheek, then leans forward and puts her elbows on the table.

'We all knew Per and Anne-Marie were unable to have children. She'd had several miscarriages in Sweden; the last one almost killed her. It was one of the reasons she and Per moved here, to get a fresh start, to find a kind of community that wasn't built around the nuclear family.'

Janet reaches for the honey jar and lets a heaped spoonful trickle into her cup. Karen has declined the offer of tea, determined to keep this visit short. She now realises she's been wrong. Again.

'At first it worked,' Janet continues. 'Anne-Marie could be a supplementary mother to both Disa's daughter Mette and Tomas and Ingela's boys, but it clearly pained her that none of the children was hers.'

Janet pauses and sips her tea.

'The irony of it was that among us, Anne-Marie was, maybe with the exception of Disa, the one who loved children the most. The truth is she looked after the boys more than Ingela did; playing, comforting, getting up in the night. Ingela gave birth and breastfed, but that's sort of where her involvement ended. The rest was Tomas' job, with Anne-Marie's help.'

'And then Ingela got pregnant again,' Karen says. 'While Anne-Marie was still childless. And that's what caused her depression.'

'Not just that, I'm afraid,' Janet says, glancing quickly at her husband, as though seeking support. But Brandon's eyes are fixed on the table top. Janet sighs and spreads her hands in a gesture of resignation.

'This time, Per was the father.'

Karen feels her stomach contract and nausea rising in her throat. The combined grief of not being able to conceive, of children coming into the world unwanted and of children belonging to someone else. Not to mention the grief when children die. Children who were both welcome and loved, but who were snatched away, between one breath and the next. Those people who have child after child without any feeling of wonder at the miracle of it. And the ones who are left without.

Anne-Marie had not only been forced to accept that her husband had been unfaithful. He was having a baby with another woman. While she struggled with her own grief at never becoming a mother, her husband was going to be a father. And it had all happened right in front of her in the house that was supposed to be her safe haven.

'Go on,' Karen says flatly.

Janet shoots her a quick look, then pushes the teapot and an empty cup toward her guest and continues.

'Like Brandon said, we'd left the farm by the time Ingela gave birth, so what we're telling you now is what Disa told us when she visited last summer. Before then, we didn't know; she never breathed a word until Tomas passed away.'

Karen nods.

'So Ingela left Susanne with Per when they moved back to Sweden? Well, he was her father, so maybe that's not entirely surprising,' she says.

I'd rather rip my own arm off than leave my child, she thinks inwardly.

'They left one child. Ingela and Tomas brought the other one with them back to Sweden.'

71

The kitchen is dead silent. Two children. Not one. And yet, it's not the revelation that Susanne had a sister that shakes Karen. She fumbles desperately for any kind of logic in what Janet just told her. To split up siblings, keeping one and giving up the other. To choose one and reject the other.

'Apparently, they had to leave quickly,' Janet says. 'One of the children was weak from the first and needed more care than Disa could provide. Ingela was in a bad state and unable to bond with either child. They tried to get her to breastfeed, but it wasn't working and the weaker girl kept losing weight, despite attempts to feed her formula. In the end, they decided to leave the farm and go back to Sweden. I think they made the decision within days of the birth.'

'Without Susanne?'

Janet nods.

'Without Susanne. Or Melody, as they called her back then. Melody and Happy.'

With a pleading look, Janet asks her husband to take over. Betraying Disa's confidence is clearly distressing for both of them. That she's a police officer is obviously making it even more difficult for these old hippies, Karen realises. She gives Brandon an encouraging nod and he presses on, reluctant but determined.

'They had no right to remain here and didn't want to get the authorities involved, so their best option was to go back to Sweden,' he says. 'The idea was probably to return as soon as the little girl had been given the care she needed and grown a bit stronger.'

'But they never did?'

'Apparently, they joined some kind of religious cult after returning to Sweden. Some kind of quasi-Hindu shit, I think. Tomas left pretty quickly, but Ingela stayed. The birth of the twins triggered some kind of psychosis, according to Disa, but I don't think that's the whole story.'

'Drugs?'

Brandon chuckles.

'I mean, we all smoked pot, but Ingela was very . . . how to put it . . . unworldly. Well, we all were, in a way, or pretended to be at least. For us, it was a deliberate struggle to break with convention, but in her case . . . let's just say she was in a league of her own. Either way, Ingela went off to India with that cult and took the boys with her. According to Disa, Tomas spent over a year trying to find them, but in the end, he gave up. Closed the door on that part of his life. And formally he had no rights, of course; the children weren't his.'

'Whose were they?'

'No idea. Tomas and Ingela were a couple when they were young, but they spent a few years apart. Ingela had Orian and Love while they were separated. But we never really talked about who the father was. Tomas and Ingela got married right before we moved to the commune, so even though he never legally adopted the boys, we honestly never gave it much thought.'

'And you're saying she took the boys? What about the girl? Happy.'

'She left her with Tomas.'

Karen feels her cheeks flush with anger. Ingela had abandoned first one girl then the other. And yet, both girls were likely better off than their brothers. Had either boy survived a childhood in a religious cult in India with a mum who had likely stoned herself into a psychosis?

And the girls, who had been taken in by others, true, but never loved by their mother. Melody and Happy. What tragic irony.

'Eventually, Tomas renamed Happy Anne,' Janet says, as though she'd read Karen's mind. 'He was a different person after Ingela left. He changed course completely and took over his father's company. Formally, he was Anne's father, since he and Ingela were married and she had been conceived in wedlock. I don't know if he ever had the marriage annulled or if Ingela's still alive, but he never heard from her again.'

Anne, Karen thinks to herself. It must be her. She resists the urge to hurry them along, to jump to when Happy, who grew up as Anne Ekman, eventually took the surname Crosby.

'So Tomas never remarried?'

'No, apparently not. He and Disa kept in sporadic contact for a few years; she kept trying to persuade him to tell Anne about her half-brothers and twin sister, but he refused. That was a closed chapter, he'd say, and he told Anne her mother was dead. And Disa kept her promise and said nothing; that's just the kind of person she is.'

'And she obviously realised she could get Per and Anne-Marie in trouble, too, if she stirred the pot,' Janet adds.

Don't stir the pot, Karen thinks. Leave the past in the past. No, successful businessman Tomas Ekman hardly stood to gain from the affair becoming public knowledge. He would have risked losing Anne, as well. It probably wouldn't have been good for Per and Anne-Marie Lindgren either. The people of Langevik already looked at them askance; if it came out that Susanne was the result of an affair between Per and one of the women in the commune, they would have found it difficult to stay.

'So she kept everything to herself all these years?'

'Yes, until Tomas passed away. Then she decided to tell both girls the truth. Anne had moved to the US and got married, but she came home for the funeral, of course, and Disa sought her out.'

'And Susanne? How did she get in touch with her?'

'As a matter of fact, we helped her find out where Susanne worked, and then the rest was pretty straightforward.'

'But why?' Karen asks. 'Why was it so important to Disa to have it all out? Surely it would have been a lot easier to stay quiet?'

'That's exactly what we wanted to know,' Brandon said. 'But Disa very firmly believed a twin robbed of its sibling will always feel a sense of loss. And in this particular case, the girls had been torn apart on her recommendation. And Anne, who always believed her mother was dead. I think Disa walked around with a sense of guilt she wanted to assuage before she died.'

'Before she died?' Karen says doubtfully.

The old lady's apparently spry enough to ramble about the Spanish countryside, she notes.

'Disa was diagnosed with breast cancer six months ago. An aggressive form, unfortunately. Apparently, there's nothing to be done.'

72

Karen starts the audio recorder and monotonously recites the date and time, who is present in the room and in what capacity. She senses what's coming; some kind of admission, a desperate attempt to demonstrate a willingness to cooperate now that a bold-faced denial is no longer possible. Linus Kvanne is very likely going to admit to being in Langevik for Oistra but reiterate that he had nothing to do with the murder of Susanne Smeed. No one's going to believe him. The question is if even Karen herself does anymore? And a forbidden voice inside her says she's on the brink of not giving a toss.

She glances down at her papers, then tries to catch Linus Kvanne's eye, to no avail. He's sitting with his head bowed and seems completely absorbed in picking at the cuticle of his right middle finger. With a sigh, she turns instead to Kvanne's lawyer, Gary Brataas.

'Right, you requested this interview,' she says. 'I take it your client has something he wants to share.'

Gary Brataas gives Linus Kvanne a quick look and puts a hand on his shoulder before turning to Karen.

'My client has remembered certain circumstances that may be useful to the investigation. But I would like to take this opportunity to point out that these circumstances in no way changes my client's position with regards to his innocence. Linus had nothing whatsoever to do with the murder of Susanne Smeed.'

'Nothing whatsoever?' Karen says, her eyebrows raised. Fancy that, she adds under her breath.

But apparently not quietly enough, she realises when Gary Brataas opens his mouth to protest. Karen beats him to it.

'All right, Linus, let's hear it, then.'

Without taking his eyes off his cuticle, Linus Kvanne mutters something inaudible.

'I think you're going to have to speak up if you want us to hear what you're saying.'

'I was in Langevik. That night, I mean.'

'Were you now? Well, that's hardly news to us. As you know, we've already established that your phone was there. And since you've not reported it stolen or lost, we've concluded you were there with it. Which you have previously denied. Why did you deny it, come to think of it?'

'Why do you think?'

Kvanne finally looks up. He stares belligerently at Karen, who calmly meets his eyes.

'You're trying to frame me for murder. I haven't fucking killed anybody.'

'Yes, Linus, you have. On New Year's Day six years ago, to be exact.'

Kvanne quickly withdraws and opens his eyes wide.

'Yes, but that was self-defence,' he says.

His tone is resentful, like a schoolboy trying to explain that it was actually the tall boy in class 5b who started the fight in the corridor.

'So you claimed. Stabbed him five times, if I remember correctly. Four times after he he'd already dropped his weapon.'

Kvanne launches across the table. His face ends up so close to Karen's, she can smell his sour chewing tobacco.

'Fuck you, you fucking—'

'Calm down, Linus,' Brataas interjects and puts a hand on Kvanne's shoulder. 'There's no need to provoke my client when he's cooperating,' he adds, turning to Karen.

Linus Kvanne seems to have calmed down as quickly as he flared up. He subsides back into his chair, glaring at Karen.

'The prick tried to stab me when I was saving my girlfriend from being raped,' he mutters. 'You can't bloody well hold that against me, can you? This is fucking pointless, you've got it in for me no matter what . . .'

He spreads his arms in a gesture of resignation and falls silent. Karen waits without comment and hears Gary Brataas clear his throat.

'As my client points out, that matter is unrelated to the case at hand.'

'So what is it you want to tell us, Linus? Are we going to keep wasting time or are you going to let us in on what really happened in Langevik the morning after Oistra?'

73

'What do you think?'

Dineke Vegen puts her coffee mug down on her desk along with the interview transcript.

'I don't know anymore,' Karen replies. 'Do I have to answer that?'

The news that Susanne Smeed had a twin sister had been met with shrugs from both Viggo Haugen and the prosecutor. Not even Karl Björken had shown much interest.

'I guess that explains why she and Susanne were in touch,' he'd said. 'But there's nothing to suggest Anne Crosby wanted to kill her sister. Quite the contrary, I reckon. I think you're going to have to drop this and just accept that it was Kvanne.'

Maybe they're right, Karen ponders. Why would Anne Crosby kill her sister? Financial motives are out of the question and while revenge and envy might be a factor, they feel distinctly flimsy next to Kvanne's proven habit of breaking and entering. The only thing left is blackmail; Susanne was hardly the type to forego a chance to turn a profit when presented with an opportunity. But in the short time they'd known about each other's existence, what could Susanne possibly have found out about her sister that would have made it necessary for Anne Crosby to off her? No, Karl's probably right; it's time to drop it.

The prosecutor leans back in her chair with a smile.

'No, not really,' she replies. 'We're very likely going to press charges against Kvanne; we have enough to move on that. He was in Langevik at the time of the murder, which is to say he had both motive and opportunity. And he's been caught lying about things. Moreover, he's already proven he's prepared to use violence if it benefits him in the moment.'

'You mean the manslaughter? Surely that wasn't for his own benefit, more like revenge. Or to defend his girlfriend, if you want to take a generous view.'

'True, but it also demonstrates a lack of boundaries. According to Arild Rasmussen, Linus Kvanne was drunk and disorderly when he threw him out of the pub; probably high, too, if you ask me. He broke into Susanne Smeed's house – either to steal valuables or just to have somewhere to sleep.'

'He should have realised someone might be home. The car was parked in the driveway.'

Dineke Vegen shrugs.

'It's not uncommon for the owners to be home when a burglary takes place. We have several examples of people waking up to find a burglar in their room.'

'Sure, but in those cases there's usually more than one offender.'

'Maybe Kvanne wasn't making entirely rational decisions. And don't forget he set the house he broke into on fire on at least two occasions.'

'And you don't think he would have taken the silver?'

Dineke shrugs.

'Maybe he was interrupted or maybe he just overlooked it. No, I don't think it could be a coincidence that good old Kvanne was in Langevik that particular morning. The only real problem is the car.'

Karen nods. No DNA other than Susanne's was found in the Toyota and only Susanne's fingerprints have been identified. There was another set of prints on the passenger-side door handle, the same unidentified prints that were found at the house. Unfortunately, they don't belong to Kvanne.

'He claims he hitchhiked. That could be true,' Karen says without conviction.

She thinks how empty the roads were the morning after Oistra. Even if a car did pass – in itself by no means a given – Kvanne would have been extraordinarily lucky to have it stop to pick him up.

Dineke Vegen quickly flips through the transcript, then reads aloud: '*I waited for about thirty minutes, then some geezer stopped. A Volvo, I think. Black, or maybe dark blue.*'

'How convenient,' Karen says. 'After just half an hour. And a Volvo, of course, what else?'

The prosecutor shrugs again.

'Yes, I suppose that's the part I'm dubious about, too. The most likely scenario is that he drove away in Susanne's car,' she says. 'I guess he simply made sure not to leave any prints.'

Karen gives her a look but says nothing about the fact that Linus Kvanne hardly seems the type to deftly avoid leaving any trace behind for the technicians to find.

'We did find the bike he claims he used to get to the village,' she says instead. 'He nicked it from one of the farms south of Grunder after crashing the yellow motorcycle. Also, the doctor tells me he has a fractured right collarbone and some scrapes and bruises on one hip, which supports that part of his story.'

The prosecutor lets out a snort of laughter.

'Poor baby. There he was, hurt and with a backpack full of stolen goods. And he had to stick to the back roads down to Langevik to avoid the police after his burglaries. A truly touching picture.'

Karen smiles against her will.

'When you have time to read the entire report, you'll notice that we've been able to verify that Kvanne did make the phone calls he claims to have made. Jörgen Bäckström, an old junkie – actually, you probably know who he is – has confirmed he had four missed calls when he woke up that afternoon, the day after Oistra. One from his mother and three from Linus Kvanne, all of which had gone to voicemail. Which is hardly surprising; I can't imagine Jörgen was in a state to talk that night. Much less in a state to drive out to Langevik to pick up his stranded mate.'

'And so instead Kvanne broke into Susanne's house, killed her and took her car. We're just going to have to do our best to explain the thing about him leaving no trace in the car. I know the boys are thorough, but can't they go over it again?'

'Unfortunately, no. The car has been released. But to be fair, Larsen would never release it unless he was 100 per cent sure. If Kvanne did drive that car, he must've been wearing both gloves and a hairnet. Or maybe he's just unbelievably lucky.'

Karen stands up. She doesn't let on what she's thinking: that Kvanne might not have broken into Susanne Smeed's house at all; that he might just have been in the vicinity, like he claims. That Linus Kvanne might in fact be unbelievably unlucky. And she says nothing about her sneaking suspicion that whoever killed Susanne Smeed is still out there. Maybe if she'd a name, or at least a plausible motive, but a vague hunch ... No, this time, Karen keeps her mouth shut.

'Well, I've done what I can,' she says. 'I'm handing the case over to you guys. You'll have the complete report in your inbox before the end of the day. And then I finally get to have some time off. Both Haugen and Smeed are pretty happy I'm going away,' she adds with a wry smile.

Dineke Vegen has stood up as well and extends her hand with a smile.

'Yes, I heard you're due a vacation. And I want to thank you. If anything comes up while you're gone, I'll take it to Jounas. Where are you off to?'

'North-east France. I own a share of a vineyard down there and was planning on helping out with whatever harvest chores still need doing.'

'It's not in Alsace, is it?'

'It is, actually. What would you say to a bet?'

'Sure. What are the terms?'

'If your charges against Kvanne hold up, I'll give you a crate of white.'

'And if they don't?'

'Then I was right. That's enough for me.'

74

'So now that you don't get to play captain anymore, you're jumping ship.'

Without turning around, Karen watches as the coffee slowly trickles down into the mug she rinsed out just about adequately in the sink. She slowly turns and blows on the hot beverage before raising the mug to her lips. Then she leans her backside against the counter and studies Evald Johannisen, who is standing in the doorway to the small kitchenette.

She doesn't let on that she just realised she forgot to add sugar and that the bitterness is making her mouth pucker.

'It's good to see you, too, Evald,' she says. 'I heard you were back. Would you like a cup?'

He pulls a revolted face.

'Faggot coffee? No thanks, I prefer a good old-fashioned cuppa.'

'Why am I not surprised? But you really should give it a try. This is good stuff.'

She runs her hand over the brushed steel. Then she flicks the steam wand with her index finger and smiles at her colleague. He eyes her, shaking his head.

'I suppose the taxpayers are footing the bill,' he says testily. 'But apparently that's just one of many messes Jounas is going to have to clean up.'

'Is that right?' she says calmly. 'What exciting gossip have you picked up this time?'

Evald Johannisen steps into the room, opens the fridge and takes out a can of Coca-Cola. Then he pops the tab, raises the can as though making a toast and takes a couple of deep swigs.

So you *did* want caffeine after all. Karen raises her own mug in response.

'Maybe you should be careful, that's strong stuff,' she suggests blandly, nodding at the fizzy drink. 'Can't be good for the old ticker.'

'Go to hell.'

'No, actually, I'm going to France. I'm off on Saturday night. I'll be sitting on my farm, drinking wine, while you keep your noses to the grindstone up here in the freezing cold.'

Johannisen takes another sip and wipes his mouth with the back of his hand.

'I guess you had to give up in the end,' he says. 'Didn't get to keep wasting time and resources on something that should have been solved in less than a week. That must've stung.'

He pulls out a chair and sits down. Then he leans back and crosses his stretched-out legs, raising the can of Coke to his lips for the third time.

'You've been running around asking questions about what happened fifty years ago instead of minding what's right in front of you,' he says before taking another sip and letting out an open-mouthed belch.

She stifles a wince and instead cocks her head and smiles.

'Oh, I see, you and Smeed have had one of your sewing bees. What else did he tell you?'

'You mean about the time you spent poring over old photo albums, running to the local pub and chatting to old hippies? No, I found that out myself. Jounas asked me to go over your notes and let me tell you, they were not an uplifting read.'

'And yet you worked your way through them all. I'm touched.'

'Don't see that I had much choice; I'm going to be taking over as the prosecutor's liaison, since you've decided to slink off with your tail between your legs.'

'Great, then you've read the transcripts from the interviews with Linus Kvanne, too. I'm sure they were enough to get you on board. They certainly convinced Vegen, Haugen and Smeed. I'm so glad you're all in agreement.'

'What the fuck's that supposed to mean?'

'Just what I said. I've given you everything you think you'll need. Have at it!'

'So you still don't think Kvanne did it? Is that what you're telling me?'

Evald Johannisen snorts and wipes a splash of foam from his chin. Karen studies him without responding, waiting for what's coming next.

'I've been over every last goddamn crumb of information you coaxed out of those ancient layabouts or managed to pick up while you were gossiping down the pub. Hippies, Danish midwifes and abandoned brats; completely useless, all of it. And, yes, I've read the interviews with Kvanne. Seems like an open and shut case to me. If you can't see that, why are you even here?'

Karen walks over to the sink, rinses out her mug and places it upside down in the dishrack. Then she turns around.

'You know what, Evald? I've been asking myself that very question.'

The last thing she hears as she steps over his outstretched legs and leaves the room is the sound of another belch as effervescence pushes its way out of Evald Johannisen's throat.

75

The moment Karen pulls the key out of the ignition, her phone buzzes. But the feeling of exhilaration that only yesterday would have accompanied seeing Anne Crosby's name on her screen fails to appear; for a couple of seconds she considers simply not picking up.

Her conversation with Brandon and Janet has already cleared up any remaining questions she had. What happened in Langevik almost fifty years ago was a tragedy. That Anne Crosby is the little girl who went back to Sweden with Tomas and Ingela is now beyond doubt. With Cornelis Loots' help – discreetly provided on the understanding that Jounas mustn't find out – she has confirmed that Happy was eventually christened Anne and grew up in Malmö with Tomas Ekman, whom she probably assumed was her biological father. In the late eighties, Anne moved to the US to study marketing and eventually married Gregory Crosby, from whom she has now been divorced for six years. The couple have no children; Anne Crosby is registered as single at a Los Angeles address.

That the two sisters, Anne and Susanne, found out about each other only months before Susanne's death, is a tragic coincidence. But it explains the phone calls to Susanne Smeed, both the ones from Disa Brinckmann and the ones from Anne Crosby herself. Most importantly, Anne is much less likely to have killed Susanne than Linus Kvanne. A woman of almost fifty, and, according to Cornelis Loots, considerable wealth, probably has no interest in beating her new-found sister to death in a remote village on Heimö. Even Karen has come to accept that.

Her mobile rings for the third time and Karen realises she has to answer. After the urgent text she sent Anne Crosby, it would be nothing short of rude not to talk to her, now that she's finally calling back. She reluctantly hits the green receiver button.

'Yes, this is Karen Eiken Hornby,' she says.

'My name is Anne Crosby. You've been trying to reach me?'

The voice is polite but sounds frazzled, almost winded, as though Anne Crosby's eager to get the call over with. Suits me fine, Karen thinks to herself.

'Yes, that's correct. I have been trying to reach you in connection with a death here on Heimö.'

Karen breaks off and there is a brief silence. Does Anne Crosby know her sister is dead? Has she gathered as much from her phone call with Mette?'

'It's about Susanne Smeed,' she says gently. 'I don't know if you're aware that she . . .'

'Yes, I know Susanne is dead. It's horrible.'

Anne Crosby speaks curtly and despite her years in the US, her Swedish is virtually perfect, at least to Karen's ear.

'The thing is that we've gone through Susanne's call log and your number appeared in it, together with Disa Brinckmann's. It was her daughter who gave me your name, which made it possible to link you to this number. Since it's a pay-as-you-go SIM, we wouldn't have known it was yours otherwise.'

'Yes, I always use pay-as-you-go when I'm abroad.'

442

'Of course, I guess that's a good idea; apparently it's easy to rack up a hefty bill pretty quickly if you use your regular contract.'

Karen thinks she can hear something that might be a construction site in the background, but Anne Crosby says nothing.

'Either way,' Karen continues, 'I think I already have the answers I need. The case is pretty much closed at this point. We have a suspect in detention and . . .'

'Pretty much closed? You're not sure?'

'Well, the case is considered solved as far as the police are concerned. Now, it's a matter of the charges holding up in court.'

There's a scraping sound on the other end and then the line goes dead silent. For a second, Karen thinks Anne Crosby must've hung up.

'Well, that's a relief,' she says.

'I myself am going on leave for a couple of weeks, but if you want, I can ask the person in charge of the case to keep you posted on any developments. If you give me your contact information, I can make sure it gets to the prosecutor's office.'

'They can call me on this number.'

'So you will be staying in Sweden for a while?'

This time, the scraping is so loud, Karen instinctively pulls the phone away from her ear.

'I'm sorry,' Anne Crosby says. 'I'm in an awkward spot.'

'I will, of course, try to get hold of Disa as well before I go,' Karen says, 'but, as you know, that's not as easy as it sounds. Her daughter tells me she's finally on her way home. Have you been able to reach her, by the way? Mette said you've been trying to get in touch with her, too.'

'What? No. I mean, not yet.'

'Well, I'll give her a ring before I leave. If I can't reach her, I might drive by Malmö on my way back. I hear it's a lovely town, and it's not much of a detour now that there's a bridge.'

I'm prattling on, she thinks. She's not interested in my vacation plans and a bit of small talk won't change the fact that her sister's dead. A few more seconds of silence and Karen is ready to end the call.

'So you're holidaying in Denmark?'

'I'm going all the way down to France, actually. I'll be taking the evening ferry over to Esbjerg on Saturday and driving down from there.'

'Then I wish you safe travels.'

'Thank you. And also,' Karen adds, 'I'm really sorry about your sister.'

76

'You won't even know I'm there. Promise.'

'And how's that going to work exactly? You'll be sitting next to me in the car, no? Or were you going to climb in the boot?'

There's a flash of hope in Sigrid's eyes.

'So, are you saying it's OK? I can come?'

Karen heaves a sigh. Two days of unremitting nagging has started to wear her down. The campaign of persuasion had begun the moment she told Sigrid she was finally free to take leave and would be driving down to see old friends in Alsace. In an angelically pleading voice, Sigrid had committed to paying half of the petrol costs and helping out with the grape harvest, saying France had always been her number one dream destination.

When that got her nowhere, she'd tried a new strategy:

She could actually really need a break from 'this fucking country' after everything that's happened, and also, Sam keeps turning up at the club, which is a 'fucking shithole', and she never wants to see him again, so she's going to quit anyway and start studying after New Year's (but not because her dad's badgering her; that 'sanctimonious prick' can go to hell). And besides, apparently, Karen won't even know she's there.

Jounas would probably have a fit if he found out I've gone on vacation with his daughter, Karen sniggers inwardly.

'Fine,' she says.

After talking to both Kore and Eirik and Marike, however, she realises there's still one problem to take care of. None of them can housesit and look after Rufus for three weeks. She's uncomfortable having the cat stay at Marike's; when the emaciated wretch appeared out of nowhere less than a year ago, he'd shown signs of having wandered. It's not unlikely he would run away from Marike's and try to get back home. He might get taken by a fox or, even more likely, run over.

Granted, she could ask a neighbour to feed him, but given how persistently he seeks out hers – and now Sigrid's – company, it feels cruel to leave him alone in the house for weeks on end. Why had she let the bloody cat in in the first place? It hadn't crossed her mind he would compromise her freedom.

Kore's suggested solution had felt equally unappealing. And yet, here she is, in her car, between two loading docks in the New Harbour, having circled the dark buildings, peering into nooks and crannies, for twenty minutes. Just as she decides to give up and drive away, Leo Friis appears without warning in her headlights. He's standing in the middle of a street she's already driven down at least twice. Seeing him arouses equal parts relief and instinctive urge to leave while she still can. Then she reminds herself the ferry to Esbjerg is leaving in less than twenty-four hours. The day after tomorrow, she could be sitting with the others, sipping a glass of last year's vintage, gazing out across the vineyard.

She shifts into neutral, opens the door and climbs out of the car.

'All right, and what's the catch?' Leo Friis says after hearing her out. 'You'd hardly be asking me if there wasn't a catch. We don't know each other.'

He's eyeing her warily and accepts another cigarette without a word of thanks.

'Kore's vouching for you. And you're hardly the one sticking your neck out here, are you? You'll simply housesit for me while I'm in France. I need someone there to make sure no one breaks in, to keep an eye on things.'

'Things . . .?'

'My cat. Make sure he's fed and watered and . . . well, stroked and petted.'

'Aha. So the cat's the catch. What's wrong with it?'

Karen can feel her patience wearing thin. Kore's suggestion to let Leo Friis housesit had sounded like a desperate remedy from the get-go. A filthy homeless guy, probably with a very long list of personal problems.

'He's a good guy, underneath it all,' Kore had told her. 'Got into all kinds of trouble when the band broke up: drugs and debts and what have you, but he's a decent sort. Besides, I'm happy to swing by from time to time and keep an eye on him if that makes you feel better. We've stayed in touch since that night at Repet. Well, you were there, so you could say you know him, too.'

'After two pints? And how have you been staying in touch anyway? I doubt he has a phone.'

'He doesn't, but I let him sleep in the studio that night and a few more times since. And I've had him over for dinner.'

'At your house? Eirik let you?'

'It caused a bit of friction, but he agreed in the end. Though I swear he was sweating bullets when Leo flopped onto that white sofa we bought last spring.'

'Yeah, I can imagine,' Karen had told him. 'Fine, do you know where I can find him? Is he still crashing in the studio or is he back under a loading dock in the New Harbour?'

'The latter, I'm afraid. The studio's really busy at the moment; we have people there around the clock, so he has to steer clear for a while. The others wouldn't like it if they know I let him borrow my keys. The equipment alone is worth millions.'

'Sure, great, better he steals what little I have . . .'

'Cut it out. Leo's not a thief; besides, do you have a better solution?'

Now she's studying the man before her with a mix of fascination and revulsion. His coat was probably nice-looking once upon a time – it might even have been his – and his boots look suspiciously new. But the headlights reveal that the red jumper underneath the coat is full of stains – she doesn't want to know where they came from – and the sleeves poking out are grey with ingrained dirt. The yarn at the bottom of one sleeve is fraying; a safety pin has been clumsily inserted through the stitches keep to them from running. The good news is the grey blanket Leo Friis wore wrapped around his shoulders the first time they met is nowhere to be seen, but his hat and the socks peeking out of his boots are probably teeming with vermin. There's probably no part of him that's not teeming with vermin, she reflects gloomily.

He should be grateful. Should jump at a chance to get food and shelter for three weeks without having to do much in return.

Instead, I'm standing here like some kind of bloody door-to-door salesman, trying to persuade him. Who the fuck does he think he is?

At the same time, Karen realises she's probably more desperate for his help than he is for hers.

'There's nothing wrong with the cat,' she says. 'He's just slightly high maintenance.'

'Are you sure it's not a female?'

Leo scratches his eyebrows, pushing his hat up his forehead in the process.

'Ah, a homeless man with a sense of humour,' Karen snaps. 'Do you have fleas or something? That hat looks like it might crawl away of its own volition.'

'How the fuck should I know? Do you have a tub?'

'Of course.'

'All right.'

'All right what?'

'All right, I'll housesit for you, look after your cat and make sure no one breaks in, while you head down to Costa del Sol to guzzle sangria.'

'To a vineyard in France. I actually own a share of it.'

'Bully for you.'

Leo clears his throat, getting ready to spit. Karen watches in disgust as he turns his head and hawks a loogy over the edge of the pier.

'I have one condition,' she says. 'You won't bring home any dodgy friends, and you won't do any drugs while you're living under my roof. Not even weed. You can drink if you want, but nothing else.'

'I knew it. There's always a catch . . .'

'I'm a police detective; I can't risk you doing that shit at my house. I mean it. Does that sound doable?'

'Look, I've got by on beer and crappy red wine for almost two years. Do you have any drink at your house, by the way?'

'Probably nothing you'd like. Just decent wine and good whiskey. And a freezer full of food, a TV and a guestroom with clean sheets,' she adds, to take the edge off the snark.

'And where is this paradise?'

'Langevik, north-east of town.'

'I know where it is. But how do I get there? As you might have gathered, I don't own a car.'

Karen's silent for a few moments, doing quick some quick mental calculations. Twenty-three hours until the ferry departs. She's hardly going to have time to drive around town looking for Leo Friis tomorrow, and she doesn't trust him to make it to Langevik on his own, even if she were to give him money for a taxi.

'By car,' she says. 'We're leaving right now. Unless you have something else going on,' she adds.

77

The noise from upstairs has subsided. The alternating rush of the tap and gurgle of the drain as dirty water has repeatedly been let out and replaced with clean has, after more than an hour, finally stopped.

'Do you reckon he's gone to bed?' Sigrid asks, absently tinkling her spoon against her teacup while she scrolls up and down on her phone with the thumb of her other hand. 'Maybe he's drowning in the tub? I've heard that happens,' she continues, tearing her eyes away from the phone for a brief moment. 'Maybe we should check on him.'

'I think Leo can take care of himself,' Karen says sourly and pushes Rufus, who has jumped up onto a kitchen chair and put his front paws on the table, down onto the floor. 'If you're done with the cheese, I'll put it back in the fridge.'

She gets up to clear the table. It's covered in crumbs from the walnut loaf of which nothing but a sad heel remains. Leo must have scarfed down at least eight slices; she opens the freezer to pull out a new loaf. If he carries on at this pace, I won't have a scrap of food left in the house when I get back.

'He's probably pretty good-looking underneath that beard. He looks well fit in old pictures online. Check it out!'

Karen turns around and looks at Sigrid who is enthusiastically holding her phone out. Without looking at it, Karen shakes her head.

'He's at least twenty years older than you,' she says disapprovingly.

Sigrid sighs and gets up.

'God, do you honestly think I'd be interested in some old fossil? I was thinking of you.'

'Thanks. But that old fossil is probably ten years younger than me.'

'Eight, actually. I checked.'

Karen lets that pass without comment.

'Have you packed?' she asks instead.

'I will. Soon. Calm down, why are you so wound up?'

Because for some reason, instead of being on my own, enjoying some peace and quiet, I have a pierced lass with tattoos all over her arms at my kitchen table and a homeless man in my upstairs bathroom, Karen retorts inwardly. Out loud, she says:

'Would you mind fetching clean sheets and putting them in the guesthouse? Turn on the radiator, too, if it's off; I forgot to check.'

'So I'm out now? You want to be alone with Mr Beard?'

Sigrid grins broadly and manages to cock just one eyebrow; for a split second, Karen can clearly see her father in her.

'Don't be silly,' she snaps. 'Leo will sleep out there tonight; after we leave, he can move in here if he wants. I want him quarantined until we know he's rabies-free.'

The gurgling starts again upstairs, but this time, it's not followed by the sound of the tap. Instead, they hear footsteps crossing the bathroom floor, a door opening and loud creaking. Next, Leo Friis appears in the kitchen door, wearing nothing but a towel wrapped around his hips. Karen looks away. Sigrid doesn't.

'Did you shave with a blender?' she says.

'I found nail scissors. Do you have any clothes I can borrow? I think mine need to be washed.'

More like burned, Karen observes.

'Sigrid, can you show Leo the washing machine and have a look in the wardrobes for something that might fit him? I have to make a phone call.'

Karl Björken picks up immediately.

'Hiya, Eiken, what are you up to now?'

'Nothing, actually. I'm in holiday mode. I'm taking the evening ferry out of here tomorrow and won't be back for three weeks. When are you off, by the way? For your parental leave, I mean.'

'Probably not until the first of December, so you'll be back before I go.'

If I come back, she thinks. At the moment, returning to work with Jounas Smeed and Evald Johannisen feels less tempting than ever.

'I just wanted to let you know I talked to Anne Crosby yesterday.'

'Oh, so she finally called you back. What did she have to say for herself?'

'Not much. She sounded very subdued.'

'What about Disa Brinckmann; have you reached her?'

'Not yet. But she should be back by now, so I'm going to try to give her a ring. I don't feel right about leaving loose ends, you know. About not explaining why I've been trying to get hold of them, I mean, even if it's redundant now.'

'I thought you were on leave. On holiday mode, isn't that what you just told me?'

'I am, but I promised Anne Crosby we would keep her posted on the case against Kvanne. After all, it is her sister, even if we have no official confirmation of their blood ties. So, I really just wanted to ask you to give me a call if anything happens.'

Even though it's patently impossible, she can clearly hear Karl Björken smiling on the other end.

'So it's not that you want to know yourself?'

Karen sighs resignedly.

'Fine,' she admits. 'I just feel really weird about dropping everything.'

'You know what they say about cats and curiosity . . .'

'Are you going to call me or not? If he confesses, I mean.'

'Sure. But do try to actually enter holiday mode for real now.'

'I promise. I'm probably not going to give any of it a second's thought once I'm down there, surrounded by mountains of grapes.

When Karen forces her suitcase shut and zips it, she catches herself humming an old nursery rhyme.

'Don't go sniffing everything
Said the old man that saved the cat
Next time, you'll have to save yourself
Or drown in the deep water.'

78

Right, I guess I'm on my own then, Karen thinks to herself as she watches Sigrid disappear in the direction of the lower-deck bar.

Sigrid had spotted some friends of hers in one of the cars ahead of them before they even got on the ferry. After making sure Karen wouldn't be offended, she'd jumped out and hurried over to the other car, tapped on the window and been let in immediately.

'I'll see you on board in a while,' she'd said. 'Which cabin are we in, again?'

Karen had handed her one of the white plastic cards stamped with the number 121.

'I think I'm going to hit the hay early. Don't wake me when you stagger in, please. I need my sleep so I can drive all the way down to Strasbourg tomorrow.'

'You won't even know I'm there,' Sigrid had assured her. Looks like she was right. Karen is suddenly overcome with worry. Is this just the first of many times Sigrid will be out of her sight this trip? What if something happens to her? Or she decides to take up with one of the blokes travelling around the various farms to help with the harvest? They have been known to be gratuitously good-looking. How would she explain something like that to Jounas Smeed? True, Sigrid is an adult, but bringing her along is still an immense responsibility.

And while she's worrying about that anyway, she takes the opportunity to fret about the situation at home as well. Leo Friis, surrounded by empty bottles and lines of cocaine, Rufus desperately padding around his food bowl. *What* had she been thinking?

Her agonising is interrupted by a car horn. The vehicles in front of her have started moving, disappearing in under MS *Skandia*'s open bow visor, one after the other.

Karen has taken a seat in one of the leather armchairs in the small upper-deck bar. She notes with disappointment that there are no ashtrays on the tables anymore. Surely this particular bar used to be exempt from the smoking ban?

'Is there anywhere I can smoke on board?' she asks the waiter, who is placing a tiny napkin on her table and setting a gin and tonic down on top of it.

'I'm afraid not. Not for the last five years. Well, it's allowed outside, obviously,' he replies, taking the card she holds out.

Karen glances over at the window. They departed on time and have already left all lights behind. A few droplets of rain on the glass quells her urge to smoke. Besides, she has already felt that familiar rolling that indicates an agitated North Sea. The waiter, sensing her apprehension, confirms her suspicions with a practised smile aimed at calming anxious passengers.

'Don't worry,' he says. 'We're looking at slightly rough seas tonight, but there is absolutely no need for concern. We wouldn't have left port if there was any danger.'

Karen shoots him an amused look. Their respective defini-
tions of 'slightly rough' probably differ considerably.

'So there's a storm coming,' she says calmly.

'They're saying Doggerland's going to be hit hard, but we
should make it over before it reaches the Danish coast. That being
said' – he cautions with a glance at the glass in front of her – 'if
you're prone to seasickness, you might want to take it easy.'

Karen smiles and shakes her head.

'No, I've thankfully never been seasick. I've been told it's
agony.'

The waiter takes back the card reader, prints the receipt and
crumples it up in his palm when she declines it with a wave of
her hand.

'Yes,' he says. 'I've heard people say they want to die when it
gets really bad. But I don't think it's necessarily going to get that
bad tonight,' he adds and leaves her with a smile.

The distant sound of a Lady Gaga song seeps into the peace-
ful upper-deck bar from the lower deck when the glass door to
the stairwell opens to admit an older couple. Just as they cross
the threshold, the boat pitches. The woman misses her step and
looks mortified. With one hand firmly clutching on the gold
chain strap of her handbag and the other on her husband's arm,
she moves further into the room. Karen turns her head to watch
as the two of them sit down at one of the small tables.

The main bar's probably packed by now, but here, the higher
prices have scared away all but twenty or so guests. The waiter
is just now serving another well-dressed, middle-aged couple a
dry martini and a double whiskey. Three older women seem to
be sharing a bottle of white wine. Beyond them, Karen can see
two men in suits nursing cognacs and above the back of a green

chesterfield armchair, she can make out the head and shoulders of a woman who seems to be searching her handbag for something. Despite her lack of fashion knowledge, Karen can tell her handbag must be expensive. Something flashes in the woman's hand; Karen realises she was looking for a small mirror, which she's now holding up to her face. She's probably refreshing her lipstick.

Well, she's unlikely to get picked up in this bar, Karen considers and takes a sip of her G&T. This is a refuge for people who chose the ferry over air travel but who can't bear the racket of the main bar. For people who are afraid of flying or who are bringing their cars. Or for those of us who are simply getting to be too old. Downstairs is for the people who consider the ferries from Dunker and Ravenby destinations in their own right, and who couldn't care less if they're going to Esbjerg or Harwich. For people who are drawn by tax-free prices, gambling machines and a chance to get laid. And for young people who are compelled by the lax enforcements of government age restrictions in the onboard bars.

It was a long time ago, but Karen remembers what it was like.

Maybe I should give Sigrid a ring after all, she ponders. Just a quick call to make sure she's not seasick. Or too drunk.

Karen glances at her watch: only 11.36 p.m. Surely Sigrid would have called if something had happened. Unless she's drugged in some cabin and . . .

'Cut it out,' she tells herself.

One of the middle-aged women turns to look at Karen, who realises she must have spoken out loud. She has noticed that she has started talking to herself quite a bit recently. Rufus normally provides good cover, but here, sitting alone on a North

Sea ferry, talking to no one at all might have an unsettling effect on the people around her.

Time for bed, she decides. I should get at least a few hours of sleep before it's time to get back behind the wheel. She knocks back what's left in her glass and gets up. Takes a quick step to the side as the ship lurches and smiles, embarrassed, at the other patrons. No one seems to have noticed. The woman who was digging through her handbag earlier half turns her head toward Karen, but immediately turns away again.

79

Evald Johannisen gives his wife an inquiring look. She has turned on her bedside lamp and sunk back into her pillows with a dejected look on her face and the phone pressed to her ear. Now she mouths something to her husband while showing with her free hand that the person on the other end is rambling on and on.

Evald glances at the clock radio, where the red digits glow like a jeering reminder of his long-since vanished youth and vigour: 10.47 p.m.

It's Saturday night and not even eleven, yet both he and Ragna had been asleep.

On the other hand, he thinks, annoyed, who the fuck calls at this hour?

Then he suddenly manages to decipher Ragna's mouthing: '*Cousin Hasse.*'

'No, don't be silly, of course we're not in bed this early,' she says with a glance at her husband. 'Oh no, much better. Yes, he's sitting right next to me, so you can talk to him yourself. Of course it's fine. My love to Eva. Yes, we really should. You too. Here's Evald now.'

With a crestfallen look at his wife, Evald Johannisen accepts the receiver from her and pushes himself up into a slumped version of sitting. His conversations with his Swedish cousin tend not only to be tedious but to make him feel inferior as well. Maybe because Hasse – who works for the Swedish Police Authority – has a habit of working in some reference to the fact that he has managed to advance further than Evald, even though there's considerably less competition in Doggerland. Or maybe it's simply the little-brother complex all islanders feel with respect to their much larger eastern neighbour.

But this time, his cousin Hans Kollind, Deputy Regional Chief of Police for Region South, proves uncharacteristically succinct. After just a few brief courtesies about Eva's health and a forced assurance from Evald that he will take it easy, Hasse seems ready to move on to the real reason he called.

'The thing is,' he says, 'that we have a bit of a strange case here in Malmö. And I was wondering if you could help us. I didn't want to call just anybody at this hour.'

Right, but bothering me is just fine, Evald thinks to himself, even though he can already feel his reflexive irritation turning into curiosity.

'I'm listening,' he says.

'Well, we have an older woman, murdered in her home, without any signs of a forced entry or sexual violence. Someone seems to have just walked in, killed her and left. According to the coroner, it happened the night before last and we haven't been able to establish a motive or find any witnesses.'

'And what makes you think I can help?'

Evald Johannisen's surprise is genuine. For his cousin to call and talk about himself and brag about everything from work to his children would be perfectly normal, but this isn't. It actually sounds like Hasse's asking him for help.

'Well, the thing is the daughter, who's naturally both shocked and upset, has told us the Doggerland police have been in contact with her, trying to reach her mother. The woman has apparently been away on some kind of hike in Spain and someone at your end has been trying to get hold of her repeatedly, according to the daughter.'

'Our end? Why would we . . .'

Before he can finish, Evald Johannisen realises who has been trying to call and who the murdered woman is. Even so, he asks the question.

'What's her name?'

'The victim, you mean? Disa Brinckmann.'

80

The fluorescent lights in the east corridor on the third floor of the Dunker police headquarters flicker before turning on, spreading their cold light over the empty office. Evald Johannisen walks straight over to his desk and starts his computer before plodding out to the kitchenette, picking up a mug from the drying rack and pushing the button marked double cappuccino. He looks at his watch and sighs.

Disa Brinckmann.

Evald had made the connection before Cousin Hasse even said the name. After all, he'd read Karen's report twice. Thoroughly. Granted, mostly to find mistakes and material for scornful comments, but even so, enough of it had stuck, despite the fact that he'd considered it utter lunacy. But then Hasse had said the thing that made Evald Johannisen throw his duvet aside and get out of bed.

How many old dears really went hiking in Spain?

And no matter how badly Johannisen wished it were otherwise, it simply couldn't be a coincidence that two people connected to the case had been murdered. And now he was going to have to contact Eiken. Goddamn it.

His wife had offered no comment when her husband, who just an hour earlier had been too tired to make love to her for the first time since he collapsed at work, suddenly and without explanation climbed out of bed, got dressed and left the house. Instead of pestering him with questions and admonitions, she'd calmly turned her bedside lamp off, turned back onto her side and gone back to sleep. Ragna Johannisen has been married to Evald for almost forty years. She knows there's no point.

Now he's leaning back in his office chair, eyes closed. He's skimmed the report a third time and found what he was looking for. No, it can't be a coincidence, he's sure of that. Exactly what's going on is less clear, but Evald Johannisen's convinced there's a connection. Despite ailments, angina and apparently now impotence as well, he's still detective enough to know when things are linked. It's no coincidence the woman Karen was trying to reach has now been murdered. Much as he's loath to admit it, it looks like Eiken was onto something. The question is what? No, he corrects himself, the first question is where that bloody woman is since she's not answering her phone.

He dials her number for the third time and is once again put through to her voicemail. Evald Johannisen slams the receiver down so hard that for a split second, he's worried he might have broken the phone. Just because she's on leave doesn't mean she gets to go off grid. Surely even that woman has some sense of responsibility?

He quickly picks the receiver back up and notes that the phone still seems to be in working order. Then he takes a deep breath and dials Karl Björken's number.

Fuck, he thinks while it rings. If Eiken's right, she's going to make me swallow it until I retire.

'Hey there, Evald,' Karl answers, true to form.

'How soon can you be here?'

464

'Yes, we're having a lovely evening, thank you for asking,' Karl replies sardonically. 'The kids are asleep and . . .'

'I'm serious. How long will it take you to get over here?'

A brief silence on the other end.

'Give me half an hour.'

'OK. Just one thing: do you know if Eiken's left already? She said something about France, I think?'

'Karen? Why do you want to . . .?'

'Never fucking mind. Do you know or not?'

'Yes, I think she's was taking the 10.30 ferry to Esbjerg tonight and driving down from there. What's this about?'

But Evald Johannisen doesn't hear the last part. He's already ended the call.

He stares vacantly at the screen, his mind racing. For exactly four minutes he sits stock still, unseeing. Then he leans forward and quickly and types in 'doggerlines.com' in the search bar. After a few clicks, he finds the information he needs and picks up the phone.

Talking to Eiken can probably wait until tomorrow, he ponders while the phone rings. After all, there's not much they can do right now to figure out the connection between the murders of Disa Brinckmann and Susanne Smeed. Naturally, the very best thing would be if he could sort everything out without her help. She would be furious.

But an inexplicable sense of unease has begun to spread inside Evald Johannisen. He can feel it in the pit of his stomach while he listens, with mounting exasperation, to a pre-recorded voice on the other end, assuring him he's in line and that it will soon be his turn. There must be some other bloody way to get through to the ferry company than to call customer services.

The problem is that in the middle of the night, with no senior managers around, he doesn't know where to look. On the other hand, getting the information he needs shouldn't require top brass intervention. It's trivial, really, and could probably just as easily wait until tomorrow.

If not for that nagging feeling that time is, in fact, of the essence.

81

Five minutes later, Karen has walked down a hallway lined with flashing fruit machines and is now surrounded by loud dance music, laughter and people contributing to the unbearable noise level by shouting to make themselves heard. The baseline thuds in her chest as she pushes though the crowded room as quickly as she's able.

It's not really out of my way, she'd told herself. I'll just swing by and see if I can spot her. Make sure she's OK. Now, she realises her mission is doomed to fail. Aside from the jostling and the noise, the shipping company has also decided that appropriate lighting consists of raking lights from the bar and some kind of strobe light from the dancefloor that's making her pulse race. Finding anyone in here is clearly impossible. A shove sends her stumbling into a young man who curses loudly when his beer spills.

'Mind where you're fucking going,' he roars.

'Sorry, someone pushed me,' she tries to explain, but then realises he's already turned away again and is shouting something into the ear of a girl whose face is illuminated by the phone she's fiddling with. Taking no notice of the guy, she suddenly shrieks and holds her phone out to another girl standing next to her.

'Oh my God, he's insane, look!'

'Seriously, like, he should fucking . . .'

Karen doesn't hear the rest. Instead, she presses on through the horseshoe-shaped room, groaning loudly with relief when she reaches the other side.

The well-dressed woman with the expensive handbag has apparently tired of the serenity of the upper-deck bar and is now standing in front of one of the fruit machines up ahead.

What do you know, Karen muses, you hardly look like you need to supplement your income. That being said, she knows a percentage of the shipping company's regulars are gambling addicts.

The well-dressed woman doesn't look like a gambling addict, however; she hasn't inserted so much as a shilling into the machine but rather looks like she's just studying the unmoving rows of cherries, clocks and sevens. Her black trousers and suit jacket signal money and taste. Not Karen's taste, granted, but the entire ensemble screams that this is a woman who cares about her appearance. Her hair completes the image. Karen's own hairstyle doesn't require frequent visits to the hairdresser and she usually takes care of the many grey hairs in it herself, at home in the bathroom. Yet even so, or maybe precisely because of it, she can clearly see that neither the woman's tidy bob nor her honey-coloured highlights are the result of home dyeing. Karen experiences a vague sense of unease, studying the woman's back. There's something sad, almost anxious about the solitary figure standing dead still, staring at a one-armed bandit.

I need a smoke after living through that nightmare. Karen takes a backwards glance at the strobe-lit dance floor. One cigarette and then to bed. She sticks her hand in her handbag and digs around but can't find her packet of cigarettes. When she sinks into a squat with her back against the wall and opens her bag wide, she notices the cold glare of her phone screen and feels her heart skip a beat. Someone has been trying to reach her.

But it's not Sigrid calling her. Karen stares incredulously at the screen and the number shining up at her. Three missed calls from a number she knows all too well; the police station switchboard. And one from her mother.

82

'Good evening, welcome to Dogger Lines, my name is Pie, how can I help you?'

Why do people insist on reading out an entire bloody essay when they answer the phone these days? Evald thinks to himself, drumming his fingers on his desk.

Out loud, he says:

'This is Detective Evald Johannisen from the Dogger Police. I need information about your departure from Dunker to Esbjerg, quickly.'

'All right, and what date?'

'Today. Now.'

A moment of silence.

'You mean the ship that's on its way to Esbjerg right now?'

'That's right. I need to know whether a passenger, Karen Eiken Hornby, is on board. If she is, I need to get a message to her urgently.'

'I'm sorry, but we're actually not allowed to give out information about individual—'

Evald Johannisen knows what the outcome of this discussion is going to be if he doesn't nip it in the bud.

'Now you listen to me, sweetheart. I'm sure you're well aware the police have a right to access every passenger list you have.'

'Yes,' Pie says diffidently. 'But we've been told not to give out any individual—'

'The lists are digital, aren't they?'

'Of course,' she says in a voice that eliminates any doubt that Dogger Lines doesn't have its paperwork in order.

'Then send me the whole bloody list, and I'll check it myself. And do it now! Do you have pen and paper?'

Pie seems to have taken down Johannisen's address correctly and also seems to have instant access to the requested information, because six minutes later, an email with an attached Excel sheet has landed in his inbox.

The list is sorted alphabetically; it takes him four seconds to find Karen's name. He picks up the phone again. This time, he gets through straight away.

'Good evening, welcome to Dogger Lines, my name is Pie, how can I help you?'

'Johannisen again. Thanks for the list, but we've already wasted ten minutes, so now you're going to listen closely and do as I say, OK?'

'OK . . .' comes the hesitant reply, as though Pie is as scared of promising things blindly as she is of denying the authoritative voice on the other end anything it wants.

'As I said, I need to get in touch with a passenger on the ferry we talked about immediately. I've been trying to call her, but she's not picking up.'

'No, the reception on board tends to come and go.'

'So what I want is for the crew to call out for her over the speakers, or go to her cabin or whatever they need to do to find her and make sure she calls me.'

'No problem,' Pie says cheerfully.

Johannisen's jaw drops in surprise. First the little bint threatens to deny him the information he could have got anyway by jumping through the required bureaucratic hoops. And now she's suddenly saying it's no problem.

'I'll make sure they send out a passenger announcement. What is your friend's name?'

Evald Johannisen almost explodes with indignation.

'Her name is *Police Detective* Karen Eiken Hornby. And she's not my *friend*! Understood?'

'I'm sorry, that was reflex. We have so many people trying to—'

'Sure, whatever, just make sure she gets the message that she needs to call Evald Johannisen as a matter of utmost urgency. She has my number. And so do you, now,' he adds while typing in the digits and sending them back to Pie via email. 'If I haven't heard from her in thirty minutes, I'll be in touch again.'

And with that threat, he ends the call.

83

Karen stays squatting, muttering curses. She barely notices the looks she's getting from passers-by and in any event doesn't care what they think of her. How did this happen? she thinks. I kept my phone with me the whole time. Then she spots the little crossed-out bell symbol and realises she's turned the sound off. To avoid calls from the police chief inspector and anyone else who might have failed to register that she's on leave, she muted her phone last night before going to bed. She has no desire to be woken up in the middle of the night while on holiday. And apparently, it had been a wise decision; three calls in the past hour alone. I'm going to have to give the police chief inspector a ring and tell him to update his call lists.

What worries her is the missed call from her mum. Karen checks the time of the call and realises her mother called just after half eight. And left a voicemail, too. Why would she suddenly call me on a Saturday night? Karen wonders and keys in her voicemail pin; we always talk on Sundays. She impatiently listens to the monotone voice.

'*You have two messages. Message one, recorded today at 9.34 a.m.*'

'*Hi sweetheart, guess where I am! No, you'll never be able to. Harry and I are in London of all places, visiting his sister, so now we're considering popping over to see you, too. Harry would love to see Langevik, he says. Just for a couple of days and we won't be a bother; we can stay in the guesthouse. There's a ferry from Harwich tomorrow around noon. Call and let me know if you want us to bring anything, otherwise, I'll see you tomorrow! Love you!'*

Karen lets the phone fall into her lap and stares vacantly straight ahead. Then she blinks and glances at her watch: 12.14 a.m. Should she call now and abort this plan or would it be better to wait until tomorrow morning? Her mum and Harry are probably asleep by now. She hasn't met the miracle that is Harry Lampard yet, but there's no doubt her mother has fallen head over heels in her old age. And now they've left Costa del Sol without warning to go on some kind tour around Europe, visiting people.

She decides to fire off a text and follow it up with an early morning phone call. Because the plan definitely needs to be aborted. The mere thought of Eleanor Eiken's reaction if she were to get to the house in Langevik and find Leo Friis in it fills Karen with horror. Leo, with his poorly trimmed beard, wearing Karen's sweatpants, which end at his ankles, and much too tight T-shirt with the Doggerland Police logo. At least that's what he'd looked like when she left him a few hours ago. He was clean, but that's really all that could be said for him.

Hi! Would have been great, but I'm on my way to France so I'll have to take a rain check. I'll call you tomorrow. Love K

The moment she sends the message, she's struck by another horrifying thought: maybe her mother will decide to head over to her former homeland despite her daughter not being there. Stay in the house for a few days and show Harry around Langevik on

474

her own. After all, Eleanor Eiken lived there for forty years and the area means a lot to her, even if Estepona has been her home for the past eight years. I need to stop her, Karen thinks, I'll have to call her the moment I wake up. Why on earth does this have to happen right now?

The urge to smoke has become overwhelming; she needs a cigarette or two to calm her nerves before she heads down to the cabin. She frantically roots through her handbag for her cigarettes and lighter, finally finds both and gets up from her squat. Her legs are practically numb; she shakes them to get the circulation going as she walks toward the door leading out on deck.

84

When Karl Björken pushes open the glass door to the east corridor on the third floor of the Dunker police headquarters, exactly twenty-six minutes have passed since Johannisen called. It's now 12.16 a.m. as he approaches Evald Johannisen's desk with a grim look on his face.

'What the fuck's going on?' he says, even though he can plainly see his colleague has a receiver pressed to his ear.

Johannisen turns to him and hangs up with a shake of his head.

'That old witch isn't picking up.'

'Old witch?'

'Eiken. I've been trying for an hour.'

Karl Björken doesn't comment on how it's rather contradictory of Johannisen to be using that expression for someone fifteen years younger than himself.

'I guess she's asleep. Do you realise what time it is? What's this about?'

'Disa Brinckmann,' Johannisen says darkly. 'She's been murdered.'

For a few seconds, Karl Björken stares blankly at his colleague. Then the penny seems to slowly drop: first the tentative connection, then the unwelcome definitive insight.

'Anne Crosby,' he says and sits down.

'The sister,' Johannisen sighs, remembering how he'd snickered at that section of Karen's report. 'Though we obviously can't be sure it's her,' he says without conviction.

'Either way, she's the link between the victims. Karen wanted to check her out, but both Haugen and the prosecutor told her no. I didn't listen, either; I was dead sure it was Kvanne. We've been idiots!'

'Well, I don't know about that,' Johannisen grumbles, 'but someone broke into Disa Brinckmann's flat and killed her.'

'How did you find out?'

'Hasse called from Sweden. Apparently, she was thrown headfirst into a door and then suffocated while she was unconscious, for good measure. But the Swedish Police have neither motive nor witnesses.'

Karl is aware Johannisen's cousin Hasse Kollind holds a fairly senior position within the Swedish Police, but he also knows they don't normally call each other to talk shop. At least not if Johannisen has anything to say about it. And as though he can read his colleague's mind, Johannisen continues.

'But Disa Brinckmann's daughter apparently told the Swedes someone from the Doggerland Police has been trying to get hold of her mother. And it doesn't take a rocket scientist to figure out who. Goddamn it, Eiken was bloody right.'

Karl realises what it must cost his colleague to admit Karen was onto something everyone else had dismissed out of hand. And yet, here he is, at work, in the middle of the night.

'And you're telling me Karen's not answering her phone. Do we even know if she's on the ferry? Maybe she took an earlier one and is already in France.'

Johannisen turns his computer screen and pushes his chair back.

'She's on the passenger list.'

Karl looks at the alphabetised Excel sheet.

Edmund, Timothy

Edgerman, Jan

Egerman, Charlotte

Eiken Hornby, Karen

He frowns. And before gut feeling has a chance to turn to conscious thought, he instinctively reaches for the mouse and scrolls up the list. He holds his breath while his eyes scan the names of the passengers.

Cedervall, Marie

Cedervall, Gunnar

Clasie, Jaan

Crawford, David

Davidsen, William

Then he lets the air out in a sigh of relief.

'At least there's no Anne Crosby on board,' he says.

Johannisen is right; there has to be a connection, just like Karen suspected, but they don't have to reach her tonight. She's probably asleep anyway, he thinks to himself. She's turned the sound off now that she's finally off work.

Karl Björken feels the adrenaline subsiding and his heart rate slowing and starts to get up. Just as he gets to his feet, he hears Evald Johannisen's voice behind him.

'God-fucking-damnit.'

85

Karen struggles a little with the door to the aft deck. The wind has picked up and the air is raw with impending rain. It's probably going to start pouring down any second, but she should have enough time to smoke a cigarette before the skies open. Two plastic chairs lie toppled onto their sides next to a round table and a handful of plastic cups role forlornly back and forth across the deck, but there's not a soul in sight. Apparently, she's the only one desperate enough to brave the chill, or maybe all the other smokers are huddled somewhere else. There must be a better spot than this.

She sets her course for some white life-vest storage bins crammed in under a protruding roof some way down the leeward deck. Just half a cigarette, she tells herself, then I'm off to bed. She keeps a safe distance between herself and the railing as she moves toward the storage bins; a sudden gust of wind buffets her. Facing in toward the wall, she pulls out cigarettes and lighter with fingers that already feel clumsy with cold. Her thumb keeps slipping; it takes her four attempts to light her cigarette. She closes her eyes and takes a deep drag.

I have to stop her, she thinks, once again imagining her mother's face if she were to get to the house and discover Leo

Friis. Potentially, in a worst-case scenario, surrounded by empty bottles and joints.

Karen's still not sure if her mum's desire to emigrate had been caused by her own return to the island, or if her moving back to her childhood home had simply given Eleanor Eiken a reason to let go of the old stone house. She'd held off for a year after Karen moved back before judging that her daughter was capable of getting by on her own. A year surprisingly free of conflicts, possibly because Karen had quickly moved out to the guesthouse. Two widows in one house was, after all, one too many.

Eleanor, for her part, had claimed she and Karen's father had always dreamt of moving to warmer climes the moment they retired. Now she was going to have to do it on her own.

'And I know the house is in good hands,' she'd said.

She's probably going to change her mind about that, unless I can get through to her tomorrow morning, Karen ponders. I'll be lucky to get a few hours of sleep at this rate, she laments inwardly and feels a yawn tickle her jaw. Suddenly, she realises the stress of her mother's message has made her forget something. There had been another voicemail on her phone. Probably just an apology from the police chief inspector for calling her in error, but she has to check it regardless. She briefly contemplates listening it to it immediately, but then decides to finish her cigarette and wait until she's back inside. Karen turns her head and watches the light streaming out through the windows further down the deck and is suddenly overcome with an almost unbearable tiredness. She takes one last deep drag and flicks away the cigarette. Watches the glow go out the moment it hits the deck.

Just then, she's shoved hard from behind. The force of it throws her head first into the railing.

86

Karl Björken spots it the moment Evald Johannisen lets out his curse. True, there's no Anne Crosby on the passenger list. But at the top of the Excel sheet they're now staring at are the last names under the letter *B*.

Bok, Anders
Bosscha, Ruud
Besscha, Marianne
Brinckmann, Disa

For a few moments, there is complete silence.

'How the fuck . . .' Evald Johannisen says, but Karl Björken is already standing at his own desk with his hand on the phone. They exchange a look and a nod. Then they get to work.

Karl Björken has to admit he's never felt more helpless in his life. At least not since Ingrid gave birth to the children.

By now, he and Johannisen have done everything they can. Without needing to coordinate, they've made the calls that need to be made, noting what the other has already taken care of before proceeding to the next step. Together, they've run down the list of possible and impossible interventions. They've contacted the police chief inspector, who has sent out a major alert. They've talked to the head of the Coastguard's helicopter fleet in Framnes, who informed them the weather is too rough to head out. The police's helicopter squad gave them the same answer. There are strong winds where the ferry is, but that's not the problem. The wind along the east coast of Doggerland has reach gale force and the visibility is much too poor for a helicopter to take off.

They've spoken to the shipping company's head of security, who promised to inform the captain immediately and call them back. It's been confirmed that a woman who according to her passport is called Disa Brinckmann holds a return ticket from Esbjerg to Dunker and that the ferry is right on the border between Doggerian and Danish territorial waters.

They've woken up Viggo Haugen, who for once listened without objection and promised to contact the Danish police immediately. They've informed Jounas Smeed, who is on his way in. Now, their only hope is that the Danish coastguard are able to send someone out. Or that the crew on board the ferry can locate Karen.

It's a big ship, Karl thinks darkly.

He puts his head in his hands and tries to think. Is there really nothing more they can do? Just then, Johannisen curses again.

'Karl, get yourself over here.'

Without getting out of his chair, Karl Björken rolls over to his colleague's desk and watches him jab a chubby finger at the passenger list on the screen.

'Look,' he says. 'Apparently everyone's on that bloody ferry. I wonder how Jounas is going to react when he finds out his little girl's on board?'

87

Her first sensation is cold. A freezing wet cold that makes her aware she's alive. Then a sliver of light that cuts through the blackness, producing a searing pain in her head.

Karen doesn't understand why she's slumped on a hard floor in the dark and cold, with her head and shoulders against an ice-cold wall. I must be outside, she thinks, noting with surprise the rain pattering against her face. The wind is roaring around her and she can hear a rhythmical, thumping sound. Then she remembers.

Instinctively, she tries to get up and hears a scream. Still only half-conscious, she's astonished to realise the sound is coming from her, that it's rising out of her only to be snatched away by the wind. Her eyes dart helplessly back and forth in the faint light from lanterns and windows, then stop to focus on a spot three feet in front of her. Only now does she realise; her left leg is sticking out at a horrifying angle between herself and the railing. She can't move.

That's when she notices the woman.

'Please, help me . . .'

Karen breaks off abruptly. This time, the sudden insight is so powerful she's immediately wide awake. The woman standing next to the wall of the ship, bent over, panting with exertion, watching Karen, has no intention of helping her. She's catching her breath before finishing what she started.

And through the rain, in the faint light from the lantern above the life vest bins, Karen recognises her. It's the woman with the expensive handbag, who dug around for a mirror to top up her lipstick, the woman who stood by herself, staring at the gambling machines. Now she straightens up and her eyes are so filled with hate Karen lets out an involuntary gasp.

There's something familiar about her features and the expensive hairdo that's now clinging wetly to her pale face. Something that's not right, that can't be true. A thought slowly gnaws its way into Karen's awareness, looking for a foothold. And she doesn't know if she says it out loud or if she just thinks it.

'You look exactly alike . . .'

She screams when the woman takes a first step toward her.

The sound is swallowed by the monotonous thudding of the ship's engines and the menacing growl of the wind around ladders and lifeboats. Terrified, Karen flails her arms about to protect herself, striking out blindly, weakly, against the body leaning over her. She fights to keep screaming when the woman grabs her arms and tries to pull her up. This time, the pain is so intense she vomits. The retching send jolts of pain through her chest and something inside her gives up. Sluggishly, as though it has nothing to do with her, she notes that at least a couple of ribs on her right side are broken.

The woman instinctively lets go and takes a step back. She stares at the vomit slowly sliding down the lapels of her suit jacket with surprise that quickly turns into revulsion.

Far away, Karen hears a door open; the din and music from inside grows louder for a second before the door closes again.

No one's going to brave this weather, no one's going to risk getting soaked and chilled to the bone for a cigarette. No one's going to see or hear her, even though there's nothing but a thin wall between her and the hundreds of dancing, laughing people inside. No one has any idea what's happening.

Gagging involuntarily again, Karen tries to turn her head to the side to avoid choking on her own vomit. The music grows louder again when another door opens. Behind her this time, further down the deck. She tries to scream, but can't get anything out before the sound from inside fades again as the door closes. I'm not going to make it, she thinks, staring at the woman in front of her.

Anne Crosby is going to kill me too.

Then she hears footsteps approaching and the woman in front of her backs up against the wall again. They're no longer alone.

A wave of gratitude washes over Karen; someone has come outside, someone's going to help her.

And then a voice, so familiar Karen's overcome with fear so intense it makes blood rush to her head. The sound of Sigrid's voice behind her.

'Karen, is that you? Didn't you hear them call . . .'

She breaks off suddenly and Karen knows Sigrid must now be close enough to realise something's not right.

'Sigrid, don't come over here,' she tries to shout, but she's too weak; her feeble voice is drowned out by the wind.

She tries again. Desperately presses her hand against her broken ribs and yells.

'Go inside and get help. Get out of here, Sigrid!'

But Sigrid doesn't go inside. Instead, she continues to move forward, entering Karen's field of vision.

'Oh my God, Karen, what happened?'

'Please, Sigrid, get out of here, you have to go and get help. She's dangerous.'

She mouths the last part, frantically trying to point with her eyes at the woman, who has now withdrawn into the shadows. The woman Sigrid still hasn't spotted.

Sigrid follows her gaze toward the wall of the ship. Karen sees her startle and grab the railing to keep upright. And then she watches helplessly as Sigrid, instead of turning around to go get help, takes a few slow steps toward the woman.

Anne Crosby is standing motionless, frozen, her arms dangling limply at her sides.

Sigrid's long, jet black hair whips in the wind, covering her face like a veil. She pushes it aside with both hands and stops a few feet from Anne Crosby. For a few seconds, they stand dead still, staring at each other. And only now does it dawn on Karen what Sigrid must be thinking. Now, when the previously elegant woman's well-coiffed hair is wet and lanky, when the dim light of the lanterns makes it impossible to tell her apart from Susanne Smeed.

It's not her! she wants to scream. She just looks like her. Get out of here; this is the woman who killed your mother. Her name is Anne Crosby, she's your aunt.

But she can't get a word out.

She had meant to tell Sigrid about her aunt. Once they were in France, when the time was right. She'd reckoned Sigrid would be happy. That it might help both her and Anne to deal with Susanne being gone. Now, all she wants to do is to bellow at Sigrid to get out of there. But her body is failing, there's not enough air. The pain is too overwhelming.

And for a moment that stretches into an eternity, Karen watches Sigrid's face change. Watches as emotions ruthlessly rush through her. Watches doubt turn into a split second of happiness before reality catches up again. An unfathomable reality.

Karen can't hear it, only sees Sigrid's lips move, forming a single word.

'Mummy?'

Something inside her breaks. She wants to jump up, fold Sigrid into her arms and protect her from this experience. Tell her it's just a bad dream. But all she can do is muster her last ounce of strength, defy the pain and shout as loudly as she can.

'It's not her, Sigrid,' she roars. 'It's not your mother.'

Maybe Sigrid hears her, maybe she doesn't. Maybe she doesn't care what Karen's trying to say, maybe she doesn't believe her. And now the woman's eyes start to dart back and forth between her and Sigrid, as if she's trying to make sense of things, too, and slowly, as she looks at Karen, the rage that had momentarily abated reawakens. She quickly walks up to Sigrid and embraces the rigid girl. Holds her tight with her hate-filled eyes still fixed on Karen.

And yet it's only when the woman opens her mouth that Karen realises how wrong she's been.

'Yes, Karen,' the woman says, 'I am her mother. Nothing you do can change that.'

Karen's mind is reeling and can find nothing to hold onto. Pictures of Susanne Smeed's dead body on the kitchen floor. The still so familiar features behind the grotesquely smashed-in face. The open dressing gown, the silicon breast peeking out, the well-manicured hands, the glossiness of her hair where it wasn't covered in blood. Karen had seen and noted all those things. Found some of them surprising, but accepted what she saw without question. The memory of Kneought Brodal's anguish at having to examine the body of a woman he'd known and socialised with once upon a time. The DNA results that had confirmed what he and everyone else already knew. That the dead woman was Susanne Smeed.

All their efforts had been focused on finding the killer. No one had questioned who the victim was.

And while the truth slowly sinks in, Karen hears the woman who is not Anne Crosby say:

'I'm sorry, Sigrid. I didn't mean for you to find out. You were supposed to think I was dead.'

Sigrid emits a sound that's somewhere between a sob and a howl. She wrenches free and takes a few staggering steps backwards. Slips, but regains her balance.

'What the fuck have you done?' she screams. 'Then who was murdered?'

And Susanne Smeed looks genuinely surprised, cocking her head and studying her daughter with a troubled expression, as though she doesn't quite understand the question.

'My sister, of course.'

Sigrid's eyes are wide with horror. Her mother doesn't have a sister. Does she?

'I didn't know about her either. At first, I was happy. Before I realised how messed up everything was. I had to kill her. You weren't supposed to find out until years from now, when I'm dead. Why are you here? What are you doing here with her?'

Her eyes wander back and forth between Sigrid and Karen with a mix of hatred and confusion; Sigrid has thwarted her plans by turning up. Horrified, Karen realises Susanne's desperation might drive her to do just about anything right now; killing her will no longer be enough. But is Susanne crazy enough to kill her own daughter?

Sigrid stares at the woman in front of her. The face that is etched into her being. Her mother, whom she has loved and hated. Sees the madness she might have sensed lurking beneath the surface all along, the madness that frightened her more than she dared to admit, even to herself.

'Why?'

She says it so quietly the question is swallowed by the wind. But Susanne can read it in her eyes.

'Don't you see? She had everything that was mine. She'd stolen my entire life. I've explained it all in a letter, Sigrid. It's in Anne's house in Sweden; I've been staying there since she died. It's *my* life now.'

Then Susanne rushes over to Karen. Bends down and bellows:

'And I'm not going to let you take what's mine, you fucking whore. Sigrid's my daughter, not yours. Don't you forget it.'

Her eyes glow with hate when she raises her hand and slaps Karen hard.

The blow knocks Karen's head into the metal wall; Susanne turns back to Sigrid.

'I'm always going to be your mother. No one can take that away from me!'

Karen barely notices the sharp beam of light suddenly sweeping across them. Barely hears the sounds of the ship's siren and of running steps. Her field of vision narrows and all sounds become suddenly remote. As though from inside a bell jar, she sees Susanne shade her eyes with her hand as she looks up at the helicopter searchlight, watches her turn back to Sigrid and slowly shake her head. Her face looks completely blank. Drained of hope of a better life. Drained of life. This is it, Karen thinks. This is when she makes her final decision.

Then Susanne grabs the railing with both hands and heaves herself up onto it; Karen sees Sigrid rush over to stop her. Sees her own arm raised in a desperate attempt to grab hold of the girl. Feels a surge of panic that Susanne will pull Sigrid down with her.

Karen's hand latches onto Sigrid's jumper; pain slices through her as her body is yanked forward. With a strength she doesn't feel like she has, but which must nevertheless exist somewhere deep inside her, hidden under layers of despair and years of grief, she forces her hand to hold on. Knowing that she's holding onto life itself. Her fingers are clinging to hope, hope of healing and redemption. Hope for Sigrid. For John. For Mathis.

For a child that mustn't be lost.

The wind tears at the woman who has now swung one leg over the railing. Her body sways; she's still clutching the white iron bar.

'Read the letter, Sigrid!' she shouts. 'You'll understand.'

Then she opens her hands and lets go.

And somewhere, far beyond herself, Karen hears Sigrid roar out her despair as her mum falls and disappears into the darkness below.

88

It's like someone's playing with a switch, turning the lights on and off around her. Relentless flashes of light that force her back to reality, alternating with a gentle darkness that lets her slip away from it all.

The sharp light when the paramedics lift her onto a stretcher, then the prick of a needle that makes the wave of pain slowly retreat. The swishing roar of the rotor blades and straps being tightened before darkness envelops her again. Faint vibrations, calming voices speaking a different language than her own, unfamiliar voices telling her not to fall asleep.

'Don't fall asleep, sweetie.'

It sounds like Marike, Karen notes. But surely she's not here?

She knows nothing of her journey to Copenhagen's main hospital, but in the sharp glare when the lights are turned on again, she sees tubes, white coats and focused eyes. For a moment, she doesn't understand why she's in a hospital. Her alarm's probably about to go off and she'll have to get up and go to work. Her next conscious thought is that there's a loud humming around her. Now, it feels like she's going into a tunnel and she thinks to herself that she's probably dying. That this must be what it feels like. That it must have been like this for John and Mathis, too.

And she thinks there's a smile on her lips when she realises it's not so bad, after all.

But then the lights are turned on again and she's forced back. Apparently, she's not dying today. The humming has stopped, replaced by voices. Murmuring voices, speaking words she can understand at first but then words she doesn't recognise and she panics. More needle pricks and soothing hands. And now, she can see kind eyes between green skullcaps and white masks. Then it finally goes dark again.

She's not sure how time passes, whether it's fast or slow. Later on, she will be told she spent almost three full days after her surgery at the hospital in Copenhagen, before she was flown back to Doggerland. That it will be some time before she can go home. Unbearably long days she has to spend motionless in a bed at Thysted Hospital in Dunker. She escaped the blow to her head with nothing worse than lacerations, a severe concussion and a skull fracture. Fourteen stitches, antibiotics and plenty of rest will take care of those things, her doctors have assured her. Her ribcage has been stabilised and is holding her broken ribs in place. Her left leg, however, which snapped just above her ankle, and her knee, where two tendons were severed, are a different story. At least two weeks at Thysted before they can even discuss discharging her. After that, she will convalesce at home and make frequent visits to a physiotherapist.

'But you are going to make a complete recovery.'

They find Susanne's letter in a house in Limhamn that Anne Crosby had inherited from her father. The house in which Susanne lived as her sister for a few weeks. She'd made no effort

to hide the envelope with Sigrid's name on it. Since it's techni-
cally relevant to the investigation, five people have read it: Karl
Björken, Evald Johannisen, Dineke Vegen, Viggo Haugen and
Jounas Smeed.

Karen is given a copy, as well, even though she's on sick leave
and no longer on the case. She's still dazed from the analge-
sics when Karl asks her if she feel strong enough to read what
Susanne Smeed wrote to her daughter.

'It's proper sick,' he warns her.

Karen nods slowly and takes the letter. With a growing sense
of unease, she looks at the crowded lines, the furious uppercase
letters, the underlining, the misspelled words. Then she begins
to read.

TO SIGRID,

*IF YOU'RE READING THIS, IT MEANS I'M DEAD. YOU MIGHT
BE AN OLD WOMAN YOURSELF, MAYBE YOU HAVE CHIL-
DREN OF YOUR OWN. MAYBE YOU'VE SUSPECTED IT WASN'T
ME WHO DIED IN THE HOUSE IN LANGEVIK. I BELIEVE A
PERSON CAN SENSE WHETHER OR NOT THEIR MOTHER'S
ALIVE.*

*BUT I HAVE KILLED AND I WANT YOU TO KNOW WHY. NOT
SO YOU CAN FORGIVE ME BECAUSE I DON'T EVEN WANT TO
BE FORGIVEN. BUT YOU HAVE TO UNDERSTAND.*

*YOUR FATHER'S A REAL ASSHOLE (I'M SORRY, BUT THAT'S
THE TRUTH) BORN WITH A SILVER SPOON IN HIS MOUTH,
GOT EVERYTHING FOR FREE WHILE I HAD TO STRUGGLE.
I ALWAYS HAD TO STRUGGLE!!!*

*AND HE WASN'T GRATEFUL EITHER. EVEN THOUGH HE WAS
A 'REAL SMEED' AND I WAS 'THE WRONG SORT' HIS WHOLE*

FAMILY THOUGHT SO. YOUR GRANDFATHER WAS THE WORST OF THE LOT!!! AXEL SMEED REQUIRED A PRENUP TO HELP US FIND A FLAT EVEN THOUGH YOU WERE JUST AN INFANT. HE EVEN THREATENED TO DISINHERIT YOUR FATHER IF WE DIDN'T SIGN IT.

I DIDN'T GET TO KEEP ANYTHING IN THE DIVORCE!!!

AND AXEL STOLE MY INHERITENCE FROM MY MOTHER, TOO. YOU SHOULD KNOW THAT ABOUT HIM. HE BOUGHT ALL THE LAND FROM MY FATHER, PIECE BY PIECE, FOR A PITTANCE, UNTIL THERE WAS NOTHING LEFT FOR ME TO INHERIT.

BEHIND MY BACK!!!

I DIDN'T KNOW ANYTHING ABOUT IT UNTIL AFTER THE DIVORCE. ALL YOUR FATHER WOULD GIVE ME WAS 'A LITTLE SOMETHING' EVERY MONTH SO YOU COULD HAVE A 'TOLER-ABLE QUALITY OF LIFE' WHEN YOU WERE WITH ME.

FUCKING PRICK!!!

YOUR FATHER WANTED TO KEEP EVEYRTHING WHILE I HAD TO STRUGGLE.

WHEN YOU MOVED OUT AS WELL, I WAS ALL ALONE. NO FRIENDS AND WORK WAS HELL. AFTER A FEW YEARS, I COULDN'T TAKE IT ANYMORE. I JUST WANTED TO DIE AND THOUGHT ABOUT KILLING MYSELF ALMOST EVERY DAY.

Karen lets the letter sink onto her chest and closes her eyes. Is Sigrid going to have to read this? Or has she already? As though he can tell what she's thinking, she hears Karl's voice from the visitor's chair.

'We had to. She's over eighteen and it was addressed to her. She received it yesterday.'

496

She's never going to be the same again, Karen concludes. Never. Then she picks the letter back up and forces herself to keep reading.

THAT WAS WHEN A WOMAN BY THE NAME OF DISA BRINCK-MANN CALLED.

SHE HAD LIVED IN A COMMUNE WITH MY PARENTS AND WAS THERE WHEN I WAS BORN. SHE TOLD ME NOT EVEN MY OWN MOTHER WAS MINE. MY FATHER HAD CONCEIVED ME WITH ANOTHER WOMAN.

BUT THEN SHE SAID I HAD A TWIN SISTER.

THEY HAD SPLIT US UP BETWEEN THEMSELVES <u>LIKE KIT-TENS!!!</u> MY SISTER GOT TO GO TO SWEDEN AND I WAS LEFT BEHIND.

I MET DISA BRINCKMANN AND MY SISTER IN MALMÖ.

AT FIRST, I DIDN'T SEE IT BECAUSE SHE LOOKED MUCH BETTER THAN ME, ON THE SURFACE. BUT THEN WE SAW IT. <u>WE LOOKED EXACTLY ALIKE!!!</u>

NO ONE HAD REALISED WE WERE IDENTICAL TWINS WHEN WE WERE BORN. NOT EVEN DISA BRINCKMANN HAD KNOWN UNTIL THAT MOMENT. WE EVEN HAD THE SAME VOICE AND TALKED THE SAME WAY BECAUSE WE'D BOTH GROWN UP SPEAKING SWEDISH AT HOME. <u>IT WAS LIKE WE WERE THE SAME PERSON!!!</u>

I WENT TO MALMÖ TWO MORE TIMES TO SEE ANNE AND WE TALKED ON THE PHONE. SHE LIVED IN THE US BUT SAID SHE WAS SELLING EVERYTHING OVER THERE AND MOVING BACK HOME.

THAT WAS WHEN I REALISED HOW RICH SHE WAS.

SHE HAD EVERYTHING AND I HAD NOTHING.

BUT EVERYTHING SHE HAD COULD JUST AS EASILY HAVE
BEEN MINE!!! IF I HAD BEEN THE ONE WHO WENT TO SWEDEN
AND SHE WAS THE ONE WHO STAYED IN LANGEVIK. IT WAS
CHANCE THAT GAVE HER EVERYTHING AND ME NOTHING!!!

THAT WAS WHEN I DECIDED TO CHANGE EVERYTHING. SHE
WAS COMING TO VISIT AND WAS GOING TO STAY OVER AT MY
HOUSE. SHE CAME ON A CRUISE SHIP THAT WAS STOPPING
OVER FOR ONE DAY AND I PICKED HER UP FROM THE BOAT.

THAT MORNING I DID WHAT I HAD TO DO. YOU DON'T
NEED TO KNOW HOW I DID IT.

THEN I TOOK HER PLACE ON THE CRUISE SHIP. JUST TOOK
OVER HER LIFE.

IT WAS ACTUALLY EASIER THAN I THOUGHT, BECAUSE NO
ONE LOOKS TWICE AT A WOMAN MY AGE.

THE ONLY PERSON WHO KNEW WE WERE TWINS WAS DISA
SO I HAD TO GET RID OF HER TOO BEFEORE I COULD FEEL
SAFE. AND NOW I HAVE TO GET RID OF ONE MORE PER-
SON WHO'S SNOOPING AROUND, ASKING QUESTIONS. SHE
WORKS WITH YOUR FATHER BUT LIVES IN THE VILLAGE. YOU
KNOW WHO SHE IS. SHE'S ALWAYS BEEN A REAL WHORE WHO
SLEEPS AROUND SO AT LEAST IT'S NO GREAT LOSS.

Karen shoots Karl a quick glance, but he's staring out the window. Then she reads the final lines.

I JUST WANTED TO LIVE THE LIFE THAT SHOULD HAVE BEEN
MINE FROM THE BEGINNING.
    ANNE GOT THE FIRST HALF AND <u>I TOOK WHAT WAS LEFT.</u>
    I HOPE YOU CAN UNDERSTAND. I ALWAYS LOVED YOU.
    MUM

The room is completely silent for several minutes.

'She must've been psychotic when she wrote it,' Karl says.

Karen makes no reply.

Then he gets up to leave. The last thing he says gives voice to the only thing she can think right now.

'Poor Sigrid.'

89

Everyone comes to visit. Crowds around her hospital bed with worried faces until they feel assured Karen's unlikely to suffer any lingering consequences. Marike, Aylin, Kore and Eirik. And Mum.

Eleanor Eiken – who has made it clear she will not be talked into going back to Spain until Karen has been discharged – has resolutely moved back into the house in Langevik and sent Harry home to their flat in Estepona.

Leo Friis is apparently still there, too. Like Rufus, he seems to have decided to stay. Karen has no idea if he's moved back into the guesthouse or if he and Eleanor are sharing the main house. She doesn't have the energy to ask, or to answer any questions herself. She's not surprised Leo hasn't come by the hospital, and how she's going to get rid of him is a question that seems completely irrelevant at the moment.

All Karen can think about is Sigrid.

'She's not doing great,' Eleanor says.

'No wonder. Where is she staying now? She's not on her own, is she?'

'Don't worry. We're keeping an eye on her.'

'It's possible she blames me for her mother killing herself. Do you think she does? Is that why she won't take my calls?'

'I think she's blaming herself, Karen. I know she does.'

'Why? None of this is her fault.'

'Don't play dumb, Karen. You of all people should understand.'

'Maybe I could talk to her . . .'

'Sigrid's afraid of everything right now. Seeing you like this, battered, bandaged, in a cast, it would just make her more anxious.'

Karen realises she can only imagine a fraction of what Sigrid's going through. But that fraction alone is too much for an eighteen-year-old girl to deal with. The shock of finding out her mother was a murderer. Losing her first once and then again. The anguish of being torn between revulsion at what her mother did and grief at the bitterness that twisted into madness. Grief for a wasted life. And the role her grandfather played, the role her own father played. If Sigrid's relationship with her father was bad before, it must be completely ruined now.

And for the first time, Karen understands how Sigrid must have been shaped by the constant need to navigate a course between her father's frosty arrogance and her mother's unstable psyche. And by the knowledge that she's inevitably part of them both.

Karen realises she can only ever understand that slightly. And yet, she wishes she could speak to Sigrid: tell her nothing's her fault, that she's not responsible for the sins of her parents. That she's not alone.

But all she can do is lie here and wait for her body to heal enough to be discharged.

'We're keeping an eye on her,' Eleanor says again. 'Leo and I. Oh, and by the way, he installed the cat flap.'

90

Then her colleagues stop by. One after the other, they pop in with grapes and newspapers and flowers her mother accepts with a patient smile before heading out into the hallways to find yet another vase. Cornelis Loots, Astrid Nielsen, Sören Larsen and an extremely embarrassed Viggo Haugen relieve each other with such precision, Karen gets the feeling someone in the department has in fact drawn up a schedule. Considerate, brief visits, worried glances when the pain in her head and knee makes Karen call the nurse to ask for more painkillers. Then a few mumbled words to her mother before they leave Karen with promises of being back soon.

On the third day, Evald Johannisen appears in the doorway.

'So, Eiken,' he says, placing the grapes he's brought on top of the others in the bowl on her bedside table before taking a seat on one of the chairs.

'So, Johannisen,' Karen replies.

'I guess you were on to something after all. Well, I suppose even a blind pig can find an acorn once in a while.'

But something's different; Karen feels no need to point out that she was simply right. That she had wanted to keep looking into something everyone else had dismissed out of hand in their eagerness to wrap things up. That there had in fact been a connection between the murder of Susanne Smeed and what happened in a commune in Langevik over forty years ago. That they had been wrong. She had been right. She mentions none of those things. Because the truth is, she was only half right.

Instead, she says:

'I wanted to thank you, Evald. For flying into action when you found out Disa Brinckmann had been murdered.'

Johannisen shrugs.

'I'm just sorry I didn't find out a few hours earlier.'

He nods vaguely in the direction of her leg, which is in a cast and secured within a metal cage to immobilise her knee.

But their new truce feels strange and the silence between them echoes in the room. They've interacted exclusively through sarcasm, needling and scowls for so long, neither one of them knows what to say now. No more than five minutes into his visit, Evald Johannisen gets to his feet, clears his throat and opens his mouth to speak. Karen beats him to it.

'You're still a prick, Evald,' she says with a smile.

Without responding, he pinches a grape from the pile in the bowl, pops it in his mouth and leaves. But Karen notices his shoulders relaxing a little and just before he pulls the door shut behind him, she catches a glimpse of a smile playing at the corner of his mouth.

Karl Björken does not smile. At least not until his third visit, when the bandage around Karen's head has been replaced with a simple compress to cover the stitches and the bruises on her face have assumed a paler, yellowish shade of green.

'You scared the shit out of us,' he says as he takes a seat by the window.

The blinds have been opened after the gloom of the first few days; Karen watches a flock of migrating birds flying south. At least you'll get further than me, she muses. There will be no trip to France for her, at least not this side of Christmas and New Year.

'Brodal's a wreck,' Karl says.

'It wasn't his fault. Not even DNA could reveal it wasn't Susanne in that kitchen.'

'That's why. He's been shaken to the core.'

'Well, he's unlikely to experience it again,' Karen says, looking away from the window. 'Though that being said, between 2 and 3 per cent of all babies born are twins,' she parrots. 'And of those, about a third shared an egg. In this country alone, there are around 10,000 pairs of twins, 3,000 of which are identical. But the likelihood of any of them being the victims, or perpetrators, of serious crimes is negligible. Cornelis came to visit yesterday,' she adds, smiling at Karl's slack-jawed expression.

'Oh, I see, good old Loots strikes again. Did he have any other facts to entertain you with?'

'Probably, but I've forgotten what they were. No, that's right. Identical twins apparently have the same DNA.'

'I could've told you that,' Karl says. 'That's why the only DNA we found was Susanne's own.'

He leans forward.

'Seriously, Eiken, how much of this did you suspect?'

'Not much,' she admits. 'I was fairly certain Kvanne wasn't our guy, though it was hard to ignore the fact that he did lie about being in Langevik. He would hardly have been able to break into the house and steal the car without leaving the smallest trace. And I felt there had to be a personal

504

connection of some sort, but what that connection might be, I had no idea. Or at least not enough of an idea to persuade Haugen to let me carry on. On the other hand, I did enough damage as it was.'

'You're referring to Disa Brinckmann?'

Karen nods mutely.

'You could hardly be expected to foresee that she was going to be killed.'

'No, I realise that. But, you know . . .'

She spreads her hands in a gesture that's intended to encompass everything she knows Karl is already familiar with. Lingering regrets about the ones you might have been able to save. If you'd just done things differently.

'You have too much time to dwell on stuff,' he says. 'Speaking of which, how long are they going to keep you here?'

'At least two more weeks, they're telling me.'

'Well, at least you have plenty of visitors,' Karl notes, with a nod at the pile of grapes.

Karen smiles wanly.

'Yes, even Johannisen stopped by the other day.'

'So, truce?'

'At least for now,' she says. 'He's a good detective, despite being a prick. If he hadn't put two and two together, I probably wouldn't be here.'

'Sigrid's the one who found you,' Karl points out.

'Yes, but she would probably never have come looking for me if she hadn't heard them calling out for me over the speakers.'

'What does she say about it all?'

'I haven't talked to her.'

Karen winces in a way she knows Karl's going to interpret as her being in pain. That wince has become her way of making visitors get up and leave her alone.

A few minutes later, when the door slides shut behind Karl Björken with a faint whoosh of air, Karen turns back to the window as grief sears her throat. She has no right to feel this way. No right to think Sigrid would want anything to do with her. No right at all. The grief of one lost child can't be lessened by another.

She recalls Susanne Smeed's words.

'She's not your daughter. Don't you forget it.'

91

On the eighth day, Jounas Smeed appears on the threshold to her room. Karen has dozed off after lunch and is roused by his voice from the doorway.

'So this is where you've been hiding?'

Without replying, she reaches for her glass of water and realises she was probably snoring loudly. The cage around her leg forces her to lie on her back and her mouth feels dry as sand. She drinks silently and greedily while she waits for a comment, but something about Jounas indicates that he's not in the mood for put-downs.

His face is pale and the dark circles under his eyes prominent in the harsh light streaming in through the windows. For a moment, Karen imagines she can see every contradictory feeling inside him: relief, irritation, concern, anger. And something she's never seen in her boss before. Uncertainty. A kind of awkward embarrassment that anxiously moves between the events that led to him standing here now.

For the first time ever, Karen feels she has the upper hand, despite the snoring and her bedbound state. She knows and he knows. His assessment of the case and his decisions are partly to blame for her lying here. Only partly, but that's enough to fill the room with unspoken guilt. She silently watches as he moves away from the door and walks around the foot of the bed.

He hasn't brought grapes – he would never go that far – but he places an evening paper on her bedside table before sitting down in the visitor's chair and crossing his long legs with practised casualness. A shadow of discomfort passes across his face when he studies her bruises and the metal scaffold around her leg.

'How are you feeling?' he asks, wincing.

'I've been better,' she replies and watches him nod. Now with the appropriately concerned look of a manager.

'Been worse, too,' she adds with a wry smile.

He returns the smile briefly, almost absently.

'So how long are they keeping you here, do you know?'

She recounts what her doctors have told her about the next few weeks and the sick leave and rehab that will follow.

'I guess you won't be back this side of New Year's, then,' he says.

She hears the underlying question and responds with silence. In an effort to delay, she reaches for the water glass again and feels his eyes on her. Then Jounas takes a deep breath and asks straight out.

'Because you are coming back, aren't you, Eiken?'

It would be easy to postpone the decision, to take the next few weeks to decide. But something in his voice makes her answer frankly. An unspoken plea for reconciliation. A hint of worry.

'I've been thinking about that,' she says honestly. 'Before I went on vacation, I had pretty much decided to apply for a transfer.'

'And now? Have you changed your mind?'

'I'm considering giving it a second chance,' she says curtly. 'But there's going to have to be some fucking changes in

508

your management style. A bit less adolescent bullshit, to put it plainly. And I don't want to be passed over when there are serious cases,' she adds.

'You're ballsy,' he says. 'Well, I guess I would be too, if I were you. And how long are you going to torture me about being right?'

'That's for me to know.'

This time, she allows herself a small smile. Jounas Smeed shakes his head and sighs.

'Fine, I guess I deserve that.'

'How are you getting on with the attacks in Moerbeck and Odinswalla? Do you have anything?'

'Nothing at all,' he admits dully. 'On the other hand, the guy seems to have either taken a break or to have stopped completely. No new cases since the one on Atlasvägen. I suppose it's the cold,' he adds. 'Even bastards like him can usually manage to keep it in their pants when the temperature dips below freezing.'

Karen thinks about the cases she read about when she studied criminology.

'It can be months between recurrences,' she says. 'There was this one bloke in Sweden a few years ago who shares some similarities with our cases. He went at it for years before they caught him.'

Jounas nods but doesn't speak; Karen continues.

'It's probably just a matter of time before our guy strikes again, and when he does, I'm going to be there to catch the prick.'

Jounas gets to his feet and stares out the window. He says nothing; she waits. She instinctively knows his thoughts have

509

already moved on from both closed and ongoing cases. And his real reason for coming here has nothing to do with checking on me, she thinks, studying his back.

'You're thinking about Sigrid,' she says and notes that he stiffens before he turns around.

For a split second, he looks like he's about to put words to the anger and frustration he must feel at Sigrid being on the ferry. At Karen bringing her along on her vacation without telling him. At Karen being on better terms with his daughter than he has been in years.

'I haven't talked to her either,' she says quietly.

His eyes are cold now, frosty and doubtful.

'Oh really? Because I got the impression you were real fucking close all of a sudden. United in your hatred of me, I suppose.'

She has an urge to be mean. To cut him, hurt him deeply and irrevocably. To unleash her own grief. And she knows she has no right.

'Believe what you want,' she says, 'but she hasn't been in touch with me, either. And she won't take my calls. Maybe she blames us both for Susanne's death.'

She can tell he realises she's right and she watches him steel himself to make one final, desperate attempt.

'You call me immediately if she gets in touch. If she tells you where she is. That's an order, Eiken. Are we clear?'

Karen looks him straight in the eyes.

'I can't promise that. Not if she doesn't want me to.'

She holds his gaze and sees the anger drain out of him, as though the effort of keeping it alive has become unsustainable. His chest seems to deflate and all expression leaves his face. The only thing left is bottomless grief. And she realises she's no longer looking at her boss, she's looking at Sigrid's father.

'I can promise you one thing,' she says. 'I would never say anything bad about you to Sigrid. I like her far too much to bad-mouth her dad.'

EPILOGUE

Two weeks later, Eleanor Eiken pushes the wheelchair with her daughter in it through the glass doors of the hospital. Karen wants to go home. Since the first week, when she was still drugged and in pain, her homesickness has grown stronger with each passing day. She longs to be in control of whether her door is open or closed, of whether there are visitors or not. Of what and when she eats. She longs to get away from the smell of disinfectants and the sound of ambulance sirens. To cry in peace.

And more than anything, she longs for a glass of wine or two and a cigarette.

She would prefer to be alone in her house, but realises she's going to need her mother's help, at least at first. That's why she's both surprised and relieved to hear her mother announce in a carefree voice that she will be hopping on a plane back to Spain the day after tomorrow.

'Harry's calling every day, asking when I'm coming home,' she says, pushing the wheelchair toward the exit. 'He sends his love, by the way. I'm going to have to bring him to Langevik as soon as you're feeling better. And, well, we'll be up for Christmas, of course, if not sooner.'

Karen doesn't know what to say. She's longed for this moment for two weeks, but now that she's catching a first glimpse of the real world out there on the other side of the glass doors, she wants to turn back to safety.

'You're going to be fine. And it goes without saying I'll be calling you every day to see how you're getting on,' Eleanor assures her as the doors to Thysted Hospital slide shut behind them.

The air outside the hospital is clear and fresh. Karen takes a few deep breaths and braces herself to switch to crutches and hobble the last few feet to one of the taxis lined up outside the entrance. But instead of stopping, Eleanor Eiken keeps pushing the wheelchair toward the car park further on.

Karen's chest contracts when she spots her own car. But it's not the sight of the dirty green Ford that makes her press her lips together to stop herself from crying with relief.

Standing next to the car is Leo Friis, taking one last drag on a cigarette before dropping it on the ground and grinding it out with his heel.

And behind the wheel is Sigrid.

If you enjoyed *Fatal Isles*, don't miss the
next in the series

AFTER THE STORM

Coming 2022